ArtScroll History Series®

Rabbi Nosson Scherman / Rabbi Meir Zlotowitz

General Editors

THEY
CALLED
HIM

Published by

Mesorah Publications, ltd

MIKE

REB ELEMELECH TRESS

*His Era, Hatzalah,
and the Building of
an American Orthodoxy*

BY YONASON ROSENBLUM
based in part on research by Dr. David Kranzler

FIRST EDITION
First Impression . . . June, 1995

Published and Distributed by
MESORAH PUBLICATIONS, Ltd.
4401 Second Avenue
Brooklyn, New York 11232

Distributed in Europe by
J. LEHMANN HEBREW BOOKSELLERS
20 Cambridge Terrace
Gateshead, Tyne and Wear
England NE8 1RP

Distributed in Israel by
SIFRIATI / A. GITLER—BOOKS
4 Bilu Street
P.O.B. 14075
Tel Aviv 61140

Distributed in Australia & New Zealand by
GOLDS BOOK & GIFT CO.
36 William Street
Balaclava 3183, Vic., Australia

Distributed in South Africa by
KOLLEL BOOKSHOP
22 Muller Street
Yeoville 2198, Johannesburg, South Africa

Typography by Compuscribe at ArtScroll Studios, Ltd.

Printed in the United States of America by Noble Book Press Corp.
Bound by Sefercraft, Quality Bookbinders, Ltd., Brooklyn, N.Y.

*...*HASHEM, *who may sojourn in your tent? Who may dwell on Your Holy Mountain? One who walks in perfect innocence, and does what is right and speaks the truth from his heart; who has no slander on his tongue, who has done his fellow no evil, nor cast disgrace upon his close one; in whose eyes a contemptible person is repulsive, but who honors those who fear* HASHEM; *who can swear to his detriment without retracting, who lends not his money on interest; nor takes a bribe against the innocent. The doer of these shall not falter forever.*

(TEHILLIM 15)

"This, then, is the essence of a true Jewish leader: total sacrifice for the klal *coupled with dedication to meeting the needs of each individual Jew."*

(RABBI CHAIM SHMULEVITZ)

They called him "Mike",
We called him "Pa".

He was wise,
He was warm,
He was wonderful.
He sang with us,
He laughed with us,
He cried with us.
He was our best friend.

May his legacy be an inspiration
to those whose lives he touched.

תנצב״ה

משפחת טרעס

Reb Elemelech Gavriel Tress, zt"l

✒️Table of Contents

Author's Preface   XI

Introduction
A Man for Mashiach's Time / A Gaon in Deeds / The Legacy
of Mike Tress / Their First Hero / A New Jew / The Challenge
of Mike Tress   15

✒️ Part One: LAYING THE FOUNDATIONS

1 Early Years
From the Shtetl to the New World / Starting a Family / Seeds
of Faith / A Summer in the Country / An All-American Boy /
Young Executive   24

2 Flight from Orthodoxy
From Shtetl to Metropolis / The Struggle for Existence / The
Quest for Education / Religious Form Without Content /
Generational Tension / The Lack of Religious Education / No
Place in Shul   35

3 Zeirei Agudath Israel
An Unpopular Cause / The Lower East Side Zeirei / The
Williamsburg Zeirei / Bnos / The ZAI Interbranch Council   46

4 Mike Joins Zeirei
The Attraction of Agudath Israel / Rabbi Gedaliah Schorr /
Zeirei Finds a Leader / The Shemiras Shabbos Campaign   63

5 Pirchei
Building a Movement / Spreading the Word / A Way with Kids
/ Bringing the Gedolim to Life / Love Of Mitzvos / A Sense of
Belonging / Off the Street and Out of Trouble / Reaching Out
/ A Vision Fulfilled   73

6 Mike — The Man
Father Figure for a Generation / A Friend of Every Jew / A
Need to Give / Salesman of Yiddishkeit / Modesty / "I Could
Never Say No to Mike" / A Builder of People   95

7 Williamsburg
Reb Shraga Feivel / Recruiting Trips / Bais Yaakov / Reb
Elchonon's Visit   114

❧ Part Two: A MOVEMENT IS BORN

8 616 Bedford Avenue
Expanding Horizons / Idealism and Inspiration / The Chanukas Habayis / New Uses for a New Home / Marriage 132

9 The Refugee Home
The Shatnes Laboratory / Rabbi Herbert S. Goldstein 150

10 Going National
Getting that Old-time Ideology / Building a Grass-roots Organization / Youth Organization / Conventions and Banquets / Bnos / The Youth Council at War's End 163

11 Getting the Message Across
Orthodox Youth and Orthodox Tribune / Flexing the Muscles / Charting an Ideology / Anti-Zionism / Versus Mizrachi / The Overriding Issue 185

12 The Jewish Serviceman's Religious Bureau
The Plight of the Orthodox Serviceman / The Jewish Servicemen's Religious Bureau / Mike as Pen Pal / The Servicemen's Paper 198

13 Camp Agudah
Camp Kiruv / Not By Bread Alone / The Chiddush of Camp Agudah / Rabbi Yaakov Teitelbaum 217

❧ Part Three: THE WAR YEARS

14 Obstacles to the Rescue
The Price of Caring / Playing Against a Stacked Deck 232

15 The Refugee and Immigration Division
The Kopyczinitzer Rebbe's Love / Affidavits and Visas / The Kranes / Washington Trips / Saving the Roshei Yeshiva / Shabbos for Reb Aharon 247

16 Relief and Rescue
Relief Projects / Fort Oswego / Food for the Ghettos / The Vienna Agudah / Fundraising 269

17 In the Corridors of Power
In Washington / Early Contacts / Latin American Documents / Averting the Final Disaster 292

❧ Part Four: REBUILDING FROM THE ASHES

18 Views from the Ruins
Eager to Help / No End to the Suffering / Growing Despair /
Sparks of Hope   308

19 First to the Rescue
Using the APO / Among the Shearis Hapleitah / Discovering
the Stoliner Rebbe / Back from the Abyss   321

20 A Message from the DP Camps
The Knessiah Mechinah / Paris / In Germany / Where Are
the Children? / We Have Only Hakadosh Baruch Hu /
Giving Lie to the UNRRA / Breaking the Spirit / Living
Among the Survivors / Grasping at Straws / For Eretz Yisrael
/ Beyond Tzedakah / Don't Forget Us   336

21 Keeping Faith with the Survivors
A Responsibility Sought / Bringing to a New Home   352

22 The Save-A-Child Foundation
Obstacles to Success / Modus Operandi / Arrest /
Unorthodox Means / Other Activities / Success and Failure   367

23 The Post-War Agudah
Another Day Older and Deeper in Debt / Jewish Pocket
Books / Focus On Eretz Yisrael / Chinuch Atzmai / The
Fourth Knessiah Gedolah / The Last Hurrah / Journey to
Morocco   384

24 At Home
A Happy Home / Quality Time / Tress Family Values / Rabbi
Avraham Gershon Tress, zt"l / A Good Investment   409

25 The Sun Sets at Midday   420

INDEX OF PERSONALITIES   428

GLOSSARY   440

AUTHOR'S PREFACE

THIS BOOK IS THE PARTIAL REPAYMENT OF A DEBT that has been outstanding since Reb Elemelech Gavriel Tress's *petirah* nearly 28 years ago. Partial — not just because of my inadequacy to capture the magnitude of his personality, but because the currency of repayment is not one that would have ever meant anything to Mike. He had little need for praise in his own lifetime and certainly has none now from his perch in Heaven close to the *Kisei Hakavod* (the Divine Throne).

The only thing that ever mattered to Mike was that more Jews live in accord with the ideals for which he gave his life. Only by striving to be more like him in our concern and willingness to sacrifice for *Klal Yisrael* and for every individual Jew making up that *Klal,* can we discharge our debt to him. By the same token, this work will be adjudged a success only if it inspires others to follow in the path Mike blazed.

This book is not only the story of the life of Mike Tress, but of an entire generation that he shaped. Many names are mentioned, and many others that should have been mentioned were no doubt left out inadvertently. Some of those mentioned are today known throughout the Orthodox world; others only in their narrow circle of friends and family. But each is a hero in his or her own way: Each is a survivor of a generation in which the vast majority of their contemporaries were lost to *Yiddishkeit*. Because of what they did, it is immeasurably easier for those of us who follow in their wake to live Torah-true lives. And for that they deserve to be recorded for posterity. Mike would have wanted those who shared in his achievements to receive the credit due them.

No book of this scope is the product of one person, and this one is no exception.

I am grateful to the Tress family for having granted me the privilege of helping to perpetuate the memory of Reb Elemelech Gavriel Tress, zt″l, and for the many hours spent sharing their own memories and reviewing the manuscript. From the time spent with the remarkable woman with whom he chose to share his life, I have gained a sense of his own *heilige neshama*. Mrs. Tress has taught me that writing Jewish history does not excuse any deviation from the Torah's commands, including that against causing pain with one's words.

Much of this book is based upon the nearly 80 interviews conducted by noted historian DR. DAVID KRANZLER over a period of years. Dr. Kranzler also organized the voluminous Tress files. Without his efforts, the task of writing the book would have been far more arduous.

Much of this work is based on the memories of the more than 100 people who were gracious enough to give of their time to be interviewed. In many cases, people in their 70s and 80s were asked to recall with precision events that occurred 50 and even60 years ago. As one born after most of the crucial events in this book occurred, and who already often has difficulty remembering the previous week's Shabbos guests, I am in awe of their ability to reconstruct events of so long ago.

RABBI MOSHE KOLODNY, archivist of Agudath Israel of America, graciously put his vast knowledge at my disposal. In addition he not only responded promptly to every request for hard to find documents, but at his own initiative unearthed many vital documents about which I would not have known.

I have benefited from the insightful reading of various chapters by: RABBI NOSSON SCHERMAN, RABBI EMANUEL FELDMAN, RABBI NISSON WOLPIN, RABBI DAVID KAMENETSKY, MATTISYAHU ROSENBLUM, AVROHOM BIDERMAN, and REVA KIRSHNER.

I am indebted to RABBIS MEIR ZLOTOWITZ and NOSSON SCHERMAN, general editors of the ArtScroll History Series, for always making me feel like a member of the family and not as an employee. It is indeed a privilege to be part of the ArtScroll family.

For AVROHOM BIDERMAN the weeks of work assembling pictures and overseeing the literally thousands of details involved in production of this book were a labor of live. Raised in the Agudah movement, he demonstrated an uncanny ability for ferreting out important pictures and documents.

SHMUEL BLITZ, director of Mesorah Publications' Jerusalem office, is a good friend and trusted advisor, and deserves much of the credit for all that I write.

The book is beautifully adorned with the cover designed by REB SHEAH BRANDER and REB ELI KROEN. Their craftsmanship is evident in the layout of every page.

MRS. FAYGIE WEINBAUM's meticulous proofreading has added immeasurably to the quality of this work. SHLOIME HENIG, MRS. BASSIE GUTMAN, and UDI HERSHKOWITZ went beyond the call of duty in the production of this book.

The burden of being separated from my family for weeks at a time during the research of this book was greatly eased by my hosts in America, RABBI AND MRS. NISSON WOLPIN. The Wolpin home not only exemplifies the *middah* of *hachnasas orchim* but every other quality for which a Jewish home is praised. It is truly a dwelling place of the *Shechinah*. The *Shabbosim* spent with Michael and Liba Markson of Monsey were an added benefit of the book.

My parents MR. AND MRS. PAUL ROSENBLUM שיחיו have provided me with a model of parenting that I hope to be able to emulate with my own children. They remain, as they have always been, the closest of friends and my most devoted supporters. May they be granted many more years of health and happiness together, and to see their children, grandchildren, and great-grandchildren fully involved in Torah and *mitzvos*. My father-in-law MR. ROBERT BLOCK שיחי' and my grandmother MRS. MAXWELL ABBEL תחי' remain sources of unstinting encouragement.

No words of *Chazal* resonate so personally as those of Rabbi Akiva to his students: "All that is mine is hers."' They describe, without elaboration, all that my wife Judith תחי' means to me. May the *Ribbono Shel Olam* grant us the ability to raise our children to personify the ideals for which Reb Elemelech Gavriel Tress stood.

My deepest debt of gratitude is to the *Ribbono Shel Olam* Who, in addition to all the other *berachos* with which He has showered me, has made it possible to spend even that time outside of the *beis medrash* in the company of great men.[1]

Wherever possible the names of women mentioned have included maiden names in parentheses. Occasionally the reference to women by their married names may cause confusion when referring to events prior to their marriage, and, in a few instances, where discussing at length a woman prior to marriage we have referred to her by her maiden name. When referring in their youth to men who went on to acquire *semichah* or other titles of distinction, we have omitted their titles.

---

1. Note on nomenclature:

The reader should be aware that while today Zeirei Agudath Israel is a division of Agudath Israel of America, between 1939 when Agudath Israel of America was founded by Rabbi Eliezer Silver and the late 40s, when the two organizations formally joined together, they were two separate organizations. Mike Tress headed Zeirei Agudath Israel, and became, after the amalgamation, the Administrative President of Agudath Israel of America. When discussing the public activities of Zeirei Agudath Israel, we have employed its English name: Agudath Israel Youth Council of America.

INTRODUCTION

A Man for Mashiach's Time

"LAST NIGHT I HAD A DREAM."

So Reb Shraga Feivel Mendlowitz began his Tuesday night *shiur* on *Tehillim* at 616 Bedford Avenue, the Williamsburg headquarters of Zeirei Agudath Israel. Those who regularly attended the *shiur* (class) already knew that it was impossible to predict where the words of *Tehillim* (Psalms) would take Reb Shraga Feivel. Though the class was ostensibly based on Rabbi Samson Raphael Hirsch's commentary on *Tehillim*, Reb Feivel was apt at any moment to launch into a long digression on *Tanya*, the classic work of *Chassidus*.

Those present were always prepared for the unexpected, but what followed was still a surprise. Reb Feivel continued:

In my dream, *Mashiach* came. Kings, presidents, and prime ministers all came to greet him. But ahead of them all were the great *rabbanim* of our generation: Rabbi Eliezer Silver in his tall stovepipe hat; Rabbi Aharon Kotler with his burning eyes; Rabbi Kalmanowitz with his long white beard. Then *Mashiach* turned to me and asked, "Who is that sitting in the back, not pushing forward — the one without the beard?"

And I answered, "That's the one who brought you. Reb Elemelech Gavriel Tress."[1]

What made Reb Feivel's retelling of his dream so remarkable was that Mike Tress was present at the *shiur,* as he was every Tuesday night. And Reb Feivel was no flatterer. He and Mike had grown close over the years, as they worked hand in hand in creating America's first flourishing Orthodox community in Williamsburg. He certainly knew how embarrassed Mike would be by his words, and how little he needed such praise. Yet a dream was a dream, and this one had to be told.

Nor was Reb Feivel alone in thinking of Mike Tress in terms of *Mashiach.* Whether it was his *temimus* (purity of heart) or his *mesiras nefesh* (self-sacrifice) for *klal Yisrael,* there was something about the man that caused the greatest Torah leaders of the generation to associate him with the ultimate redemption of the Jewish people. The Satmar Rebbe, the fiercest ideological opponent of Agudath Israel, once told Mike's youngest son Mendel, "If there were nine more in the world like your father, *Mashiach* would come. Because he is a *sonei betza,* one who cannot be swayed by money."[2]

In the middle of the war which would consume six million Jews, the Kopyczinitzer Rebbe, himself a recent refugee, also had a dream. In his dream he was in *Gan Eden* seated at the foot of a table. At the head of the table was a good-looking young American. The Rebbe's neighbor turned to him and asked, "What are you doing at the end of the table while that one without *peyos* or a beard is sitting at the head of the table?"

"What?" the Rebbe replied. "You don't know Mike?" No more needed to be said: If one knew Mike, his place at the head of the table in *Gan Eden* needed no explanation.[3]

---

1. Interview with Moshe Berger. Mr. Berger was present at the *shiur.*

2. Interview with Mendel Tress.

3. The Kopyczinitzer Rebbe related this dream one Sunday morning in his Henry Street *shtiebel* on the Lower East Side. *Berger interview.*

Though the Rebbes and Torah scholars with whom Mike worked over the years always

IN THE MIDDLE OF A MEETING OF THE MOETZES GEDOLEI
HaTorah of America in the '50s, Mike had to leave the room briefly. As

**A Gaon
in Deeds**

he walked out, Reb Aharon Kotler turned to his neighbor
and said, "You are a *gaon* (genius) in Torah; that Jew is a
gaon in *maasim* (deeds)."[4]

Reb Shraga Feivel Mendlowitz was equally effusive. One day, he was
discussing with a group of his *talmidim* (students) the *Gemara* (*Pesachim*
49b) that advises a man to marry the daughter of a *talmid chacham*. And
if he cannot find the daughter of a *talmid chacham*, the *Gemara* continues,
he should marry the daughter of the *gadol hador*.

"Is it possible," Reb Feivel asked, "that the *gadol hador* (literally, great
one of the generation) is not a *talmid chacham*?" He then cited Rashi's
explanation that *gadol hador* here refers to the *gadol hador* in actions. "And
in our generation," Reb Feivel concluded, "that is Mike Tress."[5]

IT IS DIFFICULT TO IMAGINE AMERICAN ORTHODOXY EVER
again producing a lay leader of the stature of Mike Tress. Tragic events

**The Legacy of
Mike Tress**

call forth great leaders, and the name Mike Tress
will forever be associated with the *hatzalah*
(rescue) work of a band of youthful volunteers

during the Holocaust years. The affidavits obtained by Mike and his
closest associates and the visa applications processed by the Refugee
and Immigration Division of the Agudath Israel Youth Council saved
thousands of lives.

Mike personally played a pivotal role in obtaining Special Emergency
Visitors visas for 70 of the greatest European Torah scholars and their
families. Among those who came to America on those visas were Rabbi
Aharon Kotler, Rabbi Reuven Grozovsky, Rabbi Mendel Zaks, and Rabbi
Yisrael Chaim Kaplan. The postwar growth of yeshivos in America
would have been inconceivable without the influx of *talmidei chachamim*
made possible by these visas.

Yet neither the rescue work nor the development of Agudath Israel of
America — the other great achievement inevitably associated with Mike's

addressed Mike respectfully as Reb Elemelech or Reb Meilach, some of them referred to him in
the third person as "Mike," the name by which he was universally known. The use of the English
name, far from indicating any diminution in respect, was a reflection of the love and admiration
with which the name "Mike'" was always spoken in the Jewish world.

4. Interview with Rabbi Feivel Rosenzweig.

5. Interview with Rabbi Moshe Sherer.

name — encompasses the impact of Mike Tress on the growth of American Orthodoxy. He was, together with Reb Shraga Feivel Mendlowitz and Rabbi Aharon Kotler, one of the principal architects of today's American yeshiva world.

His most enduring achievement is intangible, incapable of quantification, but no less momentous for all that. He gave a group of American-born young men and women confidence in themselves and in their future as Orthodox Jews. He called out to them, *"Mi LaHashem Alai —* let's fight for the *Ribbono Shel Olam,"* and they answered his call.[6]

In relation to the total American Jewish population, the numbers were not large, and initially the movement was largely confined to the single Brooklyn neighborhood of Williamsburg. Nor did the movement arrest the headlong assimilation of most of American Jewry. But prior to the renaissance of *Yiddishkeit* in Williamsburg led by Reb Shraga Feivel Mendlowitz and Mike Tress, the question was not whether most of American Jewry would be lost to assimilation, but whether anything would be saved for Orthodoxy.

Mike painted a picture of a bright Orthodox future in America,[7] and provided an environment in which young people could be happy in their *Yiddishkeit* without the feeling that they were objects of ridicule.[8] He gave strength to those who had previously suffered from a sense of being left out of the fast-moving American society into which they had been born. "Mike gave us the feeling that we didn't have to be afraid of our own shadows," Celia (Roth) Zanzipar remembers.

His message was that America did not have to be a land of compromised Judaism. In the words of Rabbi Moshe Wolfson: "He taught us that Judaism was not just a tradition but our most precious possession, a possession for which we had to be prepared to fight and pay a price."[9] Mike pointed to the great leaders of European Jewry and told his followers, "That's what we are aiming for: a Judaism without conditions, without leniencies."[10]

EVERY MOVEMENT NEEDS A HERO, SOMEONE WHO PERSONIFIES its animating ideals, and Mike Tress was that hero for the most idealistic

---

6. Interview with Rabbi Shlomo Rotenberg.

7. Interview with Rabbi Yaakov Goldstein.

8. Interview with Mrs. Sylvia Klausner.

9. Interview with Rabbi Moshe Wolfson. Rabbi Wolfson was in one of Mike's first Pirchei groups and is today *Mashgiach* of Mesivta Torah Vodaath.

10. Interview with Rabbi Chaim Uri Lipshitz.

young American Jews. Much of his attraction lay in the fact that he was American born, an English speaker — one of them. This was not "some

Their First Hero
old European rabbi, with a long white beard, preaching Judaism," as Rabbi Ephraim Wolf put it, but someone with whom they could identify. The fact that he was handsome, impeccably dressed, and spoke English well all contributed to his magnetism. His broad shoulders and open face conveyed a quiet strength and confidence which he transmitted to others.

The youth who followed him all knew that he was a successful businessman, someone who had made it in American society. But they also knew that he was a *baalebas* who *davened* with a *minyan* every morning; that when he found out his partners in Esquire Shoe Polish had worked on Shabbos, he did not hesitate to ask Reb Elchonon Wasserman what he should do;[11] and above all, that he had given up everything to devote himself body and soul to the plight of the Jews of Europe.[12] Stories of his knocking on doors in Washington on behalf of European Jewry and of how he slept on the cold floors in the Displaced Persons (DP) camps together with the broken survivors fueled the imagination of Orthodox youth and filled them with pride.[13]

Reb Shraga Feivel Mendlowitz imbued his students with the idea that just as Torah study takes precedence over one's mundane pursuits, so too must the needs of *Klal Yisrael* take precedence over one's personal desires. But even Reb Shraga Feivel's closest *talmidim* still needed a concrete example of what they had learned in theory. Mike Tress was that example, the living personification of sacrifice for the *klal*. He made it possible to relate to Reb Shraga Feivel's vision by translating it into reality.[14]

Mike not only aroused a generation with the desire to serve the Jewish people, "to do for *Yiddishkeit*," he also showed them how. He gave focus to youthful enthusiasm and became, says Elimelech Terebelo, "the channel through which all our energies could be united and organized for the *klal*."

Without the destruction of European Jewry, those feelings of commitment to the Jewish people would never have burned with such intensity. But if Mike Tress had not already created a generation eager to serve, the

---

11. Interview with Rabbi Ephraim Wolf.
12. Interview with Elimelech Terebelo.
13. Interview with Binyamin Urman.
14. Wolf interview.

idealism and dedication that fueled the rescue activity would not have been there in the first place.

AMERICA, SAID REB SHRAGA FEIVEL MENDLOWITZ, WOULD produce a new Jewry, one combining the best elements of Europe: the **A New** intellectual acuity of Lithuanians, the *bren* (spiritual inten-**Jew** sity) of Polish *Chassidus*, the organizational abilities of German Jewry, and the appreciation of *hiddur mitzvah* (beautification of the commandment) of the Hungarians. Above all, the American Jew would be characterized by his *temimus*.[15] Mike Tress was the embodiment of that purity. "When he said the names Reb Chaim Ozer, the Chafetz Chaim, the Chortkover Rebbe, the Gerrer Rebbe," Sidney Greenwald remembers, "it was with one breath. It never occurred to him that there were differences between them."

Perhaps there was something naive about that view, but if so, it was useful naiveté, for it allowed the creation of a united Orthodoxy, one undivided by labels. If we are more sophisticated today, we have paid a high price for that sophistication: the creation of an Orthodoxy modified by a seemingly infinite number of brand names. And in that "naive" view there was more truth than in the more "sophisticated" modern one, for what the great Torah leaders of the Jewish people share in common is much greater than what distinguishes them.

When the survivors began to arrive from Europe after the Holocaust, they and their children were not swallowed up in America as earlier generations of immigrants had been. The reason was that a beachhead of dedicated young Jews who were prepared to accept the highest standards of *halachah* had already been created. And when the remaining leaders of the European yeshivos and the great Chassidic dynasties came to America during the war and after, they found awaiting them a group of young American Jews who had been trained to look upon them as the true leaders of the Jewish people. The boys may have had only a rudimentary yeshiva background and some of the girls might still have worn short-sleeved dresses. Yet they were prepared to venerate the newcomers because their first hero, a clean-shaven American, had pronounced the names of the leaders of European Jewry, in forum after forum, year after year, with such awe and reverence.

---

15. Interview with Sidney Greenwald.

JEWISH BIOGRAPHY HAS ALWAYS TENDED TO BE BIOGRAPHY OF *gedolim* (great Torah scholars). At best, such biographies are problemat-

The Challenge of Mike Tress ic. Of necessity they suffer from a built-in distortion: That which is most intrinsic to the *gadol* in question — his Torah knowledge and teaching — can only be hinted to in a popular biography. And though such works can be inspiring, the reader usually has no trouble finding grounds to distinguish himself from the *gadol* in question and to thereby render him irrelevant as a model for his own life. From the first story about the genius spotted at three years of age, the only message for the average reader is: The *gedolim* are not like you and me.

The story of Mike Tress does not permit any such easy out for the reader. Though a man of considerable intellectual gifts, those gifts are not what distinguished him from countless others. He was favored with neither illustrious *yichus* (lineage) nor a fine Torah education.

If one thing set Mike Tress apart, it was his love of his fellow Jews and his willingness to sacrifice himself on their behalf. "When we think of most people," says his cousin and successor as president of Agudath Israel of America, Rabbi Moshe Sherer, "we picture individual limbs forming a human being. With Mike it was different. All you think of is one big heart."

For this reason Mike Tress's life challenges each and every one of us to answer why we are not more like him. What is our excuse? Was he born with a bigger heart? Did he naturally love other Jews more than we do?

Throughout the late 1940s and '50s, Agudath Israel of America went through repeated financial crises. One of those called in to help the organization put its financial affairs in order was a lawyer named Sam Feinberg. In the course of his work, Feinberg had occasion to review the financial records of the organization's officers, including those of its president Mike Tress.

Feinberg was active in the National Council of Young Israel and a staunch opponent of Agudath Israel, primarily due to what he viewed as the latter organization's lack of Zionist enthusiasm. One day, not long after receiving the records of Mike Tress, Feinberg happened to be taking the train into the city from Far Rockaway with his friend Gavriel Beer. Feinberg knew that Beer was one of the Pirchei boys who had grown up in the movement under the tutelage of Mike Tress and was an active Agudah member. The two had had many friendly political arguments over the years.

Knowing how close Beer was to Mike Tress, Feinberg could not restrain himself from sharing the results of his investigations into Mike's personal finances. He told Beer that he had been so astounded by the tale revealed in those records that he could not believe his own eyes. He had called over three other lawyers in the office to confirm that he understood the records correctly, and their amazement had been no less than his own.

> When he went to work full time for the Youth Council of Agudath Israel of America in 1939, Mike Tress was a rich man by the standards of the day, with a handsome stock portfolio and substantial savings from his job as an executive with the textile firm of S.C. Lamport, Inc. His bank records from 1939 onward revealed an interesting pattern. One day, hundreds of dollars would be removed from Mike's personal account. The next day the same amount would be credited to the account of the Agudath Israel Youth Council. (And this at a time that Mike was working day and night without taking a salary.) This pattern repeated itself throughout the war years and beyond until there was nothing left in the bank account.
>
> Next the stock portfolio began to be sold off. Block after block was sold and the proceeds immediately transferred to the account of the Youth Council to allow it to carry on its rescue work. When the shares had all been sold, the Tress apartment, in which Mike lived with a large and rapidly growing family, was mortgaged — once, twice, three times. And again the proceeds of each mortgage went right into the coffers of Agudath Israel. When there was no more equity in the house, Mike began to take out personal loans to cover the expenses of Agudah.
>
> In a decade and a half, the once prosperous businessman had become little more than a pauper, for only one reason: At a time when dollars could be translated into Jewish lives, he was incapable of not giving everything he had.

"When I saw this," Sam Feinberg confessed to Gavriel Beer, "I fell in love with Mike Tress."[16]

---

16. Interview with Gavriel Beer.

Part One

LAYING
THE FOUNDATIONS

Chapter One

EARLY YEARS

A MYSTERY SHROUDS THE LIFE OF MIKE TRESS. HOW did an American-born young man, educated in American public schools and college, without a day of yeshiva study in his life, create a movement based on the ideal that Torah scholars are the true leaders of the Jewish people? Denied a Torah education himself, how did he come to see so clearly the importance of yeshiva education for boys and Bais Yaakov schooling for girls?

It is, unfortunately, a mystery to which no final answer can ever be given. The clues from his early years are sparse. With the sole exception of Rabbi Moshe Sherer, his first cousin and more than a decade his junior, there is no one alive who remembers him prior to his early 20's, around the time he first joined the Zeirei Agudath Israel *minyan* in Williamsburg.[1]

From the Shtetl to the New World

MIKE'S PARENTS, GERSHON AND HENYA, ARRIVED SEPARATELY in New York as part of the mass emigration from the Russian Pale of Settlement between 1890 and 1914. Between 1800 and 1900 the Jewish population of Eastern Europe grew from 1,000,000 to 6,800,000. At the same time, opportunities for Jews to earn a livelihood were ever diminishing. In Russia, Jews were banned from the newer industrial cities, barred from owning land, and subjected to increasingly repressive laws.[2] The overwhelming poverty, coupled with recurrent pogroms in the early 1880s, and again between 1903 and 1907, caused over 15 percent of the Jewish population of the Russian Empire (and a much higher percentage of the able bodied between 15 and 45) to emigrate between 1898 and 1914. Nearly a million and a half Jews came to America between 1891 and 1914.[3]

Henya Morotznick arrived at Ellis Island, together with her older sister Basya, a widow with a young child, just after the turn of the century. Their journey began in the tiny *shtetl* of Steppin near Berdichev in the Ukraine. The area was largely Chassidic, and Henya and Basya's family were Karlin-Stolin *Chassidim*. From Steppin, the two sisters traveled by train to Hamburg, Germany, and from Hamburg by steamship to America. Improvements in railroad and steamship transportation had by then reduced the travel time from *shtetl* to the world's most bustling metropolis to little more than two weeks in most cases.[4]

Most of the voyage was spent confined below deck in steerage with the rest of the poorest class of passengers. The horrors of the transatlantic crossing were not soon forgotten. The smell of seasickness hovered everywhere in the air of the poorly ventilated cabins. Complete strangers were crammed into cabins with bunks piled two and three high.[5]

Upon their arrival in New York, Henya and Basya made their way to the Lower East Side, a section of filthy overcrowded tenements, which

---

1. Mike's closest friend at the time he first entered the Williamsburg branch of Zeirei was another fatherless young man by the name of Julie Liebowitz. Liebowitz was hit by a car and killed shortly thereafter. Due to his premature death, there are not even any second-hand stories of Mike's teenage years.

2. *Encyclopedia Judaica*, "United States of America," vol. 15, p. 1608 (1974).

3. Howard Morley Sachar, *The Course of Modern Jewish History*, p. 309.

4. *Encyclopedia Judaica*, op. cit., p. 1609.

5. Irving Howe, *The World of Our Fathers*, pp. 39-42.

Mike's mother, Mrs. Henya Tress

by 1914 was home to approximately half a million Jews crowded into less than two square miles.[6] Like so many younger women, Henya secured employment in the needle trades working in one of the infamous sweatshops, thus known for the sweltering, airless conditions in which as many as 15 to 20 people worked together in one room.[7]

The ready-made garment industry of the time was the nearest thing America has known to a completely Jewish industry. The large manufacturers were drawn mainly from the more established German Jewry. These manufacturers in turn subcontracted much of their work to smaller enterprises. The subcontractor himself had often been in the country only a few years. As soon as he managed to scrape together enough money for a sewing machine or two, he was ready to hire others, often newly arrived *landsleit* (those from the same town or area in Europe). Of the 11,172 clothing firms listed in the Manhattan census of 1910, employing 214,000 workers, the majority were small firms with five workers each. In peak season, the workday was often 16 hours, and 12-hour days were normal.[8]

A FEW YEARS AFTER HER ARRIVAL, HENYA MET A YOUNG TAILOR by the name of Gershon Tress. He too was originally from Steppin.

Starting a Family Perhaps they met through one of more than 1,000 *landsmanshaften* (groups of Jews sharing a common place of origin in Europe) around which the Lower East Side's social life centered.[9] Whatever the case, their families back in Steppin surely rejoiced in the news that they had each found a *frum* partner from the same *shtetl*.

---

6. Sachar (p. 317) puts the Jewish population of the Lower East Side at 700,000 by 1914. *Encyclopedia Judaica* (p. 1608) gives the much lower figure of 350,000.

7. Ibid., p. 319.

8. *Encyclopedia Judaica*, op. cit., p. 1616.

9. Ibid., p. 1619.

The young couple began married life together in a typical tenement flat in which four families shared one or two water closets and a water faucet located in a narrow, poorly lit hallway.[10]

In the first decade of the century, many of the sweatshop bosses were still observant Jews who did not work on Shabbos. With the passage of time, however, there was a consolidation of the smaller shops — in which boss and workers often worked side by side — into larger, more impersonal workplaces. In these, Shabbos was far less likely to be a day off. As more and more immigrants left their traditional observance behind, it was harder to find jobs which did not require work on Shabbos, even in the smaller operations.

For Shabbos observers like Henya and Gershon, this often meant beginning the week looking for a new job. And with thousands of new immigrants pouring in every year (more than a 100,000 a year between 1904 and 1908), finding a job until the next Friday was increasingly difficult. Thus, in addition to the lack of privacy and ubiquitous filth, Henya and Gershon had to contend with the insecurity of never even knowing where the rent money would come from.

Yet somehow the young couple prevailed in the face of adversity and even started a family. In 1907, a son Moshe (Morris) was born and two years later a second son Elemelech Gavriel (Michael). Gershon's joy in his offspring, however, was shortlived. Just six months after Mike's birth, he passed away at the age of 25. In the fetid conditions of the Lower East Side, such premature deaths were commonplace.[11]

Henya was left to support and raise two infant sons by herself. Other than her sister Basya, who had since remarried, she had no extended family to fall back on. The two sisters were two of a kind and extremely close. Asked once how he and Mike had worked so closely for 25 years, Rabbi Moshe Sherer replied, "You should have seen our mothers. Neither had any money, and yet they both did everything they could so that the other should have."[12]

---

10. Howe, op. cit., pp. 151-153. In many buildings, there was still no indoor plumbing, only backyard outhouses.

11. Tuberculosis, known as the "white plague" to residents of the Lower East Side and as "the Jewish or tailor's disease" to outsiders, afflicted 12 out of every 1,000 Lower East Side Jews in 1906. Howe, op. cit., p. 148.

12. Mrs. Sherer was a surrogate grandmother for the Tress children, who never knew their father's mother. Every week the older Tress girls picked up potato latkes that Mrs. Sherer prepared for the Tress family, and when Mrs. Sherer was ill in her later years, the Tress girls used to take turns visiting her after school.

THE PSYCHOLOGY TEXTBOOKS ARE FILLED WITH DESCRIPTIONS
of the deleterious effects on a young boy of being raised without a

**Seeds
of Faith**

father. The trauma is said to result in a generalized insecurity. But if Mike suffered any such effects, they were
never noticed. No one ever knew him as anything other
than a self-confident, outgoing person, to whom people were naturally
drawn. Though lacking a father himself, he became, in time, a father
figure to hundreds of young men and women.

His mother Henya's firm faith no doubt provides the key to her son's
ability to overcome the tragedy of his own fatherless childhood.
Though he was never one to talk much about his own life, Mike always
spoke of his mother with the greatest love and respect. She was for him
the embodiment of goodness.[13]

The Tress home was not just a religious home, but a home characterized by intense piety. Henya and her sister Basya would often recite
Tehillim for an hour in the early morning.[14] When she moved to 191 Keap
Street in Williamsburg around 1930, Henya used to feed out-of-town students from Torah Vodaath, and invite boys from the yeshiva to come on
Shabbos afternoon for cakes and drinks. One of those who used to come
on Shabbos afternoon was Rabbi Nesanel Quinn, the long-time *Menahel*
of Torah Vodaath. He remembers the joy that it gave her to see *frum* boys
together in her home and how "every word she spoke — the choice of
words, her facial expressions — reflected spirituality and holiness." In
Williamsburg, she also devoted herself to the Women's Auxiliary of the
Stoliner *shtiebel*, of which she was the president.

If the difficult circumstances of his childhood had any effect at all on
Mike, it was only to leave him with a heightened sensitivity to the
misfortune of others. "I have never met another person like him in
terms of the way he suffered the pain of another Jew," says Moshe
Berger, who worked closely with him as the first head of the Refugee
and Immigration Division of the Agudath Israel Youth Council.

That sensitivity to others was also an inheritance from his mother.
Besides reciting *Tehillim*, Henya and Basya had another favorite
early-morning pastime. Whenever they heard that a woman had given
birth, they went door to door collecting money for the new mother.
Then in the early hours of the morning, they would go to her home and

---

13. Interview with Mrs. Edith (Hinde) Tress.
14. Interview with Rabbi Moshe Sherer.

place an envelope filled with cash under the door. Mission accomplished, they would repair to one or another's kitchen for a cup of coffee together. As a young boy, Rabbi Sherer often awoke in the morning to find his mother and aunt in the kitchen giggling together over the fact that they had once again managed to get away undetected with one of their *chesed* projects.[15]

This love of doing *chesed* was transmitted directly from mother to son. "It was in [Mike's] genes," observes Rabbi Sherer. "His

Mike's aunt, Mrs. Basya Sherer

greatest thrill was when he helped somebody. Then he was truly happy. It was an almost physical, earthly pleasure of satisfaction and fulfillment."

THE HUSTLE AND BUSTLE OF THE LOWER EAST SIDE — THE cacophony of hundreds of street vendors peddling a seemingly endless

A Summer in the Country variety of wares, the elevated train and trolley cars — provided plenty of stimulation for a young boy. One thing it did not provide, however, was any sense of natural beauty or any respite from the struggle for life all around. A tree may have grown in Brooklyn, but there was precious little chance of one taking root on the concrete pavements bordered by endless tenement blocks of the Lower East Side.

One of the highlights of Mike's early years — certainly one of the few he discussed later in life — occurred when he was eight years old. In his neighborhood was the Toynbee Settlement House. During the summer, Toynbee House ran a summer camp in the country for boys from the tenements. But even the subsidized price of three dollars a week was far beyond what Henya could afford. When Mike was eight, however, he won a "scholarship" of ten free days at the Toynbee House summer camp.

For the first time in his life, he could roam in meadows filled

---

15. Ibid.

Orchard Street on the Lower East Side of New York City, c. 1900

with flowers and trees, smell air untainted by rotting garbage, play baseball on a real diamond — rather than stickball among manhole covers — and swim in the clear, blue water of a natural lake — instead of the East River, with its perpetual film of oil. The experience left him with a lasting appreciation of the effect a few weeks in the summer could have on the development of a young boy.[16]

THOUGH HENYA HAD PROVIDED HER SON WITH A DEEP FAITH that would guide him all his life, she could give him little in the way of a formal Jewish education. Yeshiva education was then virtually non-existent in America, and what there was would certainly have been beyond the struggling widow's budget. Like most of his contemporaries, Mike probably attended an afternoon *cheder*, where a poorly paid, overburdened, and usually not very learned *rebbi* taught him to read Hebrew, how to *daven*, and perhaps some *Chumash*.

An All-American Boy

---

16. The story is from a brief biography of Mike written by Bernard Estes in 1956 as part of a fundraising campaign for Camp Agudah. Estes spent a week in the offices of Agudath Israel of America and interviewed Mike personally in connection with the project.

The primary concern of every young man and woman in those days, whether Orthodox or not, was to find some escape from the crushing poverty in which they grew up. College offered the best chance of earning a decent salary without the bone-crunching labor that most of their parents knew. Everybody wanted to go to college. The only question was whether one could afford to do so or would have to begin work immediately after high school.

Mike as a young boy

Mike's excellent grades at Seward Park High School entitled him to free tuition and books at Queens College. He was one of a group of young Orthodox men and women who used to cross the 59th Street bridge several nights a week, after a full day of work, to attend classes.[17] Mike worked during the day throughout college to help the family survive, just as he had worked after school during high school delivering papers and doing whatever odd jobs he could find.[18]

Upon graduating from Queens College, Mike appeared for all the world to be the all-American boy. He was a good tennis player and an excellent swimmer and one-wall handball player. His first contribution upon joining the fledgling Zeirei Agudath Israel chapter of Williamsburg was to organize a wide variety of athletic endeavors: basketball at Brighton or Manhattan Beach, ice-skating, and bicycle riding.[19] He also possessed a wide repertoire of American folk songs with which he provided entertainment on the Zeirei boatrides.[20]

There was a serious side as well awaiting its proper expression. One of Mike's fellow students at Queens College was Aharon Menashe Dershowitz, who had studied at Torah Vodaath. After the Tress family moved to Williamsburg, Mike used to attend a *Chumash shiur* that Dershowitz gave in his home. The latter remembers him as an earnest, very sincere young man, striving to be a more knowledgeable Jew.[21]

17. Interview with Mrs. Tillie (Katz) Glassman, another member of this group of young men and women.

18. Estes biography. See note 16 above.

19. Interviews with Max Gross and Max Septimus.

20. Interviews with Mrs. Tillie (Glassman) Katz and Mrs. Henchie (Gross) Leiman.

21. Interview with Rabbi Aharon Menashe Dershowitz.

Top: Mike playing tennis in Camp Agudah
Bottom: Mike (in center) on a Zeirei boat ride, June 1936

THE B.S.S. DEGREE IN EDUCATION MIKE EARNED AT QUEENS College did not turn out to be the ticket to fortune. There was an over-

Young Executive

abundance of teachers on the market, and he found that he would have to wait months before a job opened up. Even then, he could not hope to earn more than a meager salary as a teacher. In the meantime, his mother's health had failed, and she could no longer work. Mike decided that he could not wait to find a teaching job.[22]

Instead, he took a job with S.C. Lamport, Inc., a large textile firm. It was not long before he was promoted to the head of a division. Among his responsibilities was supervision of a department in which remnant pieces of material to be sold in bulk were measured. Almost 100 young women were involved in this process.

Lamport's was one of the few large *shomer Shabbos* companies, and Mike used his position to hire *shomer Shabbos* girls in his division.[23] The work may not have been terribly interesting, but in the middle of the Depression one was happy to have a job of any kind. When there were no men around, the girls spent their time singing happily and talking together, without "any pressure or stress, and without a sharp word ever being spoken."[24]

Mike eventually found jobs in the office for many *shomer Shabbos* young women. He continued to watch out for their interests even after they had left his department.[25] Besides finding jobs for *shomer Shabbos* young women, he created a rag department and hired bearded elderly Jewish men, who would otherwise have had difficulty finding jobs, to

---

22. Estes biography. See note 16 above.

23. The list of *shomer Shabbos* young women who worked at S.C. Lamport, Inc. at one time or another includes: Harriet (Gross) Leiman, who later married Rabbi Heshy Leiman, the long-time English principal of Mesivta Chaim Berlin; Ruth (Walfish) Fruchthandler, wife of philanthropist Ephraim Fruchthandler; Debby (Quinn) Deutsch, the sister of Rabbi Nesanel Quinn; Florence (Elkind) Falik, who later married Judah Falik, one of the main supporters of Yeshivas Chaim Berlin; Irene (Greenbaum) Levy, sister of Rabbi Berel Greenbaum, founder of the Lower East Side Pirchei and later principal of The Yeshiva of Spring Valley; Anne (Mashinsky) Weisberg and Bessie (Mashinsky) Zamore, older sisters of Rabbi Heshy Mashinsky, one of Mike's first Pirchei boys; and the mother of Jack Klausner, who later edited the Pirchei youth magazine *Darkeinu* and was one of the most active Pirchei leaders in the 1940s.

When a young woman named Edith Bagry was looking for a job in 1936, it was natural that she should approach Mike, since a number of her best friends — Henchie Gross, Debby Quinn, Florence Elkind, and Ruth Walfish — were already working at Lamport's. Three years later, she and Mike were married.

24. Interview with Mrs. Tress.

25. Interview with Mrs. Henchie (Gross) Leiman.

do the light work required.[26]

Mike's talents as a leader were already evident early in his business career. He had a way with people that Samuel Lamport, the company's founder, obviously noticed in promoting him so quickly to head of a division.[27] Using positive reinforcement seems to have come naturally to him, and anger was foreign to his nature. Tillie (Glassman) Katz, another young woman who worked at Lamport's, describes the atmosphere in the department as ideal:

> Mike got along very well with all the workers. He had a very positive personality, which everyone admired. He never had to ask anyone to keep working. Everybody worked steadily, without any arguing or rivalry.
>
> He had an excellent sense of humor. He would just walk by and make a remark and everybody would start laughing. He never insulted anybody, and nobody had a bad word to say about him.

The qualities of leadership Mike showed at Lamport's would soon manifest themselves in a larger forum and on tasks more important than increasing the production of bolts of textiles.

---

26. Interview with Mrs. Florence (Elkind) Falik.

27. In his will, Lamport stipulated that Mike always have a job with the company and that his department remain *shomer Shabbos*. *Interview with Max Septimus.*

    The failure of the Lamport children to keep the company closed on Shabbos was, according to one account, the reason Mike quit his job in 1938. *Interview with Mrs. Florence (Elkind) Falik.*

Chapter Two
FLIGHT FROM ORTHODOXY

STORIES OF TEFILLIN THROWN OVERBOARD by Jews about to dock on Ellis Island may be largely apocryphal, but they are nevertheless an apt metaphor for the rapid decline in religious observance among the new immigrants to America. Even where the immigrants managed to retain their religious practices, they had scant success in transmitting those practices to the next generation.

The Jewish world in which Mike came to maturity was thus one in flight from the strictures of the Torah. Only against the backdrop of the abandonment of traditional religious practice by first- and second-generation immigrants is it possible to fully assess his achievement in building a movement centered around Orthodox youth.

THE GREAT MASS OF JEWISH IMMIGRATION TO AMERICA PRIOR
to World War I was drawn largely from the *shtetls* of Eastern Europe. The

From Shtetl to Metropolis contrast between the small towns in Russia, Poland, Lithuania, Hungary, and Romania from which the immigrants came and the bustling, commercial civilization in which they arrived a few weeks later could hardly have been more stark. Even today, dirt streets and horse-drawn wagons are commonplace in many of these Eastern European hamlets. The society the immigrants entered was, by contrast, one in which rapid change was the only constant. From a world without running water, they entered one of streetcars, electricity, typewriters, and moving pictures.[1]

The shock of leaving behind a village of a few hundred to a few thousand people for a city of millions was profoundly disorienting. So great and so quick was the transformation in the immigrants' lives that it was easy for them to convince themselves that they had truly entered a new world in which everything they had once known, including their religion, no longer applied.

Eastern European society was a profoundly traditional one, which remained in many respects unchanged from the Vilna Gaon's day until the 20th century. Most Jews, especially in the smaller *shtetls*, were religiously observant, and this observance was reinforced by both the family and communal social structures. Though the level of Jewish learning may not have been high, virtually every *shtetl* could boast of a *rav* who was a *talmid chacham*. The presence of *talmidei chachamim* in their midst helped prevent ordinary Jews from viewing Jewish observance as a set of mere rituals without deeper meaning or logic. The absence of comparable religious authorities in America, and certainly the lack of the close relationship between the *rav* and his flock that had prevailed in the *shtetl*, made it difficult for parents to convince their American-born children that the traditional religious practices were anything more than empty rituals.

The social structures which preserved religious observance in the small towns were largely absent in the modern metropolis. The anonymity of the city replaced the intimacy of the *shtetl*. That anonymity made it easier for those who wanted to shed their religious practices to do so without fear of being ostracized.

Immigration severely strained traditional family structures as well.

---

1. Interview with Rabbi Berel Belsky.

In the *shtetl,* it was not unusual for several generations to live side by side. Immigration, however, was largely for the young. Single men and women who came to America by themselves no longer had to fear parental disapproval of their modern ways. In other cases, husbands came alone and had to spend a number of years in America before they were able to afford to bring over their wives and children. It was sometimes difficult for fathers to reassert their parental authority after the long period of absence.[2]

English-speaking children, educated in American public schools, did not grow up with the expectation of following in their parents' footsteps in the same way one generation had followed another in the *shtetl.* Their parents' Yiddish, or halting English, emphasized with each word the gap between the generations and between the old world and the new.

In addition, the mass of immigrants was not drawn from the most learned elements of Jewish society. If anything, America exerted the greatest attraction for those most eager to shed their traditional observance to one degree or another. The frequently reiterated fears of the religious leaders of Eastern European Jewry of the pernicious effects of the *"treifene medinah"* on religious belief and practice had the least effect on this group.

THE PRIMARY IMPETUS FOR LEAVING EUROPE WAS DIRE poverty. In some European *shtetls* as much as 50 percent of the popula-

The Struggle for Existence tion was dependent on communal charity prior to Pesach.[3] But that poverty did not automatically abate upon arrival in the *"goldene medinah,"* where if money did not exactly grow on trees, it was at least rumored to be found in the streets. The poverty in Europe may have been more intense, but the effects of that poverty were more destructive of the family in America. In Europe, virtually everyone was poor. By contrast, Jews in America were exposed to a society in which great wealth was to be found and which prided itself on the high degree of social mobility. To be poor in America was therefore to be a failure.

Only a small percentage of immigrant families could subsist on the earnings of the father alone.[4] As a consequence, the mother, and frequently the children themselves, were expected to contribute to the

---

2. Rabbi Aharon Surasky, *Shlucha D'Rachmana* (Heb.), p. 95.

3. Salo Baron, *The Russian Jew Under Tsars and Soviets,* p. 65.

4. Arthur Hertzberg, *The Jews in America,* p. 197.

family coffers. With both parents engaged in the struggle to eke out a living, children were often left with little supervision and subject to the influences of the street.

Those influences were far from salutary. The New York City Police Commissioner published an article in *Harper's Magazine* in 1908 in which he claimed that Jews constituted one half of the city's criminal offenders. Though he was forced to retract by the protests of financier Jacob Schiff and other leaders of the Jewish establishment, the accusation was not farfetched. Especially among juveniles, petty theft and other economic crimes were rife.[5] A 1906 study showed that approximately 30 percent of those arraigned in Children's Court were Jewish. A few years earlier Jacob Schiff and his brother-in-law Louis Marshall persuaded the city to allow the Jewish community to establish its own reform school for juvenile violators.[6] As early as 1880, social critic Jacob Riis noted the inordinate fondness of young Jews for dance halls, and by the early 1900s such halls could be found on almost every block of the Lower East Side.[7]

The inability of fathers to support their families further undermined their authority and made it more difficult for them to transmit their values to their children. The widespread problem of desertion by husbands is but one indicia of a pervasive sense of failure among fathers. The National Desertion Bureau, the joint creation of the Jewish charities in major cities, dealt, over a period of 20 years, with thousands of cases of fathers who had deserted their families.[8]

With the passage of time, jobs that did not require work on Shabbos became increasingly difficult to find. Parents with many mouths to feed and no savings or social safety net to fall back upon frequently succumbed to the economic pressure to work on Shabbos. As a young boy going to *shul* with his father on Shabbos morning, Rabbi Moshe Sherer remembers seeing Jews with beards leaving the Keap Street *shul* in Williamsburg on their way to work. When he asked his father where they were going, his father would only say, "When you're older, you'll understand."

Shabbos work was a tragedy not only for the father or mother upon

5. Ibid., p. 205.

6. Irving Howe, *World of Our Fathers*, pp. 263-64.

7. Hertzberg, op. cit., p. 212.

8. Ibid., p. 199.

whom it was forced but for their families as well. Parents who worked on Shabbos felt themselves to have failed as religious Jews and were therefore less likely to provide their children with any religious education. Having been unable to withstand the economic pressures on them, they lacked the moral authority to seek from their children a more scrupulous observance.

WHATEVER THE GENERATIONAL TENSIONS EXPERIENCED by the immigrants and their children, they agreed about one thing:

The Quest for Education the importance of attaining as much education as the family could possibly afford. Parents did not want their children to repeat their economic struggles anymore than the children wished to do so. The New York City college system offered ambitious Jewish boys, and to a lesser extent girls, a university education at a nominal price, and its student body soon became overwhelmingly Jewish. The Lower East Side was the most highly radicalized area in the country — in 1914, 1916, and 1920 its voters elected Meyer London to Congress on the Socialist ticket — and it is hardly surprising that the city colleges, filled with the children of immigrants, were hotbeds of radicalism. Prolonged exposure to radical campus politics did little to encourage fealty to traditional religious practice. Lacking any Jewish learning, eager young Jewish minds had nothing to temper their enthusiasm for their studies or to juxtapose to the "high-minded values" of Western civilization.

Judaism was mocked in both the socialist press and the Yiddish theater. Yom Kippur and Tishah B'Av dances and the March of Bread on Pesach were annual features of East Side life.[9] Both the vitriol and mockery that were directed at Orthodoxy would be unthinkable today. The East Side immigrants came from a religious milieu and were aware of themselves as being in rebellion, to one degree or another, against the strictures of that world. Judaism was still sufficiently alive for them to merit aggressive attacks. Rabbi Yaakov Goldstein remembers as a young boy having his *yarmulke* knocked off his head by older men, still possessed of heavy Yiddish accents, who would challenge him, "*Vy* don't you go back to Europe *vere* you belong?"

Nor could a religious youth be assured, as he could today, that any

---

9. Interview with Rabbi Moshe Sherer.

Advertisement for a Yiddish play held on Rosh Hashanah

attacks on his beliefs issued forth from the mouths of utter ignoramuses. Returning from *shul* on Shabbos morning, Rabbi Goldstein used to dread the weekly encounter with a neighbor who always sat smoking a cigar on the front stoop. Between puffs of smoke, the neighbor would ask him, "*Vos hastu gelernt di voch* — What did you learn this week?" When he would tell him, the neighbor would reply by rattling off the *Rashi* and *Tosafos* on the *daf* (page of *Gemara*) word for word.[10]

DESPITE THE IDEOLOGICAL ATTACKS FROM THE LEFT AND THE ridicule from various quarters on Judaism, East Side life remained to a

Religious Form Without Content
large extent Orthodox in form, if not content. When Jews chose to pray, they almost invariably did so in an Orthodox *shul,* and when they marked major life events, they chose Orthodox clergymen, or those who professed to be Orthodox, to solemnize the occasion. On the High Holy Days, *minyanim* sprang up everywhere, some form of *kashrus* was

---

10. Interview with Rabbi Yaakov Goldstein.

observed in most homes, a traditional *seder* celebrated, and children recited *Kaddish* for their parents. At least in the first generation, Reform — associated with the uptown German Jewish establishment — and its close cousin Conservatism exercised little pull for East Side Jews.

Yet the Orthodox forms increasingly reflected a vague nostalgia rather than a vibrant religious culture. The hiring of stars of the Yiddish theater, which was open on Friday nights and Shabbos afternoon, as *chazzanim* (cantors) was one example of the preference for Orthodox-style over the real thing. Youth choirs were common in the bigger synagogues, whose members conveniently ignored that many of the boys in the choir traveled by public transportation to perform. Joshua Silbermintz was one of the few Orthodox boys to perform in those choirs. The money he and his brothers earned in choirs helped finance their yeshiva education. On more than one occasion, he was hit over the head for actually saying the words of *Kedushah* rather than looking at the choir director for his cues. One Yom Kippur, the choir director tried to convince him that it would constitute theft if he did not eat since he had been hired to sing and fasting would impair his voice.[11]

The first hit talking movie, *The Jazz Singer,* starring Al Jolson, epitomized this strand of nostalgia and cheap sentimentality. In the largely autobiographical account of Jolson's career, a cantor's son becomes a popular entertainer and even marries a non-Jew. But in the climactic scene, he returns to his father's *shul* to lead the *Kol Nidrei* service as his father lies dying and his mother looks on tearfully from the women's gallery. The message was one East Side Jews were eager to hear: You can taste all the fruits of American society — even marry a *shiksa* — without cutting yourself off from your roots and permanently estranging yourself from your people.

DESPITE THE MULTITUDE OF FORCES THREATENING RELIGIOUS observance, religious life on the Lower East Side and in other large

Generational Tension

Jewish enclaves was not unremittingly dark. The *shuls* and *shtiebels* were still filled with pious Jews. It is not even true, as is commonly assumed, that there were no great *talmidei chachamim* in America prior to World War II. A lengthy bibliography could be compiled of the scholarly works composed in America prior to 1940.[12] An earnest religious boy in the early

---

11. Interview with Rabbi Joshua Silbermintz.

12. Sidney Greenwald has, in fact, compiled such a bibliography.

'30s could still find a *chevra Mishnayos* whose leader knew the *Rambam's Mishnah Torah,* with its principal commentators, by heart, and in which one of the *baalebatim* could place a pin on the title page of a *Gemara* and recite every word through which it would pass to the end of the tractate. The *shochet* to which the housewife took her chickens to be slaughtered on Thursday night might be found reciting *Gemara* by heart.[13]

The sacrifice involved in preserving the Shabbos lent a special purity to the Shabbos of those who were up to the challenge. Rabbi Yaakov Goldstein recalls:

> Today you have many *shomer Shabbos* Jews, but then we had *erev Shabbos* Jews. A Jew who was fired when he announced on Friday afternoon that he would not be in to work the next day, and who knew that he would be looking for a new job on Sunday morning, truly looked forward to the Shabbos as a respite from the cares of the week. Today people rush from work to *shul* on Friday night and sit there with sour faces, still wrapped up in their business.

But the fact remains that even the most committed among the immigrants had difficulty passing on their beliefs to their children. Aish Yisrael, an East Side *shtiebel,* was open 24 hours a day with Jews learning. Yet only a handful of the children of those who *davened* and learned there remained religious.[14] Of the 200 men who *davened* in the same Marcy Avenue *shtiebel* as Louis Septimus's father, only two had children who remained observant.[15]

Like most of his fellow muckrakers, Lincoln Steffens had a taste for the melodramatic. But the picture he drew in his autobiography of generational tension between fathers and sons was a staple of East Side life:

> We would pass a synagogue where a score or more boys were sitting hatless in their old clothes, smoking cigarettes on the steps outside, and their fathers, all dressed in black, with their high hats, uncut beards, and temple curls, were going into the synagogue, tearing their hair and rending their garments. . . . Their sons were rebels against the law of Moses: They were lost souls, lost to G-d, the family, and to Israel of old.[16]

---

13. Goldstein interview.

14. Interview with Sidney Greenwald.

15. Interview with Louis Septimus.

16. Hertzberg, op. cit., p. 196.

THE IMMIGRANTS WERE NOTORIOUSLY LAX IN PROVIDING their children with a religious education. A 1918 survey found that only

The Lack of Religious Education 65,000 out of 275,000 Jewish school children in New York City were provided any kind of Jewish education, and that number includes the completely non-religious schools established by various *Yiddishist* groups, such as the Jewish National Workers Alliance, the Sholom Aleichem Folke Schools, and the Workmen's Circle.[17]

The most common form of education was a group of boys learning with a *melamed* in the afternoon. If the memoirs of both immigrant children and former *melamdim* are to be trusted, the two groups generally approached each other with a cordial hatred.[18] The boys viewed their chief purpose in being in *cheder*, rather than outside playing ball, as the torment of their would-be mentor. For his part, the poorly paid *melamed* was typically free with the use of his ruler and whatever else came to hand in his efforts to silence his unruly charges. In any event, the aspirations for *cheder* were generally minimal — that the boys should learn enough to read a *siddur* and be able to recite *Kaddish* for their parents. The *cheder* experience did little to convince the boys of the spiritual majesty to be found in the holy books, to which they were, in any event, barely exposed.

Yeshivas Rabbeinu Shlomo Kluger and Yeshivas Rabbeinu Yaakov Yosef were founded on the Lower East Side in 1911 and 1915 respectively. But they served no more than a few hundred boys at most. The minimal tuition charged placed them beyond the range of many families, and even religious parents worried that a yeshiva education would leave their children ill-suited for the struggle for survival in America.

Nor did these "yeshivos" bear any great resemblance to those of Europe. They continued only until the age of *bar mitzvah*, and the curriculum consisted of a few hours a day of religious instruction. At most, boys received the barest rudiments of *Mishnah* and *Gemara*. The yeshivos also suffered from a chronic lack of qualified teachers. The majority of the teachers were Hebraists and *maskilim*. A *rebbi* was expected to know grammar, *Tanach*, and some Jewish history. Mitzvah observance was assumed, but was not necessarily a requirement for

---

17. Howe, op. cit., p. 202.
18. Ibid., pp. 200-202.

employment.[19] A popular joke of the time based on the verse (*Devarim* 13:2), "And he will place upon you a sign (אות) or a wonder (מופת)," was that *rebbis* came in two categories: those who could teach an אות (a sign or letter) — i.e., who understood grammar — and those who could tell a מופת (a wonder story) — i.e., who possessed the Fear of Heaven.[20] The two groups were assumed to have little overlap.

The small salaries the *rebbis* received, and for which they often had to wait months at a time, did little to improve the situation. The handful of truly committed *rebbis*, men such as Rabbi Yaakov Flanzgraben and Rabbi Reuven Mandelbaum at Yeshivas Rabbeinu Shlomo Kluger, are still remembered today with great affection by their students. The former used to have a special group of students with whom he would begin learning every morning at 6:30 a.m.[21]

Why were the religious immigrants so slow to establish yeshivos? For one thing, building a yeshiva requires large investments of time and money, both of which were in short supply. In addition, the immigrants were slow to realize how different the conditions of America were from those in which they had grown up. In the *shtetl*, boys naturally grew up to be *frum*, and they assumed that the same *melamed* who had been adequate for them would be adequate for their children.[22] The lures of the surrounding civilization and of the street were something their experience had ill prepared them to anticipate.

As they realized how different America was, the attitude of the immigrants shifted from the complaisant assumption that the ways of the old world would continue to suffice to one of despair. But the result was the same: quiescence. When Binyamin Wilhelm first tried to solicit funds and students for a yeshiva in Williamsburg, he was greeted with hoots of derision by older immigrants. "This is America, and the situation is hopeless" was the standard response.[23]

In their despair, religious parents accustomed themselves to unacceptable compromises. Always the excuse was the same: This is America. After the Shabbos *cholent,* many religious mothers gave their small children a few coins for the local movie theater.[24] And at a later stage, they

---

19. Interview with Reuven Soloff.
20. Surasky, op. cit., p. 98.
21. Interview with Rabbi Yitzchak Karpf.
22. Interview with Rabbi Berel Belsky.
23. Surasky, op. cit., p. 95.
24. Ibid.

made their peace with mixed dances at Young Israel on the grounds that at least their children would meet other religious youngsters.[25]

The despair of immigrant parents was shared by those *talmidei chachamim* who were in America. They, by and large, spent their days immersed in study and writing, with little thought of influencing the youth whose flight from Judaism they viewed as a foregone conclusion.

ANOTHER MISTAKE MADE BY THE IMMIGRANT GENERATION was the failure to give their children a sense that there was a place for

No Place in Shul
them within the *shuls* and *shtiebels*. An unmarried man was never allowed to the lead the *davening* or to receive any other honor in *shul*. The founding of the Young Israel movement and the various chapters of Zeirei Agudath Israel by single, young men in their late teens and early 20's is a reflection of the alienation from their parents' *shuls* of even the more religious youth.

The development of separate *minyanim* for young, usually American-born men also indicates the extent to which even those first-generation Jews who were committed to preserving their *frumkeit* viewed themselves as set apart from their parents by language, education, and differing life experiences. They were conscious of themselves as modern in ways that their parents were not.

To save American Orthodox youth would require the development of new institutions and the leadership of those thoroughly versed in American society. Zeirei Agudath Israel was one such response.

---

25. Interview with Mrs. Sylvia Klausner.

Chapter Three

ZEIREI AGUDATH ISRAEL

IF RELIGIOUS JEWS WERE BECOMING AN INCREAS-
ingly embattled minority in America in the first decades of the

**An
Unpopular
Cause**

20th century, the group of 25 or so young
men who formed the first chapter of Zeirei
Agudath Israel (ZAI) on the Lower East Side
quickly found themselves a tiny minority

within a minority.

That initial group included both foreign-born and first-
generation Americans in their late teens or early 20's who had
joined together to strengthen one another's *Yiddishkeit*. As
such, Zeirei was only one of a number of similar groups that
dotted the Lower East Side.[1] What set Zeirei apart from other
such fraternal organizations was its affiliation with the world

---

1. For instance, when Binyomin Wilhelm, the founder of Yeshivas Torah Vodaath,
arrived in America in 1907, he joined a group of other young immi-

movement of Agudath Israel that had come into existence 10 years earlier at Kattowitz, Poland and its emphasis on Talmud study.

Zeirei was itself an outgrowth of an earlier group known as Bachurei Chemed, or The Society for Young Tal-mudists, organized by Yehoshua (Shea) Gold in 1917. The earlier group broke up as a consequence of the visit of a delega-tion of distinguished Agudah representa-tives to America in 1921 led by one of Polish Jewry's leading figures, Rabbi Meir Don Plotzky, the Ostrover Rav.[2]

R' Shea Gold

The Agudah delegation urged Bachurei Chemed to affiliate with Agudath Israel, and a resolution in support of the idea was passed by

The Agudath Israel delegation upon their arrival in America. L-R: Rabbi Asher Spitzer, Rabbi Dr. Meir Hildesheimer, Rabbi Meir Don Plotzky, Rabbi Joseph Lev, Dr. Nathan Birnbaum

---

grants in a religious fraternity known as Adas Bnei Yisrael. Much of the early support for Torah Vodaath came from fellow members of Adas Bnei Yisrael who had moved from the Lower East Side to Williamsburg. See, Aharon Surasky, *Shlucha D'Rachmana*, pp. 94-95.

2. Other members of the delegation were: Dr. Nathan Birnbaum, one of the foremost ideologues of Agudath Israel, Rabbi Dr. Meir Hildesheimer of Berlin, Rabbi Asher Spitzer of Kurdorf, Slovakia, and Rabbi Yosef Lev.

Two earlier visits by Rabbi Aharon Walkin, the *rav* of St. Petersberg, and Rabbi Dr. Meir Hildesheimer on behalf of Agudath Israel had yielded no tangible results. *The Struggle and the Splendor: A Pictorial Overview of Agudath Israel of America*, p. 37.

Bachurei Chemed. A fierce editorial denouncing the decision in the next morning's *The Jewish Morning Journal*, however, caused some members to reconsider, and a second resolution was passed that Bachurei Chemed remain unaffiliated with any other organization.

Binyomin Hirsch, one of those who had been eager to identify with Agudath Israel, began agitating for the creation of a new group to be named Zeirei Agudath Israel. "Why are you silent? Where is your *kavod HaTorah* (honor for Torah scholars)? The time has come for us to leave Bachurei Chemed," he told his fellow members.[3] Those who answered his call formed the initial nucleus of Zeirei Agudath Israel.

The decision to link themselves to the world Agudath Israel movement was to prove a fateful one for the members of ZAI. Initially, however, it did little other than subject them to widespread opprobrium. At that time, Agudath Israel was not a popular cause in America, either within the religious world or without, primarily due to its stance vis-a-vis political Zionism. The Second Zionist Congress in Basel in 1898 had declared Jewish religion to be a matter of "individual conscience," essentially irrelevant to Jewish national aspirations. Such a view was anathema to the founders of Agudath Israel, and combating political Zionism was one of the major purposes for which Agudath Israel was formed. At Kattowitz, Reb Jacob Rosenheim, soon to be chosen as the first president of Agudath Israel, enunciated a vision diametrically opposed to the Basel declaration. The goal of Agudath Israel, he declared, was the revival of "an ancient Jewish possession: the traditional concept of *Klal Yisrael*, Israel's collective body, animated and sustained by the Torah as its organizing soul."[4]

American Orthodoxy at that time leaned overwhelmingly towards Mizrachi, the movement of religious Zionists, which felt it was possible to make common cause with secular Zionists. At the first convention of Agudas Harabonim in 1935, Rabbi Ephraim Epstein of Chicago introduced a resolution that membership in Mizrachi be made a formal requirement of membership in Agudas Harabonim. Opponents of the resolution could do no better than to water down the original proposal;

---

3. Moshe Yehuda Gleicher, *History of Agudath Israel of America* (a pamphlet published by the National Council of Pirchei Agudath Israel), p.3.

4. *The Struggle and the Splendor*, p.13.

affiliation with Mizrachi was reduced from an iron-clad obligation to a suggestion.[5]

Zionism was one of the first issues over which the new immigrants asserted their independence from the uptown German Jewish establishment, which was violently opposed to any movement that would call into question Jewish loyalty to America.[6] To be anti-Zionist in the immigrant milieu was thus to invite ostracism. The leading Yiddish papers refused to accept advertisements for Zeirei, and the largest *shuls* were unwilling to rent their halls for meetings connected to Agudath Israel.

On those few occasions when Zeirei did organize meetings of a political nature, they were constantly threatened with disruptions. In 1927, Shlomo Ehrmann, one of the leaders of German Agudah, came to America on behalf of Keren HaYishuv. As soon as he got up to speak on the Lower East Side, supporters of Mizrachi on all sides of the hall rose and started singing *Hatikvah*. A fight broke out and the police were called.[7] Rocks thrown through the windows and cut electric lines were common occurrences at ZAI meetings through the '30s.[8]

---

5. The ranks of Mizrachi then included many of the leading *talmidei chachamim* in America. Rabbi Ephraim Epstein was, for instance, the brother of Rabbi Moshe Mordechai Epstein, the Slabodka Rosh HaYeshiva, who had himself been active in the Chovevei Zion movement in his youth. See Rabbi Berel Wein, *The Triumph of Survival*, p. 133 fn. 41.

Opposition to Rabbi Epstein's resolution was led by Rabbi Pinchas Teitz of Elizabeth, New Jersey, a relatively recent arrival in the United States. He was accused in *The Jewish Morning Journal* of having cursed Mizrachi rather than of having criticized it. Such a distortion was typical of the way in which any deviation from the Mizrachi viewpoint was then viewed as heresy. *Interview with Rabbi Pinchos Teitz.*

Even into the '40s, Agudath Israel was numerically insignificant in America in comparison to Mizrachi. Rabbi Moshe Sherer's first assignment as Executive Director of the Agudath Israel Youth Council was to attend a conference to strengthen Shabbos observance convened by Rabbi Yisrael Rosenberg of Agudas Harabonim. When Rabbi Rosenberg called for a show of support, Rabbi Sherer was the first to respond positively. That brought Aryeh Leib Gellman, the leader of American Mizrachi, to his feet. "Who do you Agudah people think you are?" he asked. "You're nobodies. We won't join forces with nobodies like you." *Interview with Rabbi Moshe Sherer.*

In terms of membership, Gellman's characterization was unkind, but not far from the truth. Similarly, when Orthodox groups joined to fashion a joint position paper to the first meeting of the United Nations Relief and Rehabilitation Agency (UNRRA), in 1944, no memorandum could be submitted until a way was found to keep the name of Agudath Israel from appearing first among the signatories, as would have been indicated by alphabetical order. *Interview with Rabbi Joseph Elias.*

6. Arthur Hertzberg, *The Jews in America*, Chap. 13.

7. Interview with Fishel Eichenthal.

8. Sherer interview.

R' Moshe Mordechai Epstein R' Yaakov Gordon R' Moshe Blau

The Lower East Side Zeirei

THOUGH THEIR IDENTIFICATION WITH THE WORLD AGUDATH Israel movement caused problems for the young men who formed the first Zeirei Agudath Israel chapter, it would be a serious distortion to view their purposes as primarily, or even largely, ideological. Their focus was almost exclusively on creating an environment where like-minded young men could gather to study Talmud. The members spent little time discussing either the problems of world Jewry in general or the ideology of Agudath Israel in particular.[9] Connections to the Agudah movement were intermittent at best. ZAI sent two representatives — Yaakov Mordechai Gordon and Gedaliah Schorr — to Vienna in 1929 for the Second Knessiah Gedolah of Agudath Israel. And the Zeirei *minyan* was a natural stopping point for luminaries from Europe and *Eretz Yisrael* — e.g., Rabbi Meir Shapiro, the initiator of *Daf HaYomi* and Rosh Yeshivas Chachmei Lublin, Rabbi Meir Karelitz, brother of the *Chazon Ish,* and Rabbi Moshe Blau — on their visits to the United States. The Slabodka Rosh Yeshiva, Rabbi Moshe Mordechai Epstein, was the featured speaker at the first convention of Zeirei Agudath Israel in February 1924.

The first home of the Lower East Side Zeirei branch was the basement of the Gorlitzer Chevra on 102 1/2 Lewis Street. Among the early members were Fishel Eichenthal, Yisrael Feigenbaum, Anshel Fisher, Herzl Fogel, Yosef Fogel, Avraham Gleicher, Moshe Yehudah Gleicher, Yaakov Gold, Yehoshua (Shea) Gold, Yaakov Mordechai Gordon, Binyamin Hirsch, Anshel Huberman, Mendel Metzger, Yitzchak (Itchie) Metzger, and Yisrael Wiederkehr. Most of them were European born and had come to America as children or teenagers. Yiddish continued to be the language of Zeirei, as it had been of its predecessor Bachurei Chemed.

---

9. Eichenthal interview.

Committee of Zeirei Agudath Israel of America, 1927. L-R: Nathan Horowitz, Joseph Fogel, Charles Fogel, Abba Gleicher, Fishel Eichenthal, Joseph Weinrib, Hirschel Berliner

The schedule of Zeirei members barely left a free minute anywhere in the day. Most worked full time and went to night high school. The typical schedule required rising between 5 a.m. and 6 a.m. to *daven* and reach work by 8 a.m. Work generally lasted until 6 p.m. (Ten hours of work a day, six days a week generally netted around $12 a week.) After work came night school until 9 p.m. Only then could the Zeirei members get together for their daily spiritual nourishment.

The highlight of the day from the very beginning was the *Daf HaYomi shiur* given by Shea Gold, who, like the rest of the group, worked a full day.[10] Not until 11 p.m. did the ZAI members arrive home for supper.[11] On Shabbos morning, the learning started at 6 a.m. and lasted until *davening* at 9 a.m. By two o'clock everyone had gathered again and

10. In the early days of ZAI, Rabbi Noach Garfinkel used to come every night from the Bronx to teach a *shiur* in *Mesillas Yesharim*. Soon, however, his duties as head of a yeshiva in the Bronx made it impossible to continue.

11. At the 50th-anniversary dinner of the founding of Agudath Israel of America in 1972, Reb Shea Gold paid tribute to the *mesiras nefesh* of the original members of Zeirei Agudath Israel. He repeated a story that Rabbi Shimon Schwab told on his first visit to the headquarters of the ZAI of the Lower East Side at 48 Avenue C.

As a young man, Rabbi Schwab had visited the Chafetz Chaim, and the latter drew him a picture from the days of the *Bais Hamikdash:*

A wealthy Jew with a long white beard decides to make the long journey to Jerusalem to bring a *korban todaah* offering. He is accompanied on his journey by children and grandchildren, who join him in song and dance and *Hallel* the whole way to Jerusalem. After slaughtering his sacrifice, an 18-year-old *Kohen* with a scraggly beard receives the blood in a special vessel from which it is sprinkled on the Altar. The young *Kohen* tells the distinguished old Jew that only a *Kohen* is fit to do the most important part of the Temple service — the sprinkling of the blood.

"Why," the Chafetz Chaim asked Rabbi Schwab, was the most important part of the service the

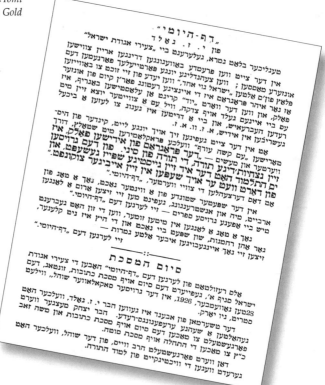

remained through *Shalosh Seudas.* This schedule was not just theoretical. Unexcused absences from the nightly learning *seder* could result in fines of up to a dollar, or almost 10 percent of the average weekly wage.[12]

At *Shalosh Seudos,* everyone was expected to take his turn delivering a *dvar Torah.* If anyone lacked confidence, Shea Gold would secretly help him prepare, but no one was excused. In later years, it was a trademark of those who had grown up in the Zeirei of the Lower East Side that they were always capable of speaking when the occasion demanded.[13]

The commitment demanded by Zeirei forged a relationship of

exclusive province of the *Kohanim?"* The Chafetz Chaim answered his own question: "Because when Moshe called out, `Who is for Hashem to me!' they responded."

"So too," said Reb Shea Gold, accepting the award on behalf of the entire founding group, "did those honored here tonight respond with *mesiras nefesh* at a time when a person who was *shomer Shabbos* could not hold a job, when there was no kosher food, and when to be religious made a person the object of ridicule." *Interview with Sidney Greenwald.*

12. Eichenthal interview.

13. Interview with Rabbi Yaakov Goldstein.

THE FOUNDERS OF ZEIREI AGUDATH ISRAEL IN AMERICA

Mr. Hirschel Berliner
Rabbi Mendel Chodorow
Mr. Fishel Eichenthal
Mr. Moshe Eichenthal
Mr. Jacob Einsiedler
Mr. Israel Feigenbaum
Mr. Anshel Fink
Mr. Anshel Fisher
Mr. Charles Fogel
Mr. Leo Gartenberg
Mr. Leo Gartenhaus
Mr. Moshe Yehudah Gleicher
Mr. Robert Gleicher
Mr. Shea Zev Gold
Mr. Max J. Gordon
Mr. Louis Greenberger
Mr. Israel Hasenfeld
Mr. Nathan Hausman
Mr. Shabse Hirschel
Mr. Avner Katz
Mr. Charles Klien
Mr. Jonah Klien
Mr. Joseph Knobel
Mr. Moshe Lanton
Mr. Pincus Mandel
Mr. David Mendlowitz
Mr. Pesachya Menkis

Mr. Isadore Metzger
Mr. Mendel Metzger
Mr. Isaac Mittman
Mr. Milton Mostel
Mr. Israel Pachtman
Mr. Abraham Plotzker
Mr. Joseph Plotzker
Mr. Elimelech Saltz
Mr. Meyer Sanft
Mr. Irving Schonbrun
Mr. Pesach Dovid Schonfeld
Mr. David Schorr
Rabbi Gedalia Schorr
Mr. Max Schreiber
Mr. Abraham Seif
Mr. Aron Seif
Mr. Louis J. Septimus
Mr. Morris Septimus
Mr. Solomon Septimus
Mr. Aaron Stauber
Mr. Alex Steinberg
Mr. Isaac Strahl
Mr. Hirsh Meilech Susswein
Mr. Jacob Tanzer
Mr. David Wachtenheim
Mr. Moshe Weinberg
Mr. Israel Wiederkehr

extreme closeness between the members. "It was all for one and one for all," says one early member. At a time when workers could be fired suddenly by any caprice of their boss, and when a week's wages barely covered the basic necessities of food and rent, the support of a group was often crucial. When one member had difficulty holding a job, the whole group met to consider all possibilities for him and committed themselves to helping him find a job. Another time one of the members contracted pneumonia, which in the days before penicillin was often fatal. The Zeirei members contributed $50 to hire the leading specialist in the city to treat him, with several members donating a whole week's salary.[14]

The convivial spirit would sometimes burst forth outside the narrow confines of the *minyan*. At the close of one festival, Zeirei met in a basement on Houston Street. Their dancing was so lively that when the storekeeper above opened his store after the holiday, he found all the cans on his shelves dancing up and down in unison with the celebrants downstairs. He called the police, and the members had to promise to refrain from dancing for six months.

WITHIN A FEW YEARS OF THE FOUNDING OF ZAI ON THE LOWER East Side, other branches had formed in the Williamsburg and

The Williamsburg Zeirei Brownsville sections of Brooklyn and in the Bronx. A Boro Park branch was formed in the early '30s.[15] The Williamsburg branch would by the mid-'30s be the largest and most active branch, as well as the forum in which Mike Tress first came to prominence, and it will therefore be the focus of our attention.

As in the case of the Lower East Side branch, the original impetus for the Williamsburg branch was the creation of Agudath Israel in Europe. A report on the first Knessiah Gedolah in Vienna in August, 1923 inspired a group of young men whose families *davened* in a *shtiebel* on Marcy Avenue and Hart Street to form a Zeirei Agudath Israel chapter. But the link to Agudath Israel was, as on the Lower East Side, for the most part in name only. Members met together at night to learn and had their own *minyan* on Shabbos, but Agudath Israel ideology was far from their purview.

There were, however, differences between the Williamsburg and East Side branches as well. Williamsburg was a second stop for immigrant families — a step up in the world. The Jews who began to move to Williamsburg in the early '20s did so in search of more room for their families than could be found on the teeming Lower East Side.

---

14. Interview with Anshel Fisher.

15. The Boro Park branch produced two of those who worked most closely with Mike over the years: Charles Klein and Charles Young. The former was actively involved as chairman of banquets and in a host of other volunteer capacities, and the latter eventually became Comptroller of the Agudath Israel of America Youth Council.

Rabbi Elias Karp gave Shabbos *shiurim* in the Boro Park Zeirei almost from the beginning. Yisrael Pachtman was another active early member, as was Yisrael Feigenbaum after his move from the Lower East Side.

Williamsburg, however, remained predominantly Irish and Italian well into the '30s.[16] Nor were the Jews of Williamsburg necessarily religious. Lee Avenue had only a few *shomer Shabbos* stores, and in the '20s a bakery thought nothing of scheduling its grand-opening celebration, replete with music, on *Shabbos Shuvah*.[17]

Williamsburg's status as a second-generation neighborhood meant that those who formed the nucleus of the early Williamsburg ZAI were far more Americanized than their Lower East Side counterparts. The majority of members of both branches were of Galician-Chassidic backgrounds, but the Williamsburg members were far more likely to be American born. Though Yiddish was still the language in the homes of the Williamsburg members, most were equally comfortable in English. Many of the early Williamsburg members — for instance, the Plotzker brothers and the Septimus brothers — went on to college and to careers in the professions.

The schedule of East Side members rarely allowed them time for more than work, school, and learning the *Daf HaYomi*. Williamsburg branch members found time for sports and an occasional card game.[18]

Despite being more Americanized than their East Side counterparts, the members of the Williamsburg Zeirei still viewed themselves as far removed from the membership of Young Israel, a movement custom tailored for English-speaking American youth. In general, Zeirei members felt themselves to be somehow *frummer* than those in Young Israel — the clearest proof being the mixed dances that were widespread in Young Israel. Young Israel was, in their eyes, more of a social organization, whereas Zeirei activities centered around *Gemara* learning.[19]

At the same time, the lines between Young Israel and Zeirei were not impermeable. Many Zeirei members also *davened* in Young Israel *minyanim* from time to time. Frequently it was geographic proximity

---

16. Rabbi Arnold Wolf remembers *davening* as a young boy in Torah Vodaath, at 206 Wilson street, one Friday night when a gang of Italian youths surrounded the building. He prayed that he would be able to get home safely.

17. Interview with Rabbi Nesanel Quinn.

18. Interviews with Max Gross and Max Septimus.

Not all the members participated in these activities. The Schorr brothers, for instance, participated only in the learning and Shabbos *davening*.

19. Rabbi Dr. David Stern was the only rabbinic advisor to the organization. The Lower East Side branch of Young Israel in which he held sway did not allow mixed dancing.

rather than ideology that primarily determined where one *davened*.[20] Young Israel forums on current events drew many from ZAI to join in the debates. Even among Zeirei members who considered themselves too religious for Young Israel, there was a general acknowledgment that the movement was a positive influence on many English-speakers who would not have felt comfortable in ZAI.

The nucleus of the original Williamsburg branch included several sets of brothers: the Septimus brothers — Louis, Morris (Mo), Sol, Harry (Heshy), Max, Abe, and Norman; the Plotzker brothers — Abe, Charlie, Joe, and Max; and the Schorr brothers — of whom Moshe, Aaron, Dovid, and Gedaliah were active. Nathan Hausman was another of the first members. Pesachya Menkis initially led the *Daf HaYomi shiur*, before it was taken over by Reb Gedaliah Schorr, and also gave a *Chumash shiur* on Friday night. By the early '30s, Anshel and Mottel Fink, Max Gross, Morris, Irving and Harold[21] Hamm, Sender Kolatch, Dave Maryles, and Pesach Dovid Schonfeld were all active in ZAI. From the ranks of those who were active in the Williamsburg branch in those years came many of Mike's closest friends and staunchest supporters in all his projects.

Around 1930, the Marcy Avenue branch joined together with another branch that had formed in Williamsburg and moved into the basement of a building at 157 Rodney Street, which was closer to the center of Jewish life in Williamsburg. The new location was next door to the house of the Stoliner Rebbe and two buildings from the Stoliner *shtiebel*. The rent of $30 a month was beyond the means of the Zeirei *minyan*. But Moshe Schorr knew someone who put him into contact with Rabbi Dr. Leo Jung, leader of the prestigious Manhattan Jewish Center. He approached Rabbi Jung for the money to pay the rent, and Rabbi Jung agreed to furnish it.[22]

---

20. Interviews with Rabbi Moshe Yechiel (Murray) Friedman, Yitzchak Levy, and Tillie (Glassman) Katz.

21. Harold Hamm was Mike's singing and dancing partner on Zeirei outings. *Interview with Mrs. Henchie Leiman.*

22. Rabbi Jung was initially active in the American Agudath Israel movement, and attended the second Knessiah Gedolah of Agudath Israel in Vienna as one of the American representatives. Until World War II, Rabbi Jung was Chairman of the American Beth Jacob Committee. Though Rabbi Jung did not remain active in Agudath Israel beyond its first years in America, he maintained a close personal relationship with Mike and was on the board of the Refugee and Immigration Division. Through his synagogue, he probably obtained more immigrant affidavits during the war years than anyone else, and many of those most active in affidavit work in ZAI were trained by him. *Interview with David Schorr.*

An early Williamsburg Bnos trip. Mrs. Mandel is in the back row on the left. The girls are the Wilhelm sisters: Claire (Gewirtz) [middle row on left], Leah (Herskowitz) [sitting], and Channah (Belsky) [on Mrs. Mandel's left]

NOTHING COMPARABLE TO ZEIREI EXISTED FOR GIRLS UNTIL 1930 when Mrs. Fruma Leah Mandel, a widow with five children, began

Bnos groups for 16- to 18-year-old girls in her Brownsville neighborhood. Two years later, she moved to Williamsburg and began another branch there. Like Sarah Schenirer, the legendary founder of the Bais Yaakov movement, with whom she corresponded, Mrs. Mandel saw a need that no one else was filling and stepped into the breach herself.

Initially, Mrs. Mandel called her groups Bnos Bais Yaakov because she was afraid that *shomer Shabbos* girls from Mizrachi families would refuse to join a group explicitly identified with Agudath Israel, and she wanted to attract the largest possible membership.

The need for some kind of organized group for older girls was, if anything, even greater than for boys. Religious education for girls was almost non-existent. The first Bais Yaakov elementary school did not open its doors until 1937, and there was no Bais Yaakov high school until the middle '40s. The most available to a young woman in terms of a Torah education was the Beth Jacob Hebrew School, the equivalent of an afternoon Talmud Torah for girls, founded in Williamsburg by Reb Shraga Feivel Mendlowitz and Reb Binyomin Wilhelm, and the National Hebrew School on the Lower East Side.

After moving to Williamsburg in 1932, Mrs. Mandel went from door to door in search of older girls with whom to start a Bnos chapter. Soon she had assembled a group which included Reb Shraga Feivel Mendlowitz's daughters Channah and Rivka, Reb Binyomin Wilhelm's daughter Channah, Henchie (Gross) Leiman, Debby (Quinn) Deutsch, and Anne (Whitehorn) Hoenig.[23] Molly (Mintz) Puritz was Mrs. Mandel's assistant.[24] The older girls eventually became the leaders for younger groups of 14- to 16-year-old girls. Within a few years, Bnos had grown to 60 girls, with the youngest group made up of 9- and 10-year olds.[25]

Mrs. Mandel began by organizing Shabbos groups, which usually included an outside speaker[26] and informal learning. Initially Reb Shraga Feivel Mendlowitz was opposed to Mesivta boys lecturing to girls. In the style of her model Sarah Schenirer, Mrs. Mandel took her case directly to Reb Feivel and convinced him of the importance of providing a Torah environment for girls.[27]

The groups also met one or two times during the week in a three-room railroad flat on Bedford Avenue for drama or other activities. Hikes, boating trips, bonfires, and outings to the park were some of the Sunday activities. Twice a year, Mrs. Mandel took the girls to cemeteries to collect money for yeshivos or for some cause in *Eretz Yisrael*.[28]

The Lower East Side also boasted an active Bnos chapter. On Friday night, Berel Greenbaum, the driving force behind the Lower East Side Pirchei, used to teach a *Chumash-Rashi* class. And on Shabbos day, the girls took responsibility for teaching one another. Each week, one girl

---

23. Anne Whitehorn, who was one of the most active leaders of the younger groups, is a good example of the permeability of the lines between different religious groups in those days. She married Rabbi Dr. Sidney Hoenig, a prominent Young Israel leader and later a professor at Yeshiva University. Hoenig himself was a frequent speaker to the Williamsburg Bnos.

24. Other Bnos members included the three Pollack sisters — Esther Landesman, Channah Kirschenbaum, and Rachel Hopfer; the Bagry sisters — Lucy Wilhelm, Donya Greenhaus, and Hinde Tress; Sarah (Samuels) Glass; Alice Septimus; and Channah (Berman) Yaffe.

25. Interview with Rebbetzin Channah Belsky.

26. Among the speakers were Shmuel Chill, Shaye Kaufman, Isaac Strahl, Sidney Hoenig, and Meyer Karlin. *Interview with Mrs. Henchie (Gross) Leiman.*

27. Interview with Rebbetzin Channah Belsky.

28. Interviews with Mrs. Henchie (Gross) Leiman and Mrs. Deborah (Quinn) Deutsch.

would be responsible for teaching *dinim*, another *minhagim*, and so on. In the summer, they learned *Pirkei Avos* together, each one sharing what she knew.[29]

With no other religious activities or learning available, Bnos played a much larger role in the life of its members than it would in later decades. Bnos kept religious girls who were going to public school, and who were of an age to be particularly susceptible to peer pressure, together in a religious environment. Tillie (Glassman) Katz, a member of the Lower East Side group, put it succinctly, "Bnos was everything to us."

Within Bnos, religious girls shared their *Yiddishkeit* with one another:

> On Shabbos afternoon we would sing and dance together. Shirley Dicker sang beautifully and Esther Rubin taught us dances. We didn't have a care in the world.
>
> We didn't have the competition of clothing and other things that you find today. We were happy with what we had. There was no rivalry among us. If anyone knew of something special happening, we all went. We helped each other in so many ways. If somebody heard of a job for a *shomer Shabbos* girl, she would immediately call a friend who was looking for a job.[30]

Besides providing a religious environment for public school girls and reinforcing the values of their homes, Bnos offered the older girls a chance to meet *frum* boys in a religious setting. Finding suitable partners was a major problem in those days. The religious community was much smaller than today, and far less institutionalized, which made it much harder for a young man or woman to become acquainted. In that context, the *Melaveh Malkahs, Lag B'Omer* walks over the George Washington Bridge, open forums at which various current issues were debated, and annual ZAI boatrides provided the only opportunities for those of marriageable age to meet one another. The alternative for a religious young man or woman was not today's system of *shadchanim*, but the dances at Young Israel.

At a *Melaveh Malkah*, the most common form of interaction between Bnos and Zeirei chapters, boys and girls sat separately, though there were opportunities to socialize. Thus young men and women met in a

---

29. Among the active early members were: Shirley (Dicker) Fensterheim, May Farkas, Amelia Drillman, Tillie (Glassman) Katz and her sister Edythe (Glassman) Septimus, Esther (Roiter) Knobel, Peshya (Halperin) Simanowitz, Kaila Halperin, and Esther (Rubin) Newman.

30. Interview with Mrs. Tillie (Glassman) Katz.

Early East Side Bnos group on an outing

group setting which emphasized the religious restrictions on them. Many *shidduchim* resulted from these joint events.[31]

From the very beginning, most Bnos members were sisters of boys who were active in Zeirei, and there was a degree of informal contact between Bnos and ZAI. It was not until 1938, however, that the Williamsburg chapter formally affiliated with ZAI. The occasion was a meeting at the home of Channah (Wilhelm) Belsky in Williamsburg attended by most of the Bnos membership. Mike Tress gave what Rebbetzin Belsky would later describe later as "one of his typically fiery speeches" on the necessity of the Agudah movement in America having a girls' division, as it did in

---

31. Mike himself was an active *shadchan. Interview with Rabbi Yisroel Belsky.*

Europe. Some idea of how impassioned his oratory was can be discerned from the fact that one of the young women present sat there riveted during Mike's lengthy presentation, despite a sharp pain in her side. The next night she had an emergency appendectomy.[32]

The ZAI Interbranch Council

THE FIVE BRANCHES OF ZAI WERE LOOSELY JOINED IN AN Interbranch Council. Each branch, however, was for all intents and purposes fully independent. Each pursued its own course, developed its own programs, and had its own character.[33] From time to time, the various branches met one another for a *Melaveh Malkah*, sometimes with one of the Bnos chapters invited along as well, and there was an annual Interbranch boatride. But with the exception of a twice-yearly collection for Keren HaYishuv, a fund to aid religious Jews in *Eretz Yisrael*, no common project united the various branches. The members of the various branches shared a common sensibility at most, rather than a sense of common purpose or goals.

Heading the Interbranch Council up until the late '30s was a young lawyer named Isaac Strahl, who was more or less drafted for the position each year. Strahl lived in Brownsville and was the leader of the Brownsville Zeirei. In addition, he worked closely with his Brownsville neighbor Mrs. Mandel in the formation of her initial Bnos groups and was a frequent lecturer on Jewish topics in a wide range of forums.[34] Even after Mike succeeded Isaac Strahl as head of the Interbranch Council, the latter remained one of the leading figures in the movement, and Mike relied frequently on his keen analytic skills and good judgment.[35]

---

32. Interview with Rebbetzin Channah Belsky.

33. Interviews with Fishel Eichenthal and Abe Plotzker.

34. Interview with Ruth (Strahl) Kaufman, Isaac Strahl's younger sister.

35. For example, in the course of sensitive negotiations between Zeirei Agudath Israel of America and Agudath Israel of America over a possible amalgamation of the two organizations, it was Isaac Strahl to whom Mike turned to join him on the Zeirei negotiating team. Strahl was also active in procuring affidavits during the war years and rendered many other invaluable services to the rescue efforts.

After the war, he was appointed to a position for which his legal acumen and analytical brilliance ideally suited him: deputy delegate of World Agudath Israel to the United Nations. In that capacity, he worked closely with Dr. Isaac Lewin, Agudath Israel's chief delegate, as well as with the president of World Agudath Israel, Reb Jacob Rosenheim, and the other members of its presidium. *Kaufman interview.*

In a long and distinguished public career, Strahl was a member of the Board of Directors of Shaarei Zedek hospital for over twenty-five years, on the Board of Governors of Lubavitch, and legal advisor to the Skulener Rebbe.

An early Zeirei group:
The Aaron brothers,
Max Grossman,
Irving Shconbrun, and
Hymie Olshin.

Meetings of the Interbranch Council were long on Robert's Rules of Order, as befitted Strahl's training as a lawyer, but short on plans for the future.[36] Though Strahl was well versed in the ideology of Agudath Israel — he attended the third Knessiah Gedolah in Marienbad in 1937 — no one was yet thinking of how an activist movement could be organized on the basis of that ideology.

The transformation of Zeirei Agudath Israel into a true national organization would require someone capable of inflaming the emotions, as well appealing to the head, possessed of inexhaustible personal warmth, and willing to devote his entire being to the rescue of Jews abroad and the revival of *Yiddishkeit* at home. Such a person had already begun his work with the youth of Williamsburg.

---

36. Interviews with Max and Louis Septimus.

Chapter Four

MIKE JOINS ZEIREI

IF LIFE WERE DETERMINED BY SOCIOLOGICAL PROFILES, Mike Tress would never have joined Zeirei Agudath Israel. The young man who first walked through the doors of the Williamsburg Zeirei at 157 Rodney Street in 1931 was modern in appearance, college educated, more comfortable in English than Yiddish, and had little background in Talmud study. Hardly the picture of the typical Zeirei member of the day.

Mike *davened* frequently in the Stoliner *shtiebel* two doors down from the basement in which Zeirei was located. During the week, many of the Zeirei members also *davened* in the Stoliner *shtiebel*, and Mike probably met them there. (Zeirei *davened* together only on Shabbos and Yom Tov.) Still it took Max Gross, the Zeirei member who first invited Mike and his friend Julie Liebowitz to try the Zeirei *minyan*, almost a year from the time he first met Mike before he extended the invitation. The reason for his hesitation is clear in the invitation itself: "Why don't you join our group? I see you come to the Stoliner Rebbe. You may be *a little more modern*, but you can join us. We're your type of guys."[1]

At the end of the first Shabbos, Mike and Julie were far from convinced that they had found their place. Mike turned to Julie and asked him what he thought. Julie replied, "They look like a bunch of *mockies* (foreigners)."[2] Nor can they be blamed for that somewhat tepid response. That first Shabbos an argument broke out between two of the sets of brothers that dominated the *minyan*. Decorum in *davening* was also far from the standards of the European yeshivos. One Shabbos, the *gabbai* became so enraged by the amount of talking that he smacked the chief offender across the mouth with his *siddur* and had him bodily removed from the *minyan*. Only after promising to henceforth refrain from talking during services was the offender re-admitted.[3]

But whatever their misgivings, Mike and Julie did join the *minyan*. Mike's own account of his reasons for coming to Zeirei may explain why he stayed despite his initial impressions of the *minyan*. He and Julie Liebowitz had been looking for more *Yiddishkeit*, and their search led them to the Brooklyn Public Library. There they came across an article by Reb Jacob Rosenheim about the ideals of Agudath Israel, and decided to accept the invitation to try out the Zeirei Agudath Israel *minyan*.[4]

MIKE WAS BY NATURE A SPIRITUAL SEEKER. HIS RESTLESS NATURE craved a grand ideal to which he could commit himself body and soul.

The Attraction of Agudath Israel

He was a man of action, but that relentless activity depended on an animating vision. The larger the vision the better — no matter how difficult its realization in practice.[5]

Mike found the type of vision he was looking in Reb Jacob Rosenheim's description of *Klal Yisrael* — the collective body of the Jewish people — united around Torah and led by the great Torah

---

1. Interview with Max Gross.

2. Ibid.

3. Ibid.

4. Mike told this story to Leon Keller when the latter first ventured into the Zeirei *minyan*. Mike was always the first to greet any newcomer. *Interview with Leon Keller.*

5. Rabbi Shlomo Rotenberg notes that the word "*shittah*," in the sense of worldview, recurred frequently in Mike's conversation.

scholars of the generation. That vision spoke to something very deep within him. "He became an Agudist not because he learned about Agudath Israel," says Rabbi Menachem Porush, "but because his soul embodied some of the basic principzxles of Agudah. He was a *chassid* of *Klal Yisrael* and *Toras Yisrael,* of the approach that all *Klal Yisrael* must be united together under the banner of Torah."[6]

In the early '30s Young Israel was certainly a far more dynamic movement than Zeirei, which consisted of a handful of *minyanim* in different neighborhoods of New York City. It had already begun to expand rapidly both within the New York area and beyond, and it played a major role in preserving Orthodoxy in dozens of communities outside the New York area.[7]

But for all its successes, Young Israel could not offer the overarching vision for which Mike was looking. Young Israel possessed no all-encompassing philosophy. It was, for all its innovative strategies, a status quo organization striving — with much success — to arrest the rapid decline of American Orthodoxy, especially among the young. Its goal could be described as the creation of a homegrown *nusach America.*

Young Israel had no pretensions to being an international organization linking Jews around the globe. Moreover, it could not offer a pantheon of heroes — in the form of the *gedolei Yisrael* — as Agudath Israel could. In its early years, the movement deliberately eschewed any rabbinic guidance. Not until the late '30s did any Young Israel synagogue hire a rabbi, and Rabbi Dr. David Stern was the only rabbi with any influence within the movement.[8]

6. In a career in Agudath Israel spanning nearly 60 years, including more than 35 as a representative of Agudath Israel in the Israeli Knesset, Rabbi Porush worked closely with all the leading figures in the movement. He ranks Mike Tress second only to the movement's founder Reb Jacob Rosenheim in his impact on the movement. And in terms of his ability to attract new adherents to the movement, he considers Mike Tress as the greatest leader the movement has known.

7. The positive work of Young Israel was widely recognized in Agudah circles, and the movement rarely, if ever, criticized. There are, for instance, no negative references to Young Israel in *Orthodox Youth* and *Orthodox Tribune,* the two newspapers put out by the Agudath Israel of America Youth Council in the 1940s. All ideological firepower was reserved for Mizrachi, the party of the religious Zionists (see Chapter 11 below). Mike personally worked hand in hand with Irving Bunim, the most prominent leader of Young Israel, on numerous projects both during the war and afterwards.

The lack of overt criticism of Young Israel and the ability to unite on common projects, of course, does not mean that Zeirei members did not view themselves as in some way distinct from Young Israel members, and this tendency grew over the years.

8. Amos Bunim, *A Fire in His Soul,* p. 33.

Rabbi Stern was the advisor to the Lower East Side Young Israel. He used to walk over the Williamsburg Bridge every Shabbos, even in the most inclement weather, to the Lower East Side

Agudath Israel was, by contrast, revolutionary in its aspirations. It sought nothing less than to reconstitute Jewish life around the globe on the basis of traditional fealty to the Torah.

THE FIRST SIGHT TO GREET MIKE ON HIS ENTRANCE TO ZEIREI'S Rodney Street basement was likely a young man, almost exactly his

Rabbi Gedaliah Schorr

own age, learning with a group of his contemporaries. On a visit to America a few years earlier, Rabbi Meir Shapiro had pronounced that young man — then only 18 years old — to have "the most brilliant mind I have come across in America and one of the most brilliant in the world."[9] And he would one day be described by Rabbi Aharon Kotler as "the first American *gadol*."[10] He was the hero and role model for the first generation of American youth to dedicate themselves to advanced yeshiva learning. His name was Gedaliah Schorr.

From his middle teens, Reb Gedaliah gave a nightly *Daf HaYomi shiur* in Zeirei. He was also the unofficial *rav* of Zeirei — a position he maintained into the '40s when his responsibilities at Torah Vodaath made it impossible to continue. Even though he was younger than many of the members, everyone looked up to him, and whatever he said was law.[11] He succeeded, for instance, in convincing some of the older members to give up going to dances at Young Israel.

There is little doubt that the presence of Reb Gedaliah was one of the major factors that drew Mike to 157 Rodney Street. Despite Mike's lack of learning background, he was immediately attracted to Reb Gedaliah. From the moment that Mike entered Zeirei, Reb Gedaliah became the central figure in his life, the one who did more than any other to shape him. "If it were not for Reb Gedaliah," Mike said years later, "I would not be who I am."[12]

Throughout his life, Mike looked to Reb Gedaliah as his personal *rebbi*, and the latter was always available to him at any time of the day or night. Reb Gedaliah was the first *talmid chacham* that Mike had met, and his presence removed the *gedolei Torah* from the realm of the abstract.

---

branch. In that branch, there was no mixed dancing. He was fearless in his criticisms. At a time when almost everyone had a New Year's party, Rabbi Stern did not hesitate to attack the practice of celebrating a non-Jewish date. *Interview with Rebbetzin Channah Belsky.*

9. Rabbi Nosson Scherman, "An Appreciation of Rabbi Gedaliah Schorr: An American-Bred Torah Genius," *The Jewish Observer*, October 1979, p. 8.

10. Ibid., p. 10.

11. Interview with Max Gross.

12. Interview with Rabbi Chaim Uri Lipshitz.

It was also through Reb Gedaliah that Mike gained much of his knowledge of the great leaders of European Jewry. Reb Gedaliah attended both the second Knessiah Gedolah in Vienna in 1929 and the third Knessiah Gedolah at Marienbad in 1937 — the latter largely due to Mike's financial assistance — and in 1938, he journeyed to Kletsk with his new bride to study under Rabbi Aharon Kotler. The impressions that Reb Gedaliah brought back of Reb Aharon and the other Torah greats he met added to Mike's awe of these figures.[13]

The relationship between Mike and Reb Gedaliah was much more than that between a *rav* and *talmid*; the two became the closest of friends. Reb Gedaliah soon discerned in Mike qualities that set him apart and did everything to nurture his potential. He used to say, "I have a friend of the

---

13. Interview with Max Septimus.

heart — Mike Tress." The two were "inseparable, as close as two people can be."[14] When Mike's first child was stillborn, it was to Reb Gedaliah that he turned for solace. And when Reb Gedaliah was going through a difficult period in his own life, he used to spend hours a day with Mike.[15] To the Tress children growing up, the Rosh Yeshiva of Torah Vodaath and his Rebbetzin were members of the family.[16]

The fact that Torah learning was the primary activity of the Williamsburg Zeirei, rather than militating against Mike's joining, was probably one of the major factors attracting him. He was never one who tried to hide who or what he was, and especially not if it could stand in the way of his becoming something more. When he spoke, he never attempted to dress up his addresses with *divrei Torah* in order to make himself appear more learned than he was. "The Chafetz Chaim *zoght* (says), Reb Elchonon *zoght* ..." was for him also a *dvar Torah*.

At the same time, he was eager to increase his own learning, and over the years attended as many *shiurim* as his schedule would allow. He was a regular at Rabbi Gedaliah Schorr's Shabbos *Gemara shiurim* as long as Reb Gedaliah taught in Zeirei, and even during the war years, when the division between day and night had long since ceased to exist, he made an effort to attend as many of the nighttime *shiurim* at 616 Bedford Avenue as he possibly could.[17]

THE VETERAN ZEIREI MEMBERS INITIALLY TOOK LITTLE NOTICE of Mike. He was in their view nothing more than "a spirited young man

Zeirei Finds a Leader who sang nicely."[18] But the younger members immediately noticed something their elders did not: Mike possessed a quiet dynamism that offered the hope of transforming Zeirei from a *heimishe* club into something much more exciting. They began to gravitate to him. Within six months of his entry

---

14. Interview with Moshe Berger. Rabbi Moshe Sherer describes Mike and Rabbi Schorr as having been "like two brothers."

15. Interview with Shmuel Baruch Tress.

16. Interview with Mike's daughter Rebbetzin Henie Meisels.

17. Mike was a regular at whatever *shiurim* Reb Shraga Feivel Mendlowitz gave to those outside his own *beis medrash: Tehillim, Pirkei Avos,* and a Shabbos evening *Chumash shiur.* The *hashkafah* and *Chumash shiurim* that Rabbi Elchonon Wasserman, *hy"d,* gave at 157 Rodney Street during his year and a half in America in the late '30s left an indelible impression on Mike.

18. This description is from a piece entitled "A Pleasant Disappointment" published by Louis Septimus on the occasion of Mike's engagement in 1938. It is unclear where this brief tribute to Mike was published.

into Zeirei, this younger group had put him forward as a candidate for president of the organization.

The older group bitterly opposed his candidacy. Prior to the balloting, they tried to invoke an "unwritten, and previously unheard-of rule" that any candidate for office had to be a member in good standing for at least a year. The senior member of the organization went so far as to argue that the election of an inexperienced leader, who had pledged his allegiance to Zeirei only a few months earlier, would prove the ruin of the organization. Yet when the ballots were counted, Mike had won a narrow victory.[19]

Five years later, Louis Septimus, one of the leaders of the opposition to Mike, would write that the veteran members who had been absent on the night of the vote "could have rendered no greater service to our organization than by their timely absence." The history of the Williamsburg Zeirei, he added, could be succinctly divided into two periods: before Mike and after Mike. Before Mike, the organization could have been more appropriately named the Shalosh Seudas Club.[20]

THE FIRST LARGE-SCALE PROJECT ON WHICH MIKE GAVE SOME taste of what lay ahead for Zeirei Agudath Israel of Williamsburg was a

The Shemiras Shabbos Campaign

shemiras Shabbos campaign aimed at closing down stores on Lee Avenue, the hub of Williamsburg's business district, on Shabbos. Every Thursday night for more than a year, Mike would mount an old roadster, which was draped with an American flag, at the corner of Lee Avenue and one of its cross streets. Over a loudspeaker system, he spoke of the importance of shemiras Shabbos and urged shoppers not to patronize stores on Shabbos or shop in stores which remained open on Shabbos. At these rallies, Mike began to develop the powerful speaking style that in time became one of his trademarks.[21]

The campaign went far beyond once-a-week harangues to passersby. It was in the follow-up work that Mike showed his organizational genius, and his sense of the tedious grass-roots work through which any organization is built up. He divided up the neighborhood into blocks, and groups of Zeirei members and older students from Torah Vodaath would canvass the neighborhood gathering signatures of

---

19. Ibid.
20. Ibid.
21. Interview with Rabbi Nesanel Quinn.

Ad for shemiras Shabbos

homeowners who committed themselves not to shop on Shabbos. Armed with these signatures, the block committees then went to talk to storeowners and tried to convince them that it did not pay to remain open on Shabbos and that they would lose business to *shomer Shabbos* competitors. The campaign achieved more than anyone thought possible at the inception; eventually more than half the stores on Lee Avenue closed on Shabbos.[22]

The culmination of the campaign was a mass Shabbos rally that started from the Novominsker *shtiebel*. No more than a couple hundred Jews were expected to join, but in the end several thousand appeared. From Novominsk, the participants marched down Lee Avenue, led by the Novominsker Rebbe and Rabbi Levi Yitzchak Kahane, *rav* of the Clymer Street shul. The crowd gathered in front of one *non-shomer Shabbos* bakery, where the owner's daughter promptly poured a bucket of water on Rabbi Kahane from her second-story window. The police were called and arrested Rabbi Kahane. When the police tried to force Rabbi

22. Ibid.

23. Interview with Louis Septimus.

Kahane into a squad car, the marchers formed a human barricade in front of the car.[23] At that point, the police contented themselves with letting Rabbi Kahane walk the two blocks to the nearby station house.

Adverse publicity from the incident caused the bakery to be sold to *shomer Shabbos* owners, a pattern that was eventually repeated by most of the bakeries on Lee Avenue.

Closely related to the *shemiras Shabbos* campaign were efforts to arouse the public

Novominsker Rebbe

against the use of non-religious cantors as a means of drawing large crowds to *shul*. One Shabbos morning, Mike stood on the steps outside the South 4th Street synagogue where Moshe Oysher was appearing that morning. Oysher had a beautiful voice, which he applied equally to *davening* in *shuls* on Shabbos morning and performing in the Yiddish theater on Shabbos afternoon. Mike urged the worshipers not to go in to hear a *chazzan* who was a public Shabbos desecrator.

Most ignored his pleas. But just as Oysher was about to begin *Mussaf*, Mike, Rabbi Gedaliah Schorr and Dave Maryles, followed by a group of Zeirei activists, marched into the synagogue and began chanting, "He sings in the morning in *shul* and in the afternoon in the Yiddish theater." Once again the police were called, but the disruption sufficiently unnerved Oysher that he did not perform that Shabbos.[24]

Important in its own right, the *shemiras Shabbos* campaign also had important repercussions for the development of Zeirei. The campaign brought Zeirei to the attention of a much wider audience. It attracted new members and galvanized both new and old members with a sense of what they could achieve if they were willing to commit themselves. The religious youth of Williamsburg became intoxicated with a sense of their own ability to make a difference, and the ranks of the Williamsburg

---

24. Interview with Max Gross.

25. Interview with Max Septimus.

A group of Zeirei members. Standing L-R: Moshe Sandhaus, Rabbi Avrohom Pam, Rabbi Anshel Fink, Yitzchok Mendelowitz, Robert Krane. Seated L-R: Moe Fensterheim, Frank Newman, Berel Belsky, Rabbi Heshy Lieman, Rabbi Gedaliah Schorr, Rabbi Alexander Linchner

Zeirei started to swell, with Mike as the magnet attracting the youth.[25]

The success of the campaign also had an important effect on Mike. He was a born leader, but like any ability, the capacity for leadership needs to be exercised or it will atrophy. The more Mike was looked to as the leader of Zeirei, the more he responded and grew into his role. "Month by month, year by year, you could see him grow," remembers Rebbetzin Channah Belsky. "He saw a need and acted, and with each successful project his stature increased." It was a situation of a group calling out to him, "Draw me after you, and we will run" (*Shir HaShirim* 1:4).

Chapter Five

PIRCHEI

ITH THE SHEMIRAS SHABBOS CAM-
paign and other projects, the Williamsburg Zeirei no longer
deserved to be called
"the *Shalosh Seudas*
club." Yet while such projects improved the
quality of life for the religious residents of
Williamsburg, they could never have formed
the basis of a broad grass-roots movement.

Building a Movement

Almost from his first days in Zeirei, Mike
set out to create precisely such a movement.
His guiding insight from the very beginning
was that such a movement would have to be
centered around the youth. He never stopped
talking about the necessity of "getting the
youth" and the dire consequences that would

follow from failing to do so. "If we get another five boys, they'll each bring in another five" was the battle plan from which he never wavered.[1]

Each new boy was, in his eyes, a building block of *Klal Yisrael*, and he never missed an opportunity to win over another boy for Pirchei or girl for Bnos. The first Shabbos that Jack Klausner arrived in America from Cracow, where he had been living with his grandparents, some non-religious cousins came to visit and took him and his sister on a trolley car. By the next Shabbos, though, he was already in the Lower East Side Pirchei group. Mrs. Klausner worked in Mike's department at Lamport's, and as soon as he heard that she had brought her children back to America, he immediately contacted Berel Greenbaum, the 15-year-old leader of the Lower East Side Pirchei group, and had him look up the newcomer.[2] Similarly, when the family of Rena (Zirkind) Ebert moved to Williamsburg, one of the first to visit them was Mike Tress. He did not forget to tell her parents about the local Bnos group for their daughter.[3]

Zeirei had begun as an organization for young men in their late teens and early 20's. Under Mike, the organization, under the name Pirchei Agudath Israel, expanded downward to boys as young as eight and nine years old.[4] The Pirchei were further subdivided into Midgets, Intermediates, and Junior-Seniors. The basement of 157 Rodney Street became the home away from home for these youngsters. A game room, with a primitive ping-pong table and mats, was set up to encourage boys to spend their time outside of school or yeshiva in the safe environs of Zeirei rather than out on the street. Boys also came there to do their homework and to conduct the once-a-week meetings of their respective groups. On Shabbos, almost the whole day was spent at 157 Rodney with the highlight being the *Shalosh Seudas* singing led by Dave Maryles, the Septimus and Silbermintz brothers, and Mike.[5]

Pirchei was the focus of Mike's energies. Virtually every night of the week, he would lead another group, and on Shabbos he spent hours singing with the Pirchei boys and telling them stories of the *gedolim*. Even during the war years, he often rushed straight from Penn Central

---

1. Interview with Eli Basch.

2. Interview with Jack Klausner.

3. Interview with Mrs. Rena (Zirkind) Ebert.

4. Max Septimus recalls a Pirchei group in Williamsburg prior to Mike's arrival, but it was Mike who first began to emphasize Pirchei as an integral part of the organization.

5. Interviews with Rabbi Avraham Abba Friedman and Rabbi Heshy Mashinsky.

station, after a day of meetings in the State Department, to 616 Bedford Avenue in order to lead a Pirchei meeting. He did not even stop at his home nearby for a bite to eat or to clean up. The Pirchei boys would see him sitting there with his head in his hands, seemingly trying to rub away the pressures of the day. He might be in excruciating pain, but would still insist on staying to the end of the meeting.[6]

At that time he was already a well-respected figure in the corridors of power in Washington, D.C., the principal contact person for the world Agudah movement in the nation's capital, and someone whose persistence and sincerity had even managed to soften a few hearts in the State Department. Yet he did not consider it beneath his dignity to spend his evenings with a group of 10-year-olds. He was not above sweeping the floor, painting the building or knocking in a few nails if the need arose.[7] When Pirchei started its own *Shalosh Seudas* at 616 Bedford Avenue, Mike was often the one to purchase the food.[8] The Pirchei boys never sensed anything incongruous about their revered leader playing ping-pong with them one minute and then getting up the next minute to address them with all the force and enthusiasm with which he would one day inspire mass meetings.[9]

IN THE LATE '30S AND EARLY '40S, AS NEW BRANCHES BEGAN TO form around the New York area, Mike was always available to speak.

Spreading the Word

Every *Motzaei Shabbos*, he traveled someplace else for a *Melaveh Malkah*. It did not matter how many boys showed up. If there were three, he would sing and speak as if there were a hundred, and when the *Melaveh Malkah* was over, he would personally walk each boy home. One time he spoke for three hours to a group on Willoughby Avenue that Josh Silbermintz led.[10]

Gershon Kranzler, Mike's chief lieutenant in the effort to build Zeirei into a unified movement, portrayed one such *Melaveh Malkah* in a reminiscence about Mike:

---

6. Interview with Gavriel Beer.

7. Interview with Rebbetzin Channah Belsky.

8. At 157 Rodney Street, Zeirei and Pirchei members ate *Shalosh Seudas* together. Not until the move to 616 Bedford Avenue in 1939 was there room for a separate Pirchei *Shalosh Seudas*. Rabbi Heshy Mashinsky recalls shopping with Mike on Havemeyer Street for the herring and other *Shalosh Seudas* staples.

9. Mashinsky interview.

10. Interviews with Rabbi Yaakov Goldstein and Rabbi Joshua Silbermintz.

A Zeirei group on an outing in the '40s. Gershon Kranzler is in the front row, right, Lother Kahn is in center of the group, Joseph Rosenberger is in back row, center.

It [was] cold. The streets [were] icy. I remember Heshy [Moskowitz's] old, broken-down, rattling roadster that took us to East New York one *Motzaei Shabbos* and to many hundreds of other places like it. There was to be a *Melaveh Malkah* in some forsaken old *shul* loft for a newly formed Pirchei group. Shaken and frozen to the marrow, we arrived at the desolate, garbage-littered place. We were met by a handful of boys between eight and thirteen ...

He shook hands with each child, and their eyes lit up. The dreariness of the place, and the frost from without and within, melted away with the warmth of the contact.

There sitting around a bare wooden table, under a yellow, naked light bulb, they even forgot the ever-present *Melaveh Malkah* diet of soda and salami sandwiches on paper plates with lots of mustard. Their eyes were glued to his face as he stood before them and said, *"Chaverim!"*

In that cold loft above the old *shul*, he set their souls and hearts aflame. When he addressed them, seriously and sincerely, the ragged little children were lifted above their small, confining worlds, just like the huge crowds I heard him address so many times at mass meetings and conventions.

... His big-heartedness struck a spark in the souls of those he led, whom he awakened and guided. Raw youngsters, as well as sophisticated *chaverim*. His sincerity struck home when he waved the magic wand of his *"chaverim"*. . . . He made all of us, all of the listeners, the *Pirchim* from East New York, the *chaverim* from the Bronx, the West Side, or Bushwick, feel like soldiers, recruited into the ranks of Hashem's army, the Maccabees of today. They were never the same after he ignited their spirit with his words.[11]

"When he said the word *'chaverim,'* recalls Sylvia Klausner, "we all felt we were somebody."

Mike did not limit his speaking to Pirchei groups. If there was a group of Jewish boys to be won over, he was there. Meyer Birnbaum grew up in the Young Israel of New Lots, and he and his friends in Young Israel all attended public high school. One week they were told that there would be a *Melaveh Malkah* that *Motzaei Shabbos* and Mike Tress would speak. They knew little about Mike other than that he had something to do with Agudath Israel, and that Agudath Israel was a group of dangerous fanatics. Birnbaum and his friends prepared to give Mike a hard time that *Motzaei Shabbos.*

As soon as Mike walked in, however, their plans went out the window. Even in the way he carried himself, they saw a modesty and sincerity that melted all skepticism. When Mike was done speaking, all the questions were positive. He responded by inviting the boys to visit the Zeirei in Williamsburg the following Sunday. The Young Israel boys were unsure about how to respond. They knew little about Williamsburg, but had always assumed that they would have little in common with boys who studied in yeshiva.

Mike, however, had struck a chord, and they went. To their surprise, they found out that boys their own age who were in Mesivta Torah Vodaath did not have horns. The boys they met from Williamsburg spent a lot of time urging them to transfer to yeshiva, but their lack of background and the long commute from New Lots to Williamsburg ruled that out.

Mike did not content himself with that one-time contact. Every

11. Gershon Kranzler, *Williamsburg Memories*, pp. 163-64.

second or third week, he traveled to New Lots to meet with the Young Israel boys. That summer he brought three or four of them with him to Camp Mesivta free of charge, and let them sleep in his room.

The following Chanukah there was a rally of Pirchei branches from around the city in Williamsburg. Mike personally welcomed each group and called out where they were from. Then he said something that Meyer Birnbaum remembers as changing his life and those of his friends: "I have left out the name of one branch. The name of this branch is not known to you. It is called the Young Israel of New Lots." From that moment on, the boys from New Lots felt completely accepted as part of Zeirei.[12]

MIKE POSSESSED A SPECIAL RAPPORT WITH YOUNG PEOPLE. WALKING down the streets in Williamsburg, he used to stop to talk to every child he

A Way with Kids

passed.[13] They were attracted to him like bees to honey.[14] Part of the attraction, of course, was that he treated them seriously and made them feel important. During the war years, for instance, he would tell his Pirchei groups about his meetings in Washington and share with them the details of his work and his frustrations in trying to move the State Department bureaucracy.[15]

He had the capacity to focus on each child separately and to make that child feel special in his eyes. When he came to a Pirchei Chanukah or Purim party, he took time for each child as if he were his own. He would talk to every boy, ask him where he learned, who his parents were. Nor was he afraid to be physically demonstrative with them. He would pat them on the head or hold them on his knee while singing a song. There are men in their 50s or 60s today who attribute their remaining religious to the experience of being held on Mike's knee as he sang "A Sukkaleh" or one of his other Yiddish favorites.[16]

Children instinctively detect artifice and anything phony. They loved Mike because there was not an artificial bone in his body. He made them feel important because to him they were. He could speak to young people at their level, without the slightest trace of condescension.

He talked to them as people from whom demands could be made and who were already capable of making significant contributions to

---

12. Interview with Meyer Birnbaum.
13. Told to Mendel Tress by Rabbi Eli Brudny.
14. Interview with Mrs. Ruth Krane.
15. Beer interview.
16. Interview with Sidney Greenwald.

advance *Klal Yisrael*. By treating them with respect, he inspired them and raised them above their own childishness. There was an extremely wild class at Torah Vodaath with whom the *rebbi* could do nothing. One day Mike, who was on the yeshiva's educational board, came to speak to the class. He only talked to them for a few minutes, but from then on it was a different class.[17]

Another time one of Mike's daughters came home from her first day in a Chassidic girls school and mentioned that she had a black teacher for English studies. She added that her classmates had been wild that day, and that the teacher had been forced to work in extremely difficult circumstances, without even a desk or chair. The next day Mike visited his daughter's class. He began by finding a desk and a chair for the teacher. Then he told the class in Yiddish, "This woman has come to teach you, and you must treat her with respect so that it will be a *kiddush Hashem*." No more needed to be said.[18]

IT WAS THROUGH PIRCHEI THAT ZEIREI DEVELOPED AS A MOVEMENT. The older Zeirei members picked up most of their knowledge of

Bringing the Gedolim to Life

Agudath Israel from overhearing Mike talking to the kids. Most of the older members, according to Louis Septimus, "knew little or nothing of the principles and religious philosophy of the parent organization [Agudath Israel] whose name and banner [they] were pledged to support,"[19] and were amazed that Mike could have learned so much about the history, philosophy, and programs of Agudath Israel after such a short while in the organization. But he had quickly seen the necessity of ideas in building a movement, and the importance of starting with the youth.

Each of the stories Mike told the boys had a clear point and was carefully designed to have a particular emotional impact.[20] From one meeting to the next, the content of his speeches might not vary greatly, but it mattered neither to speaker nor listener. Mike's goal was never to impress with his originality, but to instill certain ideals. He wanted to hammer home a few basic points that would be the *girsa d'yankusa* (learning of youth) of his boys and remain with them for the rest of their lives. Thus he

---

17. Told to Mike's daughter Eska Reidel by Rabbi David Twersky, the Skverer Rebbe of Boro Park, who was in that class.

18. Interview with Mike's daughter Leah Bloch.

19. Louis Septimus, "A Pleasant Disappointment." See Chapter 4, note 18.

20. Interview with Rabbi Yisroel Belsky.

might describe a Knessiah Gedolah week after week so that the picture of the *gedolim* gathering together to try to solve the problems of Jews around the world would resonate emotionally for the boys.[21] Whatever he said was with such warmth and emotion that the boys never grew bored or asked why Mike was repeating what he had said last week. Their attention span for what he had to say was seemingly unlimited.[22]

Certain phrases or sayings were repeated over and over in Pirchei so that they would penetrate deep into the boys' psyche. Members would repeat at every meeting: "*Avraham Avinu* was the first Pirchei leader. Avraham was a single individual against the whole world. And we are Agudists in America against the whole world. But that is nothing to be afraid of. *Avraham Avinu* was right and we are right."[23] Mike never grew tired of saying "Agudas Yisrael is *Klal Yisrael*" or of quoting the *Imrei Emes* to the effect that in the world to come each Jew will be asked, "What did you do for Agudas Yisrael?"[24] One of his favorite quotes was from the American journalist Dorothy Thompson, who compared a Zionist Congress with a Knessiah Gedolah of Agudath Israel. Thompson wrote, "At the former [i.e., the Zionist Congress], I saw Jewish statesmen; at the latter, the Jewish G-d."[25]

Above all, Mike stressed reverence for great Torah scholars and their role as the legitimate leaders of the Jewish people. He was determined to give American-born youth a new set of heroes. He wanted them to grow up with the ambition to be *talmidei chachamim*, rather than policemen and firemen. To that end, he renamed the different Pirchei groups after contemporary *gedolim* and leading figures in Agudath Israel. There was a Rabbi Chaim Sonnenfeld group, a Nathan Birnbaum group, a Chafetz Chaim group, a Gerrer Rebbe group, and a

---

21. Interview with Reuven Soloff.

22. Interview with Alter Perl.

   Rabbi David Trenk was a Pirchei leader in Boro Park from 1956 to 1964. In the late '50s, there used to be a *Melaveh Malkah* once a month for 30 or so branch leaders at which Mike would speak. Each time, he concluded by talking about the celebration of the *yahrzeit* of the *Sfas Emes* with a group of survivors in the Feldafing DP camp. In great detail, he described the individual horrors those present had gone through, and yet how they had somehow found the strength to dance at this *simchah*.

   Rabbi Trenk looked forward to this speech every month. One time, after Mike had been sick for a long time, Rabbi Trenk heard him tell the same story to a group of Pirchei boys with all his old force and passion. Rabbi Trenk broke down and cried.

23. Interview with Jack Klausner.

24. Mashinsky interview.

25. Ibid.

Mike speaking at a fundraising event for Eretz Yisrael projects.
Rabbi Shlomo Rotenberg is on the right.

Rabbi Chaim Ozer Grodzenski group.[26] With that simple name change, Mike gave American boys a whole new set of heroes to replace the baseball players they read about in the newspapers. Many boys became fascinated by the figures that their group was named after and learned everything they could about them.

The highlight of every Pirchei meeting was Mike's stories of the *gedolim.* Each week he would relate the biography of a different *gadol,* and discuss the yeshivos in which he had learned and those in which he had taught. His stories of their lives brought the *gedolim* to life. Mike took these stories very seriously and thoroughly researched each biography.[27]

"When he started speaking about the *gedolim,* you could cry," says Rabbi Shlomo Rotenberg. "Tears would come to his eyes as he told a story. He felt it." Rabbi Rotenberg, a budding *talmid chacham* from Antwerp, was familiar with the Eastern European Torah world in a way which Mike was not, and had been at the third Knessiah Gedolah at Marienbad in 1937, where he had the opportunity to observe many of the leading Torah figures first hand. Yet he was still deeply moved by the way Mike spoke about a *gadol.*

---

26. Over the years many other *gedolim* also had groups named after them in Williamsburg or other branches.

27. Beer interview.

Mike stressed to his Pirchei boys that the *gedolim* are the ultimate arbiters of every question.[28] "Why do you have to be a member of Agudath Israel?" he would ask. "Because the Chafetz Chaim says so." "Do you know how great Reb Elchonon is? All the *gedolim* hold of him."[29] There may have been something circular about proving the greatness of the *gedolim* by reference to the esteem in which they were held by each other, but no one thought to ask the question. What remained was the awe with which Mike pronounced each name.

He made the *gedolim* looming presences in the lives of the Pirchei boys. They would sing together with great fervor, *"Leben zol der alter Gerrer Rebbe* — Long live the Gerrer Rebbe," though neither Mike nor the Pirchei boys had ever seen him.[30]

Mike took a group of the older boys to see Rabbi Elchonon Wasserman at the Broadway Central Hotel shortly after his arrival. Hundreds of Pirchei, Zeirei, and Bnos members led by Mike were at Grand Central Station to greet Rabbi Aharon Kotler on his arrival in April 1941, and again a short while later when Reb Jacob Rosenheim, head of the world Agudah movement, arrived from London.[31] Mike and his Pirchei boys were also there when the first *talmidim* of the Mirrer Yeshiva arrived from Shanghai in 1946.[32] He wanted the boys to know

---

28. Interview with Murray Friedman.

29. Mashinsky interview.

30. Ibid.

31. Gershon Kranzler, *Williamsburg Memories*, p. 165.

32. Interview with Rabbi Ephraim Wolf.

that there could be no greater cause for celebration than the arrival of a Torah scholar in their city and no greater privilege than to see a *gadol*, except, of course, to learn from one.[33]

Emunas chachamim was seemingly inborn in Mike. It preceded any personal contact with *gedolim*. During Reb Elchonon's year and a half in America in the late '30s, Mike was frequently in his presence, and afterwards never stopped repeating what he had heard from Reb Elchonon. But even before that visit, *emunas chachamim* was his constant theme. He stood up for any Jew with a beard, and was always ready to do anything he could to help a *talmid chacham*. And this feeling overflowed to everyone around him.[34]

At conventions of Zeirei Agudath Israel of America and Agudath Israel of America[35] in the '40s and '50s, the honor that he showed the *gedolim* was an object lesson for all his followers in the meaning of *kavod haTorah* (honor for Torah scholars).[36] They noted how he consulted with them on any project he undertook. As the *shammas* at 616 Bedford Avenue in the '50s, Rabbi Dovid Felderbaum spent many hours together with Mike. In his opinion, Mike was the greatest *mokir rabbanim* (one who values Torah leaders) he ever met. Many times Reb Dovid heard Mike say, "My opinion was different, but since the *gedolim* say *azoi* (like this), I have to put my opinion aside and do what they say."

Usually it takes years of learning in yeshiva to attain the *emunas chachamim* that came naturally to Mike. That *emunas chachamim* was one of the reasons that *bnei Torah* and the *gedolim* themselves showed such great respect for him. They saw in him a degree of perfection of certain

---

33. Rabbi Joshua Silbermintz, who began in Mike's Midget group at the age of eight, went on to lead many groups of his own and to head the national organization of Pirchei Agudath Israel for almost half a century. He learned from Mike the importance of exposing boys to as many *gedolim* as possible so that they grow up with a clear picture of what they are striving for. As leader of the Williamsburg Pirchei after the war, he invited such luminaries as Rabbi Yaakov Kamenetsky, Rabbi Yonason Steif, and the Bluzhover Rebbe, only recently released from the concentration camps and with his beard not yet grown back, to address the boys.

34. Interview with Rabbi Chaim Uri Lipshitz.

35. Initially there was only Zeirei Agudath Israel in America. In 1939, Rabbi Eliezer Silver founded Agudath Israel of America, which, at least in theory, was to be for older members than Zeirei Agudath Israel of America. The latter organization, under Mike's direction, was, however, the larger and more active of the two. As Zeirei members aged, the distinction between a younger and older group became harder to maintain, and between 1948 and 1950 the two organizations merged, with Zeirei essentially taking over Agudath Israel of America. By that time, many of the "younger" members were already in their forties or fast approaching it.

36. Interview with Rabbi Yaakov Goldstein.

Rabbi Aharon Kotler speaking at Agudah convention. Seated L-R: Rabbi Shimon Mordechovitz, Rabbi Chaim M. Katz, Rabbi David Ochs, Rabbi Meir Schutzman, Rabbi Altusky, Rabbi Benjamin W. Hendeles, Rabbi Dovid Lipshitz, Rabbi Pinchas M. Teitz, Rabbi Moshe Feinstein, Rabbi Eliezer Silver, Rabbi Simcha Elberg, Rabbi Mendel Chodorov, Rabbi Moshe Sherer, Mike

qualities that normally comes only with years of *Gemara* study, and, even then, only rarely.[37] One of those who grew up in Pirchei under Mike's tutelage was once asked, "When you got older and had learned in *mesivta* for a number of years, did you ever look back and think, Mike is a wonderful man, but I see that I'm now a bigger *talmid chacham*?" The man was dumbfounded by the question: "The *gedolim* did not view themselves as bigger than Mike Tress. Should I?"[38]

FEALTY TO THE GEDOLIM WAS ONLY ONE OF MIKE'S CONSTANT refrains to his young charges. There was hardly a meeting that he did

Love of Mitzvos

not speak of *Eretz Yisrael* and the difficulties faced by the religious community living there. The traditional anti-Zionism of Agudath Israel did nothing to diminish his *chibas haaretz* (love of *Eretz Yisrael*). His speeches about *Eretz Yisrael* spurred the Pirchei boys into action collecting for Agudath Israel's Keren HaYishuv. Every Purim and Tishah B'Av, Mike joined them as they went around with their *pushkas* on streetcorners and subways raising

---

37. Interview with Sidney Greenwald.
38. Interview with Rabbi Shlomo Ort.

thousands of dollars for *Eretz Yisrael*.[39] Little boys who were embarrassed to stand at subway stations with a *pushka* lost their reticence when they saw Mike himself, *pushka* in hand, calling to passersby.[40]

Mike never missed the opportunity to push Torah study. It was he who went around encouraging everyone to return after the Shabbos night meal for Rabbi Gedaliah Schorr's *Chumash shiur* at 157 Rodney Street.[41] Despite the fact that he had not gone to yeshiva — or perhaps because of it — Mike realized that without a yeshiva education it would be increasingly difficult to maintain any vestige of one's *Yiddishkeit* in America. The importance of a yeshiva education was one of his recurring themes. Rabbi Heshy Mashinsky recalls that his eagerness to learn in *mesivta* was a direct outgrowth of Pirchei, and that as a result of the inspiration from Pirchei he began learning in the Mesivta Torah Vodaath at night when he was still in eighth grade.

Mike did everything he could to help boys go to yeshiva. There was a young boy named Yosef Levitan who had a tremendous thirst for learning, but whose parents did not have enough money for yeshiva. When Mike found out about his desire to learn in yeshiva, he personally went to Torah Vodaath and succeeded in having the boy's tuition waived. Levitan went on to become one of Torah Vodaath's outstanding products, but was unfortunately *niftar* at a young age.[42] Another Pirchei boy named Chaim Rapaport wanted to go to yeshiva, but because he was already of *bar mitzvah* age, no yeshiva was willing to accept him. Mike went to Rabbi Dr. Stern, the principal of Torah Vodaath, and convinced him to accept Rapaport. The parents of three brothers who belonged to a Pirchei group on the outskirts of Williamsburg once threatened to have Mike arrested for kidnaping when their sons insisted on going to yeshiva. In the end, however, Mike persuaded them not to oppose their sons' decision.[43]

One morning as Mike was *davening*, a poor man stood behind him uncertain as to whether to interrupt his prayers. Somehow Mike sensed his presence and turned around. The man explained that his son had been sent home from yeshiva because his tuition was two months in arrears. Mike immediately removed his *tallis* and *tefillin* and went into the yeshiva office, from which he emerged a few minutes later with a

---

39. Beer interview. One Pirchei boy brought in $600 himself one Purim.

40. Interview with Abe Dicker, one of the young boys who was embarrassed until he saw Mike.

41. Interview with Rabbi Avraham Abba Friedman.

42. Mashinsky interview.

43. Interview with Mike's daughter Henie Meisels.

Mike speaking at a Zeirei convention

note admitting the man's son back into class.[44]

Mike strove to create a sense of belonging to *Klal Yisrael* and of responsibility to it. "He always demanded something from you," says Rabbi Yisroel Belsky. "He lifted people up and pushed them to do things." Though Mike had the common touch, he was not a small-talk type of person. "He was," Rabbi Belsky continues, "a *gehoibeneh mentsch* (an elevated person). Everything he said rang with import."

When he spoke to a group of Pirchei leaders, he talked about their responsibility to inspire their boys with the love of *Klal Yisrael* and the Torah.[45] To those who worried that *klal* work would take away from their learning, he quoted Reb Elchonon Wasserman's answer to the same question: "If you sleep seven hours a night, sleep six and give one to Pirchei."[46]

In 1939, Mike called a meeting of all the Pirchei leaders and told them, "You are the future of *Klal Yisrael*, you have to lead and be

44. This story was one of those in a personal condolence letter to Mrs. Tress (likely from Gershon Kranzler) quoted in Rabbi Chaim Uri Lipshitz's *Jewish Press* column of August 11, 1967. See Chapter 6, fn. 12.

45. Interview with Rabbi Yisroel Belsky.

46. Meisels interview.

L-R: Rabbi Moshe Sherer, Robert Wagner, Mike at Camp Agudah, Highmount, N.Y. Note the distinctive kelley-green yarmulkes. Mr. Wagner, then New York's Postmaster, later became Mayor of New York.

involved." Some responded by working around the clock in the Refugee and Immigration Division at 616 Bedford Avenue and others through organizational activities within Pirchei and Zeirei, but few failed to answer the call.

LIKE ANY SUCCESSFUL MOVEMENT, PIRCHEI GAVE MEMBERS A sense of belonging and created a feeling of unity between the members.

A Sense of Belonging Uniforms are one means commonly employed by movements to achieve these goals. Though Mike rejected a full uniform like those worn by Boy Scouts as being too *"goyishe,"* Pirchei did have its own kelly green sweaters with a Pirchei emblem on them. Later Camp Agudah adopted kelly-green for its jackets and *yarmulkes.* In Pirchei, boys were addressed by their first names, not their family names, as in yeshiva.[47]

Mike knew how to inject just enough solemnity and mystery into the proceedings to appeal to young boys' enjoyment of secret clubs. From the very youngest Midget group, minutes were taken of each meeting

---

47. Mashinsky interview.

and read with great formality at the beginning of the next week's meeting.[48] Mike taught the groups how to conduct their meetings with a sufficient amount of decorum so that the boys felt they were engaged in an important task.

Singing was perhaps the most important means of giving the boys a warm feeling for their *Yiddishkeit* and building a sense of togetherness. The Pirchei Shabbos revolved around the *Shalosh Seudos* singing, and singing was a major part of every activity or outing. Some Pirchei leaders even brought in *chazzanim* to teach the boys Yiddish *niggunim*.[49] There were always some boys with good voices, and Mike, Dave Maryles, and some of the older boys started to bring in *niggunim* from Modzhitz and other Chassidic groups, as well as from Torah Vodaath. Pirchei adopted the Chassidic method of using singing to emphasize the group over the individual. Once the singing and dancing started, every boy felt like an equal member of the group. Singing together, the boys were enveloped in a general sense of well-being.

Even those boys who learned in yeshiva still absorbed their *ruach* (spirit) from Pirchei. On *Yom Tov*, the walls of 157 Rodney used to sway from the dancing and singing and were soaked from the sweat of the dancers led by Mike.[50] The sight of Mike, holding a grandchild on his knee and looking nostalgically at the circle of dancers one of the last Simchas Torahs of his life, stirred Gershon Kranzler's own memories of Mike leading the dancing:

> ... his collar soaked, a large handkerchief around his neck, one arm linked to the *chaver* behind him, whether a youngster of the second generation or one of our elders with beard and black hat, all of them his *chaverim*. And thus he pulled us along so often, roused us to the realm where the individual loses himself in devout inspiration.[51]

---

48. Beer interview.

49. Interview with Heshy Moskowitz.

50. Mashinsky interview.

51. Gershon Kranzler, *Williamsburg Memories*, pp. 162-63.

Interestingly, Reb Shraga Feivel Mendlowitz used singing and dancing in much the same way in Torah Vodaath to create a love of *Yiddishkeit*. He used to say that he built Torah Vodaath with the *niggun* "Al kein nikaveh," which the yeshiva sang every *Yom Tov*. Watching him dance with his students at a wedding, one *gadol* remarked, "That Jew did more with his dancing than all the *roshei yeshiva* with their Torah." On *Seder* night, he would dance in his home for three or four hours with boys from the *Mesivta*, and every *Yom Tov* the dancing in the *beis medrash* lasted

The main Pirchei group of Williamsburg was always in the same building as the Zeirei *minyan* — first at 157 Rodney Street and later at 616 Bedford Avenue. At Rodney Street, the younger boys — Heshy Mashinsky, Gavriel Beer, Herschel Schecter, Joshua Silbermintz, Moshe Weitman,[52] and Mottel Weinberg[53] — looked up to the group a few years older than themselves, which included some of Mike's first Pirchei boys: Heshy Moskowitz, Ephraim (Freddy) Wolf, Shlomo Ort, Abba Friedman,[54] Mottel Berkowitz, and Shea Schiff.[55] And both groups looked up to the Zeirei members.

The constant proximity of a group of young men a half generation older than themselves gave the Pirchei boys a sense of being part of a movement with continuity over a time. The young men of Zeirei seemed far less distant to the boys than their parents' generation and often served as role models. Besides Mike, Charlie Young, Charlie Klein, Dave Maryles, and Max Septimus all showed interest in the Pirchei boys, and Rabbi Gedaliah Schorr was a constant presence in their lives. Mike and Reb Gedaliah came to Josh Silbermintz's *bar mitzvah* in the Polisher *shtiebel* just as they would have come to the *simchah* of any Zeirei member.[56]

The close interplay between older Zeirei members and the Pirchei boys also existed on the Lower East Side. The original leaders of the Pirchei group were Berel Greenbaum and his brother Aaron.[57] The former had a remarkable ability, even as a young boy, to draw others close to him. In time, the Greenbaums were joined as leaders by Yitzchak Karpf, Herschel

---

for hours. At *Shalosh Seudas* in the *Mesivta,* the boys would sit in the dining room in the dark while Reb Feivel would call out the *niggunim.* Nobody rushed, nobody looked at the time or cared how long into the night Reb Feivel decided to extend the singing. On *Yom Tovim, meshulachim* (fundraisers) from *Eretz Yisrael* would come to the *Mesivta* and bring their own special melodies. *Mashinsky interview.*

52. Rabbi Moshe Weitman was later the founder of a day school in Montreal, Canada and Rabbi of Monticello, New York. He has served for over three decades as Dean of Torah Academy for Girls in Far Rockaway, New York.

53. Rabbi Mottel Weinberg later served on the *hanhalah* of Yeshivah Rabbeinu Chaim Berlin, was Rosh Yeshiva of Mesivta of Eastern Parkway, and was Rosh Yeshivah of Yeshiva Gedolah Mercaz HaTorah of Montreal.

54. Rabbi Avrohom Abba Freidman is among the pioneers of *chinuch* on the broader American scene. He led Yeshivah Beis Yehudah of Detroit for several decades.

55. Rabbi Sheah Schiff became a son-in-law of Reb Shraga Feivel Mendlowitz and is founding Rosh Yeshivah of Yeshivah Beis Shraga in Monsey, New York.

56. Silbermintz interview.

56. Rabbi Berel Greenbaum later married Reb Shraga Feivel Mendlowitz's daughter Rivka and was the long-time principal of Yeshiva of Spring Valley.

57. Interview with Rabbi Yitzchak Karpf.

Itche and Mendel Metzger

Fried, Fishel Simanowitz, and Berel Schwartz.[58] But in addition to the leaders, who were often only four or five years older than themselves, the Pirchei boys admired the founding members of the Lower East Side Zeirei: Yisrael Feigenbaum, later president of the Bais Yaakov of the Lower East Side, and Itche and Mendel Metzger. Shea Gold, the leader of the *Daf HaYomi shiur,* was a hero to all the Pirchei boys.[59]

Young boys were given a place in Zeirei to a degree unimaginable in their fathers' *shuls.* Pirchei boys and Zeirei members danced together on the *Yom Tovim,* and there was no hesitation about asking a boy with a beautiful voice, like Josh Silbermintz, to lead a *niggun* at *Shalosh Seudas.* Once a year, the post-*bar mitzvah* boys would lead the Zeirei *minyan.* In 616 Bedford Avenue, there was a separate Pirchei *minyan* on Shabbos to which Mike frequently came. He said he preferred the warmth of the Pirchei *minyan.*

The feeling of the boys that they had a place within Zeirei was in sharp contrast to the situation elsewhere. In most of the *shtieblach,* it was unthinkable that an unmarried man lead the *davening,* read the Torah, or even be called for an *aliyah.* Prior to marriage, the only thing a boy ever did in *shul* was to chant his *haftarah* while the older men

58. Interview with Murray Friedman.
59. Greenwald interview.

talked.[60] A boy had no status other than as an appendage of his father.

When the Silbermintz boys started to *daven* on Shabbos at 157 Rodney Street, one of the members of the Polisher *shtiebel* asked their father how he could permit such a thing, as if they were going to a baseball game and not to *shul*. That Jew learned every spare minute of his day, and there were many others like him in the Polisher *shtiebel*, which was open 24 hours a day. But neither his children or those of many of the other regulars in the Polish *shtiebel* remained religious — in large part because they never felt that their fathers' *shul* was a place for them.[61]

IN SOME WAYS THE MOST IMPORTANT INFLUENCE OF PIRCHEI WAS simply that it kept boys off the streets and together with other religious

Off the Street and Out of Trouble

boys. Sidney Greenwald and his friends in the Lower East Side Pirchei practically lived at Pirchei when they were not in school or sleeping. They did their homework there and came to play ping-pong and checkers, in addition to the structured Pirchei activities.[62] Rabbi Yitzchak Karpf, a slightly older product of the Lower East Side Pirchei, credits Pirchei with keeping him out of public school and away from the temptations of the street. Such testimony from one who went on to become a *maggid shiur* and a son-in-law of Reb Shraga Feivel Mendlowitz gives some sense of just how powerful were the attractions of the street in those days.

What happened in the hours after yeshiva was for the younger boys perhaps even more important than what occurred in yeshiva itself. Pirchei complemented the yeshiva, yet was at the same time a world apart. Boys were drawn close with love in a way that not every yeshiva *rebbi* is capable of.[63] Abilities that might have no place in the yeshiva could find expression in Pirchei. Boys who might never shine in *Gemara* studies often excelled in the *klal*-oriented projects of Pirchei, and thereby gained self-esteem not always nurtured by the yeshiva.

Not only did Pirchei keep boys in a religious environment, it provided the informal education which must complement formal yeshiva studies. In Pirchei, boys learned how to translate the lessons of yeshiva into concrete positive deeds.[64] Of his classmates in Yeshivas Rabbeinu

---

60. Interview with Rabbi Joshua Silbermintz.

61. Ibid.

62. Greenwald interview.

63. Interview with Rabbi Dr. Arnold Wolf, himself a long-time principal.

64. Interview with Rabbi Ephraim Wolf.

Shlomo Kluger, Murray Friedman says, the ones who remained strongly committed were almost all products of Pirchei and Zeirei. And Rabbi Moshe Wolfson's memory of his elementary school classmates in Torah Vodaath is the same: Of his 40 classmates, the four who remained religious were those who were most active in Pirchei.

Reaching Out

IN THOSE DAYS, THERE WAS NO AUTOMATIC PRESUMPTION THAT every Pirchei boy was learning in yeshiva. As word of the Pirchei activities, meetings, and outings to Cunningham Park, Clove Lake Park, and Prospect Park began to spread, more and more boys were attracted to Pirchei. Many boys, especially in the branches forming outside the heart of Williamsburg, went to public schools and a *Talmud Torah* after school.[65]

At 16, Joshua Silbermintz took over a group on Moore Street on the outskirts of Williamsburg. The group was so rowdy that he did not even show up for the third Shabbos. When he did not appear to lead the group, the wildest kid in the group walked a mile to Silbermintz's home, asked for *mechilah* (forgiveness) and begged him to return. That same boy once spent an entire 95-degrees Shabbos locked in an unventilated bathroom as a punishment from his father for refusing to turn on lights on Shabbos.[66] Another boy in that group used to make a *Seder* for himself and his younger sister while his father sat in the living room making fun of him and reading the virulently anti-religious *Forward*. He graduated high school at 15 and decided that he wanted to go to yeshiva. By 21 he had *semichah* from Torah Vodaath. The Willoughby Avenue branch, which Silbermintz led for several years, later had many boys who used to go to movies on Shabbos.[67] Today one is a leading rabbi, another can be seen in a *shtreimel* on Shabbos.

A Vision Fulfilled

FROM THE FIRST, MIKE SAW THE SNOWBALL POTENTIAL OF PIRCHEI — i.e., every boy brought in would in turn bring in another. And indeed within less than a decade the movement had gained tremendous momentum in precisely the way Mike had foreseen. Those who had begun under his tutelage in the youngest group were already leading groups of their own. Freddy

---

65. In one Bnos chapter in East New York, for instance, Rebbetzin Penina Goldstein estimates, almost 90 percent of the girls came from homes that were not *shomer Shabbos*.

66. Many years later, Rabbi Silbermintz ran into the same boy, long since grownup, in Jerusalem. He found him as full of energy as ever, only now he was also filled with Torah.

67. Interview with Yitzchak Levy.

Enjoying a summer at Camp Agudah, Ferndale, N.Y.

Wolf used to walk every Shabbos from Williamsburg to East New York to lead a Pirchei group. And his brother Arnold, known to a generation of boys and girls as "The Mighty Wolf" for his feats of strength at the annual Night of the Stars fundraiser, used to walk to Boro Park. Three friends from the Lower East Side Pirchei — Murray Friedman, Jack Klausner, and Sidney Greenwald — started *Darkeinu*, a Pirchei-oriented youth magazine, in the early '40s, and by the mid-'40s they, together with Meilach Silber, Bennie Ullman, and Alter Perl, had become the mainstays of the nascent national organization of Pirchei. (Rabbi Joshua Silbermintz was already Pirchei national field director.) Silber, Greenwald, and Klausner were either head counselors or assistant head counselors at Camp Agudah. Rabbi Yaakov Goldstein, another Lower East Side Pirchei boy, later headed the Williamsburg Pirchei and was the first head counselor of Camp Agudah in Ferndale.

Mike succeeded in infusing Pirchei with his own idealism. When New York State passed a Release Time law in the mid-'40s, which permitted an hour of weekly religious instruction for public school students, a large percentage of those who volunteered to teach were former

Joshua Silbernmintz inspiring the campers at Camp Agudah, Highmount, N.Y.

Pirchei leaders or Camp Agudah counselors.[68] Before the word *kiruv* was in fashion, Pirchei instilled a feeling of responsibility to help other boys become *frum*.[69] Nor did that youthful idealism necessarily wane. A disproportionate number of Mike's Pirchei boys went on to careers in *chinuch* (education) and other community-oriented endeavors.

No one personified the fulfillment of Mike's dream more than Rabbi Joshua Silbermintz. Starting out as a young boy in one of Mike's first groups, he was leading his own groups on the outskirts of Williamsburg by 16. Later he put together the first printed materials for Pirchei leaders, the Pirchei Leaders Guides. For nearly 50 years, he was "Mr. Pirchei," developing such programs as *Mishnayos B'Al Peh*, and overseeing the expansion of Pirchei from a handful of chapters to more than 80.

---

68. Greenwald interview.
69. Interview with Murray Friedman.

Chapter Six

MIKE — THE MAN

TO A REMARKABLE DEGREE THE STORY OF Agudath Israel in America is inseparable from the personality of Mike Tress. Many of the early recruits to the movement — especially the younger ones — were attracted more by Mike himself than by ideological considerations. Their feelings about their Judaism were inextricably bound to their love for Mike, and their *frumkeit* (religiosity) was to a large degree a reflection of their desire to emulate him. "When he spoke to me, it was like talking to my father," Rabbi Moshe Rivlin remembers. "I wanted to be like him. Every person with whom he came into contact developed the desire to be more like him."

The desire to be like Mike is easily understood. His was a personality of uncommon beauty and balance. The praise *"tocho k'boro* (his inside is like his outside)"

Mike speaking at the wedding of Binyamin Urman

fully describes him — the clearest proof being that everyone, from the youngest child to the greatest Torah scholar, experienced him in virtually the same way. A *"hartzige mentsch,"* one full of heart, is the description that one hears over and over from those who knew him.

He possessed almost every quality for which a man is honored without the concomitant faults often associated with those qualities. He was a forceful leader, unshakeable in his core beliefs, yet never angry or bitter to those he viewed as wrongheaded. He was dynamic and inspiring, yet the softest and most gentle of people — a man easily moved to tears and from whom a harsh word was never heard. He knew he was the leader to whom others looked, and he accepted that responsibility; yet he seemingly had no ego needs. One of his greatest strengths as a leader was his ability to bring out the best of others and to push them to the fore. He led a growing movement without ever losing sight of every individual in it. He was blessed with great charm and an easy manner with people, yet his moral seriousness was never in doubt.

TO A GENERATION OF YOUNG PEOPLE COMING OF AGE IN THE '30s and '40s, Mike was a father figure and role model. The question his **Father Figure for a Generation** Pirchei boys constantly asked themselves and each other was: "What would Mike say?"[1] For some he provided the model for being *frum* in America that their European-born parents could not; for others he was a father figure because they were becoming more religious than their parents; for still others he gave them the time that their parents did not have because every moment was taken up with the struggle to support their families. "I looked at him like a father," says Rabbi Heshy Mashinsky:

> My parents worked so hard they barely had time for me. If I had a problem, I took it to Mike. We all knew that when you had a problem you talked it over with Mike. When there was no money in the house, I spoke to him, and he got my sisters jobs at Lamport's and my father a job collecting for Keren HaYishuv.

Like a father, Mike did not wait for boys to come to him with their concerns. Often he came to them before they even knew they had a problem that needed discussing.[2]

Mike's warmth and concern wove a magic spell over all he met — whether young children, teenagers, or adults. He had an ability to enter into an immediate relationship of intimacy with a person. "You could fall in love with him" is a phrase commonly used by those describing their first meeting with Mike. Not only could they, they did. To Meyer Birnbaum, who was a 16-year-old public school kid when he first met Mike, the latter was "like a warm fire on a cold winter day. You just wanted to cuddle as close to him as you could." Rabbi Chaim Uri Lipshitz was nearly 30 when he first met Mike, and his reaction was identical: "You were immediately attracted to him and wanted to become his friend."

People instinctively trusted him after knowing him for only a short time. They sensed that he viewed their problems as if they were his own and would treat them no less seriously. Morley Auerbach was a much decorated bombardier in the Royal Canadian Air Force, the veteran of 34 combat missions, when he met Mike in England after the war. At that first meeting, Mike convinced him that he should enroll in Telshe Yeshiva as soon as he returned home. Asked whether it was not strange

---

1. Interview with Rabbi Avraham Abba Friedman.

2. Interview with Rabbi Yaakov Goldstein.

to entrust his future to someone he had just met, Auerbach could only reply, "Not if you knew Mike."

There was nothing superficial about Mike, no hale-fellow-well-met slaps on the back. He had a ready sense of humor.[3] Yet that humor was never used just to elicit laughs but to create a bond. When he put his arm around someone's shoulder upon meeting him the first time, the arm lingered and warmed the stranger in its embrace. He had, according to Rabbi Feivel Rosenzweig, who founded the Agudath Israel chapter in Toronto with Mike's encouragement:

> a way of putting his hand on your shoulder and making you feel that he was your best friend. He just had the knack. He could look at you, and you felt he cared. You never talked to him without his asking if there was anything he could do to help.

When Mike spoke with someone, he held his hand and stared intently into his face. In even the briefest conversation, he had the rare ability to make the other party feel that the moments spent talking together were precious to him, the ones to which he had been looking forward all day.[4]

His first night in America as a newly arrived immigrant from Germany, Gershon Kranzler went to the Zeirei headquarters at 157 Rodney Street. It was *Chol HaMoed Sukkos,* and the *Simchas Beis Hashoevah* dancing was in full swing. As Kranzler entered the basement headquarters, Mike immediately came over, put his arm around him and drew him into the circle of dancers. Afterwards Mike took him around and introduced him to all the members, and suddenly the lonely immigrant was no longer a stranger, but one of the boys.[5]

Rabbi Shlomo Rotenberg, who arrived in America from Antwerp via

---

3. Hints of that sense of humor, which is mentioned by almost all Mike's friends, can be found in his private correspondence. In a 1945 note to Rabbi Sherer, who was on vacation, Mike wrote, "It is a pleasure indeed to know that you are vacationing during the winter as if you `worked hard' during the summer. . . ." (The same note continues that the Tress children are constantly asking when `Uncle Moishe' is returning.)

Congratulatory telegrams to parents of new girls might include the valuable information that the Tress family included a two-year-old boy. *See e.g., telegram from Mike Tress to Mrs. Sol Septimus, Jewish Hospital-Maternity Division, December 27, 1946.* To Heshy Septimus, whose wife had recently given birth, Mike opined that the new baby must certainly be intelligent given his parents' excellent taste in friends.

None of this was thigh-slapping material; nor was it meant to be. Its purpose was to emphasize the feeling of closeness with a little humor.

4. Interview with Mrs. Hindy Krohn.

5. Interview with Gershon Kranzler.

Cuba in 1943, had the same experience as Gershon Kranzler. He thought to himself as Mike gave him his patented *"Shalom Aleichem"* and showed him around the Zeirei headquarters at 616 Bedford Avenue, "He's real. No one could fake such warmth."

THE SECRET OF MIKE'S WARMTH WAS HIS GENUINE LOVE FOR every Jew. "As close as he was to the *gedolei Yisrael,*" says Gavriel Beer,

A Friend of Every Jew who started out in Mike's Pirchei group at eight years old, "he never lost the feel for the simple Jew. When he heard of anyone with *tzores* (misfortune), he would *daven* and say *Tehillim* for him or her. He stopped people on the street to talk if he thought he could *mechazek* (encourage) them in any way. And he never met a Jew without trying to bring him closer to Judaism." The closest one ever hears to a criticism of Mike was that he was too good — too easily distracted by the suffering of any fellow Jew, too willing to commit his time and money to helping others with any problem that was brought to him.

He was available to every Jew who needed his help. From the middle '30s on, Mike was almost never seen on the streets of Williamsburg without a large crowd around him. When his future wife was looking for a position in a *shomer Shabbos* firm, she was directed to Mike and told that he could be identified by the circle of people around him as he made his way to 157 Rodney Street in the evening. After morning *davening,* particularly during the war and after, Jews would line up to discuss the status of relatives still in Europe or their own immigration problems. Mike would take out his notebook, patiently take down the details of every case, and give his assurance that everything possible would be done to help.

The walk home from *shul* often took up to an hour. No one was brushed off until later or told to make an appointment with his secretary. There was never any ceremony about talking to Mike.[6] Once he reached his office, the situation did not change. Anyone could walk into the office of the Administrative President and say, "Mike, I've got a problem, and I have to talk to you." Whatever the problem, he would try to solve it.[7]

Sometimes people would wander into the office — the kind of people no one else would talk to. Even so, Mike never cut them off.

6. Interview with Sidney Greenwald.

7. Interview with Leon Keller.

Gavriel Beer once saw him talking to such a person while suffering from a terrible headache. But he just sat there in pain until the person left.[8]

Those who had not been able to reach Mike during the week would stop him *Motzaei Shabbos* just after *Maariv* at 616 Bedford Avenue. Some of their problems — e.g., those concerning immigration issues — were within his bailiwick. Others — such as the inability to pay tuition at Torah Vodaath — were not. But it made no difference; Mike would still take the name of the parent concerned about tuition and tell him, "*Zorgt zich nicht* — Don't worry. I'll see what I can do." Eli Basch once returned an hour after *Havdalah* to find Mike still there surrounded by those seeking his help. When Basch pointed out that his family was home waiting to hear *Havdalah*, Mike replied, "My family can hear *Havdalah* a little later. But maybe I can help these people."

Of course, Mike was no miracle man and could not solve all the problems of the world, but just talking to him often gave a lift to those in need. They stopped him in the street wherever he went to discuss their problems — finding a livelihood, difficulties with children, disputes with the landlord. "Just the fact that someone was willing to listen to them with an understanding heart," says Melech Terebelo, "would pick up their spirits."

MIKE'S GREATEST DESIRE IN LIFE WAS TO GIVE TO OTHERS. HIS philosophy was summed up in a letter to a new Pirchei chapter in

A Need to Give Scranton, which had sent in a few dollars for *hatzalah* (rescue) work: "Let me once more assure you that the magic joy of 'doing good' is worth more than all our expressions of gratitude. . . ." The boys who *davened* with him in the *Shachris minyan* at Torah Vodaath's 206 Wilson building in the '30s were astounded by the way he dropped a quarter (worth at least ten times as much today) into each *pushka* that went by.[9]

He found jobs with the Agudah for Jews who were without any means of livelihood, even though each new salary only increased the pressure on the perpetually overdrawn Agudah coffers and on himself as the principal fundraiser. Beirach Rubinson arrived in America on the first ship carrying refugees after the war. He had lost his wife and children, and was barely a skeleton. With no idea of what to do for a living, he decided to try peddling, as he had done in Poland. But as soon as

---

8. Interview with Gavriel Beer.

9. Interview with Rabbi Ephraim Wolf.

Mike with newly arrived refugees after the war. Beirach Rubinson is to his immediate right. Among the others are survivors of the Katz and Solomon families. Rabbi Moshe Sherer is at far left.

Mike saw him walking around with two valises loaded with his wares, he told him that such peddling was a thing of the past in America. Instead he created a job for him with the Agudath Israel Youth Council working with other refugees.[10]

In an article published shortly after Mike's *petirah,* Rabbi Chaim Uri Lipshitz quoted at length from a condolence letter written to Mrs. Tress by an old friend of the family.[11] The letter is essentially a collection of stories of Mike helping his fellow Jews, stories which the writer suggests capture more of "the real Mike" than all the "causes, campaigns, and historical achievements wrought by his tireless efforts." One is struck by the range and variety of the incidents in which Mike was able to help — each one requiring its own particular combination of empathy and intelligence.

The writer recalls how he and Mike met a young Pirchei member one morning leaning against a fence not far from Torah Vodaath:

> Mike took one look at your face and he knew it all. He put his arm around you and you began to sob. . . . The tough outside you had put up for the assistant principal melted away, and

10. Interview with Beirach Rubinson.

11. Rabbi Chaim U. Lipshitz, "A Tribute to Mike Tress, z.l.," *The Jewish Press,* August, 11, 1967, p. 21. The style of the letter almost certainly identifies its author as Gershon Kranzler.

with it the determination to run away, or to register in the near by public high school, even if it would hurt your parents. Mike spoke to you ..., went into the Yeshiva office, and soon afterwards you were back in class.

Another story concerns an immigrant *talmid chacham* for whom Mike organized a *shiur* in one of the Zeirei branches. As a result of that *shiur*, the man's abilities as a scholar and his gift for explaining the intricacies of the Talmud became known, and eventually he became a well-known *rosh yeshiva*.

Material possessions were for Mike primarily means of doing *chesed*. From that point of view, the greatest value of an object was often that it could be given away. Shneur and Phyllis Weinberg were two of the many idealistic Williamsburg teenagers attracted to Mike. Shortly after their marriage, they decided to move to *Eretz Yisrael*, which they saw as the natural venue for their youthful energies. But before finalizing their decision, they went to talk to Mike. He convinced them that there was a crying need for committed educators in America, particularly outside the New York area. They took his advice, and have been in *chinuch* — first in Detroit and later in Toronto — for 46 years.

Mike, however, sensed that Mrs. Weinberg was not completely happy about the decision — that Detroit did not hold the same allure as *Eretz Yisrael*. A few weeks later, Mike invited her to come speak to him again. He asked her where she saw herself making a contribution for *Klal Yisrael*, and she mentioned that she enjoyed both speaking and writing. "In that case," Mike said, "please take my typewriter. Think of me when you pound the keys."[12]

Over the years, Leon Keller witnessed hundreds of cases of Mike helping someone personally. One of those beneficiaries was a shabbily dressed Jew who lived in Williamsburg during the war years. Mike approached him one day and told him that his mother-in-law had given him some money to be used for some secret *tzedakah*. "Go over to Levy's and get yourself a nice suit," Mike said, as he handed him the money to do so.[13]

---

12. Interview with Phyllis Weinberg.
13. Interview with Leon Keller.
   Mike knew how to give in the least embarrassing fashion. One of his sons-in-law came from a poor family. Before the wedding, Mike told him that it was a family custom that he purchase the *chasan's* wedding suit.

Mike had an almost instinctive sense of the needs of others. His count-less, unsolicited kindnesses reveal as much about him as the grand projects. Both came from the same source: an unlimited empathy for other Jews and an ability to put himself in their place. Soon after the Zirkind family moved near the Tress family, Mike brought them a bou-quet of flowers. On that get-acquainted visit, he added that if Mr. Zirkind was planning to build a *sukkah*, he would make sure that he had plenty of *schach* from branches cut by the Parks Department.[14] Mike always called to personally invite the widows of *gedolim* to Tress family celebrations and sent a car for them just as he had when their husbands were alive.[15]

Gavriel Beer was one of the Pirchei members closest to Mike in the early days. Beer's father barely eked out a living selling children's clothes from an outside stand. When he suffered a heart attack that made it impossible to continue standing outside in every kind of weath-er, the family was deprived of even the meager livelihood on which they had formerly subsisted. As a 14-year-old, on his first vacation home from Telshe Yeshiva in Cleveland, Gavriel went to visit Mike, and Mike told him to drop by the Zeirei office before returning to yeshiva. When Gavriel did so, Mike gave him two checks for $35, the price of a round-trip bus ticket between Cleveland and New York in those days.

Knowing of the Beer's financial situation, Mike wanted to relieve some of the pressure on his father by paying for Gavriel's trip home. The second check was spending money for the next *zman* so that Gavriel would not feel different than other boys in the yeshiva who received pocket money from home. Gavriel rushed home to tell his father about Mike's gifts. When his father heard what Mike had done, he cried tears of gratitude.[16]

Mike was frequently able to use his wide public contacts on behalf of Jews in need. During World War II, there was a draft exemption for yeshi-va boys who were pursuing rabbinic training. A special board was appoint-ed to decide who was qualified for the exemption. Unfortunately most of its members were non-religious Jews hostile to yeshiva students and eager to prove their loyalty by rejecting as many applications as possible.

One day Mike received a call at Agudath Israel Youth Council's 42nd Street offices from Alter Perl. Perl told him that Yankel Goldstein was

---

14. Interview with Rena (Zirkind) Ebert.

15. Interview with Mike's daughter Devorah Tropper.

16. Beer interview.

sitting in the back of the *beis medrash* in Torah Vodaath crying because he had been denied the exemption for rabbinical students. As soon as he got off the phone with Alter Perl, Mike called Goldstein up and asked him to come down to his office. When he arrived, Mike told him, "I'm very angry with you. Why didn't you tell me that something was bothering you?"

"Though he had the pressures of the world on his shoulders," Rabbi Goldstein remembers, "he immediately dropped everything to take care of one 18-year-old boy. When someone was in *tzores,* he went to work immediately to take care of his problem." Mike told Yaakov to gather letters of recommendation from every rabbi he knew. Mike took this packet with him on his next trip to Washington. There he went to see Irving Kaufman, later famous as the trial-court judge in the Rosenberg case, who had a high position in the Selective Service Administration.

Kaufman assured Mike that the case would be taken care of, but some time later Goldstein received a letter of induction for the second day of Rosh Hashanah. This time he ran to Mike himself without waiting for any intermediary to call. While Goldstein was still in the office, Mike called Kaufman in Washington. Kaufman told Mike that Yaakov should report three hours later than scheduled and everything would be taken care of. That Rosh Hashanah Rabbi Goldstein found himself walking 20 blocks to his draft board. When he got there, a letter from Kaufman exempting him from service was waiting in his file.[17]

Gavriel Beer was once walking with his wife on the boardwalk in Far Rockaway when they met another religious couple. They began to talk and Beer mentioned being in Mike Tress's Pirchei group as a young boy. At the mention of Mike's name, the other man became very excited. When he had gotten out of college in the late '30s, he had been unable to find a job that would not require him to work on Shabbos. Finally someone suggested that he get in touch with Mike Tress. Though he had never met Mike, it was enough for Mike to hear that he was *shomer Shabbos* and needed a job. He called up another of his contacts in public life, Albert Goldman, the New York City Postmaster, and found the man a job.[18]

In at least one case, Mike's connections were life saving. He was able to obtain erythromycin, which was then an experimental antibiotic not authorized for general use, for a critically ill immigrant

17. Goldstein interview.
18. Beer interview.

Rabbi Herbert Goldstein and a Camp Agudah camper presenting an award to New York Postmaster Albert Goldman for his efforts on behalf of Camp Agudah as Mike looks on

in the early 40s. The man lived another 25 years as a consequence of Mike's intervention.

MIKE WAS ONE OF THOSE CHARISMATIC PERSONALITIES BLESSED with the ability to move both large crowds and individuals. He was able **Salesman of Yiddishkeit** to convey to every listener in a large audience the same sense of immediacy as in a private conversation. In both public speech and private conversation, his words pierced to the heart. Rabbi Chaim Uri Lipshitz describes this ability to move others:

> When a glass of water is full, the water pours out. Similarly, Mike's heart was always overflowing, and so his words poured out into the hearts of his listeners — "words that come from the heart enter the heart." If you had any sympathy whatsoever for his point of view, he would sweep you away.
>
> He worked on your emotions. His gift had nothing to do with oratory; he spoke to the heart. When he depicted the future, it lit a spark in your soul.

Mike speaking at the Agudah dinner honoring Rabbi Eliezer Silver. Seated in front row, L-R: Rabbi Yaakov Kamenetzky, Rabbi Aharon Kotler, Rabbi Eliezer Silver, Rabbi Moshe Sherer

The best description of Mike as a speaker is that of Rabbi Feivel Rosenzweig: "He was a powerful speaker and he wasn't a polished speaker. He had both *maalos* (positive attributes)." He sought not to be admired for the beauty of the oratorical edifice he was constructing, but to get a message across. The speeches were designed to work on the elemental emotional level, to enter the hearts of his listeners. Mike himself was often so carried away by what he wanted to convey that he seemed to enter an almost hypnotic trance.[19]

At Agudath Israel conventions, he warmed the hearts of the audience with his portrayal of all that had been achieved, even as he depicted all that was left to do. He could dramatize even simple nouns and pronouns in such a way that they came alive. When he mentioned the names of the death camps — Auschwitz, Treblinka, Maidanek — his listeners felt as if they were there.[20]

Mike had the primary quality of a great salesman: an absolute belief in the quality of the product he was selling — the Torah. In Rabbi Shlomo Rotenberg's words, "Everything concerning Torah was beyond question as far as he was concerned." His voice could always be heard clearly in *davening;* the fervor of his prayers caused them to be easily

19. Interviews with Jack Klausner and Robert Krane.
20. Interview with Sidney Greenwald.

distinguished.[21] Whenever he heard of a better way to perform a *mitzvah,* he started doing so immediately.[22]

He not only preached fealty to the *gedolim* but lived it. Rabbi Yehoshua Grodzitski was a close student of Rabbi Reuven Grozovsky, Rosh HaYeshiva of Torah Vodaath and the first head of the Moetzes Gedolei HaTorah of America. Many times he saw Mike come to Reb Reuven with questions of great moment for the future conduct of Agudath Israel. "He came to be guided," says Rabbi Grodzitski, "and whatever

Rabbi Reuven Grozovsky

the answer was, he accepted it with complete equanimity, confident that he was being guided by *daas Torah.*"

In the late '40s, Mike consulted with Reb Reuven, either personally or by phone, several times a day. One *Motzaei Shabbos,* Mike and the leader of Bnos visited Reb Reuven with an important question. Mizrachi's annual convention had unmarried girls and boys together, which was a major draw. Mike's question was whether Zeirei and Bnos could hold simultaneous conventions in different wings of the same hotel. It was felt that this would help both organizations hold many of their members who were being drawn away to the mixed Mizrachi convention, and would also prove a boon for *shidduchim,* which still were a major problem for Othodox young people. Reb Reuven replied that in the view of the Torah the ends do not justify the means — both must be consonant with the demands of the Torah. For that reason simultaneous conventions could not be permitted. Reb Reuven's decision was accepted without question.[23]

Mike was incapable of meeting another Jew without trying to draw him closer to his own viewpoint. During one Agudath Israel

---

21. Interview with Rabbi Feivel Rosenzweig.
22. Interview with Rabbi Yisroel Belsky.
23. Interview with Rabbi Chaim Grozovsky.

convention at the Empire Hotel, the waiter at Mike's table was Irwin Metchik, an 18-year-old from the Bronx, who had just begun his studies at Yeshiva University. Though Mike was invariably at the center of the action at every convention, he still found a half an hour to spend alone with Metchik discussing the ideals of Agudath Israel and trying to interest him in coming to Williamsburg to visit the Zeirei branch there. Though Metchik never became a member of Zeirei, what remains in his memory more than 50 years later is that Mike did not content himself with a slap on the back and an easily ignored invitation to "Come join us." Rather, he talked to him with complete earnestness. At that moment, Metchik was made to feel as if his decision whether to join Zeirei was Mike's most important concern.[24]

MIKE'S SECOND GREAT QUALITY AS A SALESMAN WAS THAT HIS "purchasers" knew that his only concern was their own benefit. There

Modesty was nothing for him in a "sale" other than the pleasure of seeing another Jew becoming *frum* (religious). The simplicity and modesty conveyed in everything he did — the way he always stood over to the side or in the back in *davening*, the simple, unpretentious "Mike" by which he was universally known — ruled out all ulterior motives.

That simple name, of course, became in time one honored throughout the Jewish world. A Satmar *chassid* named Michoel Klaristenfeld arrived in America after the war and went to see Mike, whom he had been told would help him find a job. Mike was able to get him a job with a kosher candy manufacturer, and even called the manufacturer later in the week to make sure that everything was working out. A few days after Klaristenfeld's arrival in America some official government documents arrived at his brother's home, where he was staying. They were addressed to one Mike Klaristenfeld. When his brother saw that he had been transformed from Michoel to Mike so soon after coming to America, he told him, "*Drei teg in America, und shoen a shaygetz* — Three days in America, and already a *shaygetz*."

Klaristenfeld explained that he had received his immigration papers in Europe from Michael Tress, and when he came to the Agudath Israel offices, he heard everyone calling him "Mike" so he assumed that "Mike" would be a proper American name for him.

---

24. Interview with Irving Metchik.

"Oh, you want to be like Mike Tress," his brother said. "In that case, it's okay."[25]

After the Skverer Rebbe moved from Williamsburg to New Square, he used to return once a year to Williamsburg. On those occasions, Mike always went to visit him. Invariably the Rebbe's attendant took Mike straight in past the large crowds waiting to see the Rebbe, causing Mike untold embarrassment. So acute was his embarrassment at being pushed to the head of the line that he resolved not to go anymore. Eventually, however, an arrangement was worked out where Mike was given a time when no one else was waiting to see the Rebbe.[26]

Mike never referred to his own achievements — "I did this" — but only to what Agudath Israel had done.[27] During the last years of his life, his oldest son Shmuel Baruch spent months at a time with his father as he pursued various medical treatments. Yet no matter how many times Shmuel Baruch importuned his father to speak about "the old days" his pleas fell on deaf ears.[28]

The ultimate proof of Mike's disinterestedness, his lack of personal ego, is, of course, the way he stressed to his followers that their true leaders were the *gedolei Torah*. Being a hero is intoxicating, yet from the very beginning Mike's entire message was designed to divert the gaze of his followers from him to the great Torah leaders of the Jewish people.

MIKE'S PASSION FOR WHAT HE BELIEVED IN AND HIS PERSONAL warmth combined to give him an almost irresistible power over people.

"I Could Never Say No to Mike"

The slightest contact with him was enough to fire someone up to sacrifice for the *klal*. Morley Auerbach met Mike briefly in England on the latter's way to visit the Displaced Person's camps in Germany. A few weeks later, Auerbach was asked to translate for Rabbi Ephraim Oshry who had come to England to raise money for survivors camped in Italy. Auerbach was so aflame from his talks with Mike that when he saw that the contributions were not coming in at one hotel, he stood up and announced, "I've never been to Miami and I've always wanted to go. The entire three years I've been flying combat missions over Germany, I saved my money, and now I have 600 pounds. That

25. Told to Yitzchak Tzvi Tress by Michoel Klaristenfeld.
26. Interview with Shmuel Baruch Tress.
27. Interview with his daughter Shevy Jundef.
28. Interview with Shmuel Baruch Tress.

money was supposed to be for a trip to Miami, but I'm giving this to Rabbi Oshry. Now let's see how you're going to respond." When he sat down, the pledges poured in.[29]

Parents unable to communicate with their children — whether a son uninterested in learning or a daughter considering an inappropriate *shidduch* — relied on Mike's powers of persuasion. Mendy Dembroff was a very good baseball player, so good, in fact, that the New York Giants offered him a professional contract. Mendy's parents realized that a career in professional sports would be the end of his *Yiddishkeit* and pleaded with him to turn the contract down. Their pleas, however, were to no avail. In desperation, Dembroff's mother asked Mike to speak to him. In no more than an hour, Mike somehow managed to achieve what a mother's tears had not. Dembroff not only turned down the contract; he was profoundly changed by the encounter. In later years, he often told his children that whenever he was confronted with a difficult decision, his first question was always: What would Mike Tress have thought of this?[30]

"I could never say no to Mike" is a constant refrain in the memories of his followers. Any request from him carried a weight it would have had from no one else. Those close to him knew that whatever he asked of them was a fraction of what he had given of himself, and they could not bear the thought of letting him down."When he needed money for a project, I would take out a loan to get it," recalled Rabbi Feivel Rosenzweig, "but I never said no to Mike." Summers were always particularly precious to Rabbi Yaakov Goldstein. During the vacation from his job as a *rebbi* in Rabbi Jacob Joseph school, he was free to devote the whole day to his own learning. So when Mike asked Rabbi Goldstein to be the head counselor at Camp Agudah its first summer in Ferndale, Rabbi Goldstein told him that he never worked during the summer. But in the end, he capitulated for the same reason: "I could never say no to Mike."

Not long after he arrived back in the States after serving four years in the U.S. army, Meyer Birnbaum received a call from Mike, who wanted to know whether he was still allowed to wear his uniform. Thousands of affidavits guaranteeing that refugees would not become public charges were required for the survivors of Hitler's death

---

29. Interview with Morley Auerbach.
30. Told to Mendel Tress by Mendy Dembroff's son.

camps, and the tiny religious community in America at that time was incapable of supplying them. Mike realized that appeals would have to be made to non-Orthodox Jews, and felt that a much decorated veteran like Birnbaum, who had spent six months among the survivors, would have a credibility that no one else would. The only catch was that Birnbaum had never in his life addressed an audience of any size and did not fancy beginning civilian life by making a fool of himself. He tried to convince Mike that his idea was impossible, but in the end he too succumbed:

Rabbi Itche Meir Levine

> ... I soon learned that it was almost impossible to say no to Mike. I knew how he had worked for years around the clock on behalf of European Jews, and it would have taken someone a lot tougher than me to refuse him. His passion and sense of mission were simply irresistible.

"This is *pikuach nefesh* (saving of lives)," Mike said. "That means you have no choice. You"ll simply have to learn how to speak. You'll see, once you start, the *Ribbono Shel Olam* won't let you fail."[31]

THE ENCOURAGEMENT GIVEN TO MEYER BIRNBAUM WAS TYPICAL of Mike. He was always pushing people to develop their talents, and

A Builder of People

was a master at building up a person's confidence. When he said, "You can do it," people believed him. With Mike there was no fear of being criticized if things did not work out well. Rabbi Itche Meir Levine, son-in-law of the Gerrer Rebbe and leader of Agudath Israel in Poland and later in *Eretz Yisrael*, was a frequent visitor to America in the '40s. On one of his trips, he was scheduled to address a gathering of Bnos Agudath Israel, and Mike asked Celia (Roth) Zanzipar to introduce him. She

---

31. Birnbaum and Rosenblum, *Lieutenant Birnbaum*, pp. 182-83.

protested, but he simply told her, "I'll stand and watch; you'll do it."
And so it was.

Mrs. Zanzipar adds that Mike did the same thing for the boys and
men that he did for her.[32] He had a way of extracting talents from
people that they did not know they had. Mike's whole *modus operandi*
was predicated on getting people to do something, to contribute. He
believed that every person who made a contribution would in turn
encourage someone else to do so.

Joshua Silbermintz once came to Mike and told him that he felt
incapable of continuing with all his responsibilities with Pirchei, which
then included running a branch on Willoughby Avenue and the Pirchei
minyan at 616 Bedford Avenue. Mike lifted his spirits by sharing some
of his own experiences:

> When I go to Chicago or Detroit to raise money, I keep hearing
> thanks for all that we're doing for servicemen and so forth. But
> when I come back to 616, my old friends ask, "Why aren't you
> doing such and such?" No one comes over and says you're
> doing wonderful things. When people criticize you, you have to
> be above it and learn not to listen to it. Just know what you
> want to accomplish and that it is worthwhile, and then do it.[33]

As a leader, one of Mike's greatest strengths was his ability to spot
talent in others and give them responsibility. He never suffered from the
need to protect his own stature. He recognized, for instance, that
Gershon Kranzler's experience in the German Zeirei Agudath Israel
could be utilized in creating a truly national movement in America.
Soon after the headquarters at 616 Bedford Avenue opened, Kranzler was
put in charge of creating a national infrastructure for Zeirei, Pirchei, and
Bnos. Rabbi Ephraim Wolf remembers the way that Mike built up
Kranzler in the eyes of his followers so that they would be eager to help
him: "Mike told us how educated he was, how many languages he spoke,
and how he was one of the leaders of Zeirei in Germany. We were in
awe of him before we were even introduced. But if it were not for Mike's
introduction, he would have just been another greenhorn in our eyes."

The best example of Mike's ability to nurture talent, of course,
remains Rabbi Moshe Sherer. Mike recognized his younger cousin's

---

32. Interview with Celia (Roth) Zanzipar.

33. Interview with Rabbi Joshua Silbermintz.

Rabbi Moshe Sherer addressing an Agudah dinner in 1943.
Seated L-R: Rabbi Michael Munk, Rabbi Yechiel Elbaum, Mike

organizational abilities and brought him into the Agudath Israel Youth Council as Executive Director at the tender age of 22. From the beginning, Rabbi Sherer was given a wide range of responsibilities, without ever having to worry about being second-guessed. Over the years, he and Mike worked together hand and glove.

Mike's impact on people frequently lasted a lifetime, as in the case of Mendy Dembroff. Moshe Berger was the first head of the Refugee and Immigration Division of the Agudath Israel Youth Council. In the early '70s, he traveled to Poland at the behest of the Bobover Rebbe to bring to the United States a Jewish boy who wanted to learn in yeshiva. Subsequently, he returned to Poland and took out the boy's whole family. In all, Berger made six trips at his own expense to bring to America Polish Jews in whom the spark of Judaism still burned. A number of the younger children he raised as his own. Looking back on these efforts, he attributes them to one source: the inspiration of working closely with Mike Tress for four years.[34]

---

34. Interview with Moshe Berger.

Chapter Seven

WILLIAMSBURG

THE GROWTH OF THE WILLIAMSBURG ZEIREI IN the '30s and '40s cannot be separated from the development of Williamsburg itself as a religious neighborhood. Unlike the Lower East Side, Williamsburg was never a predominantly Jewish neighborhood — the Irish and Italian population still outnumbered the Jewish population through the '30s. Yet it was there that a vibrant religious life first flowered in America.

By the mid-'30s, Torah Vodaath was firmly established as the country's premier yeshiva, and its presence in Williamsburg attracted many religious families to the neighborhood. The first Bais Yaakov elementary school and first Bais Yaakov seminary were both established in Williamsburg.

As these religious institutions began to flourish, they each strengthened one another. There was, for instance, a close interplay between Torah Vodaath and the Williamsburg Zeirei. Through Pirchei, many boys were encouraged to go to yeshiva who otherwise would not have. At the same time, the presence of Torah Vodaath was an important factor in the unique success of the Williamsburg Zeirei. Torah Vodaath gave Mike a concrete goal towards which to direct Pirchei boys. And as more and more Pirchei boys had a yeshiva education, the level of the Pirchei groups was raised correspondingly.

The synergy generated by the parallel development of a number of Orthodox organizations created an air of excitement — a feeling that in the midst of the world's fastest-paced, most technologically advanced, richest society, a self-confident Orthodoxy might yet be fashioned.

Williamsburg provided fertile ground for all Mike's energies. In addition to his central role in the development of Zeirei, he was also involved in the other central institutions of Williamsburg Jewry, including Torah Vodaath and Bais Yaakov.

MIKE'S OWN RELIGIOUS GROWTH WAS HASTENED AS A RESULT OF his extensive contacts with many of the leading religious personalities living in Williamsburg. By the end of the '30s, Williamsburg was home to most of the leading Chassidic Rebbes living in America.[1] In addition, Torah Vodaath attracted to the neighborhood in the '30s and '40s many of the first great products of the Lithuanian yeshivos to make their presence felt in America, including Rabbi Dovid Leibowitz, Rabbi Shlomo Heiman, Rabbi Reuven Grozovsky, and Rabbi Yaakov Kamenetsky.

Reb Shraga Feivel

Yet of all the luminaries living in Williamsburg, unquestionably the one whose influence was most widely felt was Reb Shraga Feivel Mendlowitz, the dynamo who headed Torah Vodaath from 1924 until his death in 1948. Reb Feivel possessed a vision for the development of a thriving American Orthodoxy when few could see beyond their own *daled amos* (literally, four cubits).

Reb Feivel was an important influence on Mike, both directly and through his protégé Rabbi Gedaliah Schorr. The two men shared much in common, particularly their dedication to the *klal* over any particularistic interests. Both were optimists and visionaries, whose vision for the

---

1. A number of leading Rebbes, including the Kopyczinitzer Rebbe and the Boyaner Rebbe, continued to live on the Lower East Side.

Reb Shraga Feivel Mendlowitz   Rabbi Dovid Leibowitz

future encompassed all of American Jewry. These traits were seemingly inborn in Mike, but Reb Feivel helped to give them shape and to put them into an overall Torah perspective. Mike regularly attended Reb Feivel's *shiurim* (classes) in Rabbi Moshe Chaim Luzzato's *Derech Hashem* at Torah Vodaath and the *shiurim* in *Tehillim* he gave at 616 Bedford Avenue.[2]

Though Reb Shraga Feivel taught from time to time at the Zeirei headquarters[3] he was wary of being too closely identified with Agudath Israel. He was, in the words of Rabbi Gedaliah Schorr, an Agudist with a small "a,"[4] i.e., he subscribed fully to the Agudah vision of *klal Yisrael* united around the banner of Torah and led by the *gedolei Yisrael*, but eschewed any political affiliation.[5]

---

2. Interview with Rabbi Nesanel Quinn.

3. Interview with Heshy Moskowitz.

4. Interview with Sidney Greenwald.

5. Reb Feivel's wariness in this regard is partially explained by the fact that many of Torah Vodaath's principal supporters were active in the Mizrachi movement. The first president of the Yeshiva, for instance, was Rabbi Zev Gold, who was also the leader of the Mizrachi movement in America.

Reb Feivel was a master at walking the tightrope between various factions. At the dedication of Torah Vodaath's building on South 3rd Street, which was attended by Rabbi Yitzchak Isaac Herzog, the Ashkenazi Chief Rabbi of Palestine, and Rabbi Gold, there was considerable pressure to play *Hatikvah*. Reb Feivel neatly finessed the issue, however, by having Seymour Silbermintz write a *niggun* (melody) to some words of Rabbi Avraham·Yitzchak Kook, the first

Rabbi Shlomo Heiman (center) with Rav Meir Kahana of Mesivta Torah Vodaath

Mike admired Reb Feivel as someone who not only dreamed of great things but knew how to get them done. He frequently consulted with Reb Feivel before embarking on major new projects, and as the scope of Mike's activities broadened, Reb Feivel gave him more and more of his time.[6] Mike once told Heshy Mashinsky that there was no one he held in so much awe as Reb Feivel. "He speaks authoritatively and he knows what he's talking about. You can't argue with him," Mike said. In certain respects, Reb Feivel was a model for Mike of how much could be achieved in America. At the former's funeral, Mike cried like a baby.[7]

For his part, Reb Feivel viewed Mike as the embodiment of the *klal* consciousness he was trying to impart to his students.[8] He saw Mike as someone who shared his boundless energy and willingness to sacrifice all personal considerations on behalf of his fellow Jews, and who, like him, had no need for self-aggrandizement.[9]

Ashkenazi Chief Rabbi. Thus when Reb Feivel was asked why *Hatikvah* was not being played, he was able to stop the questioners in their tracks by asking whether they did not prefer the words of their hero Rabbi Kook to those of one completely alienated from all religious observance. *Interview with Rabbi Joshua Silbermintz.*

6. Quinn interview.

7. Interview with Rabbi Henoch Cohen.

8. See Introduction, pp. i-ii.

9. Reb Feivel's modesty was legendary. He steadfastly refused to answer to any title other than "Mister." (He made "Mister" into a term of the highest respect, just as Mike turned the name "Mike" into one of distinction in religious circles.) During the week of dedication ceremonies for Torah Vodaath's new building on South 3rd Street, Reb Feivel never came into the building out

Towards the end of World War II, Reb Feivel entrusted his student Avraham Abba Friedman with a cryptic message for Mike. Friedman was picked because he had been one of the first Pirchei leaders at 157 Rodney Street and was close to Mike. The message: "Tell Mr. Tress that he should accept my offer."

Reb Feivel did not tell Friedman the meaning of the message, but when the latter delivered it he could not restrain himself from asking Mike what Reb Feivel had meant. Mike told him that Reb Feivel had asked him to be his partner in an array of projects that he was then eager to undertake, such as Torah Umesorah.[10] Mike was too involved in the European rescue and relief work to consider the offer, but the offer itself is testimony to the esteem in which Reb Shraga Feivel held him.[11]

THERE WAS ONE ASPECT OF TORAH VODAATH'S OPERATIONS IN which Mike and Zeirei played a direct role: the recruiting trips designed

Recruiting Trips

to bring out-of-town boys into the Mesivta. These trips began in 1939 when Abish Mendlowitz, later the first head counselor in Camp Agudah, and his cousin Jerry Fink returned to their native Scranton, Pennsylvania for Sukkos. They organized a *seudah* for all the boys from Scranton then learning in Torah Vodaath and invited another 35 or 40 boys to join them. The non-yeshiva boys were invited back to Williamsburg for Shemini Atzeres and Simchas Torah. Twenty-seven visited Williamsburg, and of those eight stayed in Torah Vodaath to learn.[12]

The idea of actively recruiting out-of-town boys had proven itself. Over the next several years a small group of young men, inspired by Reb Feivel's repeated admonitions about how much could, and must, be done for boys growing up in cities too small to support yeshivos, began to travel to outlying regions in search of boys to come to Torah

---

of a fear of being honored by the supporters of the Yeshiva. Only when the festivities were over and there were only students in the building did he return. *Interview with Rabbi Joshua Silbermintz.*

He was an extremely charismatic personality. Men in their seventies and eighties still cry today, more than 45 years after his *petirah*, when talking about him. Yet he did not allow the students to become bound only to him. Not only did he make every effort to provide them with the greatest exemplars of Lithuanian learning, he also pushed them to become close to the leading Chassidic figures living in New York. Similarly, Mike used his tremendous prestige with his followers to push them to look to the *gedolei Torah* as their leaders.

10. Interview with Rabbi Avraham Abba Friedman.

11. Reb Feivel's offer was but the most dramatic example of his efforts to involve Mike in his projects. Mike also served on the board of directors of Torah Vodaath during Reb Feivel's lifetime. *Interview with Rabbi Nesanel Quinn.*

12. Interview with Abish Mendlowitz.

Vodaath.[13] Their forays took them to Eastern Pennsylvania — Scranton, Wilkes-Barre, and Dixon City — as far south as Baltimore, and as far west as Rochester and even Detroit. Not accidentally, almost the entire group of "recruiters," including Ephraim (Freddy) Wolf, Mottel Berkowitz, Elimelech Terebelo, Sender Francis, and Heshy Moskowitz, had grown up in Pirchei and continued to be active in the Williamsburg Zeirei. The recruiters in turn relied on friends from their Pirchei days — such as Shlomo Ort, Avraham Abba Friedman, and Binyamin Hershkowitz — to help make sure that everything was organized for the boys being bused into Williamsburg.[14]

Typically, one or two recruiters would arrive in a town armed with a list of boys who by virtue of their family's religiosity or their own interest were candidates for yeshiva. The lists were compiled with the help of boys from that town already studying in Torah Vodaath. Going house to house, the recruiters would talk to the boys' parents, who were usually reluctant to send their young sons so far away from home.

The first step to overcoming the fears of the parents and the boys themselves was interesting the boys in spending Shavuos or *Chol HaMoed Sukkos* in Williamsburg. The recruiters would enthusiastically describe the "living Judaism of Williamsburg." Among the highlights of their description was Simchas Torah at 616 Bedford Avenue.[15]

Reb Feivel emphasized that the success of the visits to Williamsburg would be judged by the number of boys who decided to go to yeshiva. To that end, the exclusive focus was on making sure that the boys had a good time and returned home filled with enthusiasm. One time some of the visiting boys began to shine their shoes on Yom Tov. Reb Feivel gave instructions that nothing should be said to them. "First we must show them a good time and bring them to Torah Vodaath, then we'll have time to teach them and take care of them religiously," he

---

13. Interview with Elimelech Terebelo.

Reb Feivel's confidence that bringing boys into the yeshiva could change their lives was amply borne out by experience. Nearly 30 years after the last of his recruiting trips for Torah Vodaath, Rabbi Ephraim Wolf was approached one Shabbos by a 17-year-old boy studying in the yeshiva he was visiting. The boy wanted to know if he was the Freddy Wolf who used to go around from town to town bringing boys back to Torah Vodaath in a bus. Assured that he was, the boy continued, "Every year at the *seder*, after we finish the *Haggadah*, my father says, 'I've told you about *Klal Yisrael's* going out of Egypt. Now I'd like to tell you about my personal *yetzias Mitzrayim*.' And then he tells the story of how Heshy Moskowitz and Freddy Wolf came to his town with a bus and took him to yeshiva." The boy's father had gone on to become a well-known *rosh yeshiva*. *Interview with Rabbi Ephraim Wolf.*

14. Interviews with Rabbi Ephraim Wolf and Elimelech Terebelo.

15. Interview with Rabbi Ephraim Wolf.

said.[16] One of the recruiters recalls with amusement the amazement on the faces of one out-of-town group when they were addressed by Rabbi Alexander Linchner, Reb Feivel's son-in-law and principal of the high school. They could not believe that a rabbi could speak fluent English. Their wonder was only increased when Rabbi Linchner spoke of some of the attractions of New York, such as the opportunity to see the Brooklyn Dodgers and New York Yankees play.[17]

Mike took an active interest in the recruiting work.[18] He often was among those there to greet the boys as they arrived, and any overflow was housed at 616 Bedford Avenue.[19] At 616, the visitors talked with boys their own age involved in wartime rescue work and got a feeling "of the importance of the individual as a member of a whole, of a creative group aiming towards a universal goal."[20]

In a letter written to Mike in the midst of one of his recruiting trips,[21] Freddie Wolf asked Mike to take care of all the arrangements for the boys who would be arriving: ensuring that they be exposed to bright out-of-town boys already studying in the Mesivta, arranging a tour for them, and grouping the boys by age, rather than by town of origin, so that they would make new friends and get a feeling of what yeshiva life is like.

Though Mike had no formal connection to Torah Vodaath other than as a member of the board of directors, Wolf asked him to set aside time to speak personally to each boy and to attempt to extract from him a commitment to come to Torah Vodaath the next year. He considered Mike, despite his own lack of yeshiva training, the person who would make the strongest impression on a group of fully Americanized youngsters and the most persuasive salesman for the importance of yeshiva learning.

In light of the fact that there would be almost a year between the visit to Williamsburg and actually enrolling in the yeshiva, Wolf also urged Mike to stress Camp Agudah, where the boys would be exposed to many yeshiva students their own age. "[Camp] will no doubt further

16. Interview with Rabbi Joshua Silbermintz.

17. Interview with Abish Mendlowitz.

18. Mike was known as one of the first addresses for any boy coming to learn in Williamsburg from out of town. Rabbi Moses J. Feldman of Los Angeles, for instance, wrote to him on September 11, 1941 requesting that he do everything possible to befriend his two sons, who were soon to arrive in Torah Vodaath, in light of "the splendid interest you take in matters of this nature."

19. Gershon Kranzler, "They Came . . . They Saw . . . And They Will Return . . . ," *Orthodox Youth*, pp. 1, 9.

20. Ibid.

21. The letter is undated, but the references to Camp Agudah, which first opened in the summer of 1942, make clear that it must have been written after that.

influence then to come to Mesivta," Wolf wrote, "so you see that the stay in camp is perhaps the most important thing for the moment, and perhaps we should get them all to camp."

One of the visiting boys was so impressed with Mike that when his parents refused to let him register for yeshiva, he called Mike long distance and asked him to speak to his parents. Mike was able to allay the parents' fears that their son would lack a secular education if he went to yeshiva, and the next September he was enrolled at Torah Vodaath. He went on to obtain both *semichah* and a Ph.D.[22]

BAIS YAAKOV EDUCATION IN AMERICA LAGGED FAR BEHIND THE development of yeshivos. It was nearly 20 years from the opening of

Bais Yaakov

Torah Vodaath until the first intrepid pioneers attempted to start a Bais Yaakov-type school in Williamsburg.

In 1935, Mr. and Mrs. Avraham Spinner opened Bais Rochel at 233 Rodney Street next door to their home.[23] The idea of a Jewish school for girls met with little initial enthusiasm. Even in Europe, Bais Yaakov was still limited primarily to the larger cities in Poland and Lithuania. The European-born mothers and grandmothers of school-age daughters had not attended anything like a Bais Yaakov school. And even the leading rabbinical authorities in America frequently showed no great interest in a religious elementary school education for girls, citing the fact that it had been unknown in their day in Europe.[24] The Spinners and the small nucleus of parents who joined them were often stymied in their recruiting efforts by parents who pointed to the fact that highly respected rabbis sent their daughters to public school.

Unfortunately, the limited enrollment of the new school proved no insurance against disputes arising between various groups of parents over the curriculum. Though Bais Rochel followed the curriculum of Torah Vodaath's elementary school, there was a substantial group of parents that objected to various aspects of the curriculum, including the teaching of Hebrew as a spoken language and *Chumash* with *Rashi*.

---

22. This story was one of those in a personal condolence letter to Mrs. Tress (likely from Gershon Kranzler) quoted in Rabbi Chaim Uri Lipshitz's *Jewish Press* column of August 11, 1967. See Chapter 6, fn. 11.

23. This was the Spinners' second attempt at opening an elementary school for girls. Previously they had started Shulamis in Boro Park, but had eventually left Boro Park for Williamsburg when more modern elements gained control of the school. *Interview with Ephraim Spinner.*

24. Interview with Reuven Soloff.

There were also objections to the English-language textbooks, and the tearing out of pages by parents became a major problem. Eventually the issues were taken to a *din Torah* before Rabbi Aharon Kotler, who was then raising funds in the United States. Though Reb Aharon largely supported the Spinners, the differences between the groups of parents proved irreconcilable and the fledgling school split in two. The Spinners reopened — under the name Bais Soroh — above the A&P on the corner of Lee Avenue and Hooper Street, and Bais Rochel moved to Division Avenue next to the *Polishe shtiebel*.[25]

Though neither Mike nor his contemporaries in Zeirei had school-age daughters — most were not even married — Zeirei played a major role in Bais Soroh. Mike, Louis Septimus, Nathan Hausman, and Dave Maryles all served on the Board of Directors of the school, and the Williamsburg Zeirei raised nearly half the annual budget of $4,000.[26] Rabbi Gedaliah Schorr, the *rav* of Zeirei, gave his first salary check from Torah Vodaath to Bais Soroh.[27] Mike was a frequent visitor to the school, where he gave impassioned speeches about Sarah Schenirer, whom he spoke about as one of the spiritual heroes of the age. He stressed the importance of bringing Bais Yaakov to America.

Mike saw that Bais Yaakov and Agudath Israel were natural allies in the United States as they had been in Europe, where there was a close relationship between Agudath Israel and Bais Yaakov. Reb Jacob Rosenheim, the first president of Agudath Israel, was one of the first to understand the importance of what Sarah Schenirer was doing, and dispatched his colleague Dr. Leo Deutschlander to Poland to assist with her organizational activities.[28] Dr. Deutschlander in turn brought along a young woman named Dr. Judith Grunfeld, who became Sarah Schenirer's closest associate.[29]

Sarah Schenirer was not only the founder of Bais Yaakov, but one of those most active in encouraging the development of Agudah-

---

25. The split of the original Bais Rochel and the subsequent re-amalgamation of Bais Soroh and Bais Rochel make it hard to identify precisely who was involved with which school. Besides the Spinners, others who were involved with one or another of the precursors to Bais Yaakov were: Rabbi Dr. David Stern of Torah Vodaath, the Follman, Pilchik, Kramer, and Soloff families, and Reb Shraga Feivel Mendlowitz.

26. Interview with Ephraim Spinner.

27. Interview with Leon Keller

28. Interview with Mrs. Daniella (Nussbaum) Buxbaum.

29. Interview with Mrs. Josephine Reichel.

| Sarah Schenirer | Rebbetzin Grunfeld | Dr. Leo Deutschlander |

ponsored Bnos groups.[30] In 1933, two years before her passing, she composed an open letter addressed to "My dear Bnos daughters." Her message was almost identical to that Mike was trying to get across in America:

> Youth means to be happy, to have the courage to face the problems of the world, optimism and belief in your own idealism. . . .
> How much joy and happiness must lay in such a youth organization! How much optimism and faith in G-d should be found in such a movement! Youth means *hislahavus*, enthusiasm! Calmness, indifference, and apathy are anti-youth.

Chava Weinberg, who had been the only American girl to study in Sarah Schenirer's seminary in Cracow, was the head teacher and in charge of the curriculum in Bais Soroh.[31] Upon Sarah Schenirer's passing in 1935, Chava had returned to New York determined to spread her revered mentor's teachings. An initial attempt to establish a Bais

---

30. To help protect the dangers that lurked beyond the school walls, Sarah Schenirer and some others established *Bnos Agudas Yisrael* for older girls, and *Basya* for children. These organizations, primarily *Bnos*, provided educational Shabbos and evening programs. Many of the group leaders were girls who had graduated from Sarah Schenirer's Cracow Seminary. These groups enabled girls who were unable to afford tuition for Bais Yaakov schools to broaden their knowledge, gain inspiration, and socialize in a supervised environment. Through Bnos, the influence of the Bais Yaakov movement reached thousands who never formally enrolled in a Bais Yaakov School. See Miriam Dansky, *Rebbetzin Grunfeld* (Mesorah Publications 1994), p. 126.

31. Chava Weinberg was the daughter of Reb Mattis Weinberg, a *talmid chacham* and successful businessman on the Lower East Side. (His other children include Rabbi Yaakov Weinberg, Rosh Yeshiva of Ner Israel, and Rabbi Noach Weinberg, the founder of Aish Hatorah.) Reb Mattis became enamored of the idea of Bais Yaakov during a visit of one of the Agudath Israel delegations to the United States in the early '20s, and began a correspondence with Sarah Schenirer. He

Yaakov on the Lower East Side failed, and she began teaching at both Shulamis in Boro Park and Bais Soroh.[32]

Bais Soroh and Bais Rochel were both too small to be either financially or educationally viable. In 1937, the former had only 45 students and the latter probably even fewer.[33] The two sets of parents had no choice but to put aside their differences and reunite if there was to be any elementary school education for girls. Binyomin Wilhelm, the founding father of Torah Vodaath, was approached by both sides and succeeded in effecting a reconciliation.[34] By 1939, the two schools had been amalgamated under the official name of Bais Yaakov, but the next few years saw a quick succession of principals. In 1943, Rabbi Avraham Newhouse, a young German immigrant, revitalized the school.

A Bais Yaakov high school and seminary took even longer to establish. Chava Weinberg taught some older girls at night above the A&P on Lee Avenue, until she married Rabbi Avraham Pincus and moved with him to Jersey City. When Rebbetzin Vichna Kaplan, a dynamic student of Sarah Schenirer, arrived in 1938, she began teaching this group in her home. Later she rented an apartment on Keap Street, where she was joined by two other former products of the Cracow seminary, Rebbetzins Bender and Wachtfogel.[35] Not until 1945 was Rebbetzin Kaplan able to open up an afternoon program for high school-age girls and those who had already graduated high school. The following year

---

wanted to send his daughter to Cracow from the time she was 12, but his wife insisted on waiting until Chava was at least 18. In one letter written shortly before her arrival in Cracow in 1933, Reb Mattis referred to Elisha's request to be twice as great as his teacher Eliyahu and enjoined Sarah Schenirer to make his daughter twice as great as her.

The *"Amerikaner"* was the subject of great curiosity on her arrival in Cracow. Her first *Tishrei* in Poland her teacher Esther Hamburger took her on a trip throughout Poland. The highlight of the trip was visiting Gur and being invited to hear the Gerrer Rebbe's *kiddush*. Thousands of *chassidim*, who had never been so privileged, were astounded that two young women had been singled out for the honor.

In her letters home, Chava described with wide-eyed wonder everything she had seen. She wrote of her first Shabbos and how Sarah Schenirer took all the girls with her to *shul*. At *Shalosh Seudas*, the custom was for one of the Seminary's graduates to say a *dvar Torah*. At that first *Shalosh Seudas*, she listened in the dark to a recent graduate describing how Moshe Rabbeinu did not eat for forty days and nights when receiving the Torah. But that was not as remarkable, the speaker concluded, as the fact that Moshe Rabbeinu did eat when he returned from Mount Sinai. That, she explained, was only because of the rule that one should not deviate from the custom of the place in which he resides. *Interviews with Rebbetzin Chava (Weinberg) Pincus and her brother Morris Weinberg.*

32. Interview with Rebbetzin Chava (Weinberg) Pincus.

33. Letter dated August 1937 from Avraham Spinner to Isaac Strahl.

34. Interview with Rebbetzin Channah Belsky, Binyomin Wilhelm's daughter.

35. Interview with Rebbetzin Chava (Weinberg) Pincus.

the first full-day program began, though the afternoon-only program also continued for some time.[36]

NO EVENT HAD SUCH A DECISIVE IMPACT ON MIKE PERSONALLY OR on the development of Zeirei in America as the presence of Rabbi

Reb Elchonon's Visit

Elchonon Wasserman in America from late 1937 to just before Pesach of 1939. Reb Elchonon came for the purpose of raising funds to relieve the desperate plight of his yeshiva in Baranovich. But while in America, he involved himself in a wide variety of communal matters, in particular the state of Jewish education.[37]

For years prior to Reb Elchonon's visit, Mike had been speaking about *gedolei Torah* and instilling in his young followers the belief that Torah scholars are the natural leaders of the Jewish people. But the prolonged exposure to a *gadol* of Reb Elchonon's stature gave these ideas a new vitality for Mike.

Reb Elchonon was an active member of the Moetzes Gedolei HaTorah of Agudath Israel Europe and one of the most powerful contemporary exponents of Agudah ideology. For Mike, whose ideology was largely culled from what he had managed to read on his own, the personal contact with a committed Agudist like Reb Elchonon was an "eye opener."[38] Reb Elchonon was, in the words of Rabbi Moshe Sherer, "the real thing, the real McCoy. He was not only an Agudist in

---

36. Interview with Mrs. Rena (Zirkind) Ebert.

A hint of Rebbetzin Kaplan's stature in the eyes of contemporary Torah leaders can be gleaned from the following story told by Morris Weinberg.

The Weinberg family was intimately connected to Bais Yaakov from its inception in America, and Morris Weinberg succeeded in interesting a non-religious coat manufacturer by the name of Simon Cohen in Rebbetzin Kaplan's seminary. In one short period in 1948-49 alone, Cohen raised $50,000 for Bais Yaakov from other rich friends in the garment industry.

All was going well until one day Cohen decided to bring a gentile woman into the seminary to teach a charm course for the girls. Rabbi Baruch Kaplan rushed to Reb Aharon Kotler and laid down an ultimatum: "either Cohen ceases all involvement in the seminary or my wife and I leave."

Reb Aharon replied, "Bais Yaakov will exist with or without Simon Cohen. *Yiddishkeit* does not depend on money. But without Vichna Kaplan to run a seminary, we won't have a seminary."

37. For a full account of Reb Elchonon's trip to America see Rabbi Aharon Surasky's *Reb Elchonon* (Mesorah Publications 1982), pp. 329-62. In the course of his stay, Reb Elchonon traveled to over a dozen cities and addressed thousands of listeners. Besides his addresses to large audiences, he left an indelible impact on hundreds of individuals with whom he had direct personal contact.

The following account focuses on his impact on Pirchei and Zeirei, but that represents only one aspect of his influence. He also spoke, for instance, in many Young Israel *shuls* and had a great deal of contact with Irving Bunim and other Young Israel leaders.

38. Interview with Rabbi Moshe Sherer.

theory, he was *kulo* (entirely) Agudath Israel." In speeches to Pirchei and Bnos groups in later years, Mike frequently spoke of the importance of Reb Elchonon in transforming him into a devoted Agudist, and he never tired of quoting him.[39]

Long before Reb Elchonon's arrival in New York on October 26, 1937, Mike had begun preparing his Pirchei boys for the fact that one of the world's greatest *tzaddikim* would be coming to America. He spoke so many times about Reb Elchonon that it was the dream of every Pirchei boy to be chosen to *meshamesh* (serve) Reb Elchonon.[40] Mike and Isaac Strahl led a sizable contingent of Pirchei boys to greet Reb Elchonon as he disembarked.[41] And throughout Reb Elchonon's stay, Mike brought different groups to the Broadway Central Hotel to meet with him.[42]

One of Reb Elchonon's recurrent themes during his time in America was the necessity of providing the youth with a proper Torah education. He did not share the widespread despair about the possibility of Torah in America. All that was lacking, he insisted, was proper education:

> Everyone told me that America is not fit for Torah. But that is not true. On my travels I have seen many pure *Yiddishe kinder* (Jewish children), *temimusdike kinder*. In some respects they are purer than the children in Europe. All that is needed is someone to teach them Torah. If people undertake to spread Torah, they will accept it.[43]

Given his interest in youth, it was natural that Reb Elchonon was drawn to Zeirei. He spoke frequently on Shabbos night at 157 Rodney Street on the weekly Torah reading. From Rodney Street, he would walk to Mesivta Torah Vodaath, accompanied the entire way by an honor guard of Pirchei boys. They would line the sidewalk on both sides as he walked, running ahead to the front of the line after Reb Elchonon had passed.[44]

---

39. Interviews with Mrs. Daniella (Nussbaum) Buxbaum and Rabbi Shlomo Rotenberg.

40. Interviews with Rabbis Joshua Silbermintz and Arnold Wolf.

41. *Reb Elchonon*, p. 333.

42. Interview with Rabbi Ephraim Wolf.

43. Silbermintz interview.

Reb Elchonon's optimism about what could be achieved in America paralleled that of Reb Shraga Feivel Mendlowitz. The two became very close during Reb Elchonon's stay, and Reb Feivel had a number of Reb Elchonon's writings printed. *Interview with Rabbi Nesanel Quinn.*

44. Interview with Max Septimus.

Fifteen hundred people crowded into the Clymer Street *shul* to hear Reb Elchonon his first Shabbos in America. But he did not consider it beneath him to speak to six boys at a Pirchei *Melaveh Malkah* two weeks later.[45] The fact that Reb Elchonon spoke so frequently at the Zeirei headquarters and for various Pirchei affairs gave Zeirei new prominence in the eyes of the larger community and helped "put it on the map."[46]

The effect of Reb Elchonon's addresses was frequently dramatic. The first time that he spoke at Rodney Street, seated in the front row was a teenage boy who had left Torah Vodaath and was spending most of his time hanging around pool halls. During Reb Elchonon's entire presentation, the boy sat transfixed. From that day on, he returned to learning Torah and in time he became one of the leading personalities in the Orthodox world, personally helping to shape thousands of young boys.[47] Rabbi Moshe Sherer and others who had the privilege of serving as Reb Elchonon's *shamash* still remember his "searing effect on [their] *neshamos* (souls)."[48]

No other contemporary Torah leader was as identified as Reb Elchonon with the concept of *daas Torah* — the principle that the Torah is the only guide to the interpretation and understanding of contemporary events, and its corollary, that those who have most fully immersed themselves in the Torah are the best interpreters of the Divine Will as revealed in history. He himself wrote widely in the European Yiddish press on current events.

On Friday night at Rodney Street, Reb Elchonon made the concept of *daas Torah* live. He would stand at the front, a *Chumash* in hand, and tell the boys that everything is found in the Torah. *"Fregt a kashe* — Ask a question," he would tell them, and they would pepper him with questions about everything that was bothering them, such as Hitler's meteoric rise to power in Germany. He would quote various verses and explain their relevance to current events.[49] Reuven Soloff, in whose parents' home Reb Elchonon stayed for a period of time, described the way in which he made the Torah seem alive in a way it never had before:

---

45. Silbermintz interview.
46. Interviews with Heshy Moskowitz and Max Septimus.
47. Interviews with Gershon Kranzler and Leon Keller.
48. Sherer interview.
49. Interview with Rabbi Ephraim Wolf.

Whenever he was asked a question, he would jump up and say, "It's an explicit verse" or "It's an explicit *Chazal*." He made me see that Torah is alive, and we are part of it, not that we are one thing and Torah is something else.

Ikvesa D'Meshicha (The Footsteps of Messiah), Reb Elchonon's last great work, in which he drew on all his vast knowledge of the Torah's prophecies and *Chazal's* descriptions of the final stages of Jewish history to interpret current events, was in part an outgrowth of his talks on Rodney Street.[50]

Reb Elchonon's talks were only a small part of the impression he made. He was used to teaching teenagers, and did not hold himself aloof from the American youngsters. He spoke to them freely and frankly. And as they observed him, they witnessed a concrete example of the Torah's power to transform those who totally submit themselves to its discipline into a completely different order of being. They saw how he walked rather than take a cab for fear of depriving his yeshiva in Baranovich of any of the money he collected and that he would not cross against a red light because of the halachic rule *dina d'malchusa dina* (the law of the land is binding).[51]

Reb Feivel used to send over different boys from Torah Vodaath to assist Reb Elchonon. One day, Yitzchak Karpf decided to join his *chavrusa* Shalom Grodensky, Rabbi Shlomo Heiman's nephew, when the latter went to be Reb Elchonon's *shamash*. When Reb Elchonon answered the door and saw two young men there, he said, "*Bitul Torah* of two? I don't have such broad shoulders. One of you must return."[52]

Reb Elchonon was always eager to make known proper Torah *hashkafah* in any viable forum. Thus when a reporter for *The Jewish Morning Journal* submitted a series of questions concerning the Zionist movement, Reb Elchonon provided him with careful and detailed answers. That interview and its aftermath were to prove one of the most painful experiences of Reb Elchonon's American stay.

When the interview was published, Reb Elchonon found to his dismay that his opinions were interspersed with a running commentary and critique by the interviewer himself. To set the record straight, Reb

---

50. Gershon Kranzler typed the manuscript and often discussed the contents with Reb Elchonon. *Interview with Gershon Kranzler.*.

51. Interviews with Rabbi Joshua Silbermintz and Leon Keller.

52. Interview with Rabbi Yitzchak Karpf.

Elchonon drafted a lengthy reply to the newspaper. But publication was withheld for so long that the average reader could no longer discern what Reb Elchonon's responses referred to. And when the response was printed, it was again surrounded by the comments of the original interviewer, who, needless to say, retained the last word for himself. The effect of the second article was to make it appear as if Reb Elchonon was engaged in a debate concerning Torah *hashkafah* with a journalist.

Once he realized that he would never be able to present his views in any coherent fashion in *The Jewish Morning Journal*, Reb Elchonon asked Mike to gather a *minyan* of ten men at the Rodney Street headquarters of Zeirei. Reb Elchonon explained to those who had gathered that he was required to publicly protest the remarks of his opponent, who had, *inter alia*, concluded his second article by accusing Reb Elchonon of lacking *ahavas Yisrael* (love of his fellow Jews). He proceeded to go through the two articles point by point, responding along the way to all the journalist's accusations and arguments. In the course of his refutation, he outlined an entire worldview of the destiny of the Jewish people and the nature of Jewish nationhood.[53]

Rabbi Anshel Fink later described the effect of Reb Elchonon's presentation on those who were there:

> We sat spellbound. This was the first time in our lives that we experienced so solemn an occasion, when matters affecting the fate of our people were concerned. I felt as if I were present . . . at a session of the Sanhedrin itself.[54]

Reb Elchonon's choice of Zeirei's Rodney Street headquarters as the forum for his protest against the articles in *The Jewish Morning Journal* indicates how close he had grown to the young men of Zeirei, and Mike in particular, in the course of his stay. He recognized in Mike the dynamism needed to breathe life into American Orthodox life. And it was he who convinced Mike to abandon a promising business career to devote himself full time to *klal* work, at a time when full time organizational work was unknown in American Orthodoxy.

Reb Elchonon also gave Mike some advice designed to keep him going in the hard times that inevitably attend any new undertaking. The

---

53. *Reb Elchonon*, pp. 342-345.

54. Anshel Fink was the son of Rabbi Yoel Fink, long-time eighth-grade *rebbi* at Torah Vodaath and a respected *talmid chacham* and *posek* in Williamsburg. Anshel Fink was one of the most brilliant and learned members of the Zeirei — it was he that Rabbi Gedaliah Schorr referred to "as my friend of the head." Fink was very close to Mike and an important influence on his development.

first was never to be disappointed by others' lack of appreciation. The second was that anything done with *mesiras nefesh* (self-sacrifice) will eventually bear fruit.[55] In return for dedicating himself to the *klal*, Reb Elchonon assured Mike, he would be rewarded with worthy, G-d-fearing children and length of days.[56]

The last people to speak to Reb Elchonon before he went on board ship for his return to Europe, and ultimately to martyrdom in the Kovno ghetto, were Mike, Gershon Kranzler, and Moshe Rivlin. At their parting, Reb Elchonon told Mike that nothing less than the fate of Torah Jewry rested in his hands.[57] Reb Elchonon recognized that whatever hope remained for the salvation of European Jewry lay with Mike and his band of dedicated activists.

Mike tried to press on Reb Elchonon *shaliach mitzvah gelt* (money to be given to charity), but Reb Elchonon resisted out of a fear that he might inadvertently intermingle the charitable monies with other monies. Finally, the money was placed in a separate envelope, on which was written, "One involved in a *mitzvah* will not come to harm," and given to Reb Elchonon.[58] But as Reb Elchonon had foreseen, he was returning to a maelstrom in which personal merit would by itself offer no protection.[59]

---

55. Reb Elchonon made this point frequently. In a letter to the organizers of the first convention of Agudath Israel of America in 1939, he wrote, "I would also remind you of the Vilna Gaon's reply to Reb Yoel Chassid of Amchislav, `If one is stubborn, he will succeed — in Heavenly matters.'" *Reb Elchonon*, p. 348.

He told some of the parents involved in founding the first Bais Yaakov that anything begun with *mesiras nefesh* (self-sacrifice) will come to fruition. *Interview with Reuven Soloff.*

56. Interview with Mrs. Hinde Tress.

57. Gershon Kranzler, "Setting the Record Straight," *The Jewish Observer*, November 1971, p. 11.

58. Interview with Rabbi Moshe Rivlin.

59. The general rule that one involved in the performance of a *mitzvah* will not come to harm does not apply in a time of widespread destruction (*Pesachim* 8b).

Part Two

A MOVEMENT
IS BORN

Chapter Eight

616 BEDFORD AVENUE

THE MOVE OF THE WILLIAMSBURG ZEIREI IN January 1939 from the three-room railroad apart-

Expanding Horizons

ment in the basement of 157 Rodney Street to a three-story mansion, built when Williamsburg was still known as the Borough of the Churches,[1] at 616 Bedford Avenue was a milestone for both the Williamsburg Zeirei and the Agudah movement in America. While the branch had long since outgrown its Rodney Street headquarters, the move was occasioned more by the suddenly expanded scope of Zeirei's activities and Mike's vision of the future than by present exigencies.

---

1. The mansion had been built as the parish house for the large church next door, which subsequently became the Hewes Street *shul*.

616 Bedford Avenue

After *Kristallnacht,* November 9, 1938, Mike and a handful of close colleagues had already begun to respond to the increasingly desperate situation in Europe, and they soon realized that their efforts would require staff and office space for which there was no room at 157 Rodney Street. In addition, Mike had a vision of transforming the moribund Interbranch Council into a truly national organization. While the Rodney Street address might have sufficed for a local meeting place, it was totally unsuitable as a national headquarters.

The immediate impetus for the purchase of 616 Bedford Avenue was the flood of refugees from Germany and Austria.[2] The gates of the United States had been slammed shut to large-scale immigration, particularly from Eastern Europe, by the Immigration Act of 1924, which imposed rigorous quotas by country of origin.[3] Nevertheless, nearly a quarter of a million refugees did enter the United States between 1933 and Pearl Harbor, 150,000 of those from 1938 through mid-1941.[4] They arrived often with little command of English, resources, and frequently without any place to stay. A number of Williamsburg families offered temporary refuge to the newcomers.[5]

The Zeirei headquarters at 157 Rodney Street became a makeshift dormitory for young unmarried immigrants, who slept on hastily collected bedding in every corner of the apartment while they acclimated themselves to their new country and began to look for work. Though many of the immigrants had relatives in America, the religious standards of the relatives were often such that it was impossible for the religious newcomers to stay with them.

A committee headed by Zeirei veterans Max Gross and Heshy Septimus was charged with raising the money to purchase a building that could serve as a refugee home and as the headquarters for Zeirei's rapidly expanding activities. The $1500 down payment alone — 10 percent of the purchase price — was far more than the organization had

---

2. Hitler's initial goal was to render Germany and Austria *Judenrein* (literally, free of Jews). The 1935 Nuremberg Laws, which deprived German Jews of citizenship and all civil rights, were designed to force the Jews out of Germany. And they were to a large extent successful. Nearly 200,000 German Jews emigrated from 1933, when Hitler ascended to power, through *Kristallnacht*, the night of November 9, 1938, during which synagogues throughout Germany and Austria were systematically vandalized and destroyed by SS troops, scores of Jews killed, and 20,000 more transported to Dachau and Matthausen concentration camps. Another 100,000 Jews fled Austria in the aftermath of the Nazi *Anschluss* (annexation) March 13, 1938.

3. Known as the Johnson Act, the Act limited total immigration to 150,000 people per year. In addition to drastically cutting total immigration, the Act was specifically designed to virtually curtail Jewish immigration. Annual quotas were set by country of origin at 2 percent of those present in the United States from that particular country as of the 1890 census. By using the 1890 census, taken prior to any large-scale Jewish immigration from Eastern Europe, rather than the 1910 census, as had the Immigration Act of 1921, Jewish immigration from Eastern Europe was almost completely foreclosed.

4. David Wyman, *Paper Walls: America and the Refugee Crisis*, p. 209.

5. Max Septimus, for instance, recalls returning from his night college courses one evening to find almost every mattress and piece of bedding in the house on the living room floor with a homeless refugee sleeping on it. Another family which provided temporary housing for many new immigrants was that of Rabbi Yoel Fink. Among those who stayed with him was David Turkel, who had been sent from Vienna to warn the Jews of the West just how far Hitler might go. *Interview with David Turkel.*

ever attempted to raise at one time. Few Zeirei members earned more than $20 a week at that time, and it took several months of active solicitations to raise the money. The largest single contribution came from Nathan Hausman, one of the first of the Zeirei members to have started a successful business.[6]

OVER THE NEXT SIX YEARS, THE FOCUS OF THE ENERGIES OF THE Agudath Israel Youth Council of America (as Zeirei called itself in its dealings with the wider public) was the effort to rescue Europe's Jews. The organization's Refugee and Immigration Division mastered the myriad technical details of securing immigration visas, and Mike personally built up a network of connections in Washington, D.C., which he used to speed up the visa process for Jews trapped in Europe. He became the principal liason for the Orthodox community on all matters connected to obtaining visas.

Idealism and Inspiration

Yet even while the bulk of his time was taken up with the work of the Refugee and Immigration Division, Mike's vision of a truly national organization was being realized. During the war years, the Youth

---

6. Interview with Max Gross.

Council began publishing two monthly newspapers — *Darkeinu* for youth and *Orthodox Youth* (subsequently *Orthodox Tribune)*; the Jewish Servicemen's Welfare Bureau was formed to protect the interests of Orthodox soldiers and to supply them with kosher food; Camp Agudah and Camp Bnos opened their doors for the first time; and National Councils of Pirchei and Bnos came into existence.

Even in retrospect, it is difficult to explain how so much could have been accomplished virtually from scratch by a previously unheralded organization. In the World to Come, the *yetzer hara* will appear to the *tzaddikim* as a tall mountain, and they will be astonished that they could have succeeded in conquering it. So too do those involved in the creation of the Agudath Israel Youth Council of America find it impossible to explain how they accomplished all they did.

What makes the achievements of this period even more remarkable is that the Youth Council relied almost exclusively on volunteer manpower. Those who combed New York City in search of Jews willing and able to sign the affidavits guaranteeing the financial support necessary to obtain an immigration visa; those who filled in the blank affidavits; those who packed the kosher food packages for American G.I.s; those who served as counselors at Camp Agudah and Camp Bnos; and those who wrote, typed, and distributed *Darkeinu* and *Orthodox Youth* all did so without any thought of remuneration.

The sheer volume of paperwork generated by the visa process would itself have kept a large office going full time. Yet the Youth Council opened its first offices at 616 Bedford Avenue with a few used desks and a typewriter supplied by Mike. The organization consisted of only two poorly paid employees, both of them recent immigrants: Moshe Berger, who was in charge of the Refugee and Immigration Division, and Gershon Kranzler, who had a vague mandate to create a national organization. Mike himself continued to work for a few months after the offices opened until it became clear that his business career could not be reconciled with his increasingly frequent trips to Washington, D.C. and his other activities. Even after Mike took charge on a full-time basis, he did not draw a salary.

The wartime work was a true young people's crusade. Mike himself was not yet 30 at the outbreak of the war, and, with the exception of a handful of his contemporaries, the volunteers were in their late teens and early twenties.

Those who were active in the Youth Council during the war years remember the period in much the way that old soldiers recall combat: It remains for them the highlight of their lives, the period in which they felt most alive. Veterans of the period acknowledge the vast transformation of American Orthodoxy in the last 50 years — the flourishing of yeshivos and Bais Yaakovs, the higher halachic standards, the reliability of *kashrus* supervision, etc. — and yet they cannot help feel a certain nostalgia for the excitement of their youth and a feeling that something very valuable has been lost. Asked whether things were better then or now, they are apt to respond, "Then we really lived; today we only compete."[7]

In many respects, the young men and women who volunteered their time so unstintingly were very different from a comparable group of young people today. The Williamsburg Pirchei newspaper "616" still ran columns predicting the results of the upcoming NFL championship game in the late '40s and carried a column by a boy in Mesivta Torah Vodaath extolling the virtues of wrestling as exercise and explaining how one should go about training.

In a 1942 memo to a Bnos leader encouraging her to push ticket sales and journal ads for an upcoming Zeirei banquet, Mike emphasized that there would be "a minimum of speakers and *a maximum of good entertainment.*" Nor did the entertainment run to the high-brow. At a typical

Ad for
fundraising rally

---

7. Interview with Mrs. Shlomo Ort.

Pirchei *Melaveh Malkah* or fundraiser, the standard fare might feature The Mighty Wolf (Arnold Wolf) and his Torah Vodaath buddy Roy Chavkin tearing up phone books, breaking chains, lifting Pirchei boys with their teeth and performing other feats of strength;[8] impersonations by Emil Adler; a performance by the Torah Vodaath acrobatic team; and A. Gassner using a set of partially filled glasses in place of a xylophone to tap out familiar tunes. The annual Night of Music (later Night of the Stars) featured well-known *chazzanim* (cantors) and Seymour Silbermintz's boys choir.

But if their standards were not yet those of today's yeshivos, this group of young people was incredibly idealistic. As a small, embattled minority, they felt an intense common bond with one another and a commitment to the *klal*. There were still too few Orthodox Jews to permit the luxury of identifying oneself with particular subgroups within the religious community — Chassidic or Litvish, this yeshiva or that yeshiva. Mike worked hard at fostering this sense of group identity, as well as the identification with the Jews in Europe. He set his followers aflame with the desire to do everything in their power to save what could be saved from Europe.

None of those close to Mike was more idealistic than Melech Terebelo. He had come to Torah Vodaath from Detroit in his late teens, with virtually no background in *Gemara* and was fully prepared to sit in *shiur* with nine-year-olds. A few years later, Mike was his *shadchan*. He told Terebelo about three girls who might be possible matches for him. Two came from families with prestigious *yichus* (lineage). The third was a poor girl. The only thing Mike knew about her was that when he gave a speech stressing that for $300 it was still possible to ransom a Jewish life from Europe, she had approached him and given him all the money she had been saving for a new winter coat. As soon as he heard that story, Melech Terebelo knew she was the wife for him. Both Melech Terebelo's reaction and his wife's sacrifice are typical of the idealism that animated these young people.

All this activity — the intense rescue work, the newspapers, the camps, the Servicemen's Bureau — was possible only because Mike was willing to give up his business career entirely and throw himself into

8. Both Arnold Wolf and Roy Chavkin went on to earn *semichah* and become *rebbeim* in Yeshiva Toras Emes.

the tasks at hand. In the estimation of Rabbi Joshua Silbermintz, "There would have been no *hatzalah* (rescue) work, no Youth Council, if Mike had not gone into it full time. A movement needs a leader who is completely devoted to it. It was not something that could have been done fitting in hours here and there." The war years produced other great Orthodox lay leaders — men such as Irving Bunim and Louis Septimus — but only Mike gave up all his personal interests for full-time *klal* work. He was the inspiration breathing life into his followers, the one galvanizing everyone into action.

Mike, of course, was more than just a source of inspiration. His innate sense of motivational psychology was just one of the abilities that made him an effective leader. In addition, he was creative, always thinking of new projects and figuring out how they could be executed with the manpower at hand.[9] His quick grasp of situations enabled him to anticipate problems that might arise.[10] Above all he had the natural leader's ability to make decisions and sell them to others.[11] It was this combination of abilities that gave Mike's opinions such weight with the *gedolim* in later years when the Moetzes Gedolei HaTorah became an integral part of the American Agudath Israel, as it had been in Europe.[12]

The Chanukas Habayis

DESPITE TAKING POSSESSION OF THEIR NEW BUILDING IN EARLY January, it took the Williamsburg Zeirei another three months of hard work on the building itself before 616 was ready to open as a refugee home. Bedding and furnishings also had to be collected. In the interim, the building was used for office space and a variety of other functions, including a large farewell party for Reb Elchonon.[13]

While work proceeded on the building, Mike and his friends were busy preparing for a festive *chanukas habayis* just after Pesach of 1939. The members of the Hewes Street *shul* next door, one of Williamsburg's largest and most impressive synagogues, generously offered their premises for the celebration. Only two conditions were placed on the use of the *shul*: The Zionist flag must be left in place throughout the festivities and *Hatikvah*

---

9. Interviews with Rabbi Boruch Borchardt and Mr. Leon Keller.

10. Interviews with Mrs. Ruth Krane and Mr. Leon Keller.

11. Interview with Rabbi Heshy Moskowitz.

12. Ibid.

13. Interview with Eugene Lamm.

The Clymer Street Shul

must be sung.[14] Mike was uneasy with the conditions and asked Reb Elchonon what he should do. Reb Elchonon told him that under no circumstances could an Agudah group accept such compromises.[15]

Though a great deal of planning had already gone into the affair — planning which would now have to start afresh — Reb Elchonon's edict was accepted without question. Mike's willingness to immediately

---

14. In those days, almost no religious affair began without the playing of *The Star Spangled Banner* and *Hatikvah*. Those who objected to *Hatikvah*, on the grounds that the words were written by a completely irreligious Jew and set to a gentile melody, were few and far between. Mike created quite a stir in the early '40s when he walked off the stage of the Torah Vodaath elementary school graduation during the singing of *Hatikvah*. *Interview with Abe Dicker.*

15. Interview with Rabbi Moshe Sherer.

Chanukas Habayis Parade — Carrying the Sifrei Torah

cancel all the previous arrangements because of Reb Elchonon's *psak* made a big impression on the Pirchei boys.[16] Fortunately, Rabbi Levi Yitzchak Kahane, one of the few prominent rabbis in those years willing to identify unabashedly with Agudath Israel, offered his equally large Clymer Street *shul* seven blocks away for the celebration.

The Sunday immediately following Pesach was chosen for the *chanukas habayis*, and it turned out to be a glorious, sunny day. All the

Chanukas Habayis Parade

16. Interview with Rabbi Joshua Silbermintz.

Zeirei chapters in the New York area were well represented. The celebration began at Zeirei's former headquarters at 157 Rodney Street. Pirchei boys, singing unrestrainedly, surrounded the procession, which was led by prominent rabbis holding a *sefer Torah*. Bnos groups followed behind. Rabbi Chaim Uri Lipshitz, who led a Zeirei contingent from Philadelphia for the celebration, vividly recalled the scene nearly 50 years later:

> The dancing and singing were overwhelming. Everyone was hugging as if we were one. There was no stopping and no one leading. The crowd just moved by itself. One person would start a *niggun* and everyone followed. And so it went along.

As the celebrants approached Clymer Street, the singing grew louder and louder. Once inside the capacious Clymer Street *shul*, the audience was treated to a number of choral arrangements specially prepared for the occasion by Seymour Silbermintz's boys choir.

The highlight of the day was Mike's speech. He began by describing the ever-worsening situation in Europe. A tremendous responsibility, he emphasized, had been imposed from Heaven on American Jews, who were fortunate to find themselves in a land of freedom and tolerance, to come to the aid of their European brethren. But all was not bleak. Mike painted an optimistic picture of an Orthodoxy that would be created in America. Even as the great centers of learning in Europe were threatened as never before, new places of Torah study would yet flourish in America. The task ahead, both at home and on behalf of those trapped abroad, was immense, but with G-d's help they would succeed.

The speeches over, the march, even larger than before, continued another seven blocks down Bedford Avenue to Zeirei's new home, which the celebrants found gaily festooned in ribbons.

ONE OF THE MIRACLES OF THE BAIS HAMIKDASH WAS THAT THE crowds stood closely packed, and yet everyone found room to prostrate

New Uses for a New Home

himself. Over the next few years, 616 Bedford Avenue showed a similarly miraculous ability to accommodate itself to a seemingly infinite array of uses. It served as a *shul* for the ever-expanding Zeirei *minyan*.[17] For the

---

17. The *minyan* was soon so crowded that those who came ten minutes late for the nine o'clock Shabbos morning *davening* found themselves standing in the hall. On Simchas Torah there was no room inside for *hakafos*.

Whenever he visited New York, the Telshe Rosh Yeshiva Rabbi Eliyahu Meir Bloch *davened*

first time, there was room for the Pirchei to have their own *minyan* and *shalosh seudos*. During the week, the young Pirchim could find much to occupy themselves in the basement game room filled with ping-pong tables and old mattresses on which any sort of activity might be improvised. At various times, the Vienner *minyan*, headed by the great Hungarian scholar Rabbi Yonason Steif, and the *minyan* of the Tzelemer Rav made their homes at 616 Bedford Avenue.[18]

The various *minyanim* were only an expansion of Zeirei's previous activities at Rodney Street. What was new was the refugee home, which occupied most of the second and third floors and a small attic on the fourth floor, and the Youth Council office, which opened with three desks and a typewriter.

A night yeshiva, headed at first by Rabbi Gedaliah Schorr and subsequently by Rabbi Shlomo Rotenberg, was opened in 1940 to meet the needs of young immigrants who did not have the opportunity to learn during the day. The night yeshiva soon became popular with the local *baalebatim* as well. Among those who taught in the night yeshiva were Rabbis Shachne Zohn, Aron Yeshaya Shapiro, Mordechai Yaffe, and Boruch Kaplan of Torah Vodaath; Rabbi Yaakov Moshe Shurkin from Yeshivas Chaim Berlin; Rabbi Simcha Wasserman ; such learned businessmen as Berel Belsky and Moshe Lieber of Lieber Chocolates; and Torah Vodaath students like Yaakov Goldstein. For six months after his arrival in the United States in 1939, Rabbi Dr. Joseph Breuer gave a *Gemara shiur* every morning to young refugees, who were almost exclusively from German-speaking backgrounds, and Reb Shraga Feivel Mendelowitz taught *Tehillim* on Tuesday night for a number of years.[19]

When he arrived from Antwerp via Cuba in 1942, Rabbi Rotenberg began a Monday night *shiur* in *Ramban* on *Chumash*, which took 13 years to complete. What struck him about the period was the thirst for spiritual growth among the Zeirei veterans and the strong bonds of friendship between then. As an example of the former, he recalls Louis

---

in the Zeirei *minyan*. Rabbi Yaakov Kamenetsky frequently *davened* there as well. Rabbi Shlomo Rotenberg even remembers the Satmar Rav *davening* at 616 Bedford Avenue until he gathered his own *minyan*.

18. The Tzelemer Rav came from Czechoslovakia in 1938. He was the first to promote the commercial production of *chalav Yisrael* (literally, Jewish milk) and did much to popularize the demand for *glatt* kosher meat. *Interviews with Moshe Berger and Charles Richter.*

19. Night yeshivos also formed on the Lower East Side, under the leadership of Rabbis Lashinsky and Tannenbaum, and in the Bronx, under the leadership of Rabbi Gelman. The Mattersdorfer Rav, Rabbi Shmuel Ehrenfeld, gave a weekly *shiur* at the Lower East Side branch. *Orthodox Youth*, December 1941, p. 7.

Septimus, whose accounting practice was already burgeoning, coming to *shiur* on the eve of the April 15 tax deadline and then returning to the office to work through the night. Mike himself was rarely able to be there for the entire 9 p.m. to 11 p.m. learning schedule due to the demands of the rescue work, but most evenings he at least tried to come for part of the *shiur*. "A *dvar Torah* was always *kodesh kadoshim* (literally, holy of holies) to him," Rabbi Rotenberg remembers.

IF THE MOVE TO 616 BEDFORD AVENUE WAS A SYMBOL OF HOW FAR the Williamsburg Zeirei had developed in the eight years since Mike

Marriage first walked through its doors and of the organization's ambitions for the future, Mike's marriage to Edith (Hinde) Bagry on June 7 (20 *Sivan*), 1939 symbolized his own religious development over the same period. With his choice of Hinde Bagry, Mike was entering into a family that had few rivals at the time in religious observance.

The future Mrs. Tress had grown up in Philadelphia as part of the closely knit Drebin-Bagry-Ackerman clan. Like Mike, she lost her father at an early age, and the role of providing the male

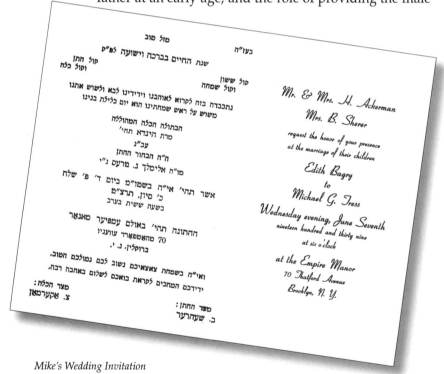

Mike's Wedding Invitation

Letter from the Chafetz Chaim to the Drebin-Bagry-Ackerman family

guidance to the family fell on the family patriarch, her mother's brother Reb Kalman Drebin.

The Drebin clan was characterized by its uncompromising stance towards any religious accommodation to the lowered standards of America.[20] Children in the Drebin family received their entire religious education at home since no Talmud Torah ever passed Uncle Kalman's rigorous standards. Every year or two, he would hear of a new Talmud Torah said to be run with the highest of religious standards, but after visiting it something was always found wanting. Once, for instance, he was appalled to find a *rebbi* teaching the blessing *borei pri ha'eitz* without making sure that the children ate a piece of fruit to eat to avoid a *berachah levatalah* (a purposeless blessing). When Uncle Kalman saw the *rebbi* erase the blessing, including the name of Hashem, from the blackboard, he stormed out of the classroom.[21] The Bagry girls were not allowed to attend high school because their mother opposed coeducation; they enrolled instead in commercial school courses, learning bookkeeping, typing, and shorthand.[22]

The family maintained close ties to the fiercely anti-Zionist old *yishuv* in Jerusalem — Mrs. Bagry's mother was remarried to Rabbi Yerucham

---

20. Mrs. Tress's first cousin Mrs. Hindy (Ackerman) Krohn has beautifully evoked her family's mindset in *The Way It Was* (Mesorah Publications, 1989), a memoir of her childhood in Philadelphia. See especially pp. 51-63 and 95-98.

21. Krohn, *The Way It Was*, p. 57.

22. Interview with Mrs. Tress.

Chapter Eight: 616 BEDFORD AVENUE □ 145

Diskin, son of Rabbi Yehoshua Leib Diskin, the leader of the old *yishuv*. Following the leaders of the old *yishuv* in Jerusalem, who fought Eliezer Ben Yehudah — the father of modern Hebrew — tooth and nail, the Drebins were strongly opposed to what they considered the desecration of *Lashon HaKodesh* (the Holy Tongue) by its transformation into a language of the street. Nor were the children allowed to forget Yiddish in favor of the language of their new country. Mrs. Bagry insisted that Yiddish be spoken in the home, a custom that was more or less adhered to in the Tress home as well.[23]

Mike and Hinde's *shidduch* was made by Deborah (Quinn) Deutsch, one of Hinde's close friends from Lamport's, and news of her match was received with great excitement by her former co-workers. The young couple was engaged for nearly two years prior to their marriage. Mike's mother Henya was already terminally ill at the time of the engagement, and he felt she still needed him at home to look after her.

The wedding at the Empire Mansion in Brownsville on June 7, 1939 was a large affair reflecting Mike's growing prominence in the American religious world. The block in front of the wedding hall had to be cordoned off for the crowd gathered for the outside *chuppah*. Virtually every prominent figure in American Orthodoxy was present, and Mike's Pirchei boys ran around trying to get the autographs of their various heroes. Meyer Birnbaum, one of the group of young men from the Young Israel of New Lots upon whom Mike had such a profound effect, remembers being bitterly disappointed not to have received a personal invitation,[24] but the Pirchei boys from Williamsburg felt no such compunction about attending, with or without an invitation. To them it was obvious that when one's leader gets married one goes to the wedding.[25]

Prior to the wedding, Mike received a letter of congratulations from Reb Elchonon, who was already back in Baranovich with his beloved *yeshiva bachurim*. The salutation began, "Peace and blessing to my

---

23. Interview with Mrs. Tress.

24. Birnbaum and Rosenblum, *Lieutenant Birnbaum*, pp. 42-45. Birnbaum could not understand how someone he considered his "best friend" could have omitted him from his invitation list. At least he had some consolation in finding others who considered Mike their "best friend" who had also been omitted.

None of these "best friends," however, saw any contradiction in the fact that so many others also thought of Mike in the same way. Just as a child does not think that his parents love him any less because he has siblings whom they also love, so they knew that Mike had enough love to be the best friend of all of them.

25. Interview with Rabbi Heshy Mashinsky.

esteemed *chasan*, the praiseworthy Reb Elemelech Tress, with love." Reb Elchonon expressed his hope that Hashem would grant that the "bond [of the *chasan* and *kallah*] be an everlasting one, for many good years —

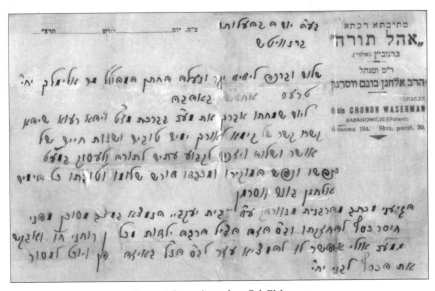

Congratulatory letter from Reb Elchonon

At the head table at Mike's weedding

a life of fortune and peace." To Mike he wished that he "be privileged to establish a schedule for [the study] of Torah, and be occupied with goods deeds." Signed: "One who is bound to his soul, one who honors and respects [him], who always seeks his peace and welfare. Elchonon Bunim Wasserman." Mike treasured that letter for the rest of his life and always kept it folded in his wallet.

The Tress wedding set new halachic standards for religious weddings in that era. All the food was *pareve* so that none of the guests should feel the least compunction about eating whatever was served. There was separate seating of men and women, which was almost unheard of in those days. For that reason, Mike's wedding was the first at which Reb Shraga Feivel Mendlowitz stayed for the meal.[26] Under the *chuppah*, Mike wore the *gartel* of the Boyaner Rebbe, which the latter had given him for the occasion as an expression of his deep affection and esteem.

The bride's decision to wear a *sheitel* after the marriage was no less of a shock. Even among young women whose mothers covered their

26. Ibid.

פיינע חסידישע חתונה
דורכגעפיהרט אין ברוקלין

אין ברוקלין איז די טעג פארגעקו־
מען א גרויסארטיגע חסידישע חתונה.
דער חתן איז געווען עלימלך גבריאל
טרעם, און די כלה הינדע באגרי. דער
חתן איז דער, פרעזידענט, פון דער
צעירי אגודת ישראל און א באקאנטער
כלל טהוער. ארום א טויזענד געסט זיי־
נען געווען אנוועזענד.
די חתונה איז דורכגעפיהרט געווא־
רען אין עכט חסידישען ניסט.

hair — as Mrs. Bagry did — the wearing of a *sheitel* was virtually unknown.

With his choice of Hinde Bagry, Mike had found the perfect helpmate for the tumultuous period ahead — someone capable of raising a family with good cheer, despite her husband's frequent travels and long hours; someone never flustered by unannounced guests for dinner or visitors who might stay for months at a time until they could find a place to live.

Chapter Nine

THE REFUGEE HOME

ETWEEN 1939 AND 1942, SEVERAL HUNDRED young men passed through the Refugee Home,[1] with approximately 12 to 15 staying there at any given time. Some of these were students at Torah Vodaath, including Don Ungarischer, today *Rosh HaYeshiva* of Bais Medrash Elyon, and Moshe Lonner, long-time principal of Torah Vodaath high school. Others were husbands who had preceded their families in the hopes that they would be better able to expedite the visa process with one family member already in America.[2] In most cases, the stay was of relatively brief duration, but some immigrants stayed for as long as five years.

---

1. Interview with Gavriel Beer.
2. Interview with Rabbi Moshe Lonner.

The four-to-a-room accommodations were far from luxurious, but the newcomers appreciated having a roof of any kind over their head and the warmth shown them by the Zeirei members — in particular Mike, Dave Maryles, and Emil Adler, who had himself recently arrived in the country.[3] Once when Don Ungarischer was sick, Mike cooked for him, and the mothers of other Zeirei members sent food and medicine.[4]

Just as he would after the war, on behalf of refugees far more broken than those who arrived in the late '30s and early '40s, Mike showed a remarkable ability to understand precisely what it meant to be completely uprooted from one's homeland and entire way of life. Though he had, of course, experienced nothing like the trauma of forced emigration, his natural empathy allowed him to put himself in their shoes. He had the patience to listen to the refugees and to see the world from their point of view.[5]

Housing was only one of the services with which the residents of 616 Bedford Avenue were furnished. The Zeirei arranged for them to eat

---

3. Interviews with Rabbi Moshe Lonner and Yosef Rosenberger.

The historian David Kranzler, who was a young Pirchei boy during the years of the Refugee Home, remembers occasional tensions between Pirchei boys, eager to assert claims to the entire building for their Shabbos "war games," and the residents of the Refugee Home, who were desirous of a well-earned Shabbos rest. None of the residents of the home with whom the author spoke, however, recalled any tensions with other groups using the building. It would seem that the younger Pirchei boys were at most an occasional annoyance.

4. Gershon Kranzler, "Setting the Record Straight," *The Jewish Observer*, November 1971, p. 12. Dr. Kranzler does not mention Rabbi Ungarisher by name, but the reference to a famous *rosh hayeshiva*, who stayed in the refugee home only until his brother and sister arrived in the United States, is almost certainly to him.

5. Interview with Mrs. Daniella (Nussbaum) Buxbaum.

their meals in the Torah Vodaath dining room, and later at Schick's restaurant. If the immigrant did not have the money for the highly discounted meals, Zeirei picked up the tab for that as well.

Mike used his wide circle of connections to try to find employment for those who were not learning full time. He understood that the most important aspect of restoring the immigrants' dignity was to help them become self-supporting. An employment bureau set up initially to find jobs for new immigrants placed over 400 Shabbos observers in positions between 1939 and 1941.[6] The Zeirei paid for several newcomers to be apprenticed as diamond-cutters or polishers, which proved to be highly lucrative professions as the center of the world diamond industry moved, due to the war, from Antwerp to New York. In another case, Mike purchased a small truck for an immigrant who had been in the scrap iron business in Europe. The truck allowed the man to successfully reestablish himself in America.[7]

The files of the Youth Council are filled with letters of introduction from Mike to dentists and doctors asking them to hold their fees to a minimum for the holder of the letter, invariably described as "a very fine gentleman."[8] The Refugee and Immigration Division sent immigrants to wealthy garment manufacturers, like Lester Udell, for the necessary suits and coats.[9] Shoe stores were requested to send the bills for pairs of shoes to the Refugee and Immigration Division, and sometimes Mike even sent his own check for hats or other items.[10]

---

6. Report of the Refugee and Immigration Division of Agudath Israel Youth, September 1941, pp. 3-5.

7. These cases are just a few of those uncovered by David Kranzler in his research in the archives of Agudath Israel of America.

Finding jobs for refugees was a natural outgrowth of Mike's services as an employment agency for Shabbos observers. He was already known as the address in the Orthodox world for those seeking *shomer Shabbos* work. When he received a request for help, he began to work on it immediately, whether or not he had any previous relationship with the person who had contacted him. The job seeker was not told to call back in a few weeks or "we'll look into it." If possible, Mike picked up the phone immediately to try to arrange a position.

The following case is typical. Mike received a letter dated February 20, 1942 from a young man looking for work as a machinist in a *shomer Shabbos* plant. Two days later, Mike had already written him with the name and phone number of a religious Jew associated with a machine shop, who would be expecting his call.

8. See e.g., the October 17, 1941 letter from Mike to Dr. Solomon Novagrodsky, a dentist on the Lower East Side, on behalf of a new immigrant in need of dental care.

9. On May 13, 1942, Udell wrote to Leon Keller, secretary of the Refugee and Immigration Division, apologizing for not having a topcoat in stock for an immigrant rabbi sent by the Youth Council, and added that "we are always glad to be of service to you and ask that you call upon us frequently."

10. In an April 11, 1949 letter to Selco Hat Company, Mike enclosed a check for two hats for himself and for the hats for the "two people I sent you."

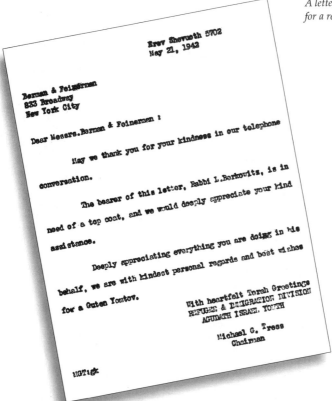

Erev Shevuoth 5702
May 21, 1942

Berman & Feinerman
833 Broadway
New York City

Dear Messrs. Berman & Feinerman :

May we thank you for your kindness in our telephone conversation.

The bearer of this letter, Rabbi L. Berkovits, is in need of a top coat, and we would deeply appreciate your kind assistance.

Deeply appreciating everything you are doing in his behalf, we are with kindest personal regards and best wishes for a Guten Yomtov.

With heartfelt Torah Greetings
REFUGEE & IMMIGRATION DIVISION
AGUDATH ISRAEL YOUTH

Michael G. Tress
Chairman

MGT:gk

The work on behalf of the residents of 616 was only a small portion of that done within Williamsburg. The vast majority of immigrants arrived with their families. They needed to be provided with apartments and furnishings. Girls in Bnos went door to door collecting the minimal necessities for recently arrived families. Homes were found and furnished for 150 immigrant families in the first two years of the Refugee and Immigration Division's existence.

Pirchei started running Refugee Suppers as fundraisers even before 616 opened. Initially these were designed to raise money for recent immigrants. Later, as immigration from abroad was cut off, the money went to purchasing supplies for starving Jews in Europe's ghettos or for relief work on behalf of new immigrants to England. The Refugee Suppers were held in the Clymer Street *shul* and catered by Mr. Hammerman free of charge.[11]

---

11. Interview with Rabbi Ephraim Wolf.

Sympathy Won't Help Them Money Will!

Mr. Y., the sole supporter of his family, was stricken with a serious illness. Cost of hospitalization had to be paid, his family had to be supported. Everyone sympathized with him — but that didn't help him recover. We paid his hospital bills and got him the best medical attention. Now, thank the Almighty, he walks around as a healthy man again.

Mrs. X. wanted to bring her relatives to America from war-torn Europe. She didn't have the necessary funds.
Sympathy didn't help — Money did!
Mrs. S., formerly a leading citizen of Leipzig, is now, like hundreds of other Jews, exposed to the hunger, torture and epidemics of Camp de Gurs (France). $350. are needed to save her.
Sympathy won't help — Money will.

The Passover holidays are approaching. Mr. W., like hundreds of other refugees in this country, is in need of matzos.
Sympathy won't help — Money will.

Help Them While There Is Still Time!
You Can Do Your Bit by Attending

THE THIRD ANNUAL

..REFUGEE SUPPER..

MARCH 22nd, 1942, at 7 P. M.

Tifereth Israel Reception Hall
Bedford Ave. & Clymer St., Brooklyn

Send Your Contribution To:

Refugee Supper Committee

616 Bedford Avenue   Brooklyn, N. Y.

To sell tickets, a group of the older Pirchei boys — Heshy Moskowitz, Sender Francis, Shlomo Ort, and Ephraim Wolf — would go down to Clinton Hall on the Lower East Side where every Saturday and Sunday night three or more *landsmanshaften* (groups of Jews sharing a common place of origin in Europe) held their meetings. The boys would go in pairs. When the sergeant-at-arms of the *landsmanshaft* opened the door, one member of the pair would stick his foot into the door to keep it from being slammed shut and the other would dart into the room yelling that they were raising money to help starving Jews in Europe. In this fashion, they usually managed to sell eight or so tickets to each organization. Most of those who purchased the tickets never attended,

A Zeirei outing. Second from left is Yosef Rosenberger, third from left is Gershon Kranzler, far right is Lothar Kahn

but occasionally someone was curious to see what these American kids were up to. The curious were treated to singing like they had never dreamed of on American soil. In addition, there was always some entertainment and a speaker.[12] Reb Elchonon himself spoke at one of the first Refugee Suppers.[13]

BY 1942, THE INFLUX OF IMMIGRANTS HAD SLOWED TO A TRICKLE, and no new residents were coming into the home. With the completion

The Shatnes Laboratory of the Torah Vodaath dormitory there was no longer any need for immigrant students to stay at 616 Bedford Avenue. All that remained in the home were a few long-term residents, the last of whom had departed by 1945.

No aspect of the Refugee Home was to have a greater impact on American Orthodox life than the Shatnes Laboratory, which had its humble beginnings at 616 Bedford Avenue. Only the single-minded — and, in the eyes of most, foolhardy — determination of Joseph Rosenberger, a denizen of the Refugee Home from 1940 through 1945, to educate the Orthodox community in America about the prohibition

---

12. Ibid.
13. Interview with Heshy Moskowitz.

against *shatnes* (garments containing mixtures of wool and linen) rescued this *mitzvah* from near total disregard. Between 80 and 90 percent of Orthodox Jews were then unwittingly wearing garments containing *shatnes*.

Mr. Yosef Rosenberger

Rosenberger arrived in America in 1940 after having spent five months in the Dachau concentration camp to which he had been sent along with thousands of other Viennese Jews. In his case, the months in the concentration camp may have actually saved his life. Despite having been able to present only a "weak" affidavit of financial support, he was granted an American visa by a sympathetic consular official, who was appalled by the suffering he had endured in Dachau.

Shortly after his arrival in the United States, Reb Yosef was approached by someone who knew that his parents had owned a clothing store in a suburb of Vienna. That person asked how one could ascertain whether a particular garment contained *shatnes*. Rosenberger did not know and began investigating. Speaking to tailors on the Lower East Side and Williamsburg, he found that there was no repository of knowledge on the subject in America, and, what is worse, little interest. From then on Reb Yosef Rosenberger was a man with a mission. His goal: to develop an accurate, quick, and inexpensive test for *shatnes*.

He began by enrolling in Manhattan's Textile High School in order to learn everything known about linen. Then he took menial jobs in the garment industry in order to understand what uses linen had in clothing design and where it was used in different types of garments. His remaining time was spent combing through learned treatises on linen in the New York Public Library. Though there were already a number of existing tests for the presence of linen, he found they all suffered from one of two crucial defects: They were either too slow or too expensive. Unless he could develop a test that was both fast and inexpensive, Reb Yosef knew, he would never be able to sell *shatnes* testing to a largely apathetic public.[14]

---

14. The use of a microscope was also precluded by the fact that it would be too cumbersome to take from place to place to do testing. Above is a publicity photograph of Mr. Rosenberger (reproduced from *Elul* 5701 edition of *Orthodox Youth*) bent over a microscope. The

Ad for Shatnes Laboratory

It took less than a year for Rosenberger to develop a test for the presence of linen that was both quick and cheap. But that was only half the battle — perhaps the easier half. There still remained the necessity of selling the Orthodox public on the necessity of *shatnes* checking. Over the years, the idea had taken hold, even among those who knew of the prohibition against wearing clothing containing *shatnes*, that linen was never used in clothing anymore. There were those who charged that the whole concept of *shatnes* checking was a racket designed only to enrich the checker himself.[15] (Even a cursory glance at the perpetually emaciated Rosenberger, who subsisted for much of this period on only bread and water, would have quickly dispelled any such notions.)

When Reb Yosef tried to speak one Shabbos in the *Nine-und-Ninesiger minyan* on the Lower East Side, he was hooted at derisively. Only after he gave a resounding bang on the *bimah* and announced that if every third person in the *minyan* was not wearing *shatnes* he would donate $1,000, was he allowed to speak.[16]

---

microscope, however, was borrowed for the occasion to publicize the work of the Shatnes Lab as a division of the Agudath Israel Youth Council. Its presence in the photo bore no relationship to the actual procedure of the Shatnes Lab.

15. Similar charges were leveled almost half a century earlier when Rabbi Yaakov Yosef tried to establish rigorous oversight on New York's *shochtim*. The local *shochtim* claimed that the half-cent surcharge for the *plumbe* to be put on all properly slaughtered chickens was nothing more than a plan to enrich the *mashgichim*.

16. Interview with Yosef Rosenberger.

Reb Yosef's idealism elicited Mike's ready support, and Mike set out to do what he could to help him. *Orthodox Youth* provided free publicity for the project, and Mike gave Reb Yosef free use of the office phone, mimeograph machine, and typewriter. Late at night, Reb Yosef would sit up in the tiny fourth-floor attic at 616 Bedford, the door closed so as not to disturb his fellow tenants, patiently teaching himself to type.[17] That skill would in the not-too-distant future allow him to put forth a seemingly endless stream of written material designed to inform an ignorant public.

But by far the most important service that Mike rendered Reb Yosef was introducing him to Rabbi Herbert S. Goldstein, the rabbi of the West Side Institutional Synagogue. Rabbi Goldstein numbered many wealthy Jews among his congregants, including a Mr. Levy, who owned Crawford Clothes, then a large chain of clothing stores.

THE COLLABORATION BETWEEN MIKE AND RABBI GOLDSTEIN ON the *shatnes* project was the first in a long series of fruitful collaborations,

Rabbi Herbert S. Goldstein

and it would perhaps be well to briefly describe the relationship between the two men. Together with Rabbi Leo Jung of the Manhattan Jewish Center, Rabbi Goldstein was the Orthodox rabbi best known to the broader Jewish public. He was at one time or another the president of the Rabbinical Council of America and the Union of Orthodox Jewish Congregations of America. He was a man of immense presence — even gentiles whom he passed on the street would bow in respect.[18]

Mike's relationship with Rabbi Goldstein typified one of his greatest talents: the ability to enlist the enthusiastic support of those outside the narrow Agudath Israel orbit. Even those who differed sharply with Mike on ideological grounds could not help being moved by his sincerity and enthusiasm. Without compromising his principles or asking others to compromise theirs, he had an ability to find the common ground on which all Orthodox Jews of good heart could unite.

In the case of Rabbi Goldstein, however, the relationship went much farther than that. The two men became very close friends, and there was no form of assistance for which Mike hesitated to ask Rabbi Goldstein. Rabbi Goldstein was devoted to Mike, remembers Sidney Greenwald, who was for a period of time the Youth Director of the West Side Institutional Synagogue.

---

17. Gershon Kranzler, *Williamsburg Memories*, p. 52.
18. Interview with Sidney Greenwald.

Rabbi Herbert S. Goldstein (speaking)

Over the years, Rabbi Goldstein headed most of the Youth Council's projects in *Eretz Yisrael* — Keren HaYishuv, The Religious Palestine Fund, and Children's Homes in Israel. He played a crucial role in raising money for the Youth Council's Refugee and Immigration Division and such postwar relief projects as the Overseas Passover Fund and Save-A-Child Foundation. One of the members of the West Side Institutional Synagogue was U.S. Congressman Sol Bloom, who headed the House Foreign Affairs Committee during World War II and who was able, in that capacity, to do a number of favors for the Refugee and Immigration Division.

Mike and Rabbi Goldstein shared much in common, and it was natural that they were drawn to one another. Both were spiritual seekers whose public activities were fueled by their personal spiritual strivings. Rabbi Goldstein was a graduate of the Jewish Theological Seminary (Conservative). Yet in time he became a devotee of the great European *roshei yeshiva* — in part due to Mike's influence[19] — publicly humbling

---

19. Ibid.

Among those to whom Rabbi Goldstein became close was Rabbi Itche Meir Levin, the Gerrer Rebbe's son-in-law and an Agudah minister in the first Israeli government.

At an Agudah dinner honoring Rabbi Goldstein. L-R: Rabbi Michel Feinstein,
Reb Yaakov Rosenheim, Manhattan's District Attorney (speaking), Mike, Lester Udell,
Rabbi Goldstein, Rabbi Zalman Sorotzkin (Lutzker Rav), Rabbi Benjamin W. Hendeles

himself before them. When 11 prominent *roshei yeshiva* pronounced a
ban on Orthodox participation in the Synagogue Council of America in
1956, Rabbi Goldstein resigned from the organization though he had
been one of the co-founders. Similarly, he left the Mizrachi movement
when its Knesset faction in Israel refused to resign from the government
over the conscription of women.

Like Mike, Rabbi Goldstein never let the widespread adulation he
received distort his own view of himself. It is not difficult for a rabbi of
a not-very-learned congregation like that of the West Side Institutional
Synagogue to convince his congregants that he is the greatest living
Jewish scholar — especially if he is a powerful orator, as Rabbi
Goldstein was. Many such rabbis succeed in convincing themselves as
well. Not Rabbi Goldstein. He used to stand out of respect for the *shammas* (beadle) in his synagogue, and if anyone asked why, he would
answer that he was his *rebbe* as well.[20] After the war, Rabbi Goldstein
requested Rabbi Aharon Kotler to send a European *talmid chacham* to

20. Ibid.

21. Rabbi Goldstein's modesty was the key to his success as an administrator. He taught Sidney
Greenwald, when the latter came to work for him as director of youth activities, that the key to
running a successful organization is to hire people who know more about the job for which you
are hiring them than you do. He made no effort to husband honor for himself. On the contrary,
he insisted that Greenwald, with his newly minted *semichah*, always be addressed as rabbi.
Interview with Sidney Greenwald.

serve as the Torah reader in the synagogue and to teach *shiurim*. And he always showed the greatest respect for the *talmid chacham* Reb Aharon sent — Rabbi Alter Pekier.[21]

Rabbi Goldstein convinced the owner of Crawford Clothes to loan Reb Yosef $250 for a series of full-page advertisements in *The Jewish Morning Journal.*[22] The advertisements announced that *shatnes* checking would be available at Crawford Clothes, free of charge, to anyone requesting it. Reb Yosef was sure that his big break had finally come and that he would soon be able to pay off the loan from what Crawford Clothes would pay him for checking suits of those who requested it. When only five such requests were forthcoming in the first week, he was on the verge of tears.[23]

But unbeknownst to Reb Yosef, the advertisements had succeeded. Crawford's competitors could not know how small the response had been, and were forced to assume that if such a large chain as Crawford's thought it was worthwhile to pay for *shatnes* checking they had better follow suit. In addition, the competitors soon learned that they could no longer assure people with impunity that there was no *shatnes* in a garment. Jews who read the advertisement began to bring garments in for checking, and if they proved to have *shatnes,* as at least one-third did, the purchaser would angrily take back his purchase to the store that had assured him the garment was free of *shatnes.*

It was still a number of years before Reb Yosef was able to earn even a meager enough living from the Shatnes Lab to avoid being laughed at whenever he sought a *shidduch.* By agreement with the cooperating clothiers, ninety cents out of every dollar paid the Shatnes Lab for checking garments was plowed straight back into additional advertising. But *shatnes* checking was launched in America.

---

22. Rabbi Goldstein also used his unparalleled institutional connections within the religious world to line up the support of almost every major Orthodox organization for the Shatnes Lab. Among the sponsoring organizations were: Agudath HaRabonim, Agudath Anshei Chasidei Chabad, Agudath HaAdmorim, Agudath Israel, Board of Rabbis of New York, Federation of Orthodox Rabbis of America, Rabbinical Council of America, Union of Orthodox Jewish Congregations, Kahal Arugath HaBothem, Agudath Israel Youth, Hapoel HaMizrachi, Mizrachi Organization of America, and National Council of Young Israel.

In a March 27, 1941 letter under the OU letterhead sent to hundreds of congregational rabbis, Rabbi Goldstein stressed the necessity that rabbis press their congregants to demand *shatnes* checking so that more and more clothiers would be pressured into providing such checking. In that letter, he estimated the percentage of garments worn by Orthodox Jews containing *shatnes* as approximately one in three.

In time, the Shatnes Lab would grow beyond anything that Reb Yosef could ever have dreamt of. Today those trained directly or indirectly by Mr. Rosenberger provide *shatnes* checking in virtually every Jewish community in America, and in many countries around the world; a number of the largest suit manufacturers routinely send the Shatnes Lab samples from all forthcoming garments for *shatnes* checking; and it is possible to have garments *shatnes*-checked in many of the finest clothing stores in major cities.[24]

---

23. Interview with Yosef Rosenberger.

24. Success only whetted Mr. Rosenberger's appetite for similar successes in encouraging *mitzvah* observance. He was also one of the founders of Hatzola, the emergency rescue service. And with the receipts from the Shatnes Lab, he founded an organization called Torah Umitzvoth, which Rabbi Goldstein served as the first president and Mike as vice-president. Torah Umitzvoth has funneled large sums to a number of different yeshivos and sponsors a *hachnassas orchim* project to provide accommodations for poor Jews, mostly from *Eretz Yisrael.*

Chapter Ten
GOING NATIONAL

THE SETTING WAS HARDLY AUSPICIOUS — THE tiny Williamsburg apartment of Mike's aunt Mrs. Basya Sherer.[1] Mike had been sick for days, and sat there bundled up, barely able to lift himself from bed. Gershon Kranzler had come to visit him with a few other new immigrants whom Mike had befriended.

Mike talked about the future. He did not have to spend much time describing the ominous threat to European Jewry. The immigrants had experienced the danger first-hand. Only a strong, committed Orthodox movement in America, Mike argued, could offer any succor for the millions of Jews trapped in Europe. The creation of such a movement was therefore the highest priority. "In

---

1. Mike lived with his aunt for approximately six months between his mother's death and his marriage.

retrospect," Gershon Kranzler would write decades later, "it seems almost uncanny how this young American Jew recognized the role that America was to play":

> He spoke of the gathering clouds of war, when so many of the heartlands of Jewish life might come under the heel of war and catastrophe, and when America would be the only place that could offer some chance of help and rescue. . . .
> We watched with growing admiration as this young man spoke of the need to set up an organization that would tie together the isolated Orthodox Jewish energies and provide some form of systematic help for the mass of Orthodox Jews trapped in Europe.[2]

For the Europeans in the group, Mike's speech was a revelation. They had long been accustomed to thinking of America as a land in which people were concerned only with their own private interests. To hear a young American speak with such passion of the collective responsibility of Jews for one another was a shock.

BUT MIKE WAS AS INTERESTED IN WHAT THE IMMIGRANTS HAD TO say as in outlining his own vision. Ever since the first young Agudah

Getting that Old-time Ideology

activists had begun to arrive from Europe, he had listened in rapt attention as they described the youth work at the 1937 Knessiah Gedolah in Marienbad and how Jewish youth from countries throughout Europe had found common ground on the basis of Agudah ideology.

In Gershon Kranzler and some of the other newcomers, he recognized a storehouse of organizational talent that had already been employed in the European Agudah youth movements on a scale far larger than anything yet attempted in America. He was eager to tap this talent and to use the thorough grounding in Agudah ideology that the Europeans brought to transform a group of clubs into a national movement.

In order to fully appreciate what so excited Mike in his conversations with the European newcomers, it is necessary to first understand some of the ways in which the development of the American Zeirei movement differed from that of Agudath Israel in Europe. Virtually every Zeirei chapter began as a *minyan* for young men, and the *minyan*

---

2. Gershon Kranzler, "He Who Saves a Soul in Israel...," *The Jewish Observer*, September 1967.

remained for most the center of their identity with Agudath Israel. But the consequence of the development around *minyanim* was that the early American Zeirei was not primarily an ideological movement. There was nothing unusual about a husband, for instance, *davening* in a Zeirei *minyan* while his wife was active in Mizrachi Women.[3]

By contrast, Agudath Israel in Europe was exclusively an ideological movement totally unrelated to where one *davened* or learned. The typical European Agudist was left slightly aghast by what he found in America. Americans thought of Zeirei as a place to *daven*, learn, sing, and share a miracle story or two. For the Europeans, on the other hand, Agudah headquarters was a place to which one came for debates.[4]

The German Agudath Israel, for instance, consisted of several sharply delineated factions divided over the issue of the proper orientation to *Eretz Yisrael* and revolving around the towering personalities of Dr. Isaac Breuer and Reb Jacob Rosenheim. Many of the newcomers had honed their debating skills in regularly scheduled public forums and sharpened their quills in the Agudath Israel youth publications.

Mike certainly had no desire to import the intense, and occasionally bitter, European ideological wars to America. His goal was finding a means to achieve greater unity of purpose, not to increase divisiveness. He shared the American's instinctive distaste for sharp ideological warfare[5] and preferred to concentrate on the immediate practical issues at hand.[6]

At the same time, he recognized that the essential elements of Agudah ideology could form the basis for organizing American youth. The basic idea of Agudath Israel was nothing other than the ancient ideal of *Klal Yisrael* — the view that the Jewish people constitute a single body and the fate of every individual Jew is therefore inextricably

---

3. Interview with Jack Klausner.

4. Interview with Rabbi Joseph Elias.

5. Throughout the war years and beyond, the task of articulating the fundamentals of Agudah ideology continued to fall primarily on those trained in the European youth movement. Agudah ideology in the pages of *Orthodox Tribune* was almost exclusively the province of products of the German Agudah movement: Reb Jacob Rosenheim, Rabbi Shimon Schwab, Rabbi Dr. L. Breslauer, Rabbi Joseph Elias, and excerpts from the works of Dr. Isaac Breuer and Nathan Birnbaum. At the "Open Forums" which Zeirei sponsored in the mid-'40s on such ideological topics as "Agudath Israel vs. Mizrachi," Mike was virtually the only speaker who was American born. The others — Rabbi Shimon Schwab, Rabbi Shlomo Rotenberg, and Reb Jacob Rosenheim himself — had all been nurtured in Europe.

6. Some of the European ideological warfare was imported of its own accord. In 1947, a group comprised almost exclusively of young German immigrants living in Washington Heights formed a short-lived, breakaway group called *Hechalutz Agudati*. The group was identified with the Breuer faction in the prewar German Agudah, and was in favor of a more activist position with respect to building up Agudist institutions in *Eretz Yisrael*.

bound with that of every other Jew. Throughout the war years, the key to Mike's success in inspiring American kids to work for their brethren in Europe was his ability to make them see themselves as members of *Klal Yisrael*, not as Jewish youngsters living in a particular neighborhood of New York City.

THE DEVELOPMENT OF A NATIONAL ORGANIZATION DEPENDED, of course, on much more than a coherent ideology. The principles of

Building a Grass-roots Organization

Agudath Israel could help bind the various Zeirei and Pirchei branches together, but only in conjunction with a great deal of nitty-gritty organizational work.

Mike recognized how critical this organizational work was. The first person he hired for the Youth Council offices at 616 Bedford Avenue was Gershon Kranzler. Kranzler's mission: to mold a national organization out of the disparate branches. Kranzler brought to this work impeccable credentials: years of organizational activity as one of the leaders of the youth wing of the German Agudah and a thorough grounding in Agudah thought.

He wasted no time getting to work. The first step was compiling an overall membership list from those of the individual branches — something that had never been done before. Next a mimeograph machine was acquired to facilitate the production of the material that began to flow freely from the national headquarters to all members. Kranzler began calling mass meetings of all the Pirchei chapters on a scale and frequency hitherto unprecedented. At these meetings, he introduced the principles of Agudath Israel along with the singing and other activities.[7]

In the pages of *Orthodox Youth*, the first issue of which appeared in December 1940, the activities of the various branches were reported in great detail, and reading about the activities of the other branches gave members a sense of belonging to a single movement. The vital role of young people in this movement was frequently emphasized.

The paper also made clear that this movement was international in scope. Biographies of distinguished Agudah leaders past and present, many of them written by Gershon Kranzler himself, appeared in almost every one of the early issues of *Orthodox Youth* and provided readers with an emotional attachment to Agudah.[8] The feeling of being part of an

---

7. Interview with Dr. Gershon Kranzler.

8. Among the contemporary Agudah leaders featured in *Orthodox Youth* were: the Gerrer Rebbe, Reb Jacob Rosenheim, president of World Agudath Israel, Dr. Isaac Breuer, Rabbi Isaiah Fuerst,

international movement linking Jews around the world infused Mike's young minions with a strength and fortitude they had not previously known.[9]

It took awhile for the realization of the transformation of what was taking place to sink in. At meetings of the Interbranch Council at 616 Bedford Avenue, Gershon Kranzler remembers, it was clear that representatives from the Bronx, Lower East Side, and other branches "didn't have a clue" as to what was happening — i.e., that the loosely federated Interbranch Council was a thing of the past. A set of clubs was in the process of becoming a national movement.

---

rav of the famous Schiff Shul in Vienna and father of Zeirei Agudath Israel of Vienna, and Rabbi Eliezer Silver, president of Agudath Israel of America. There were also tributes to deceased leaders of Agudath Israel: Rabbi Chaim Ozer Grodzenski, undisputed leader of the East European yeshiva world until his passing in 1940; Rabbi Meir Shapiro, initiator of the worldwide *Daf HaYomi*, Rosh Yeshivas Chachmei Lublin, and Agudath Israel representative in the Polish *Seym*; Rabbi Yehudah Leib Zirelson, *rav* of Kishinev and president of the Third Knessiah Gedolah in Marienbad, who was beheaded by the Nazis; and Rabbi Pinchos Kohn, one of the leading activists in the German Agudah, who had been placed in charge of the religious needs of Polish Jewry by the occupying German army in World War I. The fate of some European Agudah leaders such as Rabbi Elchonon Wasserman and Rabbi Aaron Levin, the Reisher Rav, described by Gershon Kranzler as "the most popular figure on the Jewish street of prewar Poland," was still unknown at the time tributes to them appeared.

9. Interview with Elimelech Terebelo.

Mike outdoors at a convention. Rabbi Shlomo Lorincz is speaking.

THE SUMMER CONVENTIONS, MIDWINTER CONFERENCES, AND A wide variety of banquets[10] which became such a prominent part of the

Conventions and Banquets

Youth Council activities in the early '40s reflected the extent to which Zeirei had become a coherent movement. By 1944, the three-and-a-half-day summer convention attracted 500 delegates.[11] There was nothing fancy about these conventions — the 1944 convention, for instance, was held on the grounds of Camp Agudah in Ellenville, New York. The delegates came not to see or be seen but out of a sense of a vital connection to the

10. The banquets were almost exclusively for the purpose of funding the ever-expanding work of the Refugee and Immigration Division. As Mike said at one such affair, were it not for the purpose of raising money to save Jews, it would have been forbidden to gather for a fancy dinner at a time of so much Jewish suffering.

Given their fundraising purpose, the banquets were designed to attract those not within the immediate orbit of Zeirei. Neutral, patriotic names like the "$10,000 Defense Jubilee Banquet" or the "Victory Banquet" and honorary chairmen such as New York Governor Herbert S. Lehman were designed to create the widest possible appeal.

Nevertheless the banquets are another indicia of the growth of Zeirei in the early '40s. Without a core of dedicated activists — men like Binyamin Hirsch, Charles Young, Charles Klein, Israel Feigenbaum, Bernard Gross, and Morris Weinberg — ready to take on the huge task of selling tickets and journal ads, the banquets could not have been the success they were. The success of these affairs also reflects the growing reputation of the Youth Council, and particularly the Refugee and Immigration Division, in the Orthodox world.

11. "Convention of Agudath Israel Youth Huge Success," *Orthodox Tribune*, October 1944, p. 7.

Fundraising affairs like the annual "Night of Music" featuring prominent cantors and Seymour Silbermintz's Pirchei choir attracted as many as 1,500 listeners to the auditorium of Seward Park High School on the Lower East Side. Initially the "Night of Music," which was organized by Dave Maryles, was designed to raise money for the Refugee Home. Later it was used to support Camp Agudah. "Our Organization," *Orthodox Youth*, February 1941, p. 7.

organization.[12] The conventions were devoted almost exclusively to the business of the Youth Council, and in addition to the reports on the various activities of the Youth Council, there was a good deal of discussion and debate over the desirable course of action.[13]

The Bobover Rebbe

The shared commitment of the delegates to Zeirei created a real emotional closeness among the delegates, most of whom knew each other well. On Friday night, the singing of *zemiros*, led by Dave Maryles, went on for hours outside on the lawn under the cloudless sky. The dancing too could go on for hours, just like in the old days on Rodney Street.[14] At the 1946 convention, at which the Bobover Rebbe was present, the *Melaveh Malkah* lasted until 5 a.m.[15]

Mike was the hub around which all the spokes revolved at the conventions. His State of the Organization address on *Motzaei Shabbos* was the highlight of the convention. "He was the one they came to hear," remembers Rabbi Shlomo Rotenberg. He could hold the audience enthralled for an hour and a half with his calls for young men and women to devote themselves to the Jewish people.[16] The loudest applause of the convention was typically reserved for the announcement of his reelection as president of the organization. Yet despite his

12. Elias interview.

Rabbi Elias, who did not come to the United States from Canada until after World War II, was referring to the conventions of the late '40s. What was true of those conventions was, if anything, even truer of the earlier conventions when Zeirei was less well known.

13. At the 1943 convention, for instance, nearly every speech was directly connected to the Agudah movement or the work of the Youth Council. Rabbi Shlomo Rotenberg's hour-and-a-half keynote address entitled "Our Task in a World at War" was in large part devoted to outlining the fundamentals of Agudah ideology for an American audience. Rabbi Shimon Schwab spoke on "The Historic Role of Agudath Israel," Rabbi Aaron B. Shurin on "Agudath Israel and Eretz Yisrael," and Meilach Silber on "What Pirchei Agudath Israel Means for American Orthodoxy." All day Sunday was devoted to reports on the Refugee and Immigration Division, Pirchei Agudath Israel, Camp Agudah, the problems confronting the American Jewish soldier, Keren Hayishuv, the *Orthodox Tribune,* branch activity, and the election of officers.

14. Interview with Rabbi Shlomo Rotenberg.

15. *Darkeinu,* October 1946.

16. "Victory Banquet Huge Success," *Orthodox Tribune,* April 1944, p. 6.

prominence at the conventions, what many remember best is the deference he showed to the *gedolei Torah* present.

AT THE YOUTH LEVEL, TOO, A NATIONAL ORGANIZATION WAS coming into being. In September 1942, *Darkeinu*, published by the **Youth** National Council of Pirchei Agudath Israel, made **Organization** its first appearance. That first issue reported on a large Pirchei Sukkos rally held at Mesivta Torah Vodaath. The president of the Pirchei National Council told the overflow crowd, using the type of military metaphor so popular at the time, that they were *"Klal Yisrael's* junior commandos." Mike spoke, and talked about the fact that all the European youth movements had been destroyed by the war. As a consequence, even more responsibility fell on American Orthodox youth to prepare themselves to be the Torah-true leaders of the future.

The rough edges seen everywhere in the original three-page mimeographed *Darkeinu* were to be expected given that those involved were in their mid-teens. But within two years, the same kids were producing a reasonably polished, twelve-page magazine with two-color photo offset.[17] The magazine included *gadol* biographies by Sidney Greenwald, which were far more detailed than the comparable ones from *Orthodox Youth*, news of events in the Jewish world, and a detailed list of the activities of the various Pirchei branches. One of *Darkeinu's* goals was to broaden the horizons of American youth, and to that end the religious *yishuv* in *Eretz Yisrael* was a frequent subject.[18] Tales of Rebbe Yitzchak Levi of Berdichev and other Chassidic masters lent themselves to conveying important points about *mitzvos bein adam lechaveiro* (between man and his fellow man) in easily digested nuggets, and were a staple of the magazine.

Entertainment was provided by Murray Friedman's "The Adventures of Itzikel," the magazine's most popular feature. Every month another self-imposed disaster befell Itzikel, "the leading hooky player from the Kelsey Street yeshiva" and member of the Kelsey Street

---

17. The May 1944 issue lists Murray Friedman as editor-in-chief; Meilach Silber as managing editor; Jack Klausner as associate editor; and Alter Perl as distribution manager. With the exception of Silber, the other editorial board members were all from the Lower East Side Pirchei. Later they were joined by another friend from the Lower East Side, Sidney Greenwald, who wrote the biographies of the *gedolim*, Marcus Kurzman, Bennie Ullman, and Charles Wengrovsky, described as the "story-teller of Camp Agudah." The artists included: Arnie Lieber, F.D. Rabinowitz, Marvin Weinstein, and Yaakov Greenwald.

18. Interview with Jack Klausner.

Pirchei. There was nothing didactic about this feature, no hidden *mussar* message — only pure entertainment in a vaguely religious setting. That the humor was occasionally sophomoric is hardly surprising given the age of the author and his readers. But at the same time it is not hard to see why Itzikel delighted a generation of readers. Here is a description of Itzikel's cat Devoireleh's reaction to the *latkes*, fried in cod-liver oil purloined from his mother's medicine chest, that Itzikel prepared for a Pirchei Chanukah *Melaveh Malkah*:

> Itzikel looked at them with pride, but also a little suspicion. His suspicions were partly confirmed when Devoireleh jumped up on the table and licked one of the *latkes*. Nowhere had Itzikel ever seen such amazement as that which appeared on Devoireleh's face. She shook her head twice as if in disbelief, and then she ran howling through the house as if her tail were on fire. She finally found some relief by leaping into the sink and putting her tongue under the faucet which dripped constantly. Itzikel watched her carefully, and he slowly shook his head. Devoireleh just did not appreciate good food.

Darkeinu provided Pirchei boys with common reading matter. The Leaders Guides, prepared by Joshua Silbermintz, which were first circulated to group leaders from early 1945, however, were a much more important step in creating a degree of uniformity between the various branches. Each guide contained Torah material according to the time of the year, quizzes, games, and even jokes for the group leader.[19] The Torah material in each Leaders Guide ranged over varying levels of sophistication so that there would be something for every age group.[20]

The Guides made clear that the decision to become a group leader was a serious undertaking and would involve great work. Leaders were advised to be alert to the needs of each boy in their group, and to be prepared to provide personal counseling where necessary. During the summer, the leaders were urged to write every boy at least once every two weeks. Tips included: "Don't expect devotion and self-sacrifice unless

---

19. The organization down to the last detail was a trademark of Rabbi Silbermintz. As head counselor of Camp Munk in later years, he kept a record of every joke he told and made sure never to tell the same joke more frequently than every five or six years. *Interview with Rabbi Nisson Wolpin, who worked together with Rabbi Silbermintz for many years at Camp Munk.*

20. Some of the material was at a very high level. For instance, the explanation, in one early guide, of why the commemoration of *Matan Torah* on Shavuos has no symbols like other holidays drew heavily on the lectures given by Reb Shraga Feivel Mendlowitz to advanced students in Torah Vodaath.

Rabbi Joshua Silbermintz

you practice it"; "Don't attempt to teach what you don't know"; and "Don't come late. Keep your word."

Despite the demands on leaders, over 125 boys signed up for the 1945 Leadership Seminar, which featured lectures on Agudah ideology from Rabbi Shlomo Rotenberg and Rabbi Binyamin Hendeles; on the Jewish *Weltanschauung* from Reb Shraga Feivel Mendlowitz; and on trends in education and psychology from Rabbi Heshy Leiman.

Though each meeting was to contain a Jewish message, the leaders were constantly told to remember that the Pirchei group was to complement yeshiva, not be an extension of it:

> The paramount characteristic of a good meeting is *activity*, action rather than study. The *chaverim* come to a meeting to have a good time, to be with their friends, sing songs, express ideas and to make use of their abilities and talents. . . . The meeting spirit must be a different one from a classroom spirit. Although all meetings should broaden their knowledge on some Jewish topic … yet it must be given in a different form. In a classroom the teacher takes the initiative, while at a meeting the *chaverim* should take the initiative. In a classroom the teacher arranges everything, while in a meeting there is self-government.

Even the study material focused on subjects not usually covered within the yeshiva curriculum — *middos, mussar,* and *Pirkei Avos.*

By September 1945 there were 66 Pirchei groups — nine each in Williamsburg and Washington Heights — in 29 different branches. Nearly 40 percent of the groups were newly formed ones. Almost every group had at least one weekly *shiur,* but, at the same time, 90 percent of the branches had at least one game room and their own basketball and baseball teams. In 30 percent of the branches there was a separate

Pirchei *minyan*. Some groups — e.g., those in Detroit, Scranton, and on Bushwick Avenue in Williamsburg — had been so successful in their primary purpose of sending boys to yeshiva that there were not enough boys left to sustain a group.[21]

Bnos

A PARALLEL DEVELOPMENT OF A NATIONAL ORGANIZATION WAS going on in Bnos. By 1940, there was a Bnos interbranch council, which attempted to establish some uniformity in the programs of the various branches.[22] At the March 1941 mid-winter conference of Zeirei, one of the three sessions was given over to Bnos. Speakers included Rebbetzin Kalmanowitz and Rebbetzin Bender, both products of Sarah Schenirer's seminary, and the session attracted Bnos groups from Philadelphia, Baltimore, Detroit, and Newark.[23] The first national convention of Bnos was held in December 1942, with Reb Jacob Rosenheim giving the major address.

The *Motzaei Shabbos* session of the next year's convention drew over 1,000 participants. Mike was one of the speakers, and he stressed that with so many young Zeirei members going into the service it was incumbent upon Bnos to pick up the slack. It was a message he repeated everytime he spoke to a Bnos gathering throughout the war years.

Mike backed up his words about the importance of Bnos with actions. He was the "*rebbe*" of the Bnos National Council, which came into being largely through his initiative. "We went to him like a daughter to a father to discuss anything that we needed," remembers Celia (Roth) Zanzipar, a national officer in the early '40s. "He made us feel like human beings, not as something put on the shelf."

Whenever the girls had a halachic question, Mike took care of getting it answered. He himself provided the spiritual direction. One time, for instance, the Bnos National Council was considering a theater party to raise funds for the organization. Mike told them a story of how a woman had once presented Reb Shraga Feivel Mendlowitz with a check for $2,000 — a sufficient sum in those days to pay off all the debts of Torah Vodaath. The next day Reb Feivel learned that the money had

---

21. Semi-annual report of the Executive Director of the National Council of Pirchei Agudath Israel covering the period between February and September 1945.

22. At a November 1940 membership meeting, chaired by Clara Bergman, a resolution was passed that each branch should have at least two uniform *shiurim* a week. "Our Organization," *Orthodox Youth*, December 1940, p. 5.

23. "Our Organization," *Orthodox Youth,* April 1941, p. 6.

been raised from a theater party. He immediately borrowed $2,000 and returned it to the lady. "Yeshivos are not built on theater parties," Reb Feivel had said. Mike added that Bnos too had to be built up in an *"erliche* way."[24]

In 1941, Mike appointed Daniella (Nussbaum) Buxbaum, a recent German immigrant, as executive director of Bnos.[25] Her mandate was to increase the membership within the existing branches and to oversee the creation of new branches. Mike did everything he could to help her achieve these goals. When Rebbetzin Kalmanowitz complained to Mike that the Williamsburg branch of Bnos was in decline, he told her that he had just appointed a new executive director. Shortly thereafter, he arranged a get-acquainted meeting between Miss Nussbaum and the leaders of the Williamsburg Bnos at the home of Rebbetzin Channah

24. Interview with Mrs. Daniella (Nussbaum) Buxbaum.

25. Daniella Nussbaum had escaped from Germany to England with one of Rabbi Dr. Solomon Schonfeld's Children's Transports. She arrived in the United States from England in 1940.

Her work as executive director of Bnos was on a purely volunteer basis, something typical in those days. She used to come into the Youth Council offices three or four times a week after a full day of teaching in the Bais Yaakov of the Bronx.

Mike presenting an award to Rebbetzin Channah Belsky. Seated L-R: Rabbi Moshe Sherer, Rabbi Hager, Rabbi Chaim Pinchos Lubinsky

Belsky. From then on the Williamsburg branch took off. Mike was always available to speak whenever Miss Nussbaum needed him, whether in Philadelphia, Baltimore, or one of the New York branches.[26]

Bnos was treated as an integral part of the Youth Council. Its leaders were invited to the National Council meetings. And Mike often took Daniella Nussbaum and other Bnos leaders along with him to meetings at the home of Reb Jacob Rosenheim at which *gedolei Torah* were present. The Klausenberger Rebbe, just arrived from Europe, was there for one such meeting.[27] Mike was also instrumental in getting major figures to speak at Bnos conventions. In the late '40s, Rabbi Itche Meir Levin, head of Agudath Israel in *Eretz Yisrael*, was the most sought-after speaker in the Torah world. Still he spoke at one Bnos convention, as did Rabbi Yaakov Kaminetsky.[28]

Mike gave Bnos direction and provided concrete ideas as to where its members should focus their energies. His own dedication was the inspiration for many of the Bnos leaders.[29] After the war, he

---

26. When the Baltimore branch held its first annual conference in 1944, Mike went to speak. He was accompanied by Dave Maryles, whose singing provided the entertainment. Clara (Bergman) Frankel and Lillian (Snow) Wechsler, who alternated as presidents of the Bnos National Council throughout the early '40s, also traveled to Baltimore. Miss Snow was the head of a very active branch on the Lower East Side, and known for the *shiurim* in *Pirkei Avos* that she gave at various Bnos gatherings. Miss Bergman was the founder and first head of Nshei Agudath Israel, the Agudath Israel women's organization begun in 1947.

27. Buxbaum interview.

28. Ibid.

29. Ibid.

Rabbi Wolf Jacobson

emphasized the importance of helping the survivors in Europe, and gave Bnos an international perspective.[30] Bnos "adopted" a group of Jewish girls who had been saved and brought to Sweden where they were educated under the supervision of Rabbis Wolf Jacobson and Shlomo Wolbe. When these girls subsequently went to *Eretz Yisrael*, Bnos kept up the contact and continued to send them needed items.[31]

On the homefront, Bnos girls took an active part in such projects as packing for U.S. soldiers and sorting used clothing for shipment to the DP camps.[32] The organization was also involved in teaching Jewish children in the public schools during the weekly Release Hour for religious education.

Gradually a viable national organization began to evolve. Every month, the National Council put out a leadership guide for branch leaders,[33] and twice monthly leadership seminars, led by Rabbi Dr. L. Breslauer, were instituted.[34] Sunday rallies for Junior Bnos held at Rabbi Leo Jung's Manhattan Jewish Center or Rabbi Herbert Goldstein's West Side Institutional Synagogue attracted up to a thousand girls. Girls thought nothing of coming from Philadelphia or Baltimore for one of these rallies.[35]

The influx of immigrants from Europe included many learned women, which greatly increased the quality of teaching Bnos was able to provide. Julia (Wechsler) Mandel, an immigrant from Germany, led classes in Boro Park and, after her marriage, in Williamsburg. The Zehnwirth sisters —

---

30. Interview with Mrs. Rena (Zirkind) Ebert, who succeeded Daniella (Nussbaum) Buxbaum as executive director of Bnos.

31. Ibid.

32. Ibid.

33. Buxbaum interview.

34. "Bnos Leadership Seminary," *Orthodox Youth,* June 1942, p. 8.

35. At the rallies, the host group would put on a play or musical, and there would be contests and games. The speakers emphasized some *mitzvah* with which the girls were already familiar. *Buxbaum interview.*

Bnos officers, 1944. Seated L-R: Mrs. Tillie Katz, Mrs. Clara Frankel, Zelda Zehnwirth, Rose Kowalsky, Liza Pappenheim. Standing L-R: Ruth Strahl, Daniela Nussbaum, May Farkas, Mollie Weintraub, Pearl Gold.

Channah Rotenberg and Zelda Litmanowitz — made *Chumash* "come alive" as never before for Bnos girls without too much previous learning.[36] Two sisters-in-law — Molly (Mintz) Puritz and Bracha (Levenberg) Mintz — were regular teachers in the Williamsburg Bnos. The latter was a fixture on the Yiddish radio for many years. She had inherited from her father — Rabbi Yehudah Levenberg, Rosh HaYeshiva of America's first post-high school yeshiva in New Haven, Connecticut — the talent for delivering powerful *mussar drashos.*

The Bnos National Council ran a summer camp on Engel's Farm in East Haven, Connecticut in 1944 and 1945.[37] Most of the girls came from poor families, and so the camp charged a very minimal tuition. The money to support the camp came entirely from contributions solicited by Bnos members.[38]

---

36. Interview with Mrs. Sylvia Klausner.

37. Mrs. Pesha (Halperin) Simanowitz and Shaindel (Fishbain) Finkelstein were the head counselors and Marion (Wald) Lamm the director of athletic activities. "Camp Bnos Opened in Connecticut," *Orthodox Tribune,* June-July 1944, p. 17.

38. Mrs. Daniella (Nussbaum) Buxbaum remembers how crestfallen she was the second year when she had to report to Mike that Bnos had fallen $150 short in its collections for the camp. That was the last year that the camp was under Bnos exclusive jurisdiction. In 1947, the Youth Council took over responsibility for Camp Bnos, which moved to the Catskills, where Camp Agudah was already located.

Rabbi Shimon Schwab addressing an Agudah dinner.
Seated L-R: Rabbi Moshe Sherer, Mike, Nathan Hausman.

In the early '40s, the percentage of Orthodox girls going to Bais Yaakov was still small. Bnos attempted to fill that void in their education. For that reason, the teaching of practical *halachah* played a much larger role than in Bnos groups today. Girls in the Baltimore chapter of Bnos, for instance, used to bring chickens from home, and Rabbi Shimon Schwab and his Rebbetzin would show them how to *kasher* them.[39] Even today, Daniella Buxbaum is stopped on the street by women who tell her, "I still remember when you taught me this *halachah.*"

Most importantly, Bnos helped to raise the girls' general halachic standards. In an era when mixed swimming and short-sleeved dresses were still commonplace in the Orthodox world, Bnos had a crucial role in educating the girls. The first time many girls thought seriously about covering their hair after marriage was when they saw their Bnos leaders doing so.[40] Daniella Buxbaum recalls that when she married in 1946, it was still considered something of a scandal in her Washington Heights community that her husband intended to learn in *kollel*. As

---

39. Ibid.
40. Interview with Mrs. Sylvia Klausner.

more and more Bnos leaders followed her lead, the idea of marrying *kolleleit* lost some of its strangeness.

Finally, the Bnos groups pushed the importance of a Bais Yaakov education and encouraged girls to register in Bais Yaakov. As early as 1935, the Lower East Side branch attempted to help Chava Weinberg, upon her return from Cracow, to set up a Bais Yaakov on the Lower East Side.[41] The Bnos National Council even took the initiative in organizing a Bais Yaakov school in East New York.[42] Eventually Bnos was a victim — albeit a willing one — of its own success in stressing the importance of a Bais Yaakov education. With the passage of time, more and more girls opted for a Bais Yaakov education, and Bnos inevitably had a much less significant role to play in their lives.

The Youth Council at War's End

MIKE'S VISION OF HARNESSING THE ENERGIES OF THE ORTHODOX community for the rescue of European Jewry was realized to a degree he could never have envisioned in that conversation with Gershon Kranzler in late 1938. True, no more than a small fraction of the Jews of Europe had been saved by the Youth Council, but each one of these was infinitely precious and the result of the combined activity of hundreds of young activists. By 1942, the Youth Council, which had opened an office only three years earlier at 616 Bedford Avenue with two employees and one typewriter, was employing dozens of secretaries alone and had to move into far larger quarters at 113 West 42nd Street in Manhattan.

Not only had the office staff grown, but Mike had added crucial executives to the staff. In Rabbi Moshe Sherer, who joined the Youth Council as Executive Director in early 1943, Mike found his ideal complement. Sherer was a natural administrator and had the keen eye for detail necessary to run a large organization.[43] While still a student at Ner Israel, he had already proven his mettle as one of the principal organizers of the 1941 convention of Agudath Israel of

---

41. Interview with Mrs. Tillie (Glassman) Katz.

   When Rebbetzin Vichna Kaplan was married in 1938, the members of the Lower East Side chapter of Bnos, who had heard so much about her from Chava Weinberg, helped make her *chasanah*.

42. "Branch Jottings," *Orthodox Tribune*, April 1944, p. 10.

43. That attention to detail is amply displayed in a letter written by Rabbi Sherer, while still a student in Ner Israel, to Gershon Kranzler concerning the preparation of press releases. The letter is replete with instructions as to when press releases should be submitted to insure publication, the need to avoid foreign words in releases intended for the Anglo-Jewish press, how the releases should be headlined, capitalization, and italicization of words, etc.

America[44] in Baltimore. That was the first convention at which many of the initial group of Torah giants to reach America during the war were present: Rabbi Aharon Kotler, Rabbi Reuven Grozovsky, Rabbi Yisrael Chaim Kaplan, Rabbi Moshe Shkop, Rabbi Mendel Zaks, Rabbi Simchah Zissel Levovitz, Rabbi Avraham Joffen, Rabbi Eliyahu Meir Bloch, and Rabbi Mordechai Katz.

In a letter to Rabbi Sherer on the eve of the opening of the first session of Camp Agudah in 1942, Mike wrote, "Camp business has as always reverted back on my shoulders. You have no idea how badly I need a strong hand here, and I am eagerly awaiting you." Rabbi Sherer's arrival freed Mike to spend more time charting the Youth Council's long-term goals and conceiving the projects to meet those goals. Besides freeing Mike to concentrate on the larger picture, the presence of a competent executive director allowed Mike to focus on the wartime work in Washington, D.C., which depended so heavily on the personal relationships he had established.

Another important addition to the staff was that of Charles Young as comptroller in 1945. Young had long been one of Mike's closest friends and one of the most active Zeirei members, and he provided a necessary buffer between Mike and the myriad day-to-day financial problems. But while he could take the burden of some of the financial work off Mike, he could not ultimately shield Mike, as the Youth Council's president and chief fundraiser, from the fact that there was never enough money to do everything that had to be done.

During the war the ranks of Zeirei, Pirchei, and Bnos swelled. By 1947 the combined organizations claimed over 12,000 members, broken down as follows: Zeirei Agudath Israel (young men 18 to 35) — 3,700; Bnos Agudath Israel (young women 18 to 35) — 2,600; Pirchei Agudath Israel (boys 6 to 18) — 4,400; Junior Bnos (girls 6 to 18) — 2,300.[45] The

---

44. Agudath Israel of America was formed in 1939 by Rabbi Eliezer Silver of Cincinnati at the behest of Rabbi Chaim Ozer Grodzenski, whose student Rabbi Silver had been. It was natural that when Reb Chaim Ozer decided to establish a branch of Agudath Israel in America, he turned to a recognized *talmid chacham* whom he knew well, like Rabbi Silver, rather than to the leaders of the Agudath Youth Council with whom he had had little contact. Though Agudath Israel of America was the senior Agudah organization in America in name, the Youth Council had the troops, the ability to raise money, and was, in general, the more active organization. At the same time he headed Agudath Israel of America, the indefatigable Rabbi Silver was one of the major forces in Agudas Harabonim (despite that organization's pronounced Mizrachi leanings) and the founder of Vaad Hatzalah, which did so much to rescue the European yeshivos.

45. Inasmuch as these figures are taken from a January 16, 1947 letter to the State Department trying to convince the State Department of the organization's need for 75 immigrant

Above: 1940 Convention delegates. Standing L-R: Rabbi Oscar Rand, Mike, Joe Fogel,
Chaplain Hersch Levazer, unknown. Seated: Binyamin Hirsch, Dr. Jonas Simon,
Rabbi Chaim Uri Lipshitz, Grand Rabbi Moshe Lipshitz, Isaac Strahl.
Below: R' Eliezer Silver addressing the 1941 convention in Baltimore. Behind Rabbi Silver:
Rabbi Moshe Feinstein, Boyaner Rebbe, Reb Jacob Rosenheim, Novominsker Rebbe.

rabbis to serve as religious teachers and field directors, there is reason to believe that they are somewhat inflated.

crisis in world Jewry had called forth the energies of Orthodox young people to a remarkable degree.

But the way in which the Youth Council grew so rapidly also created its own anomalies and the seeds of future problems. The war had catapulted the neophyte organization to the forefront of the rescue work. At war's end, it was the Youth Council more than any other Orthodox group in America that the surviving remnant in Europe looked to for help. And

Charles Young

the same was true of the Agudah movement in *Eretz Yisrael*, which was totally devoid of the resources to deal with the sudden influx of thousands of religious immigrants after the declaration of the State of Israel. The end of the war thus brought no diminution in the demands on the Youth Council as an international organization: In fact, those demands increased dramatically.

As a result of the continual crises in which world Jewry found itself in the '40s and the necessity for some response from the Youth Council, there were fewer resources available for the development of the organizational infrastructure starting with Pirchei and moving on up. A finite amount of dollars and manpower could only be spread so many ways. The regrettable, if unavoidable, result was that the development of the Youth Council as a religious organization was hampered. Those who charged that Zeirei had ceased to be a youth organization with a *hatzalah* division, but rather that the youth council and *hatzalah* had become synonymous, had a great deal of justice on their side. In his biannual report on the activities of the World Agudath Israel organization, Reb Jacob Rosenheim lamented that the Youth Council's leading role in social and political activities — which in normal times would be beyond the "legitimate sphere of a youth organization" — was hampering its educational task.[46]

Not that Mike had in any way forgotten the importance of Pirchei.

46. "Fifth Confidential Report to Chawerim Nichbodim of the Agudath Israel World Organization" [hereinafter Fifth World Agudah Report] covering the period July 1, 1943 through December 31, 1943, p. 23.

He first rose to fame on the strength of his work building up Pirchei, and throughout the war and for years afterwards, he continued to personally lead the oldest of the Williamsburg Pirchei groups and to speak every other week at the Pirchei *Melaveh Malkah*. During the war he frequently spoke to Pirchei and Zeirei groups in such far-flung venues as Baltimore, Scranton, Philadelphia, Montreal, and Detroit.

The urgency with which Mike continued to view the spread of Pirchei is captured in a letter to a member of the Brownsville Zeirei. Mike wrote that a group of younger boys who "do not have too much Jewish education" had expressed a desire to join Pirchei Agudath Israel, but that if an appropriate leader were not found immediately they would likely affiliate elsewhere. He concluded by urging that a suitable boy from Yeshivas Chaim Berlin be found immediately since it was a matter of *"hatzalas nefashos."*[48]

The ongoing commitment to developing American youth was expressed in the hiring of Rabbi Philip Greenstein as a full-time organizational director in 1947 and the continued emphasis on Camp Agudah. Though in 1946 (a somewhat anomalous year because of the need for massive aid to Europe) the Camp Agudah and organizational budgets were approximately 10 percent of that of the Refugee and Immigration Division, they accounted for almost all of the overall deficit. Much of Mike's financial burden over the years was due to his unwavering commitment to Camp Agudah.

Those who criticized the diversion of resources from Pirchei and other projects at home were both right and wrong. They were right that the Youth Council had to a large extent become an international relief organization. They were wrong in thinking that with the war over, the Youth Council could somehow cease its rescue and relief activities and focus on building the national infrastructure. Mike had personally given his word to the survivors in Europe that everything possible would be done to help restore some normalcy to their lives, and there was no way for the organization to simply turn its back on them.

In a sense, Mike and the Youth Council were victims of the unrealistic expectations created by their own remarkable success. So much was achieved both in terms of internal organization and on the international scene, within a few short years, that Jews both at home and around

---

47. Mike Tress to Mr. N. N. Gertzulin, January 9, 1942.

Bluzhover Rebbe visiting Zeirei's rescue operations after his arrival in America. Seated to his right is Rabbi Herbert S. Goldstein. Standing on the left is Mike, to his left are Moshe Dyckman and Rabbi Chaim Uri Lipschitz. Third from right is Nathan Hausman, at far right is Rabbi Moshe Sherer.

the world began to look to the Youth Council for the answers to all their problems. Inevitably many were disappointed when that salvation was not forthcoming — or at least not to the extent they had hoped. The burden of their disappointment was just another of those that Mike would have to carry for the rest of his life.

Chapter Eleven
GETTING THE MESSAGE ACROSS

T HE CREATION OF A DYNAMIC NATIONAL MOVE-
ment depended, *inter alia*, on finding a suitable

Orthodox Youth and Orthodox Tribune

organ to promulgate the Agudah vision. In December 1940, *Orthodox Youth*[1] appeared for the first time. The bimonthly journal in newspaper format had a threefold purpose. The first was to forge a collective identity and sense of unity among its readers. The second was to strengthen the identification of Zeirei members

---

1. The masthead of an early issue of *Orthodox Youth* listed Herman Moskowitz as managing editor, Alexander Francis as circulation manager, Michael G. Tress as Honorary Advisor, and Emil Adler, Alexander Brenner, Gershon Kranzler, Eugene Lamm, Solomon Lamm, Ben Mayer, Oscar Reichel, Abraham Tannenbaum, Aaron Silbermintz, Sidney Weiner, and Ephraim Wolf as members of the editorial staff.

with their movement and to deepen their understanding of its basic tenets. Finally, the paper addressed major issues — Zionism, Mizrachi (religious Zionism), the war — from an Agudist perspective. It was hoped that a lively and provocative journal of ideas would clarify the Agudah position to the outside world and win the movement new respect and even new members.

The name *Orthodox Youth* was a misnomer. The majority of readers might have been largely in their late teens and early twenties but the paper was never confined to that age group. In 1943, *Orthodox Youth* became *Orthodox Tribune*.[2] Though *Orthodox Tribune* was for the most part a continuation of its predecessor, there were subtle differences as well. *Orthodox Youth* tended to be more inward looking and to

2. The announcement of the name change in the May-June 1943 issue of the *Orthodox Tribune* took note of the mistaken impression created by the name *Orthodox Youth*: "We feel that our newspaper is the champion of the Torah-true viewpoint for both young and old in this country, and not, as our previous name implied, a periodical only for youth and its problems."

concentrate on creating a collective identity among its readers. The names of Pirchei and Zeirei members, from Mike on down, were preceded by "*Chaver*," and the activities of the various local branches of Pirchei, Bnos, and Zeirei were covered in detail. *Orthodox Tribune* was aimed at the broader Orthodox world, and tended to focus more on ideas and issues.[3]

Mike himself wrote much of the early copy for *Orthodox Youth*.[4] He had, according to the paper's founding editor, Heshy Moskowitz, "a quick and agile pen." More important than what he wrote was the vision he imparted. *Orthodox Youth* fully reflected Mike's view that America was about to become the center of Orthodox life. The very first issue announced, "Here in our country a new world is being created. The center of traditional Judaism has moved across the high seas to the free shores of our blessed land."[5] "America, symbolic land of hope [was] becoming the Torah center of the world," and the primary task at hand therefore was to forge American youth into a "powerful and militant movement that cherishes the ideals of our Faith and lives according to the dictates of the Torah."[6]

Yet while the Nazis had assured that America would of necessity replace Eastern Europe as a center of Torah Judaism, there was no glib assumption that anything had yet been created in America worthy of comparison to the Torah world then in the process of being destroyed.

To create a vibrant Torah world would, first and foremost, require a great increase in yeshiva learning. An early article labeled as "an ominous fallacy" the widespread view that yeshivos were primarily for the training of rabbis and *roshei yeshiva*, and thus unnecessary for boys not intending to become rabbis.[7] An obituary for Rabbi Dovid Leibowitz, founder of Yeshivas Rabbi Yisroel Meir HaKohen, glorified yeshiva learning: Reb Dovid's *shiur* "was never a lecture but an impassioned plea for a proposed solution to the complexities he found to the *halachah* in question. To be a *lamdan* — was an ideal he constantly glorified. To acquire a Torah outlook was the greatest of achievements. . . . To be a

---

3. There were also differences in the composition of the editorial board between the two papers. The editorial board of *Orthodox Tribune* tended to be slightly older, as some members of the *Orthodox Youth* staff were drafted into the army or moved to yeshivos outside of New York City. The editorial board consisted of M.J. Gleicher, Rabbi Bernard Goldenberg, Rabbi Chaim Uri Lipshitz, Michael G. Tress, and Charles Young, with Rabbi Moshe Sherer serving as de facto editor.

4. Interview with Heshy Moskowitz, the founding editor of *Orthodox Youth*.

5. "The Sun Riseth Again," *Orthodox Youth*, December 1940, p. 2.

6. "The New Era of Agudath Israel," *Orthodox Youth*, August 1941, p. 1.

7. Joseph Goldberg, "An Ominous Fallacy," *Orthodox Youth*, December 1941, p. 3.

marbitz Torah (teacher of Torah) was the crowning achievement of a *talmid chacham.*"[8] *Orthodox Tribune* carried a regular column entitled "From the Torah Front," devoted to the description of various yeshivos and Bais Yaakov seminaries.

A conscious effort was made in the pages of *Orthodox Youth* to address the specific questions of American young people. Writers of German background predominated in part because it was in Germany that Orthodox Jewry had first confronted the main currents of modern intellectual life. German Jewry had been shaped by the confrontation with modernity, and its leaders were thus the best guides for American Jewish youth faced with the allure of the relatively tolerant and open American society.

The same type of questions posed by a hypothetical young German Jew more than a hundred years earlier at the outset of Rabbi Samson Raphael Hirsch's *The Nineteen Letters of Ben Uziel* might well have been asked by American-born young men and women: "What happiness is offered by Judaism to its adherents? From time immemorial, slavery, misery, and contempt have been their lot. The Law interdicts all enjoyments and severs them from everything which adorns and beautifies life." It was thus no accident that *Orthodox Youth* excerpted *The Nineteen Letters,* and published the writings of so many of Rabbi Hirsch's intellectual heirs.[9] Rabbi Hirsch's insistence that authentic Jewish life was no less capable of flourishing in a liberal and free society than in the ghetto was a message that American Jewish youth needed to hear.

MIKE'S GRAND PROJECT WAS TO CREATE A MOVEMENT OF YOUNG men and women confident in themselves as Jews and unsullied by the

Flexing the Muscles compromises that characterized so much of the existing American Orthodoxy. It is instructive that the adjective "militant" was used frequently in the pages of *Orthodox Youth* to describe this movement — and never pejoratively. To "let there be no compromise in ... personal or collective life" was the goal.[10]

The tone of self-confident youth was all over the paper as it proceeded to tweak the nose of the Orthodox establishment[11] over such issues

---

8. "With All Thy Heart and All Thy Soul," *Orthodox Youth,* February 1942, p. 4.

9. "Extracts from 'The Nineteen Letters of Ben Uziel,' " *Orthodox Youth,* March, 1942, p. 6.

10. "Elul — Period of Teshuva and Repentance," *Orthodox Youth,* August 1941, pp. 2,4.

11. The Reform and Conservative movements were almost entirely ignored in the pages of

as synagogues receiving their support from "desecrating bingo games and besmirching card parties."[12] The Orthodox rabbinate was castigated for its tepidity in advancing the cause of Shabbos observance,[13] and the 5 percent of Jews estimated to be fully Shabbos observant were encouraged to conduct campaigns for Shabbos observance in their neighborhoods.[14] Another favorite topic was the need to root out from the Talmud Torahs teachers who could not serve as models of *mitzvah* observance and "instead of teaching *Chumash* in its entirety ... give only a synopsis with their own Bible criticism."[15]

Perhaps the sharpest pen on the staff belonged to a young yeshiva student in Baltimore named Morris Sherer, who wrote a series of "Reflections" under the pseudonym Martin Nerl. In an early piece, he characterized the English-speaking rabbis of Orthodox *shuls* as masters of the fine art of "How to win friends and not to influence people": "[They] feel that if they mollycoddle every vital issue by murmuring platitudinous nothings about 'religion' and 'democracy' they will not trample on the delicate feelings of their congregants." The problem with the modern yeshiva graduate entering the rabbinate was that:

> Usually ... he views the rabbinate either as a lucrative profession, a vocation, or a (shhh!) ... vacation. Hence ... dances, bingo, mixed pews, Zionist affiliation, clerical robe, book reviews, Bas Mitzvahs ... necessity, my boy, necessity.[16]

Elsewhere Nerl complained of the "Yankee doodle touch" given to Rosh Hashanah so that the holiday had become the occasion "for pulling congregational budgets out of the red, family get-togethers, exasperating the Post Office employees with tiny 'New Year greeting' envelopes, and earning some wholesome cash by the members of the Jewish Tin Pan Alley, pseudo-cantors, choir boys, and what have you."

Orthodox Youth and *Orthodox Tribune*. Occasionally, however, an item too sad or comical to overlook would sneak in, as, for instance, when Arthur Hays Sulzberger, publisher of The *New York Times*, presented a church with a pair of candlesticks brought by his great-grandparents to America from their synagogue in Landau, Germany. The rector of the church was assisted in blessing the candlesticks by Sulzberger's Reform rabbi, Jonah S. Wise. Rabbi Bernard Goldenberg, in commenting on this news item, could not resist noting that "the distinguished rabbi of St. Paul's in Eastchester" was also head of the United Jewish Appeal. "The Passing Parade," *Orthodox Tribune*, June-July 1944, p. 9.

12. Sidney Weiner, "A Glance at Jewish Youth," *Orthodox Youth*, April 1941, p. 5.

13. "Shmiras Shabbos," *Orthodox Youth*, April 1941, p. 2.

14. "Shabbath Wardens," *Orthodox Youth*, February 1942, p. 2.

15. Sidney Weiner, "A Glance at Jewish Youth," *Orthodox Youth*, April 1941, p. 5.

16. Martin Nerl, "Reflections," *Orthodox Youth*, March 1942, p. 4.

In place of the spiritual preparations of yore, he lamented, everybody was too busy buying new suits and dresses and cleaning and remodeling the synagogues "to even think of G-d."[17]

ABOVE ALL, ORTHODOX YOUTH AND ORTHODOX TRIBUNE WERE vehicles for articulating Agudah ideology and explaining where

Charting an Ideology

Agudah differed from other groups within the Orthodox world. In article after article, the major points of Agudah ideology were delineated. The papers' editors were not preaching to the already converted. Many readers wavered between Mizrachi and Agudah, and the battle for the hearts and minds of American Orthodox young people gave bite to the papers' treatment of ideological issues.

At one level, Agudath Israel was said to possess no ideology as such — that is, no ideology other than the Torah and no purpose other than the restoration of the authority of the Torah into collective Jewish life.[18] As such, its leaders proclaimed, Agudath Israel was not a political party nor "the instrument for political aims"[19] representing some faction or part of the Jewish people. Agudath Israel laid claim to every Jew because the Torah lays claim to every Jew as having a role to play in its collective fulfillment.[20]

Because the fulfillment of the Torah is the collective responsibility of the Jewish people, *Orthodox Tribune* preached, the Jewish people can only be conceived collectively, not as a group of autonomous individuals. Agudah philosophy emphasized that being a Jew is not a private matter between the individual and G-d, but a "public matter of the people, by the people, and for the people of the Torah."[21] As Rabbi Dr. L. Breslauer put it:

> The Torah itself frowns upon anyone who dares to approach it singly, and refers him first to the community. It is G-d Himself Who insists upon the foregoing affirmation by every Jew of our *collective trusteeship* of His will. This is the fundamental

---

17. Martin Nerl, "Reflections," *Orthodox Youth,* September 1942, p. 4.

18. Gershon Kranzler, "Testimonial to Rabbi Eliezer Silver," *Orthodox Youth,* March 1942, p. 2.

19. Ibid.

20. Rabbi Dr. L. Breslauer, "The Ideology of Agudath Israel (Part II)," *Orthodox Tribune,* June-July 1944, p. 10.

21. Rabbi Dr. L. Breslauer, "The Ideology of Agudath Israel (Part I)," *Orthodox Tribune,* October 1943, p. 7.

principle of our theocratic State. Not to individuals [was the Torah given], but to **a people, to His people.**

From this principle followed the necessity of thinking collectively, not in terms of oneself alone. Now more than ever, in the aftermath of the Holocaust, was such a frame of mind necessary, wrote Rabbi Shlomo Rotenberg. American Jews were not spared Hitler's wrath, he argued, for themselves but as part of the Jewish people "for the Jewish people as a whole cannot perish." But if American Jews were saved as members of the Jewish people, it followed that their lives no longer belonged to them but to their people: *"They died for our people! We have to live for our people! No more individual life! There is only Jewish life!* This is *our* duty!"[22]

Even yeshiva students were called upon to recognize their duties to the *klal.* When *Orthodox Tribune* republished a debate from the pages of *The Jewish Weekly* of London over how much time a yeshiva student should give to outside activities, only the opinions of proponents of outside commitments were included.[23] Meilach Silber, President of the Pirchei National Council, wrote that yeshiva students should "search their hearts to see whether at present all their time really does belong to learning":

> Is Orthodoxy rich enough in qualified leaders, are our yeshivos and Hebrew schools populated sufficiently, do enough youngsters know and care about Judaism that we can afford to sit idly by while the strength of our people, its youth, is sapped away by those to whom G-d and Torah are matters of little concern?[24]

The final pillar of Agudah ideology, as developed in the *Orthodox Tribune,* was the insistence that no aspect of individual or collective life is outside the purview of the Torah. As Dr. Isaac Breuer wrote:

> Not a bolt in the structure of national life can be withdrawn from the rule of G-d the King. What part of the State, of which the Bible speaks, was "secular"? Was the Jewish king, by reason of his kingship, less G-d's servant than the Jewish High Priest?[25]

A corollary of the view that the Torah encompasses every aspect

---

22. Rabbi Shlomo Rotenberg, "Their Inheritance — Our Goal," *Orthodox Youth,* April 1943, p. 3.

23. J. A. Starfer from Manchester Talmudic College noted that in Europe the Telshe Rosh Yeshiva had encouraged the *talmidim* to canvass for Agudah in local Jewish elections and that groups of yeshiva students organizing younger boys had been primarily responsible for the spread of *yeshiva ketanos* in Poland.

24. "The Role of the Yeshiva Student," *Orthodox Tribune,* June-July 1944, p. 14.

25. "Dr. Isaac Breuer on His Sixtieth Birthday," *Orthodox Tribune,* March 1944, p. 3.

of life was that "the leadership of the Jewish people must be vested in men of religious adherence and religious integrity."[26] Not only must leaders be men of religious integrity, but whenever it "becomes necessary to measure practical works by the pure standard of the Torah" the task must be left to "those most learned in Torah."[27]

AGUDAH IDEOLOGY AND ZIONISM REPRESENT TWO IRRECON-cilable definitions of Jewish nationhood. The former views the Torah as

Anti-Zionism

the constitution of the Jewish people, whose entire raison d'etre lies in its duty to live according to the Torah's dictates. The Zionists, however, advanced a radically different conception of Jewish nationhood — one divorced entirely from religious observance. Religious observance was reduced by the Zionists to nothing more than a matter of individual conscience.

While consistently calling for open immigration to *Eretz Yisrael* and emphasizing that "settlement of the holy soil of *Eretz Yisrael* is the fulfillment of a religious imperative,"[28] Agudah rejected the Zionist conception of state in which "the Torah has been degraded to be of a private or fractional concern."[29] A Jewish state not based on the Torah was nothing less than "a denial of Jewish history and the essence of the Jewish people,"[30] and therefore without any future,[31] according to Agudah thinkers.

Agudah thought recognized no such thing as a secular realm be it political, social, or economic realm. Again Dr. Breuer:

> ...The first aim of Zionism is the establishment of a secular sphere within the Jewish nation.... Whether this sphere is great or small ... is not the issue. The determining fact must be that the Jewish nation shall voluntarily get away from G-d and the Torah at some point.[32]

The denial of an independent political sphere led Agudah to fight the

---

26. David Turkel, "I Can't Understand It," *Orthodox Youth*, September 1942, p. 4.

27. Jacob Rosenheim, "What Does Agudath Israel Aim At," *Orthodox Youth*.

28. Fourth Report of the Agudath Israel World Organization, covering the period January 1, 1943 through June 30, 1943, p. 12.

29. Jacob Rosenheim, "Was S. R. Hirsch A Religious 'Isolationist'?" *Orthodox Tribune*, June-July 1944, p. 3.

30. Jacob Rosenheim, "The Policy of Torah Jewry Between War and Peace," *Orthodox Tribune*, October 1943, p. 4.

31. "Dr. Isaac Breuer on His Sixtieth Birthday," Orthodox Tribune, March 1944, p. 3.

32. Ibid.

widespread belief, even among religious Jews, that the Zionist leaders were the political leaders of the Jewish people.[33] For this reason the use of the Zionist flag and the singing of *Hatikvah* became such burning issues. To accept *Hatikvah* as the Jewish national anthem and the Zionist flag as the Jewish national flag was to concede the Zionist conception of nationhood and the existence of an independent political realm. An early *Orthodox Youth* editorial noted that many religious Jews

Dr. Isaac Breuer

sing *Hatikvah* with "deep fervor as if it represented everything holy in Judaism" despite the fact that it was "written by an individual [who] openly violated and desecrated the essential principles of the Torah."[34] Similarly, the Zionist flag adopted by the Basle convention, "an infamous gathering of [those] … for whom the very mention of *Tefillin*, Shabbos …, *kashrus*, and *Gedolei Yisroel* [were] anathema," noted one letter writer, "is becoming the symbol of the holy martyr people of Israel!"[35]

The Zionist claim to neutrality in religious matters was also challenged. Nowhere did the antagonism to religion manifest itself with more tragic results than with regard to the so-called Children of Teheran, a group of more than a thousand Polish Jewish children, 90 percent of whom came from religious homes, who were brought via Teheran to *Eretz Yisrael* in the middle of the war. In article after article, *Orthodox Tribune* carried reports from the leading rabbinic figures of *Eretz Yisrael* describing how the Jewish Agency had systematically attempted to destroy any religious feeling in the children and denied Agudah institutions in *Eretz Yisrael* all but a small fraction of the children.

While still in Teheran the children were denied kosher food, forbidden to say *Kaddish* for their murdered parents or from praying together, and had their *peyos* forcibly cut off. In transit to *Eretz Israel*, their *yarmulkes* were thrown overboard, and once in *Eretz Yisrael* they were

---

33. David Turkel, "I Can't Understand It!" *Orthodox Youth*, September 1942, p. 4.

34. "Have We a National Anthem," *Orthodox Youth*, April 1941, p. 2.

35. Martin Nerl, letter in "What They Write," Orthodox Youth, February 1942, p. 3.

visited by cigar-smoking Jewish Agency officials on Shabbos, who wrote down all their names.[36] Though Agudah institutions were prepared to accept hundreds of the children, between 60 and 70 percent of whom came from Agudah homes, the Jewish Agency refused to let them have more than a few dozen. According to a telegram received from Rabbi Itche Meir Levin, the former president of the Polish Agudah and son-in-law of the Gerrer Rebbe, the Jewish Agency went so far as to declare that it "would never allow any of the refugee children to attend a Talmud Torah or Yeshiva."[37]

One final charge laid was leveled at the Zionists: They had allowed their own private political agenda to take precedence over saving Jewish lives in Europe. After the failure of negotiations in Washington designed to pressure the British into rescinding the infamous 1939 White Paper, which barred any Jewish immigration to Palestine as of April 1, 1944, the *Orthodox Tribune* castigated Zionist leaders for "tie[ing] up the fate of the White Paper with the moot political question of establishing a Jewish Commonwealth in Palestine, which undoubtedly accounted in great measure for the tabling of the resolution that was introduced in Congress."[38] The delegates to an assembly called in the middle of the war by the "leaders" of American Jewry, chief among them Stephen S. Wise, were accused of having focused on postwar political issues even as "every clock beats out the dirge of Jews whom no planning will ever again help."[39]

Versus Mizrachi

THE ISSUE OF ZIONISM WAS THE CENTRAL ONE DIVIDING AGUDATH Israel from Mizrachi, then the largest Orthodox organization in the United States. Not surprisingly, then, jousting with Mizrachi took up considerable space in *Orthodox Youth* and *Orthodox Tribune*. By joining together with non-religious Jews, Mizrachi was accused of having given an Orthodox *hechsher* (stamp of approval) to those hostile to the Torah.[40] When a Boro Park rabbi addressed an anti-Fascist rally sponsored by a Popular Front group, the Mizrachi youth paper castigated him for having lent his

---

36. "Jewish Children Betrayed in Eretz Israel," *Orthodox Tribune*, May-June 1943, p. 1.

37. Jacob Rosenheim, "The Refugee Children Problem," Orthodox Tribune, July-August 1941, pp. 2, 9.

38. "A Mockery of Justice," *Orthodox Tribune*, April 1944, p. 2.

39. "Orthodoxy Must Assert Itself!" *Orthodox Tribune*, July-August 1943, p. 1.

prestige to a Communist-front group. Martin Nerl responded that Mizrachi committed the same sin every time they invited such anti-Torah leaders as Stephen Wise, Chaim Weizmann, and Israel Goldman to address their public meetings:

> **You,** by rendering homage to every tenth-rate Reform rabbi who jumps on the Zionist bandwagon have thus enabled them to weave their poisonous fangs into the souls of Jews whom they might otherwise never have reached.[41]

Mizrachi was accused of having made Zionist affiliation paramount over religious observance. Thus when Mizrachi youth petitioned Agudas Harabonim to put a group of anti-Zionist Reform rabbis in *cherem* (under ban of excommunication), Martin Nerl could not help asking:

> We wonder whether the declarants themselves could keep a straight face at reading this demand. The pork chop-eating gentlemen from Park Avenue are entitled to be recognized as "rabbis" so long as they swear allegiance to the Shekel. The Shekel is their "*smichah.*" But never, never the anti-Zion[ist] "rabbis."[42]

The tragedy of the Children of Teheran was said to reveal, at best, how little influence Mizrachi had gained over non-religious Zionists in its years of partnership with them, and, at worst, how deeply implicated Mizrachi was in Zionist outrages. "The entire structure of the Mizrachi falls like a house of cards [over the Children of Teheran]," wrote Reb Jacob Rosenheim, "and shows the world exactly how much influence it has gained over the years."[43] Worse, the Mizrachi representative to the Jewish Agency had joined with his colleagues in supporting the denial of the children to Agudah institutions in *Eretz Yisrael*. And when the Chief Rabbi of Palestine, Rabbi Yitzchak Isaac Herzog, called for a world-wide boycott of all Orthodox funding of Zionist institutions, that same representative demanded that he be

---

40. By and large, this jousting was confined to ideological issues, not matters of religious observance. But when the Houston chapter of Junior Mizrachi announced a Carnival and Dance, during the seven-week *sefirah* mourning period and replete with a fortune teller and kissing booth, the *Orthodox Tribune* took note. *Orthodox Tribune*, June-July 1944, p. 12.

41. Martin Nerl, "Reflections," *Orthodox Youth*, March 1942, p. 4.

42. Martin Nerl, "Reflections," *Orthodox Youth*, March 1943, p. 4.

43. Jacob Rosenheim, "Who Is Guilty in the Dispute over the Refugee Children," *Orthodox Tribune*, July-August 1943, pp. 1, 3.

deposed.[44] The Mizrachi representative had even opined that it was better to send the children to a Hashomer Hatzair kibbutz than to "fanatic" Agudath Israel.[45]

THE EARLY YEARS OF ORTHODOX YOUTH AND ORTHODOX TRIBUNE coincided with the war years and the annihilation of European Jewry.

The Overriding Issue With the Holocaust relegated to the back pages of the secular press,[46] it fell to the Jewish press to keep the Jewish public informed of the full extent of the horrors in Europe. The front page of virtually every issue of *Orthodox Youth* began with a lead story concerning the fate of European Jewry and a column of news items relating to the suffering and destruction of European Jews.

On its editorial page, the paper tried in vain to prick the conscience of the United States and Britain. After the Bermuda Conference between delegates of the United States and Great Britain failed to come up with a single concrete plan to save some part of European Jewry, Congressman Emanuel Celler suggested bitterly that the two countries anticipated a less severe refugee problem after the war: "After victory, disembodied spirits will not present so difficult a problem; the dead no longer need food, drink, and asylum."[47]

Great Britain was excoriated for its hypocrisy in completely closing the gates of Palestine in the face of Europe's desperate Jews while suggesting that other countries should open their doors to Jewish immigrants.[48] In an appeal from the Youth Council, addressed to the British government, Mike wrote, "We refuse to believe that at a time when the doors of Palestine are open to Poles, Greeks, Yugoslavs and other refugees escaping Nazi tyranny, the gates of the land of Israel will be closed to the children of Israel knocking at the doors of the country which is their haven by the word of the Lord."[49] And when President Roosevelt finally created a War Refugee Board in 1944, the *Orthodox Tribune* wondered what he had been waiting for

---

44. Jacob Rosenheim, "The Refugee-Children Problem," *Orthodox Tribune*, July-August 1943, p. 2.

45. Jacob Rosenheim, "Who is Guilty in the Dispute over the Refugee Children?" *Orthodox Tribune*, July-August 1943, pp. 1, 3.

46. See Chapter 14, pp. 241-2

47. Congressman Emanuel Celler, "The Bermuda Conference — What Now!" *Orthodox Tribune*, May-June 1943, pp. 3, 10.

48. "A Mockery of Justice," *Orthodox Tribune*, April 1944, p. 2.

49. Reprinted in *Orthodox Tribune*, April 1944, p. 1.

while millions of Jews were slaughtered.[50]

But above all, the paper fought against the apathy of American Jewry itself. In an early article, Rabbi Shimon Schwab lamented the "business as usual" approach of American Jews as their brothers in Europe were being starved to death, and asked how American Jews could answer the decisive question: "What are [you] doing to check the deadly assault of Hitlerism against the Jewish people?"[51] In a piece entitled, "We CAN Save Jews," Dr. Isaac Lewin countered the arguments of those Jewish groups advocating a boycott of all shipments to Nazi-occupied territory, even when directed to starving Jews.[52] And the lead editorial in the same issue attacked the American Jewish community for calling meetings and assemblies to discuss mass immigration to Palestine after the war:

> For whom are the organizations making all their grandiose post-war plans...? For the mass migration of shiploads of bones, G-d forbid? Are we all blinded to the fact — can we all not see Europe slowly turning into a vast Jewish cemetery?[53]

Nor was all the criticism directed towards the rest of the Jewish community. Some of it was addressed directly to the readership of the *Orthodox Tribune* itself. A letter from a soldier in England included the Orthodox community as well in its sweeping "we":

> Today when we read after each Nazi retreat that thousands upon thousands of Jews were wiped from the face of the earth, we are already attuned to the news. Yes, we have not the time to shed a tear for them! We call it "another news item. . . ." As long as we are safe, nothing else matters.[54]

As the full extent of the extermination of European Jewry became known, *Orthodox Tribune* warned against one final type of complacency — the complacency of despair. *"Now we must stop counting the dead and start counting the living!"* the paper urged. "We must not let the tears we shed in mourning for the dead blind us to the plight of the living. And many *are* living and *urgently* need our help. . . ."[55]

---

50. "Where is the Conscience of the World?" *Orthodox Tribune*, June-July 1944, p. 1.
51. Rabbi Shimon Schwab, "The Topic of the Day," *Orthodox Youth*, August 1941, p. 4.
52. Rabbi Dr. Isaac Lewin, "We CAN Save Jews," *Orthodox Youth*, April 1943, p. 2.
53. "Food for the Ghettos," *Orthodox Youth*, April 1941, p. 2.
54. Moshe Swerdloff, "Somewhere in England," *Orthodox Tribune*, April 1944, p. 7.
55. "The Curtain Rises," *Orthodox Tribune*, October 1944, p. 1.

Chapter Twelve

THE JEWISH SERVICEMEN'S RELIGIOUS BUREAU

I N THE MIDST OF THE WAR, WHEN THE EUROPEAN RESCUE work was the focus of Mike's energies, he was still able to transform the Youth Council into a national service organization serving the needs of the broader American Orthodox community. Both the Jewish Servicemen's Religious Bureau and Camp Agudah were examples of major undertakings by the Youth Council in response to crying needs in the religious community.[1]

RELIGIOUS SERVICEMEN FACED AN ONGOING STRUGGLE to retain their *Yiddishkeit*. Theirs was not a one-time battle, but

The Plight of the Orthodox Serviceman

a series of dozens of tests every day. Everything that had been easy and natural at home suddenly became fraught with difficulty in the service. "Little do

---

1. Camp Agudah, of course, cannot be classified as a purely service project, as opposed to part of the work of building a national Agudah infrastructure. Mike

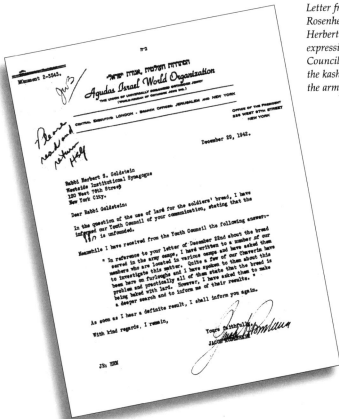

we realize what *Yiddishkeit* is or what it means to be a [Jew] until we are
faced with the crucial tests," one soldier wrote to Mike.[2] The observance
of the most fundamental *mitzvos* — Shabbos and *kashrus* — suddenly
became the subject of a seemingly endless series of calculations.

Saturday was typically inspection day, for which servicemen were
expected to appear cleanly shaven, their shoes freshly polished, and
then to march around carrying their rifles under the watchful eye of
their superior officers. Even the bread in the army was generally baked
with lard, and as a consequence the religious soldier often had to make
due on a diet of fruits, eggs, dry cereal and a few other products. His
ability to do so often depended on the good will of the mess sergeant

---

certainly viewed one of the primary purposes of the camp as indoctrination in Agudist ideology. Yet the camp, particularly in its early years, served large numbers of those with no prior connection to Pirchei and provided the first camping experience for younger boys in a fully religious
environment.

2. Undated letter of Harry A. Silber to Mike.

and the willingness of his buddies to supply him with their portions of permitted foods.

Avoiding negative prohibitions was only part of the problem. The vast majority of religious servicemen spent most of their time without a single other religious serviceman with whom they could talk on a regular basis. "The absence of any like-minded boys," wrote one sailor, "is the greatest obstacle to those Jews who care about observance." Religious servicemen were, in general, dependent solely on their own resources in withstanding the curiosity of their fellow servicemen, at best, and their hostility at worst.[3] Since there were never more than a few Orthodox soldiers on one base, commanders — even those without malice — had little familiarity with the special requirements of Orthodox soldiers.

Without a supportive community, Orthodox soldiers experienced little in the way of positive reinforcement to their religious beliefs and practices. *Davening* at the proper time was frequently impossible, and finding a place to *daven* where one would not be stared at and forced to rush through the prayers was not easy.

In an environment in which certain compromises were inevitable, it was easy to let one's religious observance slip away entirely. Even those servicemen who had some learning background, and were able to make halachically based decisions about what was and was not permissible under the circumstances, felt the yoke of *mitzvos* slipping every time they found themselves doing something that had always been forbidden. For the less learned — who constituted the majority of Orthodox soldiers — the problem was even worse because they had no sense of finely calibrating each forbidden action in a way that still emphasized the authority of *halachah*. The prayer of one servicemen — "[when], with G-d's help, I return home [and am once again able to observe the] tradition I love but couldn't follow for some time. . . . I hope to be the same kind of Jew I was before entering the army"[4] — was uttered in one form or another by virtually every religious soldier.

Most of the religious servicemen could count on little or no support from Jewish chaplains, who were drawn primarily from the Conservative and Reform seminaries. These chaplains tended to view

---

3. Anti-Semitism was an ever-present reality in the services. Many recruits, especially from the South and small towns, had never before met a Jew and brought with them deeply ingrained prejudices against Jews. One Jewish soldier reported how a platoon leader had said in front of his men, including a Jew, that "one should give Hitler credit for handling the Jews the way he did." *Orthodox Youth*, April 1943, "Those Who Fight ... Write," p. 5.

4. Arthur Hoffman to "Dear Friends," June 11, 1945.

Orthodox servicemen, with their endless stream of requests for kosher food, furloughs for the holidays, and the like, as a nuisance. One soldier wrote that the Jewish chaplain on a nearby base treated the religious soldiers like "fifth columnists."[5] In this the chaplains echoed the reaction of other non-religious Jewish servicemen for whom their more religious brethren constituted something of an embarrassment. The non-religious looked askance at any emphasis of Jewish distinctiveness, which they feared would only increase the widespread anti-Semitism.

Rather than strengthening Orthodox boys in their determination to observe *mitzvos*, the chaplains often attempted to convince them that there was a blanket *heter* (religious permission) not to do so in the army. One told a new recruit who asked about what he could eat: "We are now engaged in a *milchemes mitzvah* (a Divinely sanctioned war), and all the Orthodox rabbis of this country and England have given a blanket approval to Jewish soldiers to eat the food served in the camps." The same chaplain told another boy that he could recite *Kaddish* without a *minyan*, and assured him the G-d would forgive him for this.[6] A frequently heard "rabbinical ruling" was that the halachic principle *dina d'malchusa dina* allowed Jewish soldiers to do whatever they were ordered to do and eat whatever food was provided for them.[7]

A non-observant chaplain could make life considerably harder for Orthodox soldiers. If a soldier, for instance, told his commanding officer that he could not answer a phone on Shabbos, and the officer pointed out that the Jewish chaplain was at that moment busy talking on the phone, the commanding officer was that much more likely to feel the soldier was taking advantage of him.[8]

Nor was the mainline Jewish community prepared to concern itself with the special needs of the religious servicemen. The Jewish Welfare Board, which had semi-official status, tended to follow the lowest common denominator approach to religious needs. Thus for Pesach, there would be wine, matzah, and *haggados* provided for the *Seder*, but no provision made for those soldiers determined not to eat *chametz* for all eight days of the festival. A letter addressed to the leaders of the JWB from a serviceman stationed in England complained bitterly of the disgrace that:

---

5. "Those Who Fight ... Write," *Orthodox Tribune*, July-August 1943, p.8.

6. Ibid.

7. The halachic principle *dina d'malchusa dina*, of course, never exempts a Jew from any halachic prohibitions.

8. "Those Who Fight ... Write," *Orthodox Youth*, March 1943, pp. 9, 12.

... soldiers of the United States, members of the world's wealthiest, most powerful, least rationed community had to be advised by American Jewish chaplains to cable private organizations in New York and/or throw themselves upon the hospitality of individual British Jewish families in a country where even *matzoth* are rationed and the weekly meat ration is about twelve ounces.

"The sharp contrast between the utter failure of adequate Passover preparations and your customary efficiency," the writer hypothesized, could only be explained by the fact that:

> ... too many of your staff lack an understanding of Jewish tradition and therefore unconsciously assign low priorities to the needs of servicemen substantially above the lowest common denominator. . . . Too often a GI who approaches a JWB worker with some problem arising out of his endeavor to live up to the standards set by Judaism is given a polite brush-off as a queer, maladjusted hillbilly who has to be humored by the enlightened but tolerant social worker. Many of us have been told

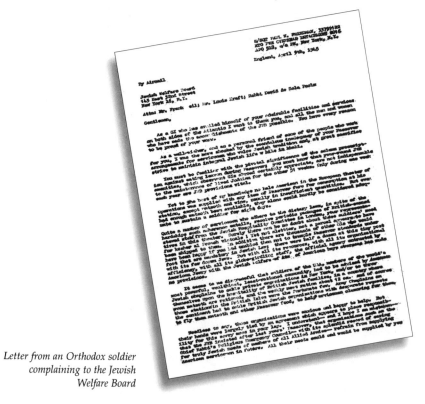

Letter from an Orthodox soldier
complaining to the Jewish
Welfare Board

"there is a war on and we all have to make sacrifices," the implication being that we, with our atavistic ideas and medieval observances, don't realize it.[9]

The Jewish Servicemen's Religious Bureau

MIKE AND THE YOUTH COUNCIL BEGAN TO FOCUS ON THE PROBlems of the Orthodox Jewish servicemen as soon as the first Zeirei members were drafted. Prior to American entry into the War, Mike led a Youth Council delegation to Washington, D.C. to discuss with representatives of the Selective Service and the War Department ways in which the needs of religious Jews to eat kosher food and observe Shabbos could be accommodated within the context of the army.[10] Those initial discussions culminated in success three years later when the War Department officially announced that its policy was to accommodate the needs of Shabbos- and *kashrus*-observant servicemen to the maximum extent possible.

In a letter to Mike, Major General J. A. Ulio stated: "The War Department policy is to afford men who celebrate the Sabbath on a day other than Sunday an opportunity to observe the requirements of their religious principles, to the maximum extent possible when military considerations permit." The Youth Council publicized this statement of policy widely, and sent copies of the Ulio memorandum to as many religious servicemen as possible in the hope that it would afford them some leverage in negotiations with their commanding officers.

By summer of 1941, the Youth Council had established a special division — which ultimately became the Jewish Servicemen's Religious Bureau — to deal with the needs of Orthodox servicemen. In an *Orthodox Youth* article on the division's activities, readers were asked to send in the names and locations of religious servicemen.[11] In this manner, among others, the Youth Council began to assemble a list of names of religious servicemen without any previous connection to the Youth

---

9. The signature of the author of this letter is omitted from the copy in the Agudath Israel archives. It appears to be dated April 9, 1945. A copy of the letter was forwarded by the Chief Rabbi's Religious Emergency Council to Reb Jacob Rosenheim, and by the latter to Mike on May 27, 1945.

10. "Kashruth and Sabbath Observance for American Jewish Youth in Army Camps Under Consideration by War Department," *Orthodox Youth*, December 1940, pp. 1, 7. The members of the combined delegation of Agudath Israel Youth Council and Agudath Israel of America delegation are not listed by name in the article. But given that Mike had the best Washington contacts of anyone in either group, it is safe to say that he played the leading role in the delegation.

11. "Kosher Food Parcels for Jewish Youth," *Orthodox Youth*, August 1941, p. 6.

*The letter from
General Ulio to Mike
guaranteeing soldiers' rights to
observe Shabbos*

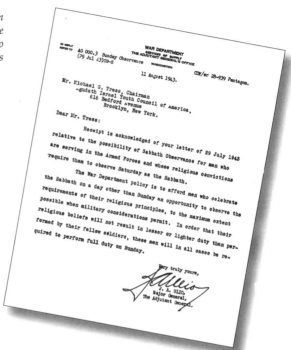

Council. Servicemen who received unsolicited Pesach packages and
other material from the Youth Council expressed their amazement at
receiving "the last package in the world [they] expected from friends
[they didn't] even know."

Among the first projects of the new division was commissioning the
translation into English of *Machane Yisrael,* the Chafetz Chaim's classic
work of halachic guidelines for the Jewish soldier. The work was dis-
seminated to as many Jewish servicemen as possible. The Youth Council
also arranged to send kosher food packages to soldiers stationed both
within the United States and abroad. Relatives of soldiers could select
from one of three types of packages, and the Youth Council would pack
and send them.[12]

---

12. In addition to the wide variety of projects on behalf of Jewish servicemen, the Youth Council
also fought to keep Jewish soldiers out of the services where appropriate. Divinity students
studying for ordination were exempt from the regular draft. Theoretically, this should have
exempted most of those learning towards *semichah*. But in practice, the New York City draft
board had set up a committee of supposedly knowledgeable Jews to advise it of the appropri-
ateness of the divinity deferment in each case where a yeshiva student sought one. Most of the
members of the advisory board were not religious and were eager to prove their patriotism by
rejecting as many candidates for the exemption as possible.

One of the few members of the board sympathetic to yeshiva students was Rabbi Herbert
Goldstein. Mike contacted him frequently for his help in pushing through the deferment for par-

The Youth Council's major project for servicemen was the provision of packages sufficient to see them through all eight days of Pesach. In 1943, 8,000 pounds of kosher for Pesach food were shipped; by 1945, this figure had skyrocketed to 55,000 pounds. Three 5-pound packages were sent to servicemen in the United States, and one 23-pound package to those serving abroad. Of the 1,400 recipients of these packages in 1944, only 400 were Zeirei members. The rest were Orthodox soldiers with whom the Youth Council had come into contact in the course of the war.[13] The high percentage of recipients with no previous connection to Zeirei is testimony to the success of the Youth Council in serving the needs of all Orthodox soldiers, and not just those affiliated with Zeirei.

One religious soldier aptly captured the feelings of many upon suddenly being contacted by an organization with which they were only dimly familiar:

> I received a letter from an organization ... with which I had not had any personal contact ... inform[ing] me that [they were]

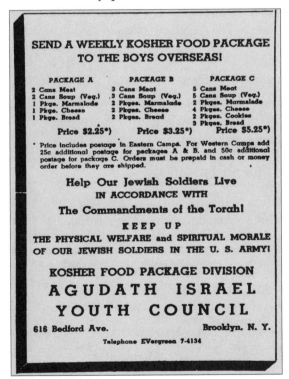

Ad for food packages to be shipped overseas

ticular students. This was one of the first instances of the two men working together, something that would take place with increasing frequency over the coming years.

sending me a package loaded with Passover provisions, and [they] had the added *"chutzpah"* to ask me to suggest any additions I might desire. . . .

As if making Passover in the army a little more like Pesach at home wasn't sufficient, I received your letter this week inviting me to suggest items for future kosher food packages. The *Malachim* are back again![14]

In the course of time the Pesach food campaign became a major undertaking requiring a full six-months of careful planning. Wartime rationing of metals meant that special permission had to be received for the tin cans in which kosher meat was packed, and the granting of that permission was by no means a foregone conclusion.[15] To ensure that the packages reached servicemen all around the globe in time for Pesach, packing had to start in early January. The more than 4,000 packages were packed by volunteers from Zeirei, Bnos, and Pirchei working out of the Youth Council's offices on 42nd Street and in Williamsburg.[16]

The responses of servicemen to these packages indicate just how important to them they were. The packages allowed servicemen to observe Pesach properly and without starving. But of no less importance was the sense they conveyed that someone at home was thinking about them and they were not completely cut off from the Jewish people. Thus even servicemen in far-flung outposts, who sometimes received their packages too late for Pesach, wrote to express their appreciation for the thought behind them.

A sample of comments from *Orthodox Tribune's* "Those Who Fight ... Write" feature captures the feelings of gratitude for the packages:

"[Your Pesach package] was the nicest gift I've received during my entire army life"; "You must have gone through a great

13. The figure of 400 Zeirei members in the armed services is taken from *Orthodox Tribune*, July-August, 1943, "Agudah Youth Convention Meets With Success," p. 5. The figure of 1,400 recipients is from *Orthodox Tribune*, April 1944, "Kosher Food Supplied to Soldiers for Pesach," p. 1.

14. *Orthodox Tribune*, May-June 1943, "Those Who Fight ... Write," p. 10.

15. Even after the intervention of Congressman Sol Bloom, Chairman of the House Armed Services Committee, the War Production Board twice refused a 1945 request that Feinberg Kosher Sausage Company of Minneapolis be allowed to pack 10,000 12-ounce cans of kosher canned meat loaf. Finally, the requisite consent was obtained in a January 23, 1945 letter from the War Production Board to Congressman Bloom.

16. Among those most actively involved in the packing work were: David Maryles, Jonah Klein, Rabbi Elias Karp, Herbert Leisser, Alter Perl, Benjamin Ullman, Rabbi Shlomo Ort, Herman Treisser, Abe Roth, David Diamond, and Private Arthur Simon. *Orthodox Tribune*, April 1944, "Among Ourselves," p. 10.

Mike and a group of Zeirei members preparing Pesach packages to be shipped overseas David Maryles is in the center (with hat).

expense to see that I have a kosher Pesach, and believe me, I can't describe how grateful I am"; "Were it not for you folks at home, the morale of the Jewish soldier would be really low"; "[The Passover package] certainly stimulated my determination to continue to live and observe the laws of our Holy Torah"; "You have no imagination of how much it means to us boys in the service to know that there is someone at home who remembers us on Passover. . . ."[17]

THROUGHOUT THE WAR, MIKE MAINTAINED AN EXTENSIVE CORrespondence both with Zeirei members in the service and with

Mike as Pen Pal

Orthodox servicemen whose names were forwarded to the Youth Council. Ever sensitive to the emotional needs of others, he realized how important that personal contact was to maintaining the spirits of religious servicemen.[18] In time, his

---

17. "Those Who Fight ... Write," *Orthodox Tribune*, May-June 1943, p. 8.

18. In a letter to Sol Septimus dated January 22, 1943, Mike lamented the loss of so many Zeirei boys to the armed services and expressed the opinion that the personal contact he maintained-with them was of a "good deal of benefit."

correspondence was supplemented by Rabbi Shlomo Ort, head of the Jewish Servicemen's Religious Bureau, and various groups of volunteers in the different Zeirei branches.[19]

Mike's letters almost invariably included some expression of his eagerness to be of help in any way possible. A typical example reads:

> We are very desirous of being of constant aid to you in every fashion possible so that you can remain a real Torah-true Jew and fulfill as many *mitzvos* as you possibly can under the circumstances. I want you to feel that you can write at all times and request ... anything that is at all possible, and you can rest assured that we will exert every effort to fulfill your request.[20]

This offer was meant be taken seriously, and it was. Mike's personal files are full of letters to soldiers providing them with names of fellow Orthodox soldiers stationed at the same base,[21] to rabbis located near bases asking them to contact religious servicemen stationed nearby,[22] to Selective Service officials requesting that induction days be changed so as not to fall on Shabbos or holidays,[23] and to commanding officers and chaplains asking for their help in gaining furloughs for religious soldiers.[24] In one letter, Mike wrote to a soldier whose mother was recently widowed and for whom he was seeking a furlough, "I have spoken to your mother ... and reassured her that you are getting along well."[25] And soldiers in turn wrote seeking everything from a place for their son in Camp Agudah for the upcoming summer[26] to information on where to obtain shaving powder, from *siddurim*[27] to a halachic responsa con-

---

19. See "Among Ourselves," *Orthodox Tribune*, May-June 1943, p. 10, for mention of a project of the Boro Park branch to correspond with members in the service.

20. Mike Tress to Pvt. Harry A. Silber, May 24, 1943.

21. Mike Tress to Pfc. Gabriel Surkis, June 4, 1943.

22. Mike Tress to Rabbi Chas. Shoulson, Fayetteville, North Carolina, March 24, 1943; Mike Tress to Rabbi Chas. Blumenthal, Waco, Texas, April 8, 1943.

23. Mike Tress to Colonel Arthur V. McDermott, Director of Selective Service, January 21, 1943 re: induction of Milton Krakowsky and Nathan Stender; Mike Tress telegram to Col. McDermott, March 4, 1943 re: induction of Joseph Wechsler.

24. Mike Tress to Commanding Officer AGF Replacement Dept, Fort Meade, Maryland, January 31, 1944 re: permission for Pvt. Alfred Sheridan to return to base Sunday, February 6 instead of Saturday night, February 5; Mike Tress to Commanding Officer, Maintenance Bn. Co. B, Los Angeles, California re: permission for Cpl. D. Sicherman to attend High Holiday services; Mike Tress to Chaplain Capt. Goldberg, Camp Abbot, Oregon, September 20, 1943 re: furlough for Pfc. Oscar Ringel.

25. Mike Tress to Pvt. Oscar Ringel, February 8, 1943.

26. Pfc. Mac Smith to Mike Tress, May 3, 1945.

27. Dave Rosenholtz to Mike Tress, date unclear.

Efforts on behalf of Orthodox men in the armed forces included helping in special situations as well as providing guidance and kosher food

cerning observance of Shabbos on the other side of the international dateline.

Of course, Mike's letters included a fair number of standard lines. But where he knew the serviceman personally or was responding to something the serviceman had written previously, his letters were highly personalized. In every letter, he sought to make the serviceman feel connected to the Orthodox world he had left behind. He did not just respond to letters, but actively encouraged them. To one former Zeirei boy, he wrote, "I want you to feel that this is not a formal letter but a desire to be in close contact with you constantly,"[28] and to another, "I am very happy that you have written to me because I have been anxious to find out where you are."[29]

Servicemen opened up their hearts in response to Mike's letters and wrote in terms of the greatest intimacy. His letters, wrote one, were "like

28. Mike Tress to Pvt. Oscar Ringel, February 8, 1943.
29. Mike Tress to Pvt. Marvin Blum, March 24, 1943.

Mike with Lothar Kahn in Camp Agudah

… a drink of water in the desert."[30] Lothar Kahn, who had been drafted not long after arriving in America from Germany, told Mike, "I have never forgotten you and never will forget a friend who has helped me so much in the short time that we have known each other."[31] One young man began a long confessional letter describing his religious struggles: "You have hinted that you are interested in my spiritual life and I will try to describe as clearly as possible how I live here and to what degree I manage to cling to my faith." The same writer concluded, "I use this letter as a basis for opening up my heart so that I may be relieved of that tenseness that I have about me."[32]

Mike's approach was always positive: He acknowledged the great obstacles confronting the serviceman in his efforts to cling to his *Yiddishkeit,* far away from his familiar surroundings and in a hostile environment, while at the same time expressing his confidence in the serviceman's ability to do so. Typical of this positive approach was a letter to Harry Silber: "You are endeavoring, despite all physical and spiritual handicaps, to remain a Torah-true Jew, and I am certain that the Almighty will give you strength and courage to carry on in your battle." To another serviceman, who had been placed in a camp where Shabbos observance was possible, he wrote, "I feel it was only through your

---

30. Harry A. Silber to Mike Tress, undated.
31. Lothar Kahn to Mike Tress, July 4, 1945.
32. Louis Roseman to Mike Tress, October 14, 1942.

deep *emunah* that you were placed in such a position."[33] Even where failures were admitted, Mike never dwelled on those in response but concentrated on encouragement for the future.

After receiving Mike's expressions of confidence in their ability to overcome all obstacles, servicemen were determined not to let him down. As one serviceman wrote, "I am extremely grateful for the encouraging letters I receive from you and will do my best to live up to the ideals and concepts of true Judaism."[34]

The extent of Mike's success in forging a connection with the servicemen with whom he was in contact can best be discerned from a small item in *The Jewish Weekly* of London. The paper reported that Orthodox servicemen in England "all carry the same passport, the name of Mike Tress. . . . They speak of the devoted efforts he gives to the youth of New York and his particular care and affection for the services."[35]

WITH THE EXCEPTION OF ISSUES OF AGUDAH IDEOLOGY, NO SUBject took up so much space in the pages of *Orthodox Tribune* during the

The Servicemen's Paper

war years as the situation of the Jewish servicemen. The paper contained paeans to the courage of the Orthodox servicemen, advice from prominent Zeirei members then serving in the armed services, and a regular feature of letters written by Orthodox servicemen themselves describing their struggles. Readers learned of Zeirei members who returned home as decorated war heroes[36] and of those who would never return home.[37]

Judging from the volume of complaints whenever the paper was late in arriving, its most avid readers were servicemen themselves. Zeirei members were eager for news of friends and their organization, and all

---

33. Mike Tress to Pfc. Gabriel Surkis, June 4, 1943.

34. "Those Who Fight ... Write," *Orthodox Youth*, April 1943, p. 4.

35. The article was subsequently reprinted in *Orthodox Tribune*, March 1944, p. 7.

36. The war heroes included two members of the Bronx branch: Lieutenant Meyer Trachtenberg and Staff Sergeant Wilfred Mandelbaum. The former was a much decorated veteran of 50 missions over the span of 88 days, and the latter's medals included the Distinguished Flying Cross and a Presidential Citation. On one bombing raid, the bomb jammed, and Mandelbaum, the waist gunner, lowered himself into the bomb bay and manually dislodged the bomb. "Two Agudah Youth War Heroes Return to New York," *Orthodox Tribune*, March 1944, p. 8. See also, "Orthodox Soldier Decorated," p. 9 of the same issue for a picture of Staff Sergeant Leon Rauchwerger being awarded a Silver Star for bravery.

37. The first Zeirei member to pay the ultimate price for his country was Seaman Second Class Morris Seif. "Among Ourselves," *Orthodox Youth*, March 1943, p. 6. Leonard Klapholz, the former secretary of the Newark Zeirei branch, was also killed in action. "Among Ourselves," *Orthodox Tribune*, November 1944, p. 10.

(Continued on Page 16)

were eager for reading with serious Jewish content, something not easy to come by in the service. The Jewish Servicemen's Religious Bureau made every attempt to circulate *Orthodox Tribune* widely, and in 1944 started a biweekly paper, *Servicemen's Tribune,* devoted exclusively to the concerns of the Jewish serviceman.

An early editorial in *Orthodox Youth* on the subject of the Orthodox soldier, "The Unsung Jewish Hero," followed Mike's approach of emphasizing the tremendous difficulties to be overcome while expressing confidence in the determination of Orthodox boys to do so. The Orthodox serviceman was described as "hour-by-hour … fac[ing] a deadly barrage of temptation and sin." The annals of Jewish military heroism, the editorialist opined, should record how the Orthodox serviceman deals with "the gnawing pangs of excruciating hunger …

Agudath Israel Youth Council of America
HONOR ROLL

★ OUR MEN IN SERVICE ★

PVT. ERNEST AARON
CPL. S. L. ACKERMAN
CPL. HERMAN ADLER
PVT. MAX ADLER
PVT. LEO ANSBACHER
PVT. GEORGE AUMANN
PVT. DAVID BADER
P.F.C. MANFRED BAER
PVT. DANIEL BARON
PVT. AARON BARUCH
CPL. SIDNEY BAUMAN
PVT. MURRAY BECKENSTEIN
CPL. IRVING J. BERGER
PVT. NATHAN BERLOWITZ
TECH. SGT. FRED BERHMAN
PVT. AARON BLUM
PVT. BENJAMIN BLUMENFELD
SGT. FRED BLUMENTHAL
PVT. SAMSON BREUER
PVT. JOSEPH BRESSLER
PVT. B. BRICKMAN
A/C W. W. BRICKMAN
CPL. ABE BURG
PVT. CARL BURG
PVT. JULIUS CHERINSKY
PVT. HERMAN CHOPP
PVT. MANNY CHOPP
PVT. A. COHEN
PVT. HYMAN COHEN
MILTON COHEN, U.S.N.
Seaman 2nd Class A. A. DAVIDSON
Off. Cand. M. DERSHOWITZ
PVT. SAMUEL DEUTCH
PVT. SEYMOUR A. DIAMOND
NORMAN DICKETT, A. S.
PVT NAT DINKELS
PVT. MEYER H. DISKIND
PVT. MAX DREYFUS
PVT. MORRIS DUBIN
PVT. IZZY EBER
PVT. BARRY EDER
PVT. DAVID EICHLER
PVT. DAVID ENGEL
LT. JOSEPH FARKAS
PVT. HARRY FEUER
PVT. M. FINK
PVT. ABE FISHER
CPL. GUSTAVE FISHER
CPL. JOSEPH FEGORNBAUM
P.F.C. JULIUS FELD
PVT. ISRAEL FLAMM
SGT. IRVING H. FLASCHEN
PVT. PAUL FORSCHHEIMER
PVT. A. S. FRANK
PVT. SAM FRANKEL
PVT. HERZEL FREED
PVT. SAMUEL FRIEDMAN
PVT. E. L. GBETZULIN
P.F.C. JOSEPH GOLDSBORO
PVT. L. GOLDSCHMIDT
A/C IRWIN DAVID GOODMAN

PVT. BERTHOLD GOTTLIEB
PVT. F. H. GREDENAU
PVT. LEO GREEN
CPL. RAY GREENMAN
Aviation Cadet GREENWALD
PVT. ALEX GROSS
PVT. MAX GROSS
PVT. SIDNEY GROSS
P.F.C. SAM GROSSER
PVT. SOL GROSSER
P.F.C. GABRIEL GROSSWIRT
P.F.C. MARVIN BRUNFELD
P.F.C. B. GRUNFELD
PVT. ERIC GRUNRECHT
PVT. BENNO GUTMAN
PVT. W. GUTMAN
PV. H. HAFTLER
P.F.C. JOSEPH HALBERSTAM
PVT. AARON HAMADA
F-5 SOLOMON HANDLER
PVT. ERIC M. HATENBACH
LIEUT. M. HEILDERN
PVT. MORTY HERTZ
PVT. MORRIS HERZEL
SGT. SID HOCHHAUSER
PVT. M. HOROWITZ
PVT. HERBERT JACOBS
PVT. MENACHEM JACOBOWITZ
PVT. HERBERT KAHN
PVT. LOTHAR KAHN
PVT. MORRIS KAHN
CPL. ABE KAPLAN
CPL. JUSTIN KAUFMAN
PVT. MORRIS KAUFMAN
PVT. MORRIS KIMMEL
SGT. WM. KAUFMAN
SGT. WILLIAM KAY
PVT. JOSEPH KAPLOW
PVT. A. KAMINSKY
PVT. I. W. KELLER
PVT. HERMAN KELLMAN
PVT. WILLIAM KELLMAN
A/C PAUL KELMANOWITZ
PVT. GERHARD KEMPE
PVT. JOSEPH KIRSCHNER
PVT. JOSEPH A. KLEIN
PVT. SIMON KLEIN
PVT. JULIUS KLUGMAN
PVT. O. KOENIGSBERG
PVT. JOSEPH KOHN
PVT. IRVING KOPS
PVT. LEON KORNBLUTH
PVT. H. H. KRANTZLER
PVT. A. KREISER
P.F.C. M. I. KRISCHNER
P.F.C. P. KURZMAN
PVT. ABE KURSZMAN
PVT. ABE LEIBERMAN
PVT. ISSIE LEHRMANN
PVT. H. LEVEN
P.F.C. ERNEST LICHTER

PVT. HARRY LICHTMAN
PVT. NAT LEIMAN
PVT. ERNEST LIPSCHITZ
CPL. JACK LUSTIG
A/C LEO MAHOHL
A/C WILFRED MANDELBAUM
PVT. ROBERT MANORSTEIN
SGT. SIMON MARYLES
PVT. MOSES MEYER
PVT. D. J. MIGDOL
P.F.C. JOSEPH MILWORM
PVT. HERMAN MOSKOWITZ
SGT. N. MUCHNICK
PVT. GOTTFRIED NEUBERGER
CPL. STEFEN NEUMAN
PVT. CHARLES NEUWIRTH
PVT. RUBIN OKUN
PVT. IRVING PACHTMAN
PVT. N. FARKESS
PVT. MAX PEHL
PVT. HANS PHILIPS
PVT. JOE PLASERIN
P.F.C. I. POLIZER
PVT. WALTER POLITZER
PVT. CHAIM POLLACK
PVT. ISIDORE RABINOVICH
CPL. SID RABINOWITZ
PVT. LOUIS RAICE
PVT. JACOB RAPPAPORT
PVT. MORRIS REICHER
PVT. HERMAN REICHMAN
PVT. WILLIAM REIMAN
PVT. J. REINHEIMER
PVT. MAX REKER
PVT. JACK RIBIAT
PVT. SEYOUR NIBIAT
PVT. O. RINGEL
PVT. JULIUS ROMANOFF
PVT. W. ROSENFELD
PVT. LOUIS ROSENMAN
PVT. D. ROSENBAUM
P.F.C. J. ROTHCHILD
PVT. S. ROKEACH
PVT. JULIUS ROSENTHAL
PVT. SOL ROSENBLATT
PVT. EDDIE RUBENSTEIN
PVT. MORRIS SWERDLOFF
P.F.C. WM. SILVERMAN
SGT. MORRIS SCHECTER
PVT. IRVING STEIN
PVT. JACK STEIN
PVT. ABE STEIN
PVT. EMANUEL STRAHL
PVT. WALTER J. STRAUSS
PVT. PHIL SCHWARTZ
PVT. A. SPIVACK
PVT. GEORGE O. STERN
CPL. JACK SAKOLS
PVT. ERNEST SALAMON
PVT. M. SAMUEL

PVT. B. SHEIN
PVT. I. SCHIFF
CPL. STANLEY SCHILDKRAUT
PVT. HENRY SCHMIDT
P.F.C. LEO SCHONBRUN
CPL. A. SCHORR
PVT. HENRY SCHREIBER
PVT. B. SCHUSTER
P.F.C. IRVING SCHWARTZ
PVT. MEYER SCHWARTZ
CPL. ABRAHAM H. SEPTIMUS
CPL. NORMAN SEPTIMUS
PVT. JOSEPH SCHACHNOW
PVT. A. SHAENBERG
MR. MOE SEPTIMUS
CPL. IRVING SICKERMAN
PVT. HARRY SILNER
PVT. JOSEPH SILBER
PVT. ARTHUR SIMONS
SGT. A. SINGER
PVT. ISRAEL SMITH
PVT. PAUL SMITH
P.F.C. LOUIS SMOLOWITZ
PVT. J. L. SOKOLOW
PVT. DAVID SPATZ
PVT. ABRAHAM SPIT
P.F.C. JOSEPH STERNBERG
P.F.C. DAVID STRIMBER
PVT. F. STRASSFELD
PVT. M. STUCKHARDT
PVT. M. STUEBLER
P.F.C. GABRIEL SUSKIS
PVT. J. TANNENBAUM
P.F.C. LEONARD TANZER
PVT. WILLIAM TARACIN
PVT. ERNEST TAUBER
P.F.C. RUDOLPH TAUBER
PVT. LOUIS THAV
PVT. M. TOLMAN
P.F.C. MORRIS WALKENFELD
PVT. LEON WANGER
PVT. JOSEPH WECHSLER
PVT. HAROLD WEINBERG
PVT. IRVING WEINBERG
PVT. M. WEINBERG
PVT. E. WEINGARTEN
PVT. ISRAEL WERNER
P.F.C. JOSEPH WEINBERG
P.F.C. MARTIN WEINSTEIN
PVT. CHARLES WEINSTEIN
P.F.C. ALEX WEINPORL
PVT. BENNO WEISS
PVT. HARRY WEITZMAN
PVT. IRVING WEITMAN
CPL. S. WERTHMAN
PVT. S. WINCELBERG
PVT. CHARLES YABLONOWITZ
PVT. I. ZAMOYER
PVT. I. ZIMMERMAN
PVT. MORRIS ZWEIG
PVT. W. ZYBMAN

List of ZAI members in the US Army, published in the Orthodox Tribune

subsist[ing] for days on tiny scraps of food. because the kosher food parcels were delayed in the mails," and his "iron will" in withstanding "the criticisms ... and ofttimes ridicule of fellow Jews and the Jewish Chaplain ... who maintain that service for Uncle Sam gives a blanket license for a total departure from daily religious practices."[38]

On the same page of *Orthodox Youth*, the paper's editor Heshy Moskowitz, then serving in the army, attacked those within the Orthodox world who maintained that it was impossible to observe the Torah while in the army. The article contained much practical information — e.g., a second pair of shoes makes it possible to polish one's boots for Saturday inspection on Friday, a *yarmulke* is legal attire in the mess hall and servicemen should not be ashamed to wear it. Parents were told how to wrap food for shipment to their sons and what foods keep well in transit, and servicemen were provided with a list of kosher foods generally available in the mess hall. Above all, Moskowitz stressed, where commanding officers are convinced of the sincerity of the recruit's religious convictions, they respect and admire him for them and are

---

38. *Orthodox Youth*, March 1943, p. 2.

Mike with Heshy Moskowitz

likely to grant dispensations necessary for Shabbos observance.[39]

Shaye Kaufman, the first director of Camp Agudah, was another who shared his experiences as a serviceman in the pages of *Orthodox Tribune*. Kaufman reiterated the message that the firmness of the recruit's beliefs would greatly influence how his commanding officers and others responded to his special needs, and added a number of other crucial points. The first was the importance of preparedness for various situations that might arise. That meant, above all, being halachically knowledgeable so that one would know with confidence how to avoid, for instance, any *melachah d'oraisa* on Shabbos. The second was the importance of persistence. Jewish chaplains could often obtain kosher food for servicemen, but unless the serviceman was firm and insistent in his requests, the Reform and Conservative chaplains would be reluctant to extend themselves. Finally, servicemen should be familiar with the army's expressed policy of accommodating *kashrus* and Shabbos observance and have a copy of the Ulio memorandum always available to show their commanding officers.[40]

39. "Is it Really Impossible?" *Orthodox Youth*, March 1943, pp. 2, 5.
40. "Religious Life in the Army," *Orthodox Tribune*, October 1943, pp. 5, 9.

*Mike with
Shaye
Kaufman
at Camp
Agudah*

Elsewhere in the pages of *Orthodox Tribune*, servicemen could learn everything from the Chafetz Chaim's advice for those about to enter combat[41] to where to find a transformer for their electric shavers in England.[42] Married soldiers were informed of the necessity of protecting their wives from becoming *agunos* (women unable to remarry) if they were lost in action.[43]

The letters of servicemen excerpted in *Orthodox Youth* echoed the main themes of the longer articles of advice. A common theme was the respect shown by fellow soldiers and officers for firmly held beliefs. One soldier described how his sergeant had ordered him to put away the *siddur* from which he was *davening* during a break between classes. As soon as the sergeant did so, a Polish-American serviceman began arguing with the sergeant. From then on, other soldiers became friend-

---

41. "When Thou Goest Forth in the Camp," *Orthodox Youth*, February 1942, p. 5. The Chafetz Chaim's advice included: (1) making a will and putting one's affairs in the hands of a responsible rabbi; (2) making a vow to be fulfilled upon one's safe return as Yaakov Avinu did; (3) praying earnestly every morning; (4) avoiding every form of strife and giving generously to charity; and (5) asking one's parents to pray for him.

42. "Those Who Fight . . . Write," *Orthodox Tribune*, October 1944, p. 15.

43. "Those Who Fight . . . Write," *Orthodox Youth*, March 1943, p. 9.

lier and even asked the Orthodox soldier to explain the major precepts of Judaism. Another soldier was excused from an exam on Shabbos after explaining to his commanding officer that he had the best interests of his country at heart since he would be praying on Shabbos for a speedy victory.[44]

The articles and letters in *Orthodox Tribune* often had a profound effect on the servicemen who read them. "Largely through [your paper] was I encouraged to break away from my Navy chow," wrote one sailor.[45] A soldier attributed to several articles in *Orthodox Youth*[46] his realization that he had no excuse for the way he had been losing ground religiously.

On its own terms the Jewish Religious Servicemen's Bureau was a major success, which greatly facilitated the ease with which Orthodox servicemen were able to observe the *mitzvos* while in the armed services. A side benefit was that the work of the Youth Council on behalf of servicemen gained it widespread respect from many who had no previous contact with the organization and a hearing for the views of Agudath Israel. One ideological opponent of Agudah wrote, "Although I disagree with many of your beliefs, I can't overlook your achievements or spirit. [Please] send me a subscription blank for your newspaper so I can better understand your views."[47] Others went further and expressed the intention to become active members of Agudath Israel on their return from the front.[48]

---

44. "Those Who Fight . . . Write," *Orthodox Tribune*, July-August 1943, p. 8.

45. "Those Who Fight . . . Write," *Orthodox Youth*, March 1944, p.7.

46. L.R. to "Chaverim," April 16, 1943.

47. "Those Who Fight . . . Write," *Orthodox Tribune*, June-July 1944, p. 15.

48. "A Marine's Approach," *Orthodox Youth*, June-July 1944, p. 11.

Chapter Thirteen
CAMP AGUDAH

FEW PROJECTS WERE AS CLOSE TO MIKE'S HEART OR had such a lasting impact on the shape of American Orthodoxy as Camp Agudah. He had never forgotten the memory of his ten days in the country under the auspices of the Toynbee Settlement House when he was eight years old, and felt sure that a similar experience of two or three weeks in a bucolic natural setting could transform a young boy's life. Time would prove him right.

It is perhaps symbolic of how dear Camp Agudah was to Mike that his last $25,000 of stocks were pledged, and ultimately lost, as collateral on a loan to buy the present campsite in Ferndale, New York.[1]

---

1. Interview with Mrs. Tress.

Main building at Camp Agudah, Ferndale, N.Y.

Rabbi Yisroel Belsky, long-time *rav* of Camp Agudah, remembers coming to the Agudah offices in the mid-'50s as a 17-year-old boy and telling Mike that more *sefarim* were needed for learning in camp. Mike told him that funds would have to be raised to purchase them and immediately made up a list of 20 people whom Belsky could contact. But before Belsky had left his office, Mike took the list back and made all the calls himself. For Camp Agudah there was no later.[2]

THE JUNE 1942 ORTHODOX YOUTH EDITORIAL "CAMP AGUDAH AT Last," announcing the opening of Camp Agudah, summarizes many of the feelings that led Mike to create the camp:

Camp Kiruv

Year after year, we viewed thousands of our Jewish youngsters going to supposedly "Jewish camps" only to find upon their return that not only did they gain nothing in the way of Jewish learning, they even lost the benefit of a whole year's training in yeshivos, Talmud Torahs, and in our own Pirchei groups.[3]

The despair at Jewish children going to non-religious camps remained with Mike the rest of his life. In Williamsburg, the Tress

---

2. Interview with Rabbi Yisroel Belsky.

3. *Orthodox Youth,* June 1942, p.2.

Rabbi Moshe Sherer and Mike (at left) and Robert Wagner (center) with campers at Camp Agudah, Highmount N.Y.

family lived just across the street from the departure point for buses taking boys and girls to coed camps sponsored by the Jewish Federation. "It used to eat him up," a daughter recalls, "to see Jewish children going to these camps rather than to Camp Agudah or Camp Bnos."[4]

In the early years of Camp Agudah, a very large percentage of the campers came from outside the New York metropolitan area and from non-yeshiva backgrounds.[5] Camp was often the first step in bringing these boys to yeshiva.[6] From the beginning this goal was central to Mike's purpose in opening the camp. He used to emphasize to the counselors the tremendous potential for *kiruv* work afforded by the camp. In a letter to Abish Mendlowitz, the first head counselor, written in the middle of the first camp season, Mike instructed him to "begin a strong campaign to induce boys who do not go to yeshivos to register for the new term."[7]

---

4. Interview with Henie Meisels.

5. Interview with Rabbi Sysche Heschel, another of the early head counselors and son of the Kopyczinitzer Rebbe. Sidney Greenwald estimates that some years half the boys came from non-religious homes.

6. In a letter dated May 7, 1942, little more than a month before camp opened its doors for the first time, Moshe Sherer wrote Mike, "This Camp, at *all* costs, must become reality — it is the *best* medium to 'save' scores of out-of-town boys." *Sherer to Tress, May 7, 1942.*

7. Mike Tress to Abish Mendlowitz July 23, 1942.
   In the same letter, Mike revealed another of his purposes in starting the camp: he saw it as a means of winning new recruits for the Agudah movement in America. He stressed:

   … It is indeed very, very vital that a full Agudah spirit and training be given to each and every camper, individually and collectively….

   I can only report that the boys who have returned home from the first trip have re-

Boys from communities outside New York City already learning in yeshiva concentrated on getting younger boys from their hometowns to Camp Agudah as the first step in bringing them to yeshiva.[8] On a trip to Boston to raise money for Torah Vodaath in 1947, Sidney Greenwald spent Shabbos with a *melamed* in Chelsea, Massachusetts named Irving Kaufman. After listening to Greenwald's descriptions of Camp Agudah, Kaufman told him that there were a number of boys in the local Talmud Torah who would benefit from camp. Many of these boys followed Greenwald to camp that summer and subsequently enrolled in yeshivos. That was the beginning of a long relationship between Irving Kaufman and Camp Agudah. One year, he sent 35 boys to camp, many of whom had only the most rudimentary Jewish background.

When camp was over, Mike would dispatch the various counselors to different cities to try to convince campers to register for yeshiva.[9] As late as 1956, it was still normal for counselors to spend two weeks after camp recruiting for the yeshivos.[10] These efforts bore fruit. Over 100 campers were influenced to enter yeshiva for the first time during the 1943 camp season alone,[11] and 200 in the first three years.[12]

CAMP AGUDAH OPENED ITS DOORS FOR THE FIRST TIME JUNE 30, 1942 in Liberty, New York with Abish Mendlowitz as head counselor

---

ceived a fine vacation but have heard very little about Agudah. . . . It is essential that this Agudah spirit and training commence as soon as possible so that we lose no members, and that we expend all energies on the basis of this policy.

In actual practice, however, it is not clear how much boys in the early years imbibed of Agudah ideological issues. What the campers did take away was a warm feeling about their *Yiddishkeit*, and this translated into both new and more committed Pirchei members.

There were other ways as well that Mike used Camp Agudah to build up the movement. In the late '40s he was eager to build up a Pirchei group in Toronto. To that end, he had the Toronto ZAI offer free scholarships to Camp Agudah.

8. Interview with Abish Mendlowitz.

9. The first year of camp, for instance, Mike sent Abish Mendlowitz and Teddy Silbermintz at the end of the camp season to Baltimore to try to sign up boys who had been at camp for yeshiva.

10. Interview with Rabbi Yisroel Belsky.

Rabbi Belsky notes that into the '50s there was still a great deal of emphasis on bringing boys into yeshivos. Each yeshiva was a neighborhood yeshiva and felt a responsibility to the neighborhood in which it was located. Thus Torah Vodaath, for instance, was no more likely to reject a boy from Williamsburg than one of the Chassidic yeshivos was likely to turn away a boy belonging to that particular Chassidic group.

11. "Among Ourselves," *Orthodox Tribune*, October 1943, p. 9.

12. Semi-annual report of the executive director of Pirchei Agudath Israel for the period February 1945 through September 1945.

Camp Agudah, Highmount, N. Y.

and Shaye Kaufman and Eugene Lamm as co-directors. For the next several years, the camp was at a variety of rented sites — Spring Glen in **Not by** 1943, Drucker's Hotel in Ellenville in 1944 — until a **Bread Alone** camp was purchased in Highmount, New York in 1946.[13]

In those early years, there was none of the superb organization and preplanning for which the camp is known today. As late as May 28, 1942, Mrs. Tillie (Glassman) Katz was still surveying possible campsites for Mike to determine where the camp would be, even though opening day was a month away.[14] On-site preparations for the camping season commenced a couple of days before camp opened, not weeks earlier as

13. Ephraim (Freddy) Wolf was the head counselor in Spring Glen in 1943 and Eugene Lamm and Emil Adler the directors. The next year, in Ellensville, Leon Machlis was the head counselor. In 1945, there was no camp for lack of a proper site. The first head counselor in Highmount was Meilach Silber, and Shaye Kaufman, just back from the army, returned to his 1942 position as director. Sidney Greenwald was head counselor from 1947 through 1949. Dave Maryles was the director in Highmount for one year before Charles Young took over the position for many years. *Greenwald interview.*

14. Letter from Mrs. Tillie (Glassman) Katz to Mike Tress, May 28, 1942, describing the pros and cons of two sites. Mrs. Katz, one of the early members of the Lower East Side Bnos, was charged with this task because she and her husband lived all year round in nearby Mountaindale.

The dining room at Camp Agudah, Highmount, N. Y.

today.[15] The first year there was only one bathroom for nearly 200 boys and no doctor or nurse on the premises.[16]

From the very beginning the camp was a major financial drain on the Youth Council coffers. Few boys could pay the full fee or even a major part of it.[17] In addition, a large percentage of the campers came from

15. Borchardt interview.

16. Interview with Eugene Lamm. Lamm was co-director with Shaye Kaufman the first year in Liberty and with Emil Adler the second year in Spring Glen.

17. Fund-raising efforts for the camp focused on the fact that it was providing a positive summer experience for poor boys, as opposed to the religious nature of the camp. Typical of this approach is a July 15, 1942 letter from Louis Septimus, Chairman of the Administrative Committee, to would-be supporters. "These critical days demand a strong youth. Our future depends upon a healthy young generation who is loyal to our faith and country," the letter began. Because "many of our finest children do not have the necessary means to receive a summer vacation...," Septimus continued, "we have founded Camp Agudah to give those boys an opportunity to gather strength and health for the whole year and fond memories for the rest of their lives."

Similarly, the Children's Rehabilitation Fund, which was created in the 1950s primarily to raise scholarships for Camp Agudah, laid almost exclusive stress on helping poor boys and recent immigrants become better Americans through a summer camping experience.

The consistent downplaying of Agudath Israel in these fund-raising efforts demonstrates how small the pool of financial donors sympathetic to Agudah aims was in the '40s and '50s, and how much the Youth Council depended on emphasizing general, non-controversial goals in those years.

Above: At Camp Agudah, Highmount N.Y. L-R: Joshua Silbermintz, unknown, Charles Young, Rabbi Moshe Sherer, Robert Wagner, Mike, Moshe Spiegel, Director of Camp
Below: Robert Wagner with four refugee children at Camp Agudah, Highmount N.Y.

Chapter Thirteen: CAMP AGUDAH ☐ 223

homes where religious observance was minimal, and only the offer of scholarships enticed their parents into letting them come. For his part, Mike could never bear to turn away any boy whom he felt had the potential to grow spiritually in camp, even though this policy only increased his financial burdens.

Even before Camp Agudah had opened its doors for the first time, Mike complained in a letter to his cousin Moshe Sherer in Baltimore, "Our deficit for the camp is mounting and the financial headache is even greater than we thought." Nevertheless, he wrote Rabbi Sherer, "we can always find room for any worthwhile boy, regardless of his ability to pay." [18]

The limited financial resources available were reflected in the level of accommodations and especially in the food. In a spoof on camp life in *Darkeinu*, the Pirchei monthly magazine, the camp dinner is described as "the meal they don't give you much of because we're having *fleishigs* for supper — tomorrow."[19] The boys joked about the zealousness with which the rule at meals of only one plum per boy was enforced, and speculated that the watermelon must have been sliced with a razor blade. But there was a good cause to be stingy. Campt Director Charlie Young was often he was not able to pay off all the debts to local merchants until the opening of the next camp season.[20]

But as is so often the case, the strained financial circumstances were inversely related to the spirit of the camp. Rather than diminishing the boys' enjoyment, the spartan conditions only seemed to increase their sense of camaraderie. Chicken may have appeared only on Shabbos — each bird divided into 15 parts — recalls Rabbi Sysche Heschel, yet "the summers at camp were among the happiest times of our lives." Those years were filled with excitement, growth, and commitment. On Shabbos and at the *Motzaei Shabbos* campfires, the singing went on for hours. Just as in Pirchei, the emphasis was on activities that gave each boy a sense of being part of a group and a warm association with his *Yiddishkeit*. Singing was something everyone could do, and the familiar camp songs brought out the group identity.[21]

---

18. The only thing Mike requested from Rabbi Sherer was that an attempt be made to obtain scholarships from the Baltimore Agudah chapter for boys who could not pay the camp fee. Mike Tress to Morris Sherer, June 17, 1942.

19. *Darkeinu*, November 1944.

20. Interview with Mr. Young's widow Mrs. Belle Young.

21. Interview with Abish Mendlowitz, the first head counselor.

The counselors were possessed with a sense of mission. They received neither a salary nor tips, and yet every year the number of applicants exceeded the number of positions for counselors.[22] The counselors carried their youthful idealism with them as they grew older, and many went on to be leaders within Agudah and in other *klal* activities. In camp, they learned to be leaders both in their dealings with their campers and with the campers' parents.[23]

For those boys too old to be campers and not yet old enough to be counselors, positions were created. One year there were 14 cooks in the camp. When there were more cooks than pots, previously unheard-of positions, like silverware polisher, were added. From a business point of view, the policy was disastrous, but Mike realized how few positive activities were open to teenage boys in the summer. In his view, making sure that they did not backslide from their yeshiva studies during the summer was just one more of the camp's purposes, and he was able to maintain this policy over the protests of some of the camp's leading supporters.

The Chiddush of Camp Agudah

THE TYPICAL "RELIGIOUS" CAMP, CIRCA 1942, WAS LIKELY TO PERmit boys to play ball on Shabbos within the *eruv*, and even to swim on hot Shabbos days. *Bentsching* after meals was often limited to the first blessing, and *davening* to Shabbos. As remarkable as it may seem today, the three-time-a-day *davening* in Camp Agudah and the way the whole camp sang the entire *bentsching* aloud were both innovations in their time, as was the rigorous adherence to proper halachic standards of *kashrus* and Shabbos observance. Perhaps the biggest innovation of all was the twice daily learning sessions. Though often no more than a half an hour each, these learning sessions were for many of the boys the first real exposure to any form of learning. Camp Agudah tried to impart to them the basic knowledge of Jewish belief and practice they were lacking. One of the goals of the learning, for instance, was that the boys know all the categories of forbidden activities on Shabbos.[24]

Another of Camp Agudah's major contributions to Orthodox camping was exposing boys to major Torah figures throughout the summer.

---

22. Interviews with Rabbi Sysche Heschel and Mrs. Belle Young.
23. Greenwald interview.
24. Ibid.

Gedolim visiting Camp Agudah. L-R: Rabbi Aharon Kotler, the Chuster Rav, R' Efraim Nussbaum (Toronto), Rabbi Thumim, Rabbi Yonasan Steif, the Kopyczinitzer Rebbe

The camp *rav*, Rabbi Yaakov Teitelbaum, had himself been one of the leaders of the Vienna Agudah and was a *talmid chacham* of note. In addition to him, the Telzer Rosh Yeshiva Rabbi Eliyahu Meir Bloch, the Novominsker Rebbe, Rabbi Gedaliah Schorr, and Rabbi Yitzchok Schmidman all began to spend several weeks each summer at Camp Agudah.[25]

Above all, the camp strove to imbue the boys — many of whom thought of themselves as Americans first and Jews second — with a feeling that being *frum* and being American were not contradictions — that one could be *frum* and perfectly normal. For several summers, in the late '40s, the Camp Agudah staff had the best softball team in the Catskills. They used to play teams from other camps and from nearby hotels. One year, they discovered to their dismay that they had scheduled a game on the fast day of *Shivah Asar B'Tammuz*.

Unsure of what to do, the players consulted with the camp *rav*, Rabbi Yaakov Teitelbaum. He told them to play — that watching their unshaven, parched and famished counselors playing with their *tzitzis* flying would be a positive experience for the campers. And indeed, there are those who were campers then who still remember how the Camp Agudah All-Stars prevailed on Sidney Greenwald's home run in the bottom of the sixteenth inning.[26]

---

25. Ibid.

26. Greenwald interview.

Among the team's stars were Mickey Weinberger and Aaron Schwebel. In the late '40s, there was still a military draft, and many older yeshiva students received divinity student exemptions.

Rabbi Eliyahu Meir Bloch speaking at Camp Agudah. Mike is on the left.

That incident neatly captures the contrast between that era and today. In the late '40s, the task was to create a self-confident Orthodox

This, however, made it risky for them to spend the summer as camp counselors because it might be used as evidence that they were not full-time students. Nevertheless, when Sidney Greenwald approached Reb Shraga Feivel Mendlowitz and told him that he was having difficulty getting the quality of counselors he needed for Camp Agudah, Reb Feivel asked him whom he wanted from the Torah Vodaath *beis medrash.* Reb Feivel felt that the work of Camp Agudah was so important that it outweighed the danger of potential problems with the draft board. Weinberger and Schwebel were the first counselors Greenwald selected.

youth, comfortable with their *Yiddishkeit*. To that end, watching the same counselors who taught *Chumash* and *Rashi* playing baseball could be a positive experience. Today's campers are, by contrast, yeshiva students, themselves children of those who learned in yeshivos. They do not have to be convinced that being *frum* is normal; they have grown up in communities where being Orthodox is the norm. For them playing baseball on a fast day would be as unthinkable as it would be unnecessary. But different times require different responses.

ONE OF MIKE'S GREATEST CONTRIBUTIONS TO CAMP AGUDAH WAS bringing Rabbi Yaakov Teitelbaum, leader of the prewar Zeirei in Vienna, to Camp Agudah as the official *rav* of the camp. Not only did Mike bring Rabbi Teitelbaum to the camp, he consistently defended him

Rabbi Yaakov Teitelbaum

against those on Camp Agudah's Board of Directors who objected to the pace at which he was instituting changes in the camp program.

From the first day he arrived in camp, Rabbi Teitelbaum pushed for an increase in the time devoted to learning. He insisted, for instance, on a half an hour of learning after the nighttime activities and before *Maariv*. Only after he repeatedly expressed his opinion in the most vociferous terms did the counselors decide that it was more trouble than it was worth to dispute the issue with him. Over the years, he consistently competed with the night activities, dragooning older boys for a *shiur* at night in place of the scheduled activities.

Whatever offended his sense of proper *middos*, he fought against, no matter how deeply ingrained in camp practice. Thus Camp Agudah was the only camp at which the boys did not wear shorts because Rabbi Teitelbaum felt they were not proper attire.

He did his best to extirpate the *grammen* and light-hearted teasing that formed a large part of camp life. Any form of *latzanus* (scoffing) was anathema to him. One of his favorite stories to illustrate the evil of *latzanus* involved Rabbi Akiva Eiger. The best boy in Rabbi Akiva Eiger's yeshiva was engaged to his daughter. One morning at breakfast, Rabbi Akiva Eiger asked "*Vie is de eiye* — Where is the egg?" The quick-witted young man answered immediately, "*Ha'eiye m'kedem*," a play on the words of the verse in *Bereishis* (12:8), to indicate the location of the egg. Rabbi Akiva Eiger immediately broke the *shidduch*. He refused to let his daughter marry someone who could use the Torah to make a joke.

Dining room at Camp Agudah, Ferndale, N.Y., 1964. Among those in the picture are: Yussie Brick, Yossi Plotzker, Baruch Grossman, Yisroel Gelbwachs, Yehudah Frankel, Shmuel Fishelis, Avraham Chaim Young, Avrohom Zweig, Asher Miller, Yitzchok Feuereisen, Yossi Lieber, Yitzchok Wenger, Feivel Brody, Shimon Zweig.

From Rabbi Teitelbaum, the boys learned that America did not have to be a land of compromises. Near the camp in Highmount was a well-known hotel catering to a religious clientele. Rabbi Teitelbaum happened to walk by once on *Shivah Asar B'Tammuz* and noticed that not only was there swimming at a time of the year when it is forbidden, but also that it was mixed. He immediately enlisted Mike's help in stopping the mixed swimming. Mike spoke to the owners of the hotel, but without success. Finally, a large protest meeting was held at Camp Agudah. Leading rabbis, Rabbi Teitelbaum, and Mike all spoke on the need for *kedushah* (holiness) in the Jewish world. The demonstration created such a scandal that the owners of the hotel could not receive an *aliyah* in *shul*. Though the hotel did not do away immediately with all mixed swimming — there was still a large clientele that insisted on it — the owners did, at least, create periods for separate swimming every day.[27]

27. The material on Rabbi Yaakov Teitelbaum is all based on an interview with his successor as *rav* of Camp Agudah, Rabbi Yisroel Belsky.

MIke relaxing in camp

Throughout his life, Mike was closely identified with Camp Agudah. He loved to spend the weekends there, and his visits were always treated as major occasions. One day he was walking around the camp when he came to a bunk on which a "No **Tress**passing" sign had been placed. He enjoyed the joke.

Today Mike's picture hangs in the lobby of Camp Agudah. He is pointed to as an example to the boys that an American-born boy like themselves can have an impact on the entire Jewish world. Camp Agudah itself is only one aspect of that impact.

Part Three

THE WAR YEARS

FROM LATE 1938, WHEN HE FIRST BECAME involved in efforts to procure United States visas

The Price of Caring for Jews desperate to escape Europe, until the end of World War II, there was scarcely a waking hour in which Mike's thoughts were removed from the plight of Europe's Jews. Those, like him, who dedicated themselves to doing whatever was possible on behalf of their Jewish brothers doomed themselves to repeated and bitter disappointment. Both the efforts to obtain visas for individuals and great rabbinic leaders and the daring plans to ransom tens of thousands of Jews hatched by Yitzchak and Recha Sternbuch in Switzerland and Rabbi Michoel Weissmandl in Slovakia ended, in almost every case, in frustration. The successes were measured one at a time — a few thousand souls at the most; the failures, in the millions.

Nor was this just any kind of failure. When a visa application was arbitrarily turned down at the whim of a consular official abroad, that denial was in most cases a death sentence for an entire family. And when Britain and the United States failed to pursue indications that the Romanian government, desirous of currying favor with the soon-to-be victorious Allies, was eager to be rid of the 75,000 Jews still surviving from the 125,000 it had exiled to Transnistra in appalling conditions, that apathy was a death sentence on tens of thousands.

For those who knew what was happening in Europe — and Mike was one of the first to know in detail from cables of the Polish government-in-exile passed on to Reb Jacob Rosenheim in September 1942 — the knowledge was almost too much to bear. The same month that Rosenheim was informed of the murder of 100,000 Jews in the Warsaw Ghetto, the front page editorial of *Orthodox Youth* — likely written by Mike himself — expressed the torment of too much knowledge:

> The pitiful cries of anguish and terror that come from the millions of Jews are so heartrending in their agony that they can drive the human mind to insanity.
>
> This is not a horror story — but a realistic picture of a bit of the truth. Never will we know what has really happened. Too many lives have been lost, too many children orphaned, too many cities and towns destroyed to make it possible to record the facts and figures. The truth is too ghastly for the human mind to conceive, and it is best that we know only that which we read if we wish to remain with our complete senses intact.[1]

For some, despair gave way to inaction. After the failure of Britain and the United States, at the Bermuda Conference in March 1943, to undertake any serious steps to rescue Jews, mainline Jewish American organizations gave up any hope that anything could be done for European Jewry. Rescue was not even on the agenda at the American Jewish Conference in September 1943, at which all the major American Jewish organizations, with the exception of Agudath Israel and Agudas Harabonim, were represented. (The failure to place rescue on the agenda was one of the primary reasons that the latter two groups withdrew

---

1. "Rosh Hashanah — 5703," *Orthodox Youth*, September 1943, p. 1.

from the Conference.[2]) The call to the Conference specifically limited the agenda to discussions of "the rights and status of Jews in the post-war world" and "implementation of the rights of the Jewish people with respect to Palestine." A resolution calling for the creation of a Jewish state in Palestine passed overwhelmingly despite warnings that such a resolution would only harden British opposition to Jewish immigration during the war.[3]

Both in early 1944, when there were indications that Hungarian ruler Admiral Horthy was eager to ransom hundreds of thousands of Hungarian Jews, and later, after Hitler invaded Hungary and sent Adolph Eichmann to engineer the extinction of Hungarian Jewry, mainstream Jewish groups were almost totally uninvolved. Their energies were wholly consumed in a futile effort to pass a Palestine Resolution in Congress.[4]

But Mike and the other leading Orthodox activists never permitted themselves to push out of mind the thousands being slaughtered every day. No matter how often their attempts to sway the American government were rebuffed, they had no alternative but to keep trying. They could never forget that no matter how numerically insignificant the successes were in comparison to those who could not be saved, nevertheless each success represented a Jewish life. "He Who Saveth A Soul In Israel Createth A World" was the motto affixed to the September 1941 Report of the Refugee and Immigration Division and it was a motto that Mike and his followers lived by.

He never stopped pushing himself and others to remember what was at stake. In a letter to Joseph Rosenzweig, a wealthy leather goods manufacturer and major supporter throughout the war years, Mike revealed how hard he himself fought against complacency:

> *Erev Yom Tov,* I spoke to Switzerland and received the most tragic and distressing news about our great *gedolim* and fellow

---

2. David Wyman, *The Abandonment of the Jews: America and the Holocaust 1941-1945,* p. 162. Wyman, who is not Jewish, is the preeminent student of American governmental responses to the destruction of European Jewry, and this chapter relies heavily on both *The Abandonment of the Jews* (Random House, 1984) and his earlier *Paper Walls: America and the Refugee Crisis 1938-1941* (University of Massachusetts Press, 1968). Meticulously researched and passionately argued, Wyman's work is a damning account of the general indifference of both the American government and the American people to the slaughter of millions of Jews.

3. Ibid., pp. 161, 164.

4. Ibid., p. 252.

Jews in Poland. I couldn't sit at the *Seder* table with the stark and realistic truth revolving in my mind. I berated myself at how completely indifferent we had become to the entire situation and that it was vital for us to drop our complacency and do everything possible to give quick and immediate aid to those thousands of Jews who are living in such abject misery in the ghettos of Poland.[5]

How well Mike succeeded in keeping constantly in front of him the plight of those on whose behalf he was working is attested to by all those who worked with him. When he learned that Rabbi Menachem Ziemba had been killed in the Warsaw Ghetto, he fainted.[6]

Talking about reports received from Europe that Jewish bodies were being used to manufacture soap, Mike would weep uncontrollably.[7] In the midst of discussing his Washington meetings with his Pirchei groups, he would sometimes start sobbing so violently that he could not catch his breath, as he described how Jews could be saved and nothing was being done.[8]

His joy at success was no less intense. When the call came through from Rabbi Aharon Kotler in Kobe, Japan that he had reached safety, Mike was, recalls Rabbi Chaim Uri Lipshitz, "as happy as if his father had been saved. You couldn't believe the way he was dancing, even though he had never seen Reb Aharon or read anything he had written." The same dancing for joy greeted the news that Julius Steinfeld had been granted a visa to enter the United States from Cuba. As head

Julius Steinfeld

---

5. Mike Tress to Joseph Rosenzweig, April 23, 1942.

6. Told to Mendel Tress by Rabbi Moshe Sherer. The Refugee and Immigration Division had earlier succeeded in procuring a visa for Rabbi Ziemba, but plans for his escape from Poland were thwarted by the Nazis.

7. Interview with Robert Krane.

8. Interview with Gavriel Beer.
   Rabbi Yaakov Goldstein has similar memories of Mike crying about how much could be done

of the Vienna Agudah, Steinfeld was forced to maintain extensive contacts with Nazi officials for two years as the Agudah carried out its relief projects in Vienna. But those contacts created suspicions on the part of the State Department that he was a German spy, and it took Mike almost two years of continuing pressure to win an American visa.[9]

Nor did Mike spare others the agony of what was happening in Europe. A fundraising letter written in March 1942 concluded:

> I don't think you will be content to sit down at your *Seder* table knowing that you might have aided many of our brethren to have some semblance of a *Yom Tov*, but that due to your indifference they will have to do without any help whatsoever.
> This letter may sound a little harsh, but in these desperate times we must be direct and emphatic.[10]

American Jewish leaders in general were unable to break out of their business-as-usual mode. As historian David Wyman concludes his scathing indictment, "Too few schedules were rearranged. Vacations were seldom sacrificed. Too few projects of lesser significance were put aside." Polish underground agent Jan Karski was sent in 1942 to alert the world to the fate awaiting Warsaw's Jews with the sardonic comment:

> Jewish leaders abroad won't be interested. At eleven in the morning, you will begin telling them about the anguish of the Jews of Poland, but at one o'clock they will ask you to halt the narrative so they can have lunch.[11]

---

with a little more money as they walked on Wythe Avenue together after the nighttime *shiurim* at 616 Bedford Avenue.

As critical as he was of the mainstream Jewish organizations and leaders such as Stephen Wise for not doing more, Mike never attacked those leaders publicly other than to say, "They just don't understand; they just don't understand." *Interview with Rabbi Ephraim Wolf.*

9. The visa was finally procured when 24 young men then serving in the American army went to Washington to testify in support of Steinfeld, and an English M.P. submitted an affidavit that he had been responsible for saving many lives. *Interview with Charles Richter, Steinfeld's son-in-law.*

10. Fundraising letter dated March 20, 1942 on behalf of the Refugee and Immigration Division and signed by Michael G. Tress, National Chairman, and Louis J. Septimus, Administrative Chairman.

11. Wyman, *The Abandonment of the Jews*, pp. 329-330.

Nor were the sins of the mainstream Jewish establishment limited to ones of omission. The leading Zionist organizations were so fearful of the growing influence of the Revisionist Zionist group led by Peter Bergson that they sought to stymie all the Bergsonites' efforts to arouse American public opinion for large-scale rescue. When the Bergsonites, aided by such Hollywood

By contrast, Mike insisted throughout the war that there could be no normal life while fellow Jews were being murdered.

Even as they kept their minds focused on the fate of the their brothers in Europe, rescue activists could never give full vent to their anger. The State Department bureaucrats working so assiduously to foil every rescue plan may have been accomplices in genocide. But the rescue activists could not simply say so, no matter how emotionally satisfying doing so might have been. Nothing would be achieved without the good will of the State Department, and today's frustrations could therefore never be allowed to explode at the expense of tomorrow's opportunity.[12] Rabbi Avraham Kalmanowitz, Rabbi Aharon Kotler, Mike, Irving Bunim, and others had to keep trying to arouse feelings of human sympathy in those who often appeared to be entirely devoid of

talent as Ben Hecht, Kurt Weill, Edward G. Robinson, and Paul Muni, mounted a pageant entitled "We Will Never Die," which drew 40,000 viewers to Madison Square Garden, and 60,000 more in five cities around the country, mainstream Jewish organizations orchestrated a campaign to dissuade sponsoring committees from mounting the pageant in other cities. This despite the fact that the pageant had proven itself to be the most successful instrument to date in arousing the American public to the plight of European Jews. Wyman, *The Abandonment of the Jews*, pp. 90-92.

Similarly, mainline Zionist organizations worked behind the scenes to prevent passage of a Rescue Resolution, which urged the President to create a commission to save the surviving Jews of Europe "from extinction at the hands of Nazi Germany," in late 1943 because the primary sponsor of the resolution was the Bergsonite Emergency Committee. Stephen Wise, the preeminent American Jewish leader, made clear in his Congressional testimony that he was opposed to the resolution unless it was coupled with a demand for the immediate opening of Palestine to Jewish refugees. Yet it was the likelihood of passage of the resolution that forced Roosevelt to create the War Refugee Board in January 1944. Though the WRB was severely limited by budgetary constraints and continued State Department obstructionism, it proved to be the only effective American effort to save Jewish lives and in the end played a crucial role in rescuing as many as 200,000 Jews. Ibid., pp. 193-206, 285.

12. There were countless ways in which all rescue activities were dependent on the State Department. For example, the Refugee and Immigration Division used State Department cables to contact consuls abroad for information on the progress of visa applications. The use of these cables was designed to expedite the process, but it was expensive.

The files of the Refugee and Immigration Division are filled with thousands of letters to relatives of applicants for visas asking them to reimburse the expense of cable transmissions. The perpetually financially strapped Refugee and Immigration Division could not afford to cover the transmissions itself nor could it afford to ignore dunning letters from the State Department since it required continued access to State Department cables. Thus even where use of the cables only elicited negative responses concerning the visa application, there was no choice but to seek reimbursement from the sponsoring relative.

At one point, the Refugee and Immigration Division ran up a huge bill of $3,335.89 with the State Department for cables to Kaunas (Kovno), Moscow, and Japan with lists of the names of rabbis for whom visas had been authorized. Mike was forced to turn to Rabbi Eliezer Silver — as was so often the case where money was needed — to make up the shortfall of $2,336.96 from the Refugee and Immigration Division's fundraising efforts. In a September 17, 1941 letter to Rabbi Silver, Mike emphasized the importance of maintaining "our good reputation with the Department of State."

R' Avraham Kalmanowitz

Irving Bunim

them. Their self-control, however, ultimately won for them significant concessions that a more adversarial posture would not have.[13]

On the one hand, constant reflection on the situation in Europe posed the danger of insanity. On the other hand, there was the danger of growing numb from the seemingly endless paperwork involved in processing visa applications — the visa application form instituted in July 1943, for instance, was four feet long and had to be filled out six times on both sides. And the constant exposure to cold bureaucratic doublespeak could cause one to lose sight of what was actually involved in each case. The finding of the U.S. Embassy in Moscow that the salaries of the Telshe Roshei Yeshiva Rabbi Eliyahu Meir Bloch and Rabbi Chaim Mordechai Katz were "not considered sufficient to support the large number of persons they must maintain," reads like a Dun and Bradstreet rating of credit worthiness. In reality, however, the denial of visas based on that finding sealed the fate of their wives and 17 children.[14] The files of several Jews provisionally approved for visas by the Berlin consul, but already deported to Poland, contains a note that "persons residing in German-occupied Poland ... are experiencing difficulty in obtaining

13. See Chapter 15 (pp. 266-8) for a discussion of Assistant Secretary of State Breckenridge Long's attitude to the Orthodox rescue activists.

14. The State Department finding was sent to Mike April 12, 1941. In July, the Jews of Telshe were wiped out.

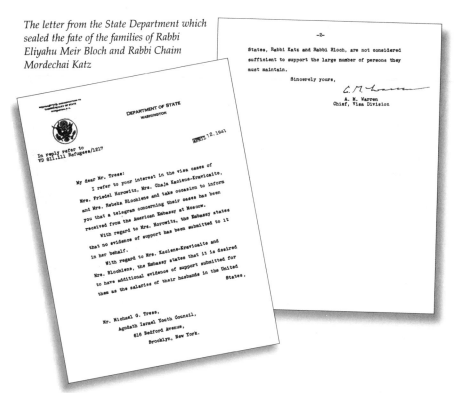

The letter from the State Department which sealed the fate of the families of Rabbi Eliyahu Meir Bloch and Rabbi Chaim Mordechai Katz

-2-

States, Rabbi Katz and Rabbi Bloch, are not considered sufficient to support the large number of persons they must maintain.

Sincerely yours,

A. M. Warren
Chief, Visa Division

DEPARTMENT OF STATE
WASHINGTON

APRIL 12, 1941

In reply refer to
VD 811.111 Refugees/1217

My dear Mr. Tress:

I refer to your interest in the visa cases of Mrs. Friedel Horowitz, Mrs. Chaja Kaciene-Kravicaite, and Mrs. Rebeka Blochiene and take occasion to inform you that a telegram concerning their cases has been received from the American Embassy at Moscow.

With regard to Mrs. Horowitz, the Embassy states that no evidence of support has been submitted to it in her behalf.

With regard to Mrs. Kaciene-Kravicaite and Mrs. Blochiene, the Embassy states that it is desired to have additional evidence of support submitted for them as the salaries of their husbands in the United States,

Mr. Michael G. Tress,
Agudath Israel Youth Council,
616 Bedford Avenue,
Brooklyn, New York.

permission to emigrate from Germany."[15] Again, the tone is that of a weatherman's travel advisory rather than what it really was: a reflection of the promise of General Frank, the Nazi military governor of Poland, that not a single Jew would escape Poland alive.

MIKE WAS IN ALMOST DAILY CONTACT WITH THE STATE DEPART-ment over the entire course of the war, and it is therefore impossible to

Playing Against a Stacked Deck

appreciate the frustrations he experienced without an understanding of the attitudes toward immigration and the rescue of Jews then prevalent in the State Department. State Department obstruction-ism proved to be the major obstacle to saving hundreds of thousands of European Jews. The middle echelons of the State Department and many of the consular offices abroad were filled with extreme nativists[16]

---

15. Files of Etta and Schimon Lejb Nachman and Max Roth.

16. Wyman, *The Abandonment of the Jews*, p. 313. David Wyman, himself the descendant of Protestant ministers, describes the State Department as being filled with "old-stock Protestants." But being Protestant was, of course, neither a necessary or sufficient condition for anti-Semitism. Though the Treasury Department was headed by Henry Morgenthau Jr., the Roosevelt

profoundly suspicious of Eastern European immigrants in general and Jews in particular.[17]

Sometimes the indifference of State Department bureaucrats — indifference that bordered on wanton cruelty — became simply overwhelming. Mike once complained to Reb Aharon Kotler that a certain State Department official was shortening his life with his obstreperousness. Reb Aharon replied, *"Ehr kertzert dayneh yahren? Ehr kertzert zayneh yahren.* He's shortening your life? He's shortening his own life." The next day the man died an abnormal death.[18]

Nevertheless, it would be a mistake to view the State Department as a malevolent body betraying the good intentions of the American people and their president. State Department policy fully reflected the desires of the majority of Americans. Two thirds of Americans, in one 1938 poll, opposed any immigration at all, and between 71% and 85%, in a series of polls, were against increasing the existing quotas in response to the Nazi rise to power. Even a proposed one-time exemption for 20,000 refugee children to enter the country over a two-year period was opposed by over three fifths of those asked. Roosevelt's Third War Powers Bill was overwhelmingly defeated in late 1942, in large part due to Congressional suspicions that it would permit suspension of immigration quotas. And a similar fate befell a bill to simplify naturalization of aliens already living in the United States and who had children

---

Administration's most prominent Jew, most of the leading Treasury officials who pushed for a more sympathetic response to the extermination of European Jewry, such as Josiah E. Dubois and John Pehle, later executive director of the War Refugee Board, were not.

Moreover, Jews were capable of expressing nativist sentiments no different than those of other State Department officials. In a telegram to the chief architect of State Department immigration policy, Assistant Secretary of State Breckenridge Long, Laurence A. Steinhardt, American Ambassador to Russia, characterized the typical Eastern European immigrant as the same type of "lawless, scheming, . . . criminal Jews who crowd our police docket in New York. . . . Wyman, *Paper Walls*, p. 146. (Later, as ambassador to Turkey, Steinhardt did act to open up Turkey as a sanctuary.) And it was frequently President Roosevelt's Jewish advisors, such as Samuel Rosenman, who were most adamant that he should not be seen as devoting special attention to the fate of Europe's Jewish population.

17. Wyman concludes that anti-Semitism was rife in consuls abroad. Ibid., p. 190. One relief worker in Unoccupied France was told by a consular official that he hoped she was not involved in helping Jews emigrate to the United States. When she asked what he thought should be done with them, he imitated someone holding a machine gun mowing down a line of people in front of him. Wyman, *Paper Walls*, p. 163. A Yugoslavian refugee in Switzerland had the impression her visa request was being held up because the consul thought she was Jewish. As soon as she made clear that she was not, her visa was forthcoming.

18. Heard by Yitzchak Zvi Tress from Rabbi Avraham Chaim Spitzer.

There is an interesting parallel to this story. Once Mike was subjected to constant heckling during a speech in Toronto. That heckler died of a heart attack the next day. *Interview with Morley Auerbach.*

serving in the American armed services. Even after the full horrors of the concentration camps were revealed, only 5 percent of Americans supported any relaxation of immigration restrictions.[19]

Anti-Semitism played a significant role in this anti-immigrant sentiment. The '30s and early '40s in America witnessed the rise of several prominent anti-Semites on the national scene, including Father Charles E. Coughlin and Gerald L. K. Smith. In New York City and Boston, incidents of vandalism against Jewish institutions and attacks on Jewish children by youth gangs proliferated in the early '40s. Over half of Americans perceived Jews as greedy and dishonest, and an even larger percentage felt they wielded too much power. Polls taken between 1938 and 1945 showed that 15 percent of Americans would have supported an anti-Jewish movement, and another 25 percent would have been sympathetic. Audiences, in one study, responded with seven times more revulsion to information concerning Nazi atrocities when the Jewish identity of the victims was hidden.[20]

Rampant anti-Semitism was one of the reasons that President Roosevelt — frequently on the advice of his Jewish advisors — was so reluctant to give any appearance of special solicitude for Jewish victims of the war in Europe. He did not wish to furnish opponents of the "Jew Deal" any further ammunition. Thus it was almost a year after State Department confirmation of the Nazi intention to wipe out European Jewry before the President even mentioned in one of his weekly press conferences the Nazis' plan or how far they had gone towards realizing their goals.

The almost total absence of press coverage of the Holocaust reflects both the general apathy of the American public to the deaths of millions of Jews and helps explain that continued apathy. The most widely covered event of the early years of the Holocaust was the deportation of thousands of Jews from Vichy France in July and August of 1942. Yet even *The New York Times,* which provided the most extensive coverage, only put the story on the front page twice — each time when it involved the attempted intervention of a Catholic official — and only at the foot of the page. Few papers even carried the story of 4,000 children being crammed into boxcars, unaccompanied by adults, for shipment to the East.[21] Though many of the deportees were old, infirm, or children too

---

19. Wyman, *The Abandonment of the Jews,* pp. 10, 56-57, 151.

20. Ibid., pp. 10-15, 157.

21. Ibid., p. 38.

young to work, no American newspaper drew the obvious inference: the Nazi cover story that they were intended for slave labor was patently false.

When the State Department, after months of dallying, finally confirmed on November 24, 1942 the existence of the Nazi extermination camps and the murder of 2,000,000 Jews to date, only five of the leading national papers placed the story on the front page, and none prominently. President Roosevelt's meeting with Jewish leaders two weeks later, at which time he confirmed the figure of 2,000,000 murdered, was relegated to page 20 of *The New York Times*. In the five weeks following confirmation of the killing camps, the Holocaust merited only one small item in *The New York Times* 10-page week-in-review section. Two years later, press coverage was still no better. A report that 400,000 Hungarian Jews had been deported to the extermination camps in Poland and another 350,000 were scheduled for imminent deportation merited only page 12 mention in *The New York Times*.

While the State Department's policies were consistent with the general attitudes of the American people, its antipathy to Jewish immigration went far beyond any legislative mandate. Seventy-five thousand Jews had sought a tenuous refuge in Unoccupied France for two years before the Nazis and their Vichy collaborators began large-scale deportations. During that time, the relevant immigration quotas for those refugees were 90 percent unfilled.[22] That percentage of unused slots remained constant from Pearl Harbor to the end of the war.[23]

From mid-1940, Assistant Secretary of State Breckenridge Long, supported by J. Edgar Hoover, Director of the FBI, became obsessed with the idea that the Germans intended to slip spies into the United States posing as refugees, and ordered every possible barrier to be put in the way of the issuance of visas. In an internal memo, Long spelled out his intentions clearly:

> We can delay and effectively stop for a temporary period of indefinite length the number of immigrants into the United States. We could do this by simply advising our consuls to put every obstacle in the way and to require additional evidence and to resort to various administrative devices which

22. Ibid., p. 38.
23. Ibid., p. 136.

would postpone and postpone and postpone the granting of the visas.[24]

Given the precarious situation in which most visa seekers found themselves, that postponement was usually forever.

A year later, after having obtained legislation requiring the exclusion of all aliens who might pose a threat to national security, the State Department put into effect an even more impregnable bureaucratic maze for visa seekers. Each application had to pass an interdepartmental security review. That process took at least nine months. The four foot long form required such detailed personal information about the applicant's sponsors that only the most determined sponsor would not have been deterred. In addition, the State Department enunciated a new rule that those with close relatives in enemy-occupied territory were presumptively barred on the grounds that once in America they would be subject to pressure from enemy agents. Since virtually every area of Europe with a large Jewish population was then under Axis control, the rule effectively barred all Jewish immigration.[25] A group of Treasury

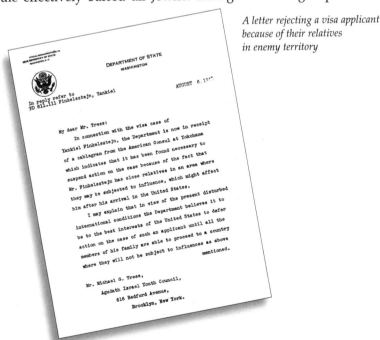

A letter rejecting a visa applicant because of their relatives in enemy territory

---

24. Wyman, *Paper Walls*, p. 173.

25. Wyman, *Paper Walls*, Chapter 9; Wyman, *The Abandonment of the Jews*, pp. 127-128.

officials reviewing State Department regulations concluded:

> If anyone were to attempt to work out a set of restrictions specifically designed to prevent Jewish refugees from entering this country, it is difficult to conceive of how more effective restrictions could have been imposed than those already imposed on grounds of security.

Just in case any Jewish immigrants managed to slip through all these barriers, the State Department had a few more "Catch-22" provisions up its sleeve. Those in Axis-controlled countries could not get visas because there were no American consuls to issue them, and those who managed to escape to neutral countries were often denied visas on the grounds that they were no longer in immediate danger.[26] Another trap was the requirement that refugees complete their travel arrangements prior to the issuance of a visa. Thus the would-be immigrant was forced to spend whatever little money was left on the purchase of tickets without any assurance that he would be able to use them.[27]

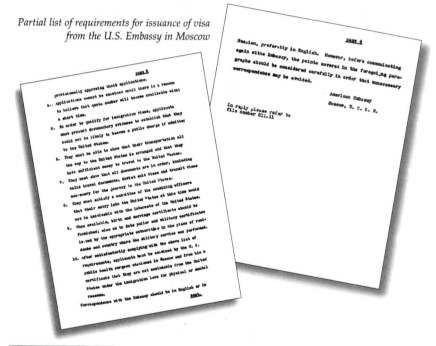

Partial list of requirements for issuance of visa from the U.S. Embassy in Moscow

---

26. Ibid., p. 127.

27. A particularly cruel version of this trap was practiced on a group of refugees who had managed to escape to North Africa. U.S. naval commanders were prepared to transport them across the Atlantic to safety but only on the condition that they had visas and quota numbers. The Visa

Immigration matters were only one area of Mike's contacts with the State Department. As the circle of his Washington connections grew, he became one of those most actively involved in pushing plans for the rescue of thousands of Jews trapped in areas held or dominated by the Nazis. Here too, he faced a steady pattern of State Department obstructionism.

It is no exaggeration to say that the overriding concern of State Department policymakers was not that Jews would die if nothing were done but the opposite: that Hitler might actually agree to release captive Jews on a world that did not want them. Treasury official Randolph Paul characterized the leading State Department policymakers dealing with the issue as an "underground movement ... to let Jews be killed."[28]

Typically, the British were more cold blooded and forthright in their attitude. The British Foreign Office worried openly that "the Germans or their satellites may change over from the policy of extermination to one of extrusion, and aim as they did before the war at embarrassing other countries by flooding them with alien immigrants."[29] Consistent with that worry, Foreign Secretary Anthony Eden warned Secretary of State Cordell Hull that the Allies should be very wary of any effort to rescue 70,000 Bulgarian Jews threatened with imminent extinction: "If we do that, then the Jews of the world will be wanting us to make similar offers in Poland and Germany. Hitler might well take us up on any such offer. ..."[30] In other words, no efforts should be made to approach Hitler for the release of Jews, not because such an approach was futile but because it might succeed.

Soon American officials were echoing the British line. One Visa Division official criticized rescue proposals as designed to "take the burden and the curse [i.e., the Jews] off Hitler." And another asked reporters on the eve of the Bermuda Conference, "Suppose [Hitler] did let 2,000,000 or so Jews out of Europe, what would we do with them?"[31]

State Department actions fully reflected concerns that Hitler or his satellites might dump the Jews in their lap. In September 1942, Gerhard Riegner of the World Jewish Congress in Geneva was the first to convey to the West a report of the Nazi decision taken at the Wannsee Conference in Berlin in January 1942 to wipe out all of Europe's Jews. In

Division of the State Department, however, refused to issue quota numbers until transportation arrangements were finalized. Wyman, *The Abandonment of the Jews*, p. 128.

28. Ibid., p. 190.
29. Ibid., p. 105.
30. Ibid., p. 97.
31. Ibid., pp. 99, 120.

early 1943, he sent a second message through the American consul in Bern detailing on a country-by-country basis the number of Jews murdered to date. The State Department ordered the consul not to transmit any more such cables in an effort to prevent pressure from building for some type of American rescue operation.

The demonstrable falsity of many of the reasons given for not doing more for European Jewry is another indication of the general indifference of the State Department. The most commonly given excuse for the failure to transfer Jews in imminent danger to safe havens in North Africa or elsewhere was that no ships could be spared without impairing the war effort. The same reason was given for the failure to pursue feelers from the Romanian and Hungarian governments eager to ransom their Jewish populations. Not a single ship was specifically requisitioned for rescue of Jews. Yet, as David Wyman notes:

> During 1942, 1943, and 1944, the Allies evacuated large numbers of non-Jewish Yugoslavs, Poles, and Greeks to safety in the Middle East, Africa, and elsewhere. Difficulties that constantly ruled out the rescue of Jews dissolved. Transportation somehow materialized to move 100,000 people to dozens of refugee camps that sprang into existence.[32]

Ships bringing supplies from American to Europe were returning to America empty while Jews were dying because "no ships were available."

The provision of food to starving Jews in Nazi-held territory was another issue on which the Allied hypocrisy was evident. The British insisted that shipments to hostage Jews somehow aided the Nazi war effort, and America by and large went along with that view.[33] Yet when the Greeks were suffering terrible famine under Nazi occupation — albeit their average daily caloric intake was 50 percent higher than that of Jews in Polish ghettos — the Allies chartered ships to move in tens of millions of dollars of foodstuffs over a period of three years.[34]

Jews, as always, were different.

---

32. Ibid., p. 328.

33. Beginning in 1942, the United States permitted the shipment of $12,000 per month of foodstuffs to captive territory, a pittance. The War Refugee Board, created in 1944, took the position that there was no justification for existing restrictions and some larger amounts of food began to be moved to starving Jews in late 1944 and 1945. Wyman, *The Abandonment of the Jews,* pp. 283-84.

34. Wyman, *The Abandonment of the Jews,* pp. 281-83.

Chapter Fifteen

THE REFUGEE
AND IMMIGRATION DIVISION

U NFORTUNATELY, THE INDIFFERENCE OF THE STATE
Department was not the only type that Mike had to

**The Kopyczinitzer
Rebbe's Love**

overcome in his rescue
efforts. Even in the
American Orthodox
world, apathy was widespread. In early 1944, for
instance, Rabbi Chaim Uri Lipshitz tried, at Mike's
urging, to arrange a meeting in Philadelphia in
response to urgent pleas for funds from Rabbi
Michoel Ber Weissmandl. Of the between 150 and
200 Orthodox Jews he called, only one — Rabbi Max
Borchardt — showed up.[1]

A guest at a kosher resort in Saratoga Springs was
told when she read aloud from Holocaust coverage in

1. Interview with Rabbi Chaim Uri Lipshitz.

The Kopyczinitzer Rebbe

the Jewish press, "We don't want to hear. We're here to have a good time."[2] That response was not atypical.

Rabbi Sysche Heschel was once asked to explain the tremendous love his father the Kopyczinitzer Rebbe had for Mike Tress. He answered with the following story:

Shortly after his arrival in the United States from Vienna, the Rebbe was approached by a Jew seeking a blessing for livelihood. In Vienna, the Rebbe had witnessed the Nazis rounding up Jews and sending community leaders to Dachau and other concentration camps, and he told the man that for $500 it was still possible to purchase the necessary papers to help a family out of Europe. The man looked at the Rebbe as if he were crazy.

The Rebbe continued, "You don't understand. I've seen what's going on, and if you don't help, these people are going to die. You must give."

The Jew replied that $500 was an enormous sum and far beyond his means. With that, the Rebbe started crying. The Rebbe's crying left the man uncomfortable, but essentially unmoved, and he pleaded with the Rebbe to stop: "Please, Rebbe, stop crying. Just tell me what your cut is from the $500, and I'll give it to you."

"When my father heard that," says Rabbi Heschel, "he realized that the Jews of Europe were doomed and that there would be no salvation from American Jewry." The Kopyczinitzer loved Mike because he was one American Jew for whom there was no rest as long as there was any possible way of saving Jewish lives in Europe.

---

2. Interview with Rebbetzin Rose Isbee.

Mike not only made the plight of European Jewry his own, he inspired hundreds of others to do the same. The work of the Refugee and Immigration Division could not have been done by Mike alone, or even by five Mikes working around the clock. Every week hundreds of letters came to 616 Bedford Avenue from around the world; every day 50 or 60 cables.[3] In the first two years of its existence, the Refugee and Immigration Division provided advice on immigration matters to 7,500 people.[4] For those without a sponsor in the United States, the Refugee and Immigration Division was virtually the only venue to which they could turn for help.[5] An article on the Division in *Orthodox Youth* invited all readers to come the office and lend their time and energy to the cause. They were assured, "Everyone can be used."[6]

The Refugee and Immigration Division office buzzed nearly around the clock. "There was no day or night," recalls Moshe Berger, who ran the Division. As often as not, Berger found himself sleeping at 616 Bedford Avenue rather than in his own bed. Young idealists, like Heshy Moskowitz, would return to Williamsburg from their night college classes at 11 p.m. and come to the offices at 616 to type out visa applications for a few more hours. Appointments were made for the small hours of the morning when no other time could be found,[7] and Mike and others often went out pleading for affidavits of financial support until well after midnight.[8]

Affidavits and Visas

ZEIREI WAS ALREADY INVOLVED IN SOME VISA WORK BY 1938, BUT the Refugee and Immigration Division did not really take off until the move to 616 Bedford Avenue. Gershon Kranzler and Moshe Berger were given some hurried training in the technical aspects of visa work by Meir Schenkolewski,[9] and the work began.

The Refugee and Immigration Division thus came into being at the very height of wartime immigration to the United States. At the July

---

3. *Orthodox Youth*, April 1941, p. 7.

4. Report of the Refugee and Immigration Division of Agudath Israel Youth, September 1941, p. 4.

5. Harry Sherer, "The Immigration Problem Today," *Orthodox Youth*, June 1942, pp. 3, 10.

6. *Orthodox Youth*, April 1941, p. 7.

7. Interview with Moshe Berger.

8. Interview with Max Gross.

9. Schenkolewski, who immigrated from Germany in the early '30s, headed the American fundraising for the European Bais Yaakov movement. At the same time, he gained experience in visa procedures working for Rabbi Leo Jung, who, besides being an active supporter of the European Bais Yaakov, was one of the first to see the need for active visa work.

1938 Evian Conference dealing with the issue of Jewish refugees from Germany and Austria, President Roosevelt pledged that the United States would fully utilize available immigrant quotas from Germany and Austria.[10] (After the German takeover of Austria, in March 1938, the quotas of the two countries were lumped together by presidential order, which gave refugees from Austria, with its far smaller quota, an opportunity to emigrate they otherwise would not have had.) Clerks were added to consular offices in Vienna, Berlin, and Prague in order to expedite the processing of visas.[11]

The most crucial step in the immigration process was the first: obtaining an affidavit of financial support from an American sponsor. At least until 1940, when the State Department became obsessed with "fifth columnists" entering the country, the primary concern of consular officials abroad was establishing that the prospective immigrant and his family would not become public charges in the event that he could not find work or became unemployed. Each consul had, under the law, absolute discretion with respect to the granting of visas, and there was substantial diversity between various consular offices as to what was considered an adequate affidavit. The "stronger" the affidavit, the better the chance of the visa being granted.

Unfortunately, the Orthodox world in the early '40s could claim few members with sufficient resources to fill out affidavits that would not be rejected. In addition, the language of the affidavit appeared to subject the affiant to potentially large liability — i.e., the support of the

---

10. Wyman, *Paper Walls*, p. 49, 168.

11. Ibid., p. 169.

The immigration quotas were relevant primarily for Jews able to qualify under the German quotas. Because immigration quotas were set according to the percentage of Americans from different European countries in the 1890 census, which was prior to the major Jewish immigration from Eastern Europe, the Eastern European quotas were very small.

By November 1939, Jews in Germany and Austria were having increasing difficulty emigrating directly from those countries because foreign steamship companies would no longer accept German currency. As a consequence, an increasingly large percentage of the German quota numbers were being used by families that had already escaped Germany. Many had reached relative safety in England or Cuba, others were in neutral Switzerland, still others in imminent danger in Unoccupied France, and finally, a large group of German refugees faced an uncertain future in Spain, Portugal, or Shanghai.

Even though the procurement of visas for those who had already reached some neutral countries or England was not immediately lifesaving, it was nevertheless crucial. The greater the number of refugees that could be moved through neutral countries, the more refugees those countries were prepared to accept. In addition, many of the refugees lived under conditions of extreme hardship. A large percentage of those in Spain and Unoccupied France and Spain, for instance, were interned, and those in France were in grave jeopardy, as subsequent events proved.

immigrant's entire family. Only the most idealistic were prepared to take on such a risk. Finally, the affidavits required the affiant to provide a wealth of financial data about himself, something many potential sponsors were unwilling to do.

Overcoming these obstacles required ingenuity, energy, and heart. Mike came up with the idea of transferring money from the bank accounts of his few wealthy supporters to the bank accounts of others who were willing to sign to make it appear that the latter possessed sufficient resources.[12] To reassure those afraid of incurring a large financial liability, the Youth Council undertook to reimburse the affiant for any expenses he might incur if the government sued him to support an indigent immigrant.

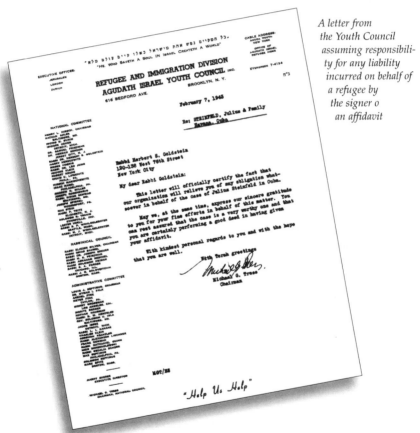

A letter from the Youth Council assuming responsibility for any liability incurred on behalf of a refugee by the signer o an affidavit

---

12. Interview with Charlie Klein.

This ploy took many forms. Shea and Jack Gold and their brother-in-law Abe Staum used to transfer the assets of their partnership from the bank account of one partner to that of another so that each of them could in turn sign affidavits that would hold up under consular scrutiny. *Interview with Rabbi Avie Gold.*

Mike, Gershon Kranzler, Moshe Berger, and a variety of volunteers combed New York City and the Eastern seaboard in search of Jews willing to sign affidavits. On one occasion, Berger came to the office of a dentist in Newark, who had a patient in the chair. While the uncomprehending patient lay tilted back in the chair, the dentist proceeded to sign a number of forms. He told the patient, "These people need my help now."[13]

The Septimus brothers obtained hundreds of affidavits — most of them from clients of their growing accounting practice. They would acquire pads of 50 forms and urge clients to sign a number at a time. Once they had the signatures, the Septimus brothers would fill out the forms. Every night Louis Septimus was at 616 Bedford Avenue helping people fill out affidavits so that there would always be extra affidavits on file to be used as the need arose.[14] Asked for the secret of their success, Louis Septimus had a one-word explanation: tears.

Tears were, in fact, the primary weapon in the young activists' arsenal. Moshe Berger heard of a Jewish real estate magnate named Slutsky, who was reputed to "own half of Brooklyn." Though the man was not known to give charity of any kind, the young immigrant decided there was nothing to lose by trying and called Mr. Slutsky at his home. He was given an appointment for the next day at Slutsky's office in the Empire State Building. Arriving at the office, Berger informed the secretary that he had an appointment and waited expectantly. The secretary, however, took one look at him, recognized that he was not a business associate of her boss, and told him that he must be mistaken. Berger insisted, and she reluctantly went in to Slutsky's office to ask. Coming sheepishly out of the office, the secretary motioned Berger in.

Berger found himself ushered into a capacious office, where a little man sat behind a huge desk. Mr. Slutsky indicated that Berger should begin. The young man froze momentarily. When he regained the power of speech, the words tumbled out in an emotional torrent as he described the situation of the Jews in Europe (from which he had so recently arrived.) When the breathless Berger had finished, Mr. Slutsky told him in a still Yiddish-inflected accent, "I've been in this country 40 years and I've never done a favor for anyone. I'm going to start now." He then pushed a buzzer on his desk summoning his son, whom he told, "Write this man whatever he tells you." When the son started to

---

13. Interview with Moshe Berger.

14. That practice only worked in the first year or so of the affidavit work. Afterwards, most consuls required that the affiant be a close relative unless he was a person of substantial means. Wyman, *Paper Walls*, p. 170.

protest, his father shut him up. Before Berger left, Mr. Slutsky told him to bring to his office any immigrant who came to the country on one of his affidavits and he would furnish the immigrant's family with an apartment rent free for a year.[15]

In time, Mike acquired a group of supporters who provided the Refugee and Immigration Division with a major source of affidavits. Irving Bunim, Nathan Hausman, Earl Spero, and Lester Udell signed affidavits, in Moshe Berger's words, "right and left." Though there was no limit on how many affidavits a person could sign, and affiants were not asked how many other affidavits they had signed, the number of Udell's affidavits was so great that it eventually aroused suspicions in Washington, D.C. He was called by the Visa Division of the State Department, and asked whether he was related to all those for whom he was taking responsibility. He replied that all Jews are cousins.

A letter from Mr. Udell, long-time chairman of the Refugee and Immigration Division, soliciting affidavits since his were no longer accepted

---

15. Berger interview.

Thereafter, the government placed tighter restrictions on those who could sign affidavits.[16]

AMONG THOSE WHO FILLED OUT MANY AFFIDAVITS WERE ROBERT Krane, a successful Wall Street lawyer, and his wife Ruth. Even before

The Kranes they met Mike, the Kranes, who had no dependents of their own, had started to fill out affidavits, but they were eager to become more heavily involved in saving Jews in Europe. Shortly after moving to Williamsburg, they learned from Reb Shraga Feivel Mendlowitz about a group of young people working around the clock on immigration matters.

Mrs. Krane went to 616 Bedford Avenue one Sunday morning to meet with Mike, and found him in the midst of a large group of young boys. The din was too great for Mrs. Krane to discuss with Mike the purpose of her visit, and she asked him what all the children were doing there. He explained that Pirchei was sponsoring a boatride that day at 50¢ a head, but that some of the boys did not have the money. In order to be rid of the children so she could speak with Mike, Mrs. Krane pulled a large bill from her pocketbook, and told Mike, "Let them all go on the ride."

At last able to talk with Mike, Mrs. Krane expressed her and her husband's eagerness to help with affidavits. Mike immediately recognized the Kranes' special qualities, and, in addition to using all the affidavits they could supply, set out to draw them closer to his circle. He began by inviting Mrs. Krane to join a *Tz'enah Ur'enah* study group organized by Rebbetzin Shifra Schorr. Acceptance in the group, however, required the approval of Mike's mother-in-law Mrs. Bagry, who wanted to be sure that only those who shared similar ideals were invited.

Mike arranged a meeting between Mrs. Krane and Mrs. Bagry. Luckily, Mrs. Krane, who was a prominent milliner, always wore a hat, and she passed Mrs. Bagry's inspection — more, the two quickly became close friends. Soon Mr. Krane began learning Gemara together Mrs. Bagry's oldest son Velvel. Mrs. Krane used to rock the cradle of

---

16. See note 14 above.

Louis Septimus once asked one of the Refugee and Immigration Division's most active sponsors to provide a bond for several members of the Boyaner Rebbe's family. The man, who had already lent the Division thousands of dollars, agreed, but only on the condition that the Boyaner Rebbe provide a written undertaking that he would make good on the bond if any liability was ever incurred. The Rebbe refused to do so on the grounds that it would be *geneivas daas* (deceitful) to sign such a promise since the potential liability was far beyond his means. When the sponsor heard that, he said, "For such a Jew, I'll give the bond anyway." *Interview with Louis Septimus.*

Robert Krane learning with Mike's son-in-law Rabbi Moshe Bloch

Velvel's oldest child so that Velvel and her husband could learn. (Mr. Krane finished *Shas* twice before he passed away.)

The Kranes supplied Mike with hundreds of affidavits. Among those were affidavits for the parents and sister of Dr. Naftali Hertz Bursztyn, a beloved Williamsburg physician.[17] Mike called the Kranes one night and told them that Dr. Bursztyn's parents and sister were booked on the last ship leaving Vienna, but that $450 were desperately needed to cover their transportation. When Mrs. Krane's father, Menachem Mendel Brawer, heard the story, he said, "I want this *mitzvah* for myself."

In time, the Kranes were numbered among the Tress family's closest friends. They were Uncle Robert and Tante Ruth to the Tress children, to whom they were always available to provide a sympathetic ear, a piece of sound advice, or a special treat. The Tress children have hundreds of letters written to them by Mrs. Krane at camp, and a number of Tress grandchildren and great-grandchildren are named after Mr. Krane or one of the Kranes' parents. The relationship the Kranes established with the Tress children soon extended to other

---

17. In Mike's last years, Dr. Bursztyn was frequently called to the house to ease his suffering, and he treated Mike with the solicitude of a brother. He was one of a group that dropped by the Tress home after Shabbos *davening*, if Mike had not been at 616 Bedford Avenue that morning, to offer encouragement.

families in Williamsburg and later Monsey, and though they never had children, they were blessed with as many "grandchildren, nieces, and nephews" as anyone could wish for.

The young people involved in the immigration work were operating in largely unchartered waters without any clear precedents to guide them. When conventional channels failed, they were always prepared to try something else. A good example of their innovative strategies was the case of Mrs. Rachel Kahan who arrived in the United States together were her infant son. Mrs. Kahan and her husband Benno had been living in Finland at the outbreak of the war and succeeded in obtaining American visas. Mr. Kahan's visa, however, was delayed, and as a consequence he could not depart with his wife and child as they left Finland and headed across the Soviet Union to Kobe, Japan, and from there to America. By the time the father's visa arrived, Japan was no longer issuing transit visas, and the father's only hope of rejoining his family lay in going West via neutral Sweden. Sweden, however, was then totally sealed to refugees.

Mrs. Kahan knew Gershon Kranzler from Germany, and she brought her problem to the Refugee and Immigration Division. Somehow Mike and Gershon Kranzler learned that there was a meeting of Scandanavian consul generals scheduled at the Waldorf-Astoria Hotel, and they arranged for Mrs. Kahan to meet with the Finnish consul Procope. The latter was so moved by her story that he spoke to the Swedish consul general Bostien, who agreed to see Mrs. Kahan. As a result of that meeting, Bostien sent a telegram to the King of Sweden, who personally secured a transit visa for Mr. Kahan.[18]

While the Kahan case was one of the most dramatic, it was just one of hundreds in which the Refugee and Immigration Division was involved. In the 12-month period beginning April 1940, nearly 1,300 affidavits were obtained, and as of September 1941, almost 1,000 visas

---

18. Interview with Chaim Kahan, the son of Mr. and Mrs. Kahan.

Mr. Benno Kahan provided the details of the story. Gershon Kranzler has a much more dramatic memory of what occurred. According to him, he and Mike came up with the wild idea of cabling the King of Sweden directly. See David Kranzler and Eliezer Gewirtz, *To Save a World*, pp. 135-36.

Mr. Kahan's travails did not end with the procuring of the Swedish transit visa. En route from Gotenberg, Sweden to Argentina, his ship was intercepted by a German ship. The German captain informed his Swedish counterpart that he knew there were Jewish stowaways aboard. The Swedish captain told Mr. Kahan to hide below deck under some grain. In the meantime, he invited the German captain aboard and plied him with Swedish rum before returning him to his ship dead drunk.

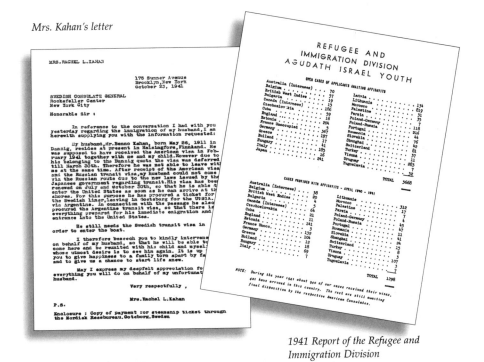

1941 Report of the Refugee and
Immigration Division

had been issued and more than 400 families had entered the United States in the calendar year 1941.[19]

Washington Trips

ALMOST FROM THE BEGINNING OF THE REFUGEE AND IMMIGRAtion Division, Mike began to travel at least once a week or so to Washington, D.C. in order to expedite the cases on which the Division was working.[20] The interest of a determined sponsor in a particular case could often hurry along the visa process considerably and make a favorable disposition far more likely.[21]

Though the 1924 Immigration Act vested the final decision on the issuance of a visa in the overseas consuls, nevertheless pressure could be applied in Washington on the State Department, and through the State Department on the consulates abroad. The consuls depended on

---

19. Report of the Refugee and Immigration Division of Agudath Israel Youth, September 1941, p. 5.

20. See, Harry Sherer, "The Immigration Problem Today," *Orthodox Youth*, June 1942, pp. 3, 10 for a discussion of Mike's successes in pushing cases ahead.

21. Wyman, *Paper Walls*, p. 160.

After the requirement of a formal security review by an interdepartmental committee was instituted in 1941, it became almost impossible to speed up the process in even the most urgent case. The security review took at least nine months.

their State Department superiors in Washington for their assignments and advancement, and were therefore unlikely to deny a visa where they knew that their superiors at home were favorably disposed.[22]

Mike began to cultivate important legislators in Washington, who could use their influence in the State Department. Rabbi Eliezer Silver introduced him to Senate Minority Leader Robert Taft of Ohio. And on the House side, Congressman Sol Bloom, chairman of the House Foreign Affairs Committee, helped Mike in a number of individual cases.[23]

Mike also had a keen sense of how many important favors low-level functionaries in a large bureaucracy can render if they so choose. He treated even the lowliest secretaries in the Visa Division with the type of consideration they received nowhere else, sending them boxes of chocolates to show his appreciation.[24]

In mid-1941 the State Department issued new regulations which had the effect of greatly complicating the visa process by requiring security

---

22. Unfortunately the State Department superiors were not favorably disposed, and overseas consuls, therefore, had a decided incentive to be reticent in the issuance of visas. Given Assistant Secretary of State Breckenridge Long's obsession with spies, the consuls knew that if a spy did enter the country on one of their visas, their career was in grave jeopardy. Wyman, *Paper Walls*, p. 166.

23. Bloom was unquestionably helpful in a number of cases involving leading rabbinic figures. In 1947, he was even the honoree at an Agudah banquet on the occasion of his 77th birthday. On general rescue issues, however, his record was far less good. He was a member of the American delegation to the Bermuda Conference, and afterwards defended the paltry results as the best that could have been achieved, which they certainly were not. As a result of the sharp criticism of the Bermuda Conference in general and Bloom in particular by the Bergsonite (Revisionist Zionists) Emergency Committee to Save the Jews of Europe — one ad read, "We would not be happy in your place Mr. Bloom. . . . We would feel blood, Jewish blood on our hands" — Bloom conceived an undying hatred for the Bergsonites. That hatred led him to bottle up the Bergsonite-sponsored Rescue Resolution indefinitely in the House Foreign Affairs Committee.

David Wyman summarizes his efforts critically:

> Despite his influential position in Congress, [Bloom] attempted next to nothing for the Jews of Europe. True, he arranged for several individual refugees to enter the United States. And he assisted the ... Vaad Hahatzala in some small ways. But when possibilities for major action arose, he consistently allied himself with the State Department.

Wyman, *The Abandonment of the Jews*, pp. 201-202.

24. A December 11, 1945 memo to Mike from his administrative secretary Mrs. Donya Bagry mentions the receipt of a thank-you note from Mrs. Griffith of the Visa Division for a box of chocolates Mike had sent her. Answering the letter, Mrs. Bagry asked for the names of all the girls assisting a certain Mrs. Bossert so that they too could be sent candy.

Mike remembered the birthdays of important officials as evidenced by a May 14, 1952 letter from Eliot Coulter, head of the Visa Division, thanking Mike for a birthday telegram. A month later, Coulter wrote again to thank Mike for "two beautiful suitcases" Mike had sent him in anticipation of an upcoming vacation: "I have appreciated your friendship during the years and know that I have your good wishes. . . . You really shouldn't have sent the suitcases for they must have cost a very sizeable sum."

checks by at least five agencies on any prospective immigrant. With the issuance of the regulations, Mike's Washington trips took on added significance.

In response to protests from James McDonald, chairman of the President's Advisory Committee on Political Refugees (PAC), and others that the regulations had effectively ended the issuance of visas just when the need was most pressing, President Roosevelt agreed to the creation of a Board of Appeals to review the findings of the interdepartmental committees responsible for the security evaluation.

The Boyaner Rebbe

The Board of Appeals proved far more sympathetic to the plight of the refugees than the State Department bureaucrats and overseas consuls, and explicitly rejected the assumptions upon which many of the State Department decisions were predicated.[25] In approximately a quarter of the cases, the Board of Appeals reversed the State Department. Decisions of the Board of Appeals were made on the basis of a written record produced at a Review Committee hearing at which representatives of the visa applicant were allowed to testify.[26] Mike was the representative at these hearings on behalf of all those on the Refugee and Immigration Division caseload whose visa applications had been denied.[27]

For high-level meetings in Washington, Mike was often accompanied by some of the most distinguished personalities in the Orthodox world. He felt that nothing could better convey what kind of people he was attempting to save from Europe than the *hadras panim* of the Kopyczinitzer Rebbe or the Boyaner Rebbe, both of whom

---

25. For instance, State Department regulations required that "enemy aliens," i.e., natives or former citizens of enemy countries, had to establish that they would be a positive benefit to the United States. The Board of Appeals, however, took the position that the benefit of the traditional American policy of providing refuge for decent people in distress and peril was sufficient, and no decent person should be excluded for failure to establish some more specific "positive benefit" from his presence.

The Board members also did not share Breckenridge Long's fear that those with relatives in enemy territory would be subject to pressure by the enemy power. They pointed out that any attempt to exercise control over immigrants once they were in the United States would force the Nazi agent to risk exposure and arrest. Wyman, *Paper Walls*, pp. 201-203; Wyman, *The Abandonment of the Jews*, pp. 129-31.

26. Ibid., p. 201.

27. Harry Sherer, "The Immigration Problem Today," *Orthodox Youth*, June 1942, pp. 3, 10.

accompanied him from time to time, even though they did not say a word at the meetings.[28]

Saving the Roshei Yeshivah

WITH THE FALL OF FRANCE IN JUNE 1940, A NUMBER OF LEADING anti-fascist intellectuals who had previously fled to France from Germany were placed in great danger. Several prominent Americans urged the State Department to immediately issue special emergency visitors visas to the endangered anti-Nazis, and the State Department's initial response was favorable. Immediately other groups, including the politically powerful American Federation of Labor and the Jewish Labor Committee, submitted their own lists for consideration.

Orthodox groups were quick to realize that the special emergency visitors visas might offer a ray of hope in rescuing leading Jewish figures from Eastern Europe. Visitors visas carried with them the advantage of being outside the normal quota system, and therefore offered the best opportunity for those in Eastern Europe where the quotas were very small. On the other hand, visitors visas normally were limited to six-months duration and required the applicant to show that he had some place to which he could return at the end of his stay in the United States. But the State Department indicated early on that it would overlook both the time restrictions and the requirement of a place to which to return, and virtually all recipients of the special emergency visitors visas ended up remaining in the United States.[29]

Within days of the issuance of the first emergency visitors visas, Mike was in Washington seeking approval of the use of the visas for leading Eastern European rabbinic figures. On his first trip, he was granted 50 dossiers. (Each dossier could include dozens of collateral relatives of the person for whom the dossier was issued.) He made two more trips in an attempt to increase the number of dossiers allocated, and each time was granted an additional ten.

That left the heart-rending task of deciding who would receive the allotted spaces, each of which would hopefully enable the beneficiary to bring out with him his entire family, including children and grandchildren. In the course of the deliberations, the Kopyczinitzer Rebbe announced that he could not continue. "We are deciding *dinei nefashos* (questions of life and death)," he said, "and I do not feel capable of

---

28. Berger interview.
29. Wyman, *Paper Walls*, p. 140.

sitting in such judgment." He withdrew despite the fact that one of those being discussed was his own brother-in-law and his family. In the end, most of the onus of deciding fell on Rabbi Eliezer Silver, who had the greatest familiarity with the Eastern European yeshiva world.

At last the list was pared down to 71. Just then, Rabbi Silver received word from Vilna that the *gadol hador*, Rabbi Chaim Ozer Grodzenski, had passed away in Vilna. Mike turned white as a sheet and then broke down completely at the news of Reb Chaim Ozer's passing. When he had somewhat regained his composure, he murmured softly to himself that the selection had been made *min Hashamayim*.[30]

Preparing the applications for each of those on the list was an immensely complicated task requiring constant telephone contact with Rabbi Noson Shup in Kovna, who provided the necessary biographical information on all those to be listed on each of the 70 applications. When the 70 dossiers were completed, Mike again traveled to Washington to submit them.

While he was in Washington, an emergency telegram reached the Youth Council offices that space must somehow be found for another two names. That usually meant that someone had arrived in Moscow, where the only Eastern European consular office issuing visas was located, and faced imminent expulsion and with it any chance of receiving a life-saving visa. Mike had already submitted his lists in Washington, and the next day duplicates were to be submitted to the New York office of the President's Advisory Committee on Political Refugees (PAC), a quasi-governmental body which had been given the task of coordinating requests for the special emergency visitors visas among the various groups seeking them. Any discrepancy between the lists already submitted to the State Department and those submitted to the PAC could compromise the reputation for scrupulous honesty that Mike had built up in Washington and upon which much of the goodwill he had garnered depended.

Moshe Berger came up with the idea of adding the two names to one of the 70 dossiers already prepared. Since each dossier included many relatives, the discrepancy between the two dossiers might well not be noticed, and even if it was, it could be explained away as a last-minute clerical error.

Among the towering figures who eventually came to America on the first set of special emergency visitors visas secured by the Youth Council

30. Interview with Moshe Berger.

were Rabbi Reuven Grozovsky, Rabbi Yisrael Chaim Kaplan, Rabbi Aharon Kotler, Rabbi Avraham Joffen, Rabbi Simcha Zissel Levovitz, Rabbi Dovid Lipshitz, Rabbi Moshe Shatzkes and his son Rabbi Aharon Shatzkes, Rabbi Moshe Shkop, (the Modzhitzer Rebbe), Rabbi Shaul Yedidya Taub, and the Chafetz Chaim's son-in-law Rabbi Mendel Zaks, together with the Chafetz Chaim's widow, son, and daughter.[31]

In early August, Mike and Meir Schenkolewski succeeded in winning State Department approval for another 400 names for special emergency visitors visas.[32] Unfortunately, no more than 40 of those 400 were able to use the authorized visas by the end of 1943.[33] (Others may have been able to renew the visas and use them after the war.) In this group of 400 were included many of the major *talmidei chachamim* whose names appear in the files of the Refugee and Immigration Division: Rabbi Isaac Ausband, Rabbi Leib Bakst, Rabbi Michel Barenbaum, Rabbi Elya Chazan, Rabbi Gedaliah Eiseman, Rabbi Shabse Frankel, Isaac Lewin, Rabbi Yehudah Nekritz, and Rabbi Chaim Shmulevitz.[34]

Each one of the applications for the special emergency visitors visas required a short biography of the applicant. By mid-1941, this requirement had been expanded to all visa applications as part of the overall security check. The biographies submitted by the Refugee and Immigration Division emphasized the anti-Nazi *and* the anti-Communist credentials of the applicant. The biography prepared for Rabbi Shlomo Rotenberg, who was then in Marseilles in Unoccupied France, for instance, stressed that after completing his studies in the Mirrer Yeshiva he had been active in the Eastern sector of Poland, bor-

31. David Kranzler and Eliezer Gevirtz, *To Save a World*, pp. 140-41, and Report of the Refugee and Immigration Division Agudath Israel Youth, September 1941, pp. 1-2.

32. Mike apparently obtained two sets of special emergency visitors visas. Moshe Berger mentions 70 dossiers that were granted prior to Rabbi Chaim Ozer Grodzenski's *petirah* on July 12, 1940. But both the 1941 Report of the Refugee and Immigration Division and the Fifth Agudah Report prepared by Reb Jacob Rosenheim speak of 400 visas obtained for *talmidei chachamim* in August 1940. The August date is consistent with a letter from Breckenridge Long to President Roosevelt in early August 1940 in which he stated that more than a quarter of the 2,583 special visas approved to date were Jewish religious leaders submitted by Orthodox rabbis.

It is not altogether clear in which group of visas any of those mentioned in this chapter fell.

33. Authorization of the visas and their actual issuance were two very distinct stages. By the end of September, 1940, for instance, visas had only been issued to 40 of the 567 people whose names were submitted by the PAC and approved by the State Department. The consul still retained the discretion not to issue or to delay issuance after State Department approval.

34. Some of these names may have been on lists submitted by the Vaad Hatzala to the State Department, but for which the Refugee and Immigration Division did all the actual visa work.

DEPARTMENT OF STATE
WASHINGTON

MAY 15, 1941,

In reply refer to
VD 811.111 Refugees/1304

My dear Mr. Tress:

The Department has received a telegram from the American Consulate at Kobe which states that visas have been issued to the following persons who were recommended to the Department by your organization:

Szabse and Szarlota Fraenkel; Izaak, Pessla and Natan Lewin; Mojsze Lejba Luski, wife Szejna Rywka, and daughter Chaja Rajzel; Chaim Lejba Szmuelowicz, wife Chana Miriam, and three children, Etel, Rywka and Rafael.

Sincerely yours,

C. M. Lawson

A. M. Warren
Chief, Visa Division

Mr. Michael G. Tress,
Agudath Israel Youth Council,
616 Bedford Avenue,
Brooklyn, New York.

dering Russia, "combating Communism" and was "well-known for his activity in stamping out Communism" as he traveled and lectured throughout Latvia and Lithuania.[35] Even membership in Agudath Israel was used as evidence of fervent anti-Communism. In the biographical portrait of Rabbi Avraham Pejsach, head of the Talmudical Academy Yesode Hadath in Antwerp, the founding of Agudath Israel at Kattowitz in 1912 was attributed to the need to "combat the growing danger of Communism both in Poland and elsewhere."

The most effusive of these biographies was that sent to Assistant Secretary of State Breckenridge Long in early 1941 on behalf of the Gerrer Rebbe and his entire family, who were seeking a temporary

---

35. For other leading rabbis and European Agudists interned in Southern France, the stress was put on the danger they faced from German authorities. That danger was proven by such activities as having published "articles in Jewish journals against anti-Semitism and racial legislation," having been "mentioned in German newspapers for disciplinary action," or merely playing a "prominent role in Jewish activities." *Biographies of Rabbi Mendel Singer, Abraham Shreiber, and Mr. and Mrs. Julius Einstadter.*

The biographies also played up the "positive benefit" and patriotism the applicants would bring to the United States, as evidenced by having volunteered for the French Foreign Legion or having been praised by former president Herbert Hoover for prewar educational activities. *Biographies of Theodore Biberfield and Mrs. Julius Einstadter.*

Chapter Fifteen: REFUGEE AND IMMIGRATION DIVISION □ 263

May 6, 1941

Hon. Breckenridge Long
State Department
Washington, D.C.

BIOGRAPHIC SKETCH OF HIS HOLINESS

RABBI ABRAHAM MORDCHA ALTER.

(Sainted Rabbi of Ger)

His Holiness Rabbi Abraham Mordcha Alter, or better known to the world as the " Sainted Rabbi of Ger " is at the present writing living in Jerusalem, Sfath Emeth 6, Palestine .(The street is named after his illustrious father who was called "Sfath Emeth ",i.e. " The Well of Truth ").

Rabbi Abraham Mordcha Alter is descended from a long line of famous and saintly Rabbis and scholars and his ancestral lineage can be traced directly to that of King David. His great and brilliant father was known throughout the Wrold with the unique title of " The Well of Truth " (Sfath Emeth).

His Holiness, Rabbi Abraham Mordcha Alter had resided all of his years in Poland and his birthplace and home were in the celebrated city of Ger. He was not only the spiritual leader of the Jews of Poland (3,000,000) but is also the Saint and Sage of our generation. Hundreds of Thousands of Jews pilgrimaged to the city of Ger to pay homage to this great Saint, and his disciples and followers throughout the world number over a half a million. In the United States, the foremost Rabbis, Religious Leaders, professional laymen and out standing business men are the devout followers and disciples of His Holiness.

When Rabbi Abraham Mordcha Alter wanted to leave Poland in 1934 and sojourn in Jerusalem, the late Marshall Pilsudski and other Polish leaders came to Ger and asked him not to leave Poland because his great spiritual guidance would be sorely missed. Wherever and whenever Rabbi Alter came to other cities or countries the Chief officials and leading statesmen would come to greet him and offer him the hospitality of the country. When he attended the Religious Congress held in Vienna in 1929 the former Chancellor of the Austrian Government came to welcome him. Rabbi A.M.Alter is known as the uncrowned spiritual and religious King of World Jewry and he is the beacon light of our Faith.

When the Germans entered Warsaw in September 1939 the Gestapo immediately began to search for the Saintly Rabbi of Ger. He was , however, in hiding and suffered untold privations until the American Embassy in Warsaw had offered him its protection and a place of refuge. He remained hidden until his American followers arranged for him and his family to leave the country for Jerusalem.

Rabbi A.M.Alter is now in Jerusalem with his family amongst whom are his noted son-in-laws, Rabbi Lewin and Rabbi Yoskowitz, Rabbi Wojne and their immediate families. Rabbi Lewin was formerly member of the Polish Parliament and the Chairman of the Agudath Israel of Europe. Rabbi Lewin is one of the foremost Jewish religious leaders.

The situation in the Near East is a very dangerous one and the religious Jews of the United States are in constant dread of the German march on Jerusalem. We fear that if ever the Nazis entered the Holy Land they would immediately arrest and persecute the Saintly Rabbi of Ger and his family. He has with the help of the Almighty, and after a great deal of suffering and privation miraculously escaped from the Gestapo and we must under no condition ever permit him to again fall a possible victim to the Nazis.

We, the religious Jews of the United States and also the religious Jews of the entire Universe, come to you, Hon. Breckenridge Long, as representative of our Government and ask you to offer a temporary haven of refuge to His Holiness, Rabbi Abraham Mordcha Alter, the Sainted Rabbi of Ger and his family. The history of the United States is based on the democratic principles of freedom and religious worship and our country is famed for its " gates of mercy and refuge ". Rabbi Abraham Mordcha Alter is the spiritual light of millions of Jews. His Holiness serves our persecuted people as a bulwark of strength, for them, to remain staunch to the eternal precepts of our Faith. He is our " Rock of Salvation " and we ask you to grant our request and to save for us our great and Holy Leader. The Saintly Rabbi of Ger, Rabbi A.M. Alter, will enrich this country, as he has done the entire world, with his great spiritual and moral strength. Thousands of Jews of America anxiously await to receive His Holiness, Rabbi Abraham Mordcha Alter.

Respectfully,

AGUDATH ISRAEL YOUTH COUNCIL OF AMERICA

visitors visas to come from Palestine to the United States. The Rebbe was described as "not only the spiritual leader of the [three million] Jews of Poland but also the Saint and Sage of our generation ... [whose] followers around the world number over a half a million." The biography went on to relate how the late Marshall Pidulski and other Polish leaders had begged the Rebbe not to leave Poland in 1934 because of the spiritual void that would be left by his absence.

NONE OF THOSE WHO CAME TO AMERICA ON THE SPECIAL EMERgency visitors visas would have a greater impact than Rabbi Aharon

Shabbos for Reb Aharon

Kotler. One Shabbos evening in the winter of 1940, several months after Reb Aharon's visa was approved, Mike had settled in for a relaxing Shabbos meal with his family. It had been a particularly draining week, and Mike was savoring the *menuchas Shabbos* when suddenly the Shabbos peace was pierced by the sound of the doorbell. The presence of a Western Union messenger at the door spelled trouble. The cable read:

> Came to American Embassy in Moscow to receive Emergency Visa. None waiting. Staff knows nothing about it. Must leave Moscow within twenty-four hours. [Signed] Aharon Kotler

Without that visa, Reb Aharon could not make his way across the Soviet Union to Vladivostok on the Pacific coast, and once expelled from Moscow there would be no other way to obtain the visa. The Moscow embassy was the only one issuing visas in the Soviet Union, and the Soviet authorities did not permit it to issue visas outside of Moscow.[36] Jews, especially identifiably religious ones, wandering through Russia could look forward to Siberian exile — at best.

Mike rushed to the home of his most trusted advisor and closest friend Rabbi Gedaliah Schorr, and the two went to consult with Rabbi Shlomo Heiman, the Rosh Yeshiva of Torah Vodaath. Reb Shlomo assured them that there was no question that they must prepare a new visa application on Shabbos. "If I knew how to type, I would do it myself for Reb Aharon," Reb Shlomo added.

It was 10:30 that night when Mike and Reb Gedaliah reached the apartment of the third member of their team, Moshe Berger. For Berger it was only the second night that week he had slept at home.[37] The three

---

36. Wyman, *Paper Walls*, p. 149.

37. This entire story is based on the account of Moshe Berger.

Rav Gedaliah Schorr and Mike

hurried to 616 Bedford Avenue where they let the blinds down before turning on the lights and getting to work. The task ahead was a daunting one: Reb Aharon's dossier included 50 to 60 people and had to be completely reconstructed from information in the files. By 5 a.m., the dossier was complete, and Mike was ready to head off for Washington, D.C. on the long shot that he would find someone working at the State Department with the authority to transmit a second visa application to Moscow. Before leaving, he did not forget to ask Reb Gedaliah how he should carry his train ticket so as to minimize *chilul Shabbos.* (Reb Gedaliah told him he should stick it in the band of his hat.)

When Mike arrived at the State Department it was already the middle of the morning and there were few signs of activity inside. Meanwhile the clock was ticking for Reb Aharon, who had only a few hours left before he had to leave Moscow.

At last, Mike saw an office with a crack of light under the door. Fortunately, the office was that of Assistant Secretary Breckinridge Long, in whose jurisdiction the Visa Division fell. There was no question of his authority to cable a new application to Moscow. But Long was an extreme nativist, whom Secretary of the Treasury Morgenthau once explicitly confronted with the charge that he was anti-Semitic, and his assistance was far from assured.[38]

---

38. Wyman, *The Abandonment of the Jews,* pp. 185, 190.

This time, however, Long was cordial, even friendly. He recognized Mike from previous meetings and realized that only the greatest of emergencies could have brought him to Washington on a Shabbos. Mike explained the problem with Reb Aharon's visa, and held his breath. Long took him to the State Department code room, where he cabled the redone application to Moscow. For good measure, he ordered the embassy to send a car to bring Reb Aharon back to the embassy.

In the end, the dramatic rescue attempt did not help Reb Aharon leave the Soviet Union. On Tuesday, a heart-broken Mike was informed by the State Department that Reb Aharon had not returned for his visa nor had the Moscow Embassy been able to locate him. Two weeks later, however, in the course of a conversation with Frank Newman, the emissary of the Youth Council and Vaad Hatzala in Kobe, Japan, Newman mentioned that there was someone in the office who wished to speak with him. Over the line, Mike heard the words he most longed to hear, "This is Kotler."

Confirmation of Reb Aharon's passage to America

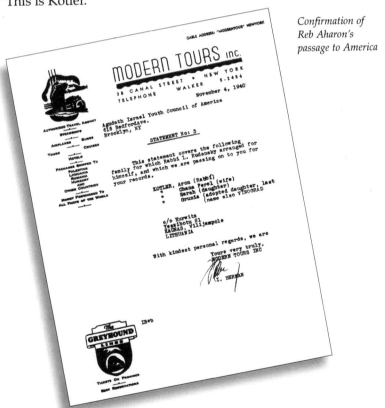

With his time in Moscow running out, a desperate Reb Aharon had gone to the train station and purchased a ticket for the 11-and-a-half-day journey to Vladivostok. As he went to board, a Soviet official stood at the door to his cabin barring the way. Reb Aharon stared directly at him and walked past, and the official miraculously did not ask to see his travel documents. The same scene was repeated in Vladivostok, where Reb Aharon was allowed to board a ship for Kobe, Japan despite the lack of an American visa or a Soviet exit visa.

One question remains: Why was Breckenridge Long, the architect of the State Department's restrictive immigration policy and one who did so much to thwart hopes for rescue throughout the war, willing to extend himself for Mike? Curious as it may seem, Long appears to have been more comfortable dealing with religious Jews like Mike. Long had a paranoid streak that led him to confide to his diary that he was under constant attack from "Communists, extreme radicals, Jewish professional agitators, refugee enthusiasts, [and] ... Jewish radical circles." On the other hand, his relations with the religious activists, who did not openly criticize him in the press, were cordial.[39] Long's sympathy for Torah scholars was revealed in Congressional testimony concerning the approval of special emergency visitors visas for a large number of yeshiva students, in which he described the yeshiva students in the most glowing terms:

> These young men were being educated by the best minds of the Jewish people in that area. . . . Their teachers were trying to educate them in the way of the religious leadership of their people. They were the light of the Church, who carry the torch of truth and the essence of Jewish religion.[40]

Those sentiments may well have been a result of the restraint that Mike and other Orthodox rescue activists showed in all their dealings with the State Department.

---

39. Wyman, *The Abandonment of the Jews*, p. 191.

40. Quoted by Reb Jacob Rosenheim in the biannual report to Chawerim Nichbodim of the Agudath Israel World Organization covering the period from July 1, 1943 to December 31, 1943, p. 1.

Chapter Sixteen
RELIEF AND RESCUE

DUE TO THE EXTENSIVE PAPERWORK INVOLVED, VISA and affidavit work took up most of the manpower of the Rescue and Immigration Division. But the visa work was only one aspect of the Division's activities. Other activities included: attending to the spiritual and physical needs of Jews who had managed to find refuge in far-flung venues around the world; finding housing and jobs for those who succeeded in reaching America; continuous lobbying of the American and other governments; providing whatever food and other relief could reach Jews in Nazi-occupied areas; and raising funds for the rescue activities of the Sternbuchs in Switzerland, Rabbi Weissmandl in Slovakia, and Dr. Jacob Griffel in Turkey.[1]

1. *Orthodox Tribune,* March 1944, p. 9.

All this work required two things: energy and money. The former Mike had in abundance. Throughout the war, he seemed not to sleep at all,[2] and he once told Rabbi Shlomo Rotenberg that he could not remember the last time he had been able to sit down and eat supper with his family.[3] Rabbi Shabse Frankel, a Vaad Hatzala activist,[4] marveled at Mike's dedication:

> To save people, to help people, he worked day and night. He was never tired, and he never said no. One time, I had an urgent meeting in Washington, and I felt his presence was necessary. His wife was just back from the hospital with a new baby. But he said that he would go if his wife agreed and we could find some help for her. Mrs. Tress, of course, agreed.
>
> There was never a time when he pleaded that he was too busy to make an appeal or help in raising money.

But if the energy flowed from deep wellsprings, the money did not, and Mike had to spend much of the former to raise the latter. "Sympathy Won't Help Them — Money Will" was an ongoing theme of the Refugee and Immigration Division advertising. Sol Septimus, stationed for a period of time in Charleston, South Carolina, wrote Mike in mid-1943 expressing surprise that he had not received any fundraising appeals of late, from which he deduced that Zeirei's financial situation must have improved. Mike quickly set him straight: "Don't worry about the financial condition of the Zeirei, it is as broke as ever, if not more so … so if you had contemplated sending in [any money] do so before you have a change of heart."[5] Six months later, he wrote Septimus again in the same vein: "Here in the Zeirei things are at the usual pace, more work and few people to do it, and of course financially we are always seeking the Utopia and have never yet come near it."[6]

The strain of the non-stop work and fundraising eventually took its toll on Mike. His friends worried about his health and the burden, financial and otherwise, on his family. Sol Septimus wrote asking

---

2. Interview with Robert and Ruth Krane.

3. Interview with Rabbi Shlomo Rotenberg.

4. Rabbi Frankel was one of the few from Poland to reach America during the war. He came via Japan on a visa arranged by the Refugee and Immigration Division. Today Rabbi Frankel is best known as the publisher of the world-famous "Frankel Rambam."

5. Mike to Sol Septimus, January 22, 1943.

6. Mike to Sol Septimus, July 20, 1943.

Fundraising ad for Hatzalah activities

whether he had yet "'degraded' to the point of thinking of [him]self for a change." Mike replied that he had reached the point of "degrada- tion,"[7] but if he ever had thoughts about quitting, they were soon banished by the realization that Jewish lives were at stake.[8] Even after the war, the pace did not slacken. Jerry Bechofer, Rabbi Joseph Breuer's son-in-law, wrote wishing Mike a full recovery after some minor surgery in 1947. At the end of his note, however, Bechofer added, "I am leaving the word 'speedy' out on purpose, since I — like everyone else — believe that you should take an unspeedy rest."[9]

---

7. Ibid.

8. According to Rabbi Shlomo Rotenberg, Mike had a good offer to return to the business world in 1945. At that time, his rapidly growing family was living in a small apartment on Clymer Street. But, in the end, Mike could not abandon the rescue work.

9. Jerry Bechhofer to Mike Tress, February 21, 1947.

Chapter Sixteen: RELIEF AND RESCUE □ 271

JEWS FLEEING FROM EUROPE HAD TAKEN REFUGE IN A WIDE ARRAY
of exotic locales around the world — in many of which there had been
Relief little previous Jewish presence. By far the largest of these
Projects wartime refugee communities was that in Shanghai, but
others could be found in Manila, off the coast of Africa on
the island of Mauritius,[10] in Cuba, and on various West Indies islands.[11]
Jews who succeeded in reaching these places were grateful to be alive,
but at the same time they found themselves without any of the
infrastructure of institutions and services upon which Jewish life
depends. Nor was it easy for the refugees — many of whom had been
forced to leave everything behind — to earn a livelihood in societies so
foreign to all they had known.

The Agudath Israel Youth Council was one of the first addresses to
which religious Jews in these communities turned. From Manila came a
request for funding to send a member of the community to Shanghai to
study *shechitah*.[12] A group of Orthodox Jews in Trinidad requested *sifrei
kodesh* (holy books),[13] as did German-Jewish refugees interned in
Australia and Canada. The large Jewish refugee community in Cuba
depended on the Youth Council for *shemurah matzos* for Pesach.[14] Even
the established British community had to request *sifrei kodesh* due to
wartime paper rationing, which made it impossible to reprint *siddurim*
and *chumashim* as they became worn.[15]

The Youth Council did everything possible to fulfill the requests
directed towards it. A check for $500, for instance, reached Manila two
hours before *Kol Nidrei* of 5701 (1940), and quickly became the talk of the
community. The heads of the non-religious Jewish Committee, which
had denied the request of the small Orthodox community for funding

---

10. Mike wrote to the Joint Distribution Committee, December 27, 1944, asking them to supply
food packages at regular intervals for a group of Jews in Mauritius that had written to the Youth
Council. He offered the services of the Youth Council in preparing and forwarding packages to
them if funding could be arranged.

11. In a March 23, 1942 fundraising letter, Mike referred to the many cables from "newly founded settlements in the British and Dutch West Indies . . . plead[ing] with us to send . . . religious
articles . . . so that they may have the possibility of remaining loyal Jews and of educating their
children in the Jewish Faith."

12. *Orthodox Youth*, December 1940, p. 1.

13. *Orthodox Youth*, March 1942, p. 20.

14. See the extensive correspondence between Mike and Julius Steinfeld in Havana with regard
to 80 pounds of *shemurah matzoh* sent to Mr. Steinfeld March 29, 1943.

15. See letter of Harry A. Goodman, Chairman of the British Agudah Israel, requesting 1,000 *siddurim* and 250 *chumashim*, reprinted in *Orthodox Youth*, February 1941, p. 3.
    The Refugee Supper run by the Williamsburg Pirchei in February 1941 was specifically to
raise funds to help the Jews in bomb-shattered England. *Orthodox Youth*, February 1941, p. 2.

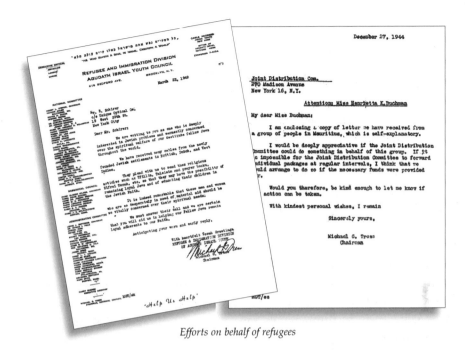

Efforts on behalf of refugees

to train one of its members as a *shochet* in Shanghai, were amazed that assistance had come from faraway America.[16] Even where the requests could not be met, the Youth Council maintained contacts with these tiny Orthodox communities to lessen their sense of isolation from the rest of the Jewish world.[17] Meanwhile the efforts continued unabated to bring the refugees, stranded so far from the centers of Jewish life, to America.

Thousands of Orthodox Jews found wartime refuge in Shanghai, including most of the student body of the prewar Mirrer Yeshiva. This large community was the object of special solicitude from the Youth Council, as well as Vaad Hatzala, which was originally organized specifically for the purpose of saving the European yeshivos. Prior to Pearl Harbor, Frank Newman, an active member of the Williamsburg Zeirei, was sent as an emissary of Vaad Hatzala and the Youth Council to Kobe, Japan. There he spent several months working on visas and arranging ship passage for hundreds of Torah scholars who had managed to escape from Lithuania.[18] Throughout the war, Mike was

---

16. Letter of H. Hirschhaut to Agudath Israel Youth Council, reprinted in *Orthodox Youth*, February 1941, pp. 1, 8.

17. Report of the Refugee and Immigration Division of Agudath Israel Youth, September 1941, p. 3.

18. David Kranzler, *Thy Brother's Blood*, p. 157.

involved in an ongoing series of efforts to secure permission for the yeshivos to leave Shanghai, where there was a constant danger that the Japanese would suddenly change their relatively benign policy toward the Jewish community at the behest of their German allies.[19]

Shanghai boasted not one but two Agudah chapters — one made up of German Jews and the other of Polish Jews. Together the two chapters maintained a soup kitchen large enough to feed 1,000 people and a Bais Yaakov school for 150 girls. A *shemiras Shabbos* campaign run by Agudah kept 90 percent of the Jewish shops closed on Shabbos. Most of the funding for the religious community came through the Vaad Hatzala, but the Youth Council was also in constant touch with the Agudah offices in Shanghai.

Shortly after his arrival in America from Shanghai, Rabbi Mordechai Schwab, one of the leaders of the Shanghai Agudah, paid a visit to the Youth Council offices.[20] He arrived in the midst of a meeting of the Youth Council executive, and, after asking which one of those present was Mike Tress, he immediately ran over and embraced Mike and each of his colleagues in turn. Rabbi Schwab explained that one of the things that had kept the community going throughout all its travails was the knowledge that there was a group in America that was doing everything possible to help them.[21]

THROUGHOUT THE WAR, WORLD AGUDATH ISRAEL, VAAD Hatzalah, and other groups concerned with the rescue of Jews had **Fort** pressed the Allies to establish large camps in North **Oswego** Africa or elsewhere where any Jews permitted to leave Nazi-controlled areas could be maintained until after the war. On July 12, 1944, Mike, together with Rabbi Aharon Kotler and Rabbi Baruch Korff, submitted a memorandum to Under Secretary of State Edward Stettinus on behalf of a number of organizations involved

---

19. Mike, Rabbi Avraham Kalmanowitz, and Rabbi Herbert Goldstein met October 11, 1944 with the Spanish Ambassador to the United States to urge his government, which represented Japanese diplomatic interests with the Allies, to encourage the Japanese to let the Jewish community leave Shanghai for a neutral port. The following January, Mike and Rabbi Kalmanowitz discussed with the War Refugee Board the progress of Rabbi Shlomo Wolbe's efforts to secure Swedish agreement to a plan for the Mirrer group to come to the United States westward through Russia and Sweden. Cables were sent by the WRB to American Ambassador Averell Harriman in Moscow asking him to discuss this plan with the Soviets.

20. Rabbi Schwab was later the Mashgiach in Mesivta Bais Shraga in Monsey, New York. He was widely known as "the *tzaddik* of Monsey."

21. Gershon Kranzler, "Setting the Record Straight," *The Jewish Observer*, November 1971, p. 13. See also, David Kranzler and Eliezer Gevirtz, *To Save a World*, p. 150.

in rescue work.[22] The memorandum referred to reports that the government of Hungary was prepared to allow 500,000 Jews to leave via Turkey, and called on the American government to enter into negotiations to realize that goal. The submitting organizations recognized that no country or group of countries was prepared to accept such a large number of Jews and therefore urged the establishment of large camps for the released Jews in North Africa.

> It would be necessary for the Allied Nations to open temporary camps in Africa, Libya or [some] other area to receive these Jews, and in this respect we wish to state that these destitute people would be willing to go to the desert and the farthest isles so that their lives might be saved. They could be interned in those temporary camps until the war is over.

The War Refugee Board (WRB) also sought to convince President Roosevelt to announce that America was ready to receive all refugees in temporary camps in which they would be interned until the end of the war, at which time they would be repatriated. Such an announcement, the Board felt, would have a twofold effect. First, it would encourage neutral countries to similarly open up their borders to refugees. Secondly, it would demonstrate to the Nazis, and more importantly to the governments of Hungary and Romania, which while under Nazi domination were formally independent, that the world was concerned with the fate of the Jews and there might be something to be gained by favorable treatment of their surviving Jewish populations.[23]

All that ever came of this idea, however, was President Roosevelt's approval of a plan to bring close to 1,000 refugees, 90 percent of them Jewish, from Southern Italy to Fort Oswego, an abandoned army base thirty-five miles north of Syracuse. So niggardly was the program in the context of the need that its symbolic effect was virtually the opposite of what the WRB had intended — it signaled to the world how minimal was the American interest in rescuing large number of Jews.[24] The Fort Oswego plan, in fact, was as much a response to logistical problems caused by the sudden influx of refugees into Southern Italy from

---

22. The signatory organizations were: Vaad Hahatzala, American Jewish Congress, Union of Orthodox Rabbis of the United States and Canada, Agudas Israel of America, Rabbinical Council of America, Union of Orthodox Jewish Congregations of America, Young Israel of America, and the Emergency Committee to Save the Jewish People of Europe.

23. *The Abandonment of the Jews*, p. 266.

24. Ibid., p. 267.

Louis J. Septimus

Yugoslavia and elsewhere as it was an expression of concern for Jews.[25] Though many of those brought to the United States had suffered greatly, by the time they reached Southern Italy they were out of any imminent danger.

But whatever the merits of the Fort Oswego plan in the larger picture, the arrival of over 900 refugees in the United States on August 5, 1944 clearly demanded an immediate response from the Jewish community. Among the very first visitors to the camp were Dr. Isaac Lewin, representing Agudath Israel of America, and Louis Septimus, representing the Youth Council. Within 24 hours of their visit, Rabbi Eliezer Silver had already made arrangements to have sufficient kosher meat shipped to the camp for the 200 or so Jews who expressed an interest in kosher food, along with various *tashmishei kedushah* (religious objects).[26] By the second Shabbos, a kosher kitchen, equipped with both *milchig* and *fleishig* utensils and serving over 200 refugees, was functioning under the joint auspices of Agudath Israel of America and the Youth Council.[27] A few months later, work was begun on a *mikveh* for which Rabbi Eliezer Silver raised the funds.[28]

It would be nice to think of Fort Oswego as a well-deserved respite after years of suffering for the refugees, many of whom had been without homes for nearly ten years. That unfortunately was not the case. By January there had already been one suicide and more internees were on

25. Ibid., p. 264.

26. Louis J. Septimus, "The Refugee Shelter at Fort Ontario," *Orthodox Tribune*, October 1944, pp. 3, 14.

27. Rabbi Sidney Bialik, "The Emergency Refugee Shelter," *Orthodox Tribune*, November 1944, pp. 2, 9.

28. Since the refugees were only permitted to go to nearby Oswego, which did not have a *mikveh*, the construction of one was of critical importance. A request for a special dispensation for visits to the Syracuse *mikveh* was turned down by the Interior Department, which was responsible for supervision of the camp, with a note that surely some religious dispensation must be available given the impossibility of residents using a *mikveh*. Memorandum of Mr. Joseph Smart to Rabbi Tzechoval, October 23, 1944.

the verge of mental breakdowns.[29] The refugees were not allowed to work outside the camp, and became extremely depressed at having nothing to do other than to stare at the camp fence all day or go to Oswego.[30] Menial jobs maintaining the camp itself, for which the pay was so small that most of the internees felt it was not worth it, were the only ones available. In this respect, the refugees' situation had been much better in Italy, where many of them had been working and they were far less confined.[31]

The tensions were increased by the crowding together of Jews from 17 different countries in converted barracks, whose paper-thin walls offered little privacy and in which families had to share bathrooms with their neighbors. Though the camp director Mr. Joseph Smart and his assistant Dr. Ruth Gruber were genuinely concerned with the state of the internees, they operated under some severe constraints. President Roosevelt was under fire from the anti-immigration forces over the program, which the latter portrayed as a ruse to let another 1,000 immigrants into the country. He therefore wanted to make clear that the internees were not being treated as welcome guests but as desperate people who should be grateful for whatever they received. Medical care, for instance, was provided, but only for the express purpose of maintaining the immigrants in the condition in which they arrived. Any medical intervention to remedy the effects of years of privation was left to the Jewish charitable organizations to supply.[32]

On October 26, 1944, Mike visited Fort Oswego at the head of a combined Youth Council and Agudath Israel delegation.[33] He was very upset by the mental state of the internees. In a letter the next day to Rabbi E.M. Eller, the Torah Umesorah emissary in charge of the *cheder*, in which 60 children learned, he wrote, "I was deeply disturbed by the constant bickering that goes on. . . . It's an acute problem and one that should be solved quickly." In the report of the visiting delegation, he detailed the bitterness of the internees, who thought that they were being "brought to America for a rest and recuperation from their long

---

29. *The Abandonment of the Jews*, p. 270.

30. As General William O'Dwyer, the second head of the WRB, wryly put it, "Anybody who would be satisfied to spend six hours in the town of Oswego in the middle of winter hasn't had much fun out of life." *The Abandonment of the Jews*, p. 271.

31. Ibid., p. 270.

32. Ibid., p. 269.

33. Other members of the delegation included Rabbi Moshe Sherer, Mr. I. Firstenberg, Mr. Julius Steinfeld, and Mr. Herman Treisser.

years of suffering ... [and] were instead ... placed in ... another form of internment camp. . . . . They feel that they have suffered enough and that they should be treated better than enemy prisoners of war."[34]

Mike could not hide his eyes from some unattractive aspects of the internees' behavior, but ever the sympathetic student of human nature, he tried to understand it as well:

> These people have suffered untold misery and have deteriorated to a form of "animal" life where they fight for self-preservation. After years of being hunted and having had to use every means at their command to escape the Nazi death trap, they have formed a mental attitude of the persecuted and [have] a completely different [way of evaluating] common, everyday existence. Great and important matters mean little to them and small, puny problems are magnified and assume tremendous importance.[35]

Mike and his co-workers returned from Fort Oswego with a long list of problems requiring their immediate attention. The most pressing was the kosher kitchen. Operation of the kitchen required at least 16 workers a day, and the workers were refusing to continue unless their pay was supplemented. The delegation estimated that if the kitchen closed, no more than 40 Jews of the 220 then eating in the kosher kitchen would continue to eat only kosher food. Therefore it was necessary to raise another $400 a month to supplement the pay of the kitchen staff. Moreover, the delegation found many internees, particularly children, who needed special diets that they were not receiving. Mike undertook to supply their needs as well.[36]

Rabbi Moshe I. Tzechoval,[37] the religious leader of the refugees, was asked to prepare a list of the clothing needs of the children in the camp, which would be supplied by separate packages to each of the children listed. The delegation also resolved to take up the issue of the poor state of the eyes and teeth of the children with Mr. Smart, the camp director.[38]

---

34. Report of the Visit to Emergency Refugee Shelter, Oswego, New York, October 26, 1944, p. 3.

35. Ibid., p. 3.

36. Ibid., pp. 1-3.

37. Rabbi Tzechoval had been a *rosh yeshiva* in Belgium, as well as a leader in the Belgium Zeirei Agudath Israel. "Kosher Kitchen Arranged for Oswego Refugees," *Orthodox Tribune*, October 1944, p. 1.

38. Report of the Visit to Emergency Refugee Shelter, Oswego, New York, October 26, 1944, p. 2.

The shul at Fort Oswego

The Youth Council and Agudath Israel were just two of a large number of Jewish groups ministering to the needs of the internees. For the most part the efforts of all groups were well intentioned, but there were nevertheless certain tensions between the religious and non-religious groups. The first concerned the publicity given to the whole program. From the start, Mike urged a very low-profile approach in the hopes that Fort Oswego would be the first of many such camps. The less publicity the program received, he reasoned, the less political heat the President would take from anti-immigration forces and the greater his willingness to expand the program. Whether such a program could have been kept secret is impossible to say, but we will never know because other Jewish organizations began publicizing their efforts, and soon Fort Oswego was crawling with photographers and journalists.[39]

Several of the mainline groups also objected to the provision of religious education to the children. Questions were raised, too, as to whether kosher kitchens should be provided and Shabbos observed in the camp. Louis Septimus, the Youth Council representative to the council of Jewish groups working in the camp, refused to agree to a vote on these matters. The outcome of such a vote was irrelevant, he argued, since no religious

39. Kranzler, *Thy Brother's Blood*, p. 167.

Jew would agree to work on Shabbos or eat *treife* food no matter what the vote. His arguments proved persuasive and no vote was held.[40]

The Oswego saga ended happily for most of the internees. A year and a half after they arrived, President Truman declared that they could remain in America under the applicable immigrant quotas.[41] But as part of an overall rescue plan, Fort Oswego is just a footnote in the history books, a bitter reminder of how much more could have been done along the same lines to save desperate Jews from the inferno.

Food for the Ghettos

BY THE SUMMER OF 1942, THE NAZI EXTERMINATION CAMPS IN Poland were ready for operation, and the Nazis had the capacity to efficiently murder thousands of Jews a day. Prior to that, the Germans were content to herd Jews into the large ghettos of Warsaw, Lodz, Cracow, Lvov, and other Polish cities and let them die off from starvation and disease. As long as the Nazis were not sure that the world would react with little more than a barely stifled yawn to their plan to extirpate European Jewry, the slower form of murder by starvation had the advantage of not clearly revealing their intentions.[42]

Jews in Polish ghettos received one-third the food ration of other Poles, were barred from purchasing non-rationed articles that were still available, and could not scavenge in the countryside for food like Poles, who enjoyed freedom of movement. In addition, Jews, including pregnant women, nursing mothers, and children, were denied milk rations.[43] In the overcrowded ghettos, disease, particularly typhoid, soon reached epidemic proportions and did the Nazis' work for them. Cables to the Youth Council from Chaim Eiss of the Swiss Agudah pleaded for funds to provide serum to fight the dreaded typhoid.[44]

---

40. Ibid., p. 168.

41. *The Abandonment of the Jews*, p. 274.

42. Nor was the use of starvation as a technique of murder limited to Poland. More that half of the 200,000 Jews living in Transnistra at the beginning of the war perished due to starvation and disease. Fifth Confidential Report to the Chawerim Nichbodim of the Agudas Israel World Organization covering the period July 1, 1943 to December 31, 1943, p. 5.

43. These facts are based on a memorandum submitted by Agudas Harabanim. Only a part of the memorandum was found in the Tress files, making it impossible to identify the intended recipient or the date. Many of the memorandum's proposals for action by the American government — e.g., warnings to Axis satellites that they would be judged after the war by their treatment of their Jewish populations, widespread propaganda among the German people informing them of the atrocities of their government — echo those put forth by Reb Jacob Rosenheim throughout the war.

44. "Serum Needed to Combat Typhoid Epidemics in Warsaw," *Orthodox Youth*, December 1941, p. 1. Eiss cabled the Youth Council July 8, 1942 seeking $5,000 for serum.

Cable from Chaim Eiss requesting funds for serum

RECEIVED BY PRIVATE WIRE SYSTEM
POSTAL TELEGRAPH

Postal Telegraph

JULY 8 1942

AGUDARH ISRAEL YOUTH
615   BROOKLYNEWYORK

IMMEDIAELY FIVE THOUSAND DOLLARS WE WILL BE
NEEDED SERUM TO GHETTO STOP NEEDLESS TO
MOST IMPORTANCE DO EVERYTHING POSSIBLE

CHAIM EISS

"OVERSEAS EMERGENCY APPEAL"

REFUGEE AND IMMIGRATION DIVISION
AGUDATH ISRAEL YOUTH COUNCIL   BROOKLYN, N.Y.

616 BEDFORD AVE.

May 18, 1942

We are at war - not only against the Nazi forces of men, tanks and planes, but also against disease, starvation, death and the brutal shattering of human lives caused by Nazi persecution.

The stark tragedy of our fellow Jews overseas does not permit us to forget their plight for even a single moment. Their harrowing misery, their bleak and desperate position cannot let us rest and we must answer the piercing cries for help that come from their ghettos, hovels and graves. Our brethren are living through the darkest period of history, and we in the United States are the only ones left to give them succor.

It is now possible to bring them aid through the medium of our organization in Switzerland and it is imperative for us to put everything else aside and definitely to contribute more than our share in this moment of abject sorrow.

We are asking you to contribute "ONE DAY'S EARNINGS" to this "Overseas Emergency Appeal."

I wish I could talk to each of you individually and explain the true picture of events. I am certain that your response would not be given as a donation in the usual fashion, but really in the spirit of "wholehearted and inspired sacrifice."

Let us be grateful that we are in the position to give aid and do not have to receive it. Don't wait - let your help be forthcoming immediately - in several weeks we may not even be able to offer our aid.

Help us help those who cannot help themselves!

sincerely yours,

Michael G. Tress
National Chairman

Chairman, National Committee

Louis B. Septimus
Chairman, Admin. Committee

Help Us Help

Overseas Emergency Appeal

The Youth Council responded with an "Overseas Emergency Appeal" calling on Jews to contribute a day's earnings to be sent to the Swiss Agudah on behalf of Polish Jews. At the same time, Agudath Israel of America — on whose board Mike served as Director of Welfare[45] — began to send food parcels to Poland from Portugal and Yugoslavia. By mid-1941, 4,512 packages containing rice, farina, coffee, tea, cocoa, sardines, beans, meat, sugar, matzos, and soup had been sent. Most were paid for by relatives of the recipients, and any excess of receipts over expenses went to purchasing parcels for

---

45. Mike signed a May 12, 1942 letter on behalf of Agudath Israel of America as Chairman, Division of Welfare. The letter expressed Agudath Israel's desire to cooperate with other Jewish organizations in providing aid for the Jews of Poland. At the time of the 1941 food packages, however, Charles Richter, a recent immigrant from Vienna, was the Secretary of the Relief Division of Agudath Israel of America, and it was he who had primary responsibility for the food packages to Poland.

Mike inspecting packages destined for Europe

approximately 100 Polish rabbis.[46]

The amount of food sent was little more than a drop in the bucket of what was needed. Yet to the recipients the packages were literally the difference between life and death. Though most of those who received the packages eventually shared the fate of the rest of Polish Jewry, the packages were a brief respite from unmitigated suffering, as the letters from grateful recipients made clear. Rabbi M. Kowalski received a letter from his mother in Poland expressing her delight at having had matzos for Pesach:

> My dear children. Imagine our surprise when on the eve of the Holidays, at four o'clock in the afternoon we received a package of matzos in the best order. Our happiness was indescribable; nor did I enjoy [them] alone, but [with] many sick people, and they blessed you and wished you the best.[47]

46. Affidavit of Charles Richter submitted in support of Agudath Israel of America's application for a foreign exchange license, July 1941.

47. From excerpts of letters attached as appendices to the affidavit of Charles Richter described in note 46 above.

In some cases, the extra food no doubt provided the wherewithal to fight off rampant disease and the chance, however slim, to survive the war.

The food packages were important for more than the immediate relief they afforded. The Nazis used the food shortage in Poland to fan Polish anti-Semitism — something not too hard to do under the best of circumstances — and to win Polish support for the murder of Jews. All over Poland, they plastered thousands of posters proclaiming, *"Ein Jude Weniger — Ein Brot Mehr* (One Jew Less — One Bread More)." If it could be shown that food for Jews did not come out of Polish mouths but from abroad, Dr. Isaac Lewin argued, then Poles would no longer have reason to rejoice in Jewish deaths and the Nazi propaganda would lose its effect.[48]

Incredible as it seems, the provision of these paltry amounts of food to starving Jews raised the ire of both the British authorities[49] and the Jewish Boycott Committee. The latter group, headed by Dr. Joseph Tenenbaum, who was also the president of the Federation of American Polish Jews, picketed the offices of Agudath Israel of America to protest its violation of the British boycott.[50] It is difficult today to reconstruct the mindset of Jews more concerned that the Nazis might steal the food for themselves than that their fellow Jews might be denied life-saving sustenance. The Boycott Committee had become so wrapped up in its own grand gestures — which in fact were no more than pathetic fist-waving at Hitler — that it lost all sight of the human consequences of those gestures. Even if the Nazis had eaten all the food themselves, the amounts were so minuscule as to have been totally irrelevant to their fighting capacity.

As it was, the fears of the Boycott Committee that the Nazis would derive any benefit, however slight, from the food shipments were grossly exaggerated. In an affidavit submitted in support of an application for a foreign exchange license, Charles Richter, the head of the program,

---

48. Dr. Isaac Lewin, "We CAN Save Jews," *Orthodox Youth*, April 1943, p. 2.

Dr. Lewin's belief that Poles would rise up in revulsion against the German extermination campaign if the incentive of more food were removed is a remarkable testament to the Jewish capacity to believe in the innate goodness of human nature despite all the contrary evidence furnished by Jewish history. Reb Jacob Rosenheim's frequent calls for moral appeals to the German people fall into the same category.

49. The British ultimately brought the program to a halt by threatening to intern Jewish refugees from Germany living in England unless the shipments stopped. *Interview with Charles Richter.*

50. For another glaring example of Tenenbaum putting British interests ahead of Jewish lives see, Bunim, *A Fire in His Soul*, p. 81.

cited proof that the packages reached their intended recipients in virtually every case.[51] Rumors that the Nazis simply deducted the amount of food received from the recipient's allotted food rations were also shown to be untrue. Finally, the shipments gave no monetary benefit to the Nazis because all the foodstuffs were purchased in neutral Portugal.

The food issue again came to the forefront in the last year of the war. Until that time, the International Red Cross had steadfastly refused to bring food packages into the concentration camps on the grounds that any sympathy shown for Jews would anger the Nazis and thereby prejudice the ability of the Red Cross to protect the interests of captured Allied servicemen. Towards the end of the war, however, the International Red Cross's stance on this issue began to soften.[52] On September 28, 1944, John Pehle informed Mike that the War Refugee Board was already sending food shipments with the Red Cross, and two months later, in the course of another Washington meeting, Pehle told Mike that 76,000 packages had already been sent and another 100,000 were on the way.[53] When transportation of the packages became difficult, the WRB purchased trucks of its own, which were then fitted out with Red Cross markings, in order to speed delivery.

These last-minute deliveries by the Red Cross were extremely critical for inmates of the Nazi concentration camps. As the German food situation deteriorated at the end of the war, even the meager diet of the inmates — less than 1,000 calories a day — was cut. Moreover, in the chaos of the rapid German retreat, many smaller concentration camps

---

51. At a later stage, the Germans did start to confiscate greater numbers of packages. In 1942, the American government broke slightly with the British government over the blockade issue and authorized the shipment of $12,000 of foodstuffs from Lisbon to Poland. Of 9,000 parcels sent from Lisbon under the program, there was good evidence that at least 3,000 were confiscated by the Nazis and receipts for only 600 were returned. Fourth Annual Report to Chawerim Nichbodim of Agudas World Organization, covering the period January 1, 1943 to June 30, 1943, p. 16.

In any event, the food was of no strategic significance to the war effort. As John Pehle, first director of the War Refugee Board, said in early 1944, "It [i.e., the food] can no longer in any way interfere with the war effort, . . . the war is going to be decided on the military side and this won't make any difference." *The Abandonment of the Jews*, p. 283.

52. The Sternbuchs in Switzerland had been pushing the International Red Cross throughout the war to be more forthcoming in providing aid to starving Jews both within and without the concentration camps. These efforts finally bore fruit in the last months of the war. See Joseph Friedenson and David Kranzler, *Heroine of Rescue: The Incredible Story of Recha Sternbuch*, pp. 143-44.

53. Mike's minutes of meetings with John Pehle on November 27 and November 29, 1944.

The figures supplied by Pehle appear to have been too optimistic. Although a shipment of 300,000 packages was authorized by the President in August of 1944, the destruction of the German transportation system made their delivery difficult, and by February only 45,000 parcels had been delivered.

were consolidated into a few large ones, sometimes tripling the population of the remaining camps and creating a major problem of food distribution.[54] Thus the Red Cross deliveries in the last months of the war in Europe were crucial in averting many deaths by starvation. And the presence of Red Cross workers in the camps as witnesses may have also discouraged last-minute atrocities against Jews.[55]

JEWS IN THE POLISH GHETTOS WERE NOT THE ONLY CAPTIVE JEWS to benefit from the Agudah food packages. Such packages also reached

The Vienna Agudah

the Jews of Vienna. Indeed the relationship between the Youth Council and the Vienna Agudah was much more extensive and direct than that with Polish Jewry, which was almost exclusively through intermediaries.[56] Unlike Polish Jews, those in Vienna were still able to emigrate between 1939 and 1941, and there was intensive contact between the Refugee and Immigration Division and the Vienna Agudah to speed the processing of visas.

Soon after the Nazi takeover of Austria, the Vienna Agudah sent David Turkel, editor of its *Juedische Presse*, to the United States to begin working on visas for the Viennese Agudah community, which hoped to emigrate en masse.[57] In Vienna, Charles Richter, son-in-law of community leader Julius Steinfeld, was appointed by Mike as the official Youth Council representative.

The achievements of the Vienna Agudah in the three years following the Nazi takeover in March of 1938 were nothing less than miraculous. Over that period, nearly 9,000 Jews were helped to emigrate to nearly 30 countries.[58] End visas were purchased for every country in the world whose consuls could be bribed to issue them. Julius Steinfeld, head of the Vienna Agudah, left Vienna several times between the Nazi takeover and September 1939, and each time returned to oversee the

---

54. Friedenson and Kranzler, *Heroine of Rescue: The Incredible Story of Recha Sternbuch*, pp. 142-43.

55. *The Abandonment of the Jews*, pp. 283-84.

56. The Polish government-in-exile was a frequent source of information to Agudist groups throughout the war, and its diplomatic cables were frequently used by the Sternbuchs in Switzerland to transmit information to their allies in the United States in circumvention of American censorship.

57. The community was a very tight-knit one. Viennese Jews came from a wide variety of backgrounds — Polish, Hungarian, and Galician — but these distinctions were not preserved in Vienna, which was something of a melting pot. It was also a very religious community. *Interview with Charles Richter.*

58. David Turkel, "Three Years Under Hitler," *Orthodox Youth* August 1941, pp. 8-9.

Rabbi Solomon Schonfeld

work on emigration.[59] That work included close contacts with Rabbi Solomon Schonfeld in England, on whose Children's Transports many Viennese children escaped to England, and with Dr. Perl of the Revisionist Zionists on illegal immigration to Palestine.[60]

The attitude of the Vienna Agudah to the visa work was exactly the same as that of the Youth Council in New York: "details" could not be allowed to stand in the way of saving Jewish lives. A Viennese resident born in a small Romanian village came to Charles Richter for help in obtaining a visa to the United States. Already well schooled in the intricacies of the American quota system, Richter realized that the man had no chance of obtaining a visa under the already oversubscribed Romanian quota. But he assumed that the consular official would not know the location of an obscure village, and told the man to write on his application that it was in Russia. Using this ruse, the man obtained a visa under the unfilled Russian quotas. In another instance, a mother was granted a visa but her handicapped son was refused. Richter asked the United States consul what could be done to obtain a visa for the handicapped youngster, and was told that an affidavit from someone of great wealth would be needed. Richter contacted the Youth Council and such an affidavit was forthcoming.[61]

In addition to visa work, the Viennese Agudah undertook to supply kosher food and Pesach supplies to 3,000 families. This food was obtained by writing hundreds of communities in Hungary, Slovakia, and Yugoslavia, where Jews were still living in relative tranquility in 1941.[62] From these communities came the food, in the form of half-pound parcels, upon which most of the Orthodox community survived for three years. Nearby Bratislava (Pressburg) was particularly

---

59. Steinfeld stayed in Vienna until May 9, 1941. *Richter interview.*

60. Ibid.

61. Ibid.

62. Ibid.

generous. All these various activities involved the expenditure of $130,000 per year by the Agudah at a time when Viennese Jews had lost their businesses to "Aryans" and few had any means of livelihood.[63]

THE WAR YEARS WERE ONE LONG FUNDRAISING CAMPAIGN BY THE Youth Council on behalf of the Jews of Europe. It would be impossible

Fundraising to detail the seemingly endless series of fundraising campaigns, dinners, and "nights." Nor did the Youth Council keep precise books of how much was raised by each campaign or banquet. And even if such books had been kept, they would not fully describe the extent of Mike's fundraising efforts. Throughout the war, his signature appeared under the letterheads of various organizations other than the Youth Council, including Agudath Israel of America and Vaad Hatzala.

In the end, the most powerful testimony to Mike's fundraising is not captured by gross receipts, but rather in hundreds of stories of simple Jews who were moved to reach into their pockets to give money they did not have: Rabbi Shlomo Weiss pawning his entire *Shas* (set of Talmud), apart from the tractate he was then learning; another Jew, not even remembered by name today, giving his life savings of $1,000;[64] Berel Belsky selling his car and contributing the proceeds to the Refugee and Immigration Division;[65] "persons with large families and small earnings" borrowing $500 to $1,000 to contribute.[66] No contribution was too small to be disdained — even contributions of a quarter were answered with a thank-you note.

The most dramatic of the fundraising campaigns was triggered by letters received in late November of 1943 and signed by the Satmar Rav, the Nitra Rav, Rabbi David Ungar, and his son-in-law Rabbi Michoel Ber Weissmandl. These letters described the possibility of saving thousands of Jews hiding in the forests on the Polish-Hungarian border by bringing them to Hungary. The price was put at $250 per Jew.[67] Funds

---

63. David Turkel, "Three Years Under Hitler," *Orthodox Youth*, August 1941, pp. 8-9.

64. Interview with Rabbi Heshy Mashinsky.

65. Interview with Rabbi Berel Belsky.

66. Fifth Report to Chawerim Nichbodim of Agudas Israel World Organization, covering the period July 1, 1943 through December 31, 1943 [Fifth Agudah Report], p. 16.

67. The exact date of these letters is unclear. In the Fifth Agudah Report, Reb Jacob Rosenheim mentions letters from the Satmar Rav, the Nitra Rav, and Rabbi Weissmandl written in September of 1943 that reached him in late November and the contents of which were confirmed by cable from Isaac Sternbuch in Switzerland in early December. In a fundraising letter dated January 23, 1944, however, Mike mentions a letter from the Nitra Rav and his son-in-law Rabbi

Rabbi Michoel Ber Weissmandl

collected in America were wired from the Polish Embassy in Washington, D.C. to the Polish Embassy in Zurich.

Another cable from Rabbi Weissmandl arrived at 616 Bedford Avenue just before *Kabbalas Shabbos* in early January. No one who was present will ever forget the next morning's *davening*. Prior to the Torah reading, Rabbi Gedaliah Schorr stepped in front of the *bimah* and banged his fist on the table. With tears streaming down his face, he screamed:

> How dare we follow our own personal pursuits at a time like this? Where is your conscience? Jewish lives can be bought for money, and you think of jobs, careers? You have the heart to sit and learn when each moment may be too late?[68]

Gershon Kranzler described the dramatic response to Rabbi Schorr's appeal:

> At Rabbi Schorr's and Mike's appeal, *yeshivos*, day schools for boys and girls everywhere were closed. Some of these youngsters manned the telephones for 72 hours. Others organized hundred of teams of boys who searched the streets for money with spread-out tablecloths, not mere *pushkas*. The subways, apartment houses and housing projects resounded with the music of the appeals our children made everywhere. They attended every meeting of any Jewish organization, from the tip of the Lower East Side to Washington Heights and the Bronx.[69]

Mike himself stood on the corner of Delancey Street shouting for

---

Weissmandl that arrived through diplomatic cable on December 20. It is from this letter that the figure of 1,000 Swiss francs ($250) for the rescue of each Jew was taken. It seems, then, that there was more than one letter concerning the Jews hiding near the Hungarian border. The major fundraising campaign in response to these letters did not start until early 1944 after what was apparently yet another letter from Rabbi Weissmandl. Kranzler, *Thy Brother's Blood*, p. 158.

68. Gershon Kranzler, "Setting the Record Straight," *The Jewish Observer*, November 1971, p. 12.

69. Ibid.

ransom money to save Jewish lives, a sheet spread out at his feet to gather the coins and bills thrown in his direction. Over the space of a few short weeks, the various Agudah groups raised nearly $100,000 to be sent to Rabbi Weissmandl via Isaac Sternbuch in Switzerland.

The January 1944 fundraising effort was probably the largest and most dramatic, but in late July another major campaign was under way. That campaign was the outgrowth of a complex series of negotiations involving Adolph Eichmann and a variety of Jewish groups in Hungary. In May 1944, Eichmann proposed to Joel Brand, a Hungarian Zionist leader, the release of 1,000,000 Jews in exchange for 10,000 trucks and large amounts of various foodstuffs and non-strategic commodities such as soap. With that offer in hand, Brand traveled to Aleppo, Syria to discuss the offer with Moshe Shertok of the Jewish Agency. There he was arrested by the British and subsequently incarcerated in Cairo.[70]

Meanwhile Dr. Rudolph Kastner, another Hungarian Zionist leader, informed Eichmann's agents in June that he had received word from Turkey that the Allies agreed to his proposal in principle, and requested that the Nazis show their good faith by permitting a train of 750 Zionist leaders — including large numbers of Kastner's friends and relatives — to depart for a neutral country. Philip Freudiger and Gyla Link, two leaders of the Orthodox community of Budapest, managed to bribe Eichmann's chief deputy Dieter Wisliceny into adding another 80 prominent Jews to the transport, including the Satmar Rav, the Debreziner Rav, Rabbi Yonason Steif, and Adolph Deutsch, head of the Budapest Agudah. By the time the train was scheduled to leave Budapest in late June, it was carrying almost 1,700 Jews.

The Nazis meanwhile had become skeptical of the intent of their negotiating partners to deliver on their promises and refused to let the train depart. Here Rabbi Weissmandl intervened with a daring gambit. Using the pseudonym Ferdinand Roth, he had a cable sent from Switzerland that 250 trucks were immediately available in Switzerland. The cable was passed on by Freudiger to Wisliceny. At the same time, Freudiger contacted Isaac Sternbuch and instructed him to immediately purchase at least 40 trucks or tractors at a cost of 700,000 Swiss francs.

---

70. *The Abandonment of the Jews*, pp. 243-44.

Sternbuch, however, had only 150,000 francs at his disposal. He first approached Saly Mayer, the Joint Distribution Committee's Swiss representative, who not only refused his request for additional funds in the mistaken belief that the transport consisted exclusively of rabbis but also informed Roswell McClelland, the War Refugee Board representative in Zurich, who opposed all such ransom plans.[71] The funds at Sternbuch's disposal were inadequate to purchase enough trucks to secure Nazi agreement to let the transport proceed to neutral Spain, and the train was diverted to Bergen-Belsen.

In desperation, Sternbuch cabled New York on July 20 that he must have another 550,000 francs immediately.[72] Within a week, Vaad Hatzala transferred $100,000 to Sternbuch, much of it borrowed in great haste in recognition of how crucial every moment was. Included in this amount were $5,500 from the Youth Council directly and other monies that Mike had raised through Rabbi Herbert Goldstein.[73] Mike also played a role in arranging the wire transfer of money from the Vaad to Sternbuch.[74]

Using the funds he already had and those sent by the Vaad, Sternbuch was able to deposit a letter of credit for 10 tractors. As a consequence, 318 of the 1,684 Jews in the Kastner transport were released from Bergen-Belsen and arrived in Switzerland on August 21, 1944.[75] In that first group were the leading rabbinic figures whose

---

71. Mayer expressed the view that it was inappropriate for rabbis, as captains of the ship, to save themselves, while their followers remained behind. Friedenson and Kranzler, *Heroine of Rescue*, p. 114.

   Mayer did eventually lend substantial sums for the ransom scheme. Sternbuch informed the Vaad Hatzala on September 26, 1944 that Mayer had loaned the sum of 260,000 Swiss francs. Another 310,000 francs were passed from Mayer to Sternbuch over the next two months. *The Abandonment of the Jews*, p. 248.

72. Sternbuch's cable is included as part of a July 20 telegram from Mike to Rabbi Herbert Goldstein.

73. Mike to Rabbi Herbert Goldstein, August 1, 1944.

74. Mike's minutes of a meeting with John Pehle of the WRB on July 26, 1944 include the notation that sufficient Swiss francs would be available for the transfer by July 28.

75. There has been considerable dispute among historians about the apportioning of credit for the removal of these two groups from Bergen-Belsen to Switzerland. Saly Mayer consistently claimed that his own ongoing negotiations with the Germans were responsible, and it is true that the first group of 318 Jews arrived in Switzerland on August 21, the same day that Mayer commenced discussions with a German negotiating team on the Swiss-Austrian border. See *The Abandonment of the Jews*, p. 246.

   Sternbuch, on the other hand, bitterly castigated Mayer for his original delay in transferring funds to purchase trucks. In a September 7 cable, he quoted the Nitra Rav as blaming the failure of the entire transport to arrive in Switzerland on Sternbuch's inability to conclude the necessary financial arrangements in time for lack of funds. Sternbuch attributed the ultimate success of the negotiations to the transfer of 12 tractors to the Germans and the promise to transfer at least 30 more. In support of his view is an August 21 telegram from the U.S. Ambassador to Switzerland Leland Harrison. That telegram, sent the same day the first group of Jews arrived from Bergen-

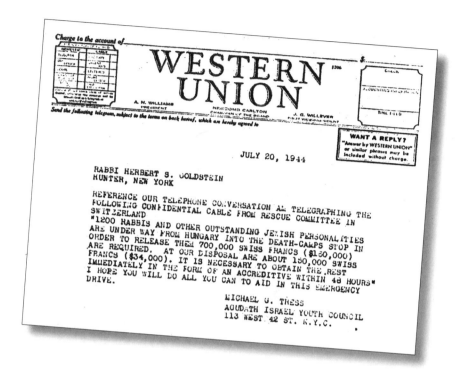

Cable from Mike to Rabbi Herbert Goldstein for funds to ransom "Kastner Train"

release from Hungary had been negotiated by Freudiger and Link.[76] In early December, the remaining Jews from the original transport arrived in Switzerland, thus concluding one of the few chapters of Holocaust rescue work with a happy ending.

Belsen, attributed to the tractor deal the Gestapo's refraining from sending more than 17,000 Jews to Auschwitz, including:

> 1,690 [actually 1,684] . . . sent later to the camp of Bergen-Belsen, . . . approximately 15,000 [actually 18,000] . . . sent to an unknown destination in Austria to be kept "on ice," and 600 persons still confined in Budapest.

Friedenson and Kranzler, *Heroine of Rescue*, p. 115.

76. On August 26, 1944, John Pehle, head of the WRB, informed Rabbi Avraham Kalmanowitz that 320 Jews had arrived in Switzerland, including rabbis "from among the 1,200 you have been so concerned about." The 1,200 figure did not include last-minute additions to the transport that brought the total figure to nearly 1,700.

Chapter Seventeen

IN THE CORRIDORS
OF POWER

I N ADDITION TO HEADING THE VISA WORK AND RELIEF projects of the Refugee and Immigration Division, Mike was the *de facto* representative of the World Agudath Israel in Washington. This role was a natural outgrowth of his other activities in the capital, through which he had established the most extensive Washington contacts of anyone in the Agudah orbit. At the same time, his effectiveness and access was increased by being able to speak in the name of a major international Orthodox organization.

Mike also served as the World Agudah representative on a variety of joint bodies. When Stephen S. Wise convened a Joint Emergency Committee of leaders of all major American Jewish organizations, after he and Reb Jacob Rosenheim received separate reports from Europe confirming the Nazi intent to wipe out European Jewry, Mike was one of the three representatives of Agudath Israel. The other two were Reb Jacob Rosenheim and Dr. Isaac Lewin. Mike's inclusion in the delegation with the most veteran members of World Agudath Israel reflects his status as the preeminent American Agudah leader and the extent to which Rosenheim relied on him in all matters requiring a forceful English presentation.[1]

Wise unilaterally dissolved the Joint Emergency Committee after one fruitless meeting with President Roosevelt on December 8, 1942, in which the President spent most of the meeting jovially discussing other topics, and the Jewish leaders present failed to offer any concrete suggestions other than a presidential war crimes warning.[2] Thereafter a United Orthodox Committee was formed under the sponsorship of Agudas Harabonim. Again the Agudah representatives were Dr. Lewin and Mike. Together they drafted a memorandum proposing the use of mercy ships to move food to starving Jews, the large-scale rescue of Jews, especially children, through the Balkans, and an Allied propaganda campaign directed to the German people via radio and the dropping of leaflets. This memorandum provided the basis for subsequent discussions with Secretary of State Cordell Hull.[3]

In September 1944, Mike again joined Dr. Lewin to represent World Agudah, this time at the Second Conference of the United Nations Relief and Rehabilitation Administration (UNRRA).[4] The most pressing issue on the agenda as far as the Jewish organizations present were concerned was the status of German and stateless Jews. Under the then operative UNRRA regulations, German Jews were considered enemy aliens and would have been treated just like German nationals. The Agudah memorandum called for surviving German Jews to be treated as citizens of the United Nations with priority in the provision of all aid. The memo further urged that survivors not be forcibly repatriated to their native lands, where the postwar political and security situation was unpredictable, at best.

The central role of the Agudah delegation was focusing attention on the needs of religious survivors. To that end, UNRRA was asked to begin

---

1. Fourth Confidential Report of the Agudas Israel World Organization, covering the period January 1, 1943 through June 30, 1943 [Fourth Agudah Report], p. 5.

2. *The Abandonment of the Jews*, pp. 71-2.

The Joint Emergency Committee was again convened prior to the March 1943 Bermuda Conference, but after the failure of the Conference to decide upon any decisive action, it was again disbanded after one gloomy post-Conference meeting. Fourth Agudah Report, p. 5.

3. Fourth Agudah Report, pp. 6-7.

4. Meir Schenkolewski also served on the delegation. The delegation was joined by Montreal residents Dr. Henry Biberfeld, Hartog Harogsohn, and Rabbi Joseph Elias.

Dr. Isaac Lewin addressing the 1941 Agudah Convention

stockpiling canned kosher meat and vegetable fats, which would be needed after liberation, and to allow ritual slaughtering as soon as livestock
became available. Kosher food was requested for hospitals, orphanages,
and other communal institutions under UNRRA auspices. World Agudah
promised to submit concrete proposals for the inclusion of Orthodox
community and social workers within the UNRRA regional teams to aid
in the reconstitution of Jewish communal life. Finally, the memorandum
requested that the needs of Shabbos observers be taken into account in the
assignment of work and that they not be disadvantaged as long as they
agreed to make up lost work time.[5] The Agudah proposals in this regard
were eventually endorsed by the other Jewish groups represented.[6]

AS THE WORLD AGUDAH REPRESENTATIVE IN WASHINGTON, MIKE
was one of the small group of Orthodox rescue activists in ongoing

In Washington

contact with American officialdom. From July 1944
through February 1945, for instance, Mike made at
least 17 separate trips to Washington on matters

---

5. Memorandum submitted to the Second Session of the Council of the United Nations Relief and
Rehabilitation Administration by Agudas Israel World Organization.

6. Joseph Elias, "UNRRA and the Jewish Problem," *Orthodox Tribune*, November 1944, pp. 1, 6.

other than visa work.[7] On many of these trips, he was alone; on others he was accompanied by such leading rescue activists as Rabbi Aharon Kotler, Rabbi Avraham Kalmanowitz, Reb Jacob Rosenheim, Rabbi Herbert Goldstein, Irving Bunim, and Meir Schenkolewski. Those with whom he met ranged from Mrs. Roosevelt to the leading officials of the War Refugee Board (WRB) and the State Department to the ambassadors of South American countries and the Vatican.

Mike's notes of his meetings include no instances of cold-hearted bureaucrats suddenly experiencing epiphanies of understanding and sympathy in response to his heartrending pleas or well-chosen parables. (Many of the meetings were with officials of the WRB, which was, in any case, fully committed to rescuing as many Jews as possible.) Even if such metamorphoses had occurred, dramatic accounts of his own activities were far from Mike's way. Moreover, the work in Washington, D.C. rarely involved major reversals of policy and sudden breakthroughs. To be sure, some such breakthroughs — such as Rabbi Avraham Kalmanowitz's fainting in the office of Secretary of the Treasury Henry Morgenthau — are well documented.[8] But, in general, the efforts in Washington involved the much more mundane tasks of continually updating information to and from government sources, exploring leads, no matter how unlikely of success, maintaining good relations with the leading policymakers, and keeping the issue of Jewish rescue constantly in front of crucial government officials.

Though the greatest flurry of Orthodox activity in Washington took place in the last year and a half of the war, after the creation of the WRB, with a specific mandate to rescue Jews, Mike's Washington involvement in non-visa matters went back to America's initial entry into the war.

ONE OF THE FIRST MAJOR ISSUES IN WHICH MIKE WAS INVOLVED was the status of yeshiva students in Russian-held territory. He was part

Early Contacts

of a delegation that included Rabbi Aharon Kotler, Rabbi Eliezer Silver, Rabbi Simcha Wasserman, and Rabbi Herbert Goldstein, which met with officials of the American Red Cross in December 1941 concerning the supply of food,

---

7. These minutes were largely prepared for the benefit of Reb Jacob Rosenheim, head of World Agudath Israel. Given the somewhat chaotic state of the vast Tress files, there is the possibility of trips other than those for which minutes were found.

8. For other instances where a well-chosen parable or impassioned plea is said to have caused State Department officials to change their former policy see, Bunim, *A Fire in His Soul.*

clothing, and medical supplies to rabbis and yeshiva students in Siberia and other parts of the Soviet Union.[9]

The next year he was active in efforts to obtain permission for 800 yeshiva students who had reached Turkmenistan on the Russian-Iranian border to go to Palestine. Though the students were Polish citizens, the Soviets viewed Polish nationals from areas of Poland under their control as Soviet citizens, and deemed the desire to leave the Soviet Union by their "nationals" as treasonous. Mike helped organize a delegation of leaders of mainline organizations to meet with Soviet Ambassador Litvinoff on November 10, 1942 to discuss the plight of these yeshiva students. That same day the delegation met with Secretary of State Cordell Hull and presented him with a memorandum seeking his intervention with both the Soviet and Iranian governments to secure the free passage of this group to Palestine.[10]

Two years later, as Soviet forces pushed rapidly westward into Poland, the situation of Jews in Soviet-controlled areas once again became of paramount importance. Of particular urgency was establishing contact with the newly liberated areas of Poland to determine how many Jews had survived and what their needs were. Orthodox organizations were eager to send representatives to Poland to assess the situation first hand and to begin reestablishing religious schools and yeshivos.[11]

John Pehle of the WRB told Mike on July 26, 1944 that the United States government had received little cooperation from Soviet authorities concerning contacts with the liberated areas of Poland, but promised to cable the U.S. Ambassador to the Soviet Union Averell Harriman asking Harriman to forward any information he could gather on Jewish survivors.[12] Mike and Rabbi Avraham Kalmanowitz heard the same discouraging message a week later from Assistant Secretary of State Adolph Berle: The Soviets still considered Poland a war zone and showed little inclination to allow direct cable contact with Jews in Poland or Lithuania, or to permit representatives of American Jewish organizations to visit these areas.[13] Furthermore, as long as the

9. "Red Cross Promises Aid," *Orthodox Youth,* December 1941, p. 1.

10. The delegation was headed by Congressman Adolph Sabbath of Illinois.

11. Minutes of August 3, 1944 meeting between Mike and Rabbi Avraham Kalmanowitz and Soviet Charge de Affairs Mr. Alexander Kapustin.

12. Minutes of July 26, 1944 meeting between Mike and John Pehle.

13. Minutes of August 3, 1944 meeting between Mike and Rabbi Kalmanowitz and Assistant Secretary of State Adolph Berle. Mike and Rabbi Kalmanowitz heard the same message that day from Chester Bohlen, Chief of the State Department's Division of Eastern European affairs.

Soviets considered the liberated areas war zones, any attempt to communicate directly with Jews in these areas was also subject to strict American military censorship.[14]

One of Mike's crucial early contacts was with Secretary of the Treasury Henry Morgenthau. That relationship took on even more importance with the formation of the War Refugee Board in 1944, since most of its leading officials were drawn from the ranks of the Treasury Department and Morgenthau

Henry Morgenthau
Secretary of the Treasury

remained quite involved in its activities. The initial meeting with Secretary Morgenthau took place as a consequence of a telegram sent to the Youth Council by the Polish government-in-exile. In it the Polish government sought funding from the Youth Council to allow it to remove 700 Polish Jewish children interned in Switzerland from internment camps to suitable hostels or children's homes.

Mike went to Washington to secure a $50,000 transfer license so that the requested money could be sent. Over two hours of conversations with Secretary Morgenthau and other leading Treasury officials, the Treasury indicated its willingness to issue the license. Mike was pleased with the meetings, and wrote to Reb Jacob Rosenheim:

> The general impression that I have gained … is that we have established a friendship in the Treasury Department with the highest officials. The name of Agudath Israel and the purpose for which it strives have been explained and will no longer be unknown to Mr. Morgenthau or his associates.[15]

Mike once gave David Hershkowitz a more dramatic account of this meeting. His meeting with Morgenthau was preceded by one with

---

14. Minutes of Mike's September 13, 1944 meeting with Mr. Lawrence Lesser and Dr. Aksin of the WRB. Mike added that he intended to pursue the matter further with the Censor Bureau in New York City.

15. The first page of these minutes is missing making it impossible to ascertain the precise date of the meetings or the name of those who accompanied Mike. It seems that these meetings took place in early 1943.

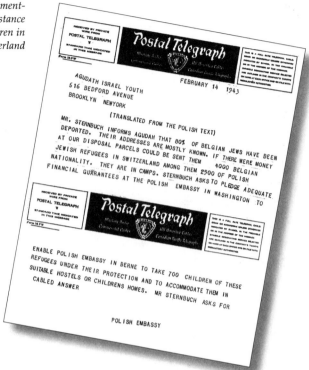

Cable from Polish government-in-exile requesting assistance for refugee children in Switzerland

RECEIVED BY PRIVATE WIRE FROM
POSTAL TELEGRAPH
STANDARD TIME INDICATED IN THIS MESSAGE

Postal Telegraph

FEBRUARY 14 1943

AGUDATH ISRAEL YOUTH
616 BEDFORD AVENUE
BROOKLYN NEWYORK

(TRANSLATED FROM THE POLISH TEXT)

MR. STERNBUCH INFORMS AGUDAH THAT 80% OF BELGIAN JEWS HAVE BEEN DEPORTED. THEIR ADDRESSES ARE MOSTLY KNOWN. IF THERE WERE MONEY AT OUR DISPOSAL PARCELS COULD BE SENT THEM 4000 BELGIAN JEWISH REFUGEES IN SWITZERLAND AMONG THEM 2500 OF POLISH NATIONALITY. THEY ARE IN CAMPS. STERNBUCH ASKS TO PLEDGE ADEQUATE FINANCIAL GUARANTEES AT THE POLISH EMBASSY IN WASHINGTON TO

RECEIVED BY PRIVATE WIRE FROM
POSTAL TELEGRAPH
STANDARD TIME INDICATED IN THIS MESSAGE

Postal Telegraph

ENABLE POLISH EMBASSY IN BERNE TO TAKE 700 CHILDREN OF THESE REFUGEES UNDER THEIR PROTECTION AND TO ACCOMMODATE THEM IN SUITABLE HOSTELS OR CHILDRENS HOMES. MR STERNBUCH ASKS FOR CABLED ANSWER

POLISH EMBASSY

Secretary of State Cordell Hull, who told the delegation that Jewish bodies were being made into soap at Auschwitz. When he heard that, Mike broke down in tears, as he did everytime he subsequently spoke about the Nazis' use of Jewish bodies for this purpose.[16]

The Hull meeting put the delegation in a highly charged mood when they met later with Secretary of the Treasury Morgenthau. The meeting was originally scheduled to last 15 minutes, but the Secretary kept the delegation over an hour and a half. Towards the end of the meeting, Morgenthau told the group, "Gentlemen, I knew I was *born* a Jew. Now I know I *am* a Jew. What can I do for you?" Mike then asked for permission to make the wire transfer to Switzerland, which was granted.

Morgenthau's attitude contrasted sharply to that of Jewish financier and presidential advisor Bernard Baruch, with whom the delegation met next. He told Mike and his colleagues after a few minutes perfunctory conversation, "We are now in the midst of a war. When the war will be over, the Jewish Problem will be solved," without even inviting the delegation into his inner office.

16. Interview with Robert Krane.

Latin American Documents

DESPERATE JEWS SEARCHING FOR ANY WAY POSSIBLE OUT OF EUrope in the late '30s were happy to have a visa to anywhere as long as it was out of the Nazis' immediate path. Some found that the consuls of various Latin American governments were willing to issue passports — out of an admixture of humanitarian and pecuniary concerns that varied from consul to consul. The value of these documents, even for those unable to escape from Europe in time, soon became clear. Those unable to use the Latin American passports in time were treated by the Nazis as foreign nationals and segregated in special camps where they received much more favorable treatment than other Jewish prisoners. The Germans apparently hoped to exchange them for thousands of German nationals living in South and Central America.[17]

As soon as the value of the Latin American documents became known, rescue activists in Switzerland, including Chaim Eiss and the Sternbuchs, began to purchase them wholesale. Relatives of Jews trapped in Nazi-held territory also purchased passports and smuggled them back to Europe. In September 1943, however, the government of Paraguay, whose Swiss consul had issued the largest number of these documents, recalled its consul and revoked all the passports he had issued. Two months later, the Germans gathered up the passports from internees in Vittel, one of the special camps for foreign nationals located in northeastern France, and the holders were readied for transport to concentration camps.[18] When the news reached Switzerland, the alarm was sounded.

Saving the holders of Latin American passports required three separate steps — none of them easy. The first was convincing the Latin American governments to explicitly affirm the validity of the passports in the hands of the interned group. Next, neutral governments, such as those of Spain and Switzerland, which represented the diplomatic interests of Latin American countries with Germany, had to push the Germans into treating the holders of these passports like other foreign nationals. Finally, it was necessary to prove to the Germans that Jews holding these passports might well be exchanged for German nationals.[19]

A combination of American pressure and the intervention of the Vatican, at the behest of various Orthodox activists, succeeded in secur-

---

17. Wyman, *The Abandonment of the Jews,* p. 277.

18. Ibid.

19. Friedenson and Kranzler, *Heroine of Rescue,* pp. 104-05.

ing the agreement in early 1944 of 14 Latin American countries whose consuls had issued passports to recognize the validity of those passports. At the same time, the WRB prepared a strong telegram to the American consul in Bern instructing him to press the Swiss government to protest the confiscation of the passports on behalf of the Latin American governments which issued them. The State Department, however, held up transmission of the telegram for seven weeks, during which time 214 Polish Jews in Vittel were deported to Auschwitz and killed.

Only the tears of Rabbi Avraham Kalmanowitz succeeded in finally dislodging the WRB telegram. Rabbi Kalmanowitz visited Secretary of the Treasury Morgenthau, together with Rabbis Shabse Frankel and Boruch Korpf, and, as Morgenthau wrote in his diary, "wept, and wept, and wept," until Morgenthau personally intervened with Secretary of State Cordell Hull. The rabbis also applied pressure by releasing news of the State Department's recalcitrance to nationally syndicated columnist Drew Pearson, who published a highly critical story.[20]

There still remained the necessity of demonstrating to the Germans that there was advantage to be had in treating Jews holding Latin American passports as foreign nationals. On September 13, 1944 Mike held discussions with the WRB concerning the preparation of lists for prisoner exchange which would include Jewish internees. In January 1945, 149 Jews in Bergen-Belsen holding Latin American passports were part of a prisoner exchange.

At the same time, efforts to ensure that neutral governments forcefully represented the interests of the passport holders with the German government continued. In October 1944, a three-man delegation, consisting of Mike and Rabbis Kalmanowitz and Goldstein, met with the Spanish Ambassador to the United States to secure Spanish intervention on behalf of the passport holders. And in December, Mike met with WRB officials concerning the failure of the Swiss to act as protective power for holders of passports from El Salvador. The WRB sent a strongly worded telegram to the Swiss government expressing the deep concern of the American government in the matter.[21]

Though the combined efforts of all those involved with the Latin American passports did not succeed in saving the deportees from Vittel,

20. Interview with Rabbi Shabse Frankel.

21. Tress minutes of December 11, 1944 meeting with Miss Hodell and Mr. Freedman of the War Refugee Board.

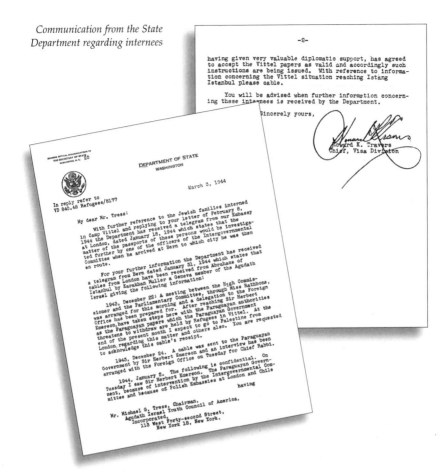

Communication from the State Department regarding internees

-2-

having given very valuable diplomatic support, has agreed to accept the Vittel papers as valid and accordingly such instructions are being issued. With reference to information concerning the Vittel situation reaching Istang Istanbul please cable.

You will be advised when further information concerning these internees is received by the Department.

Sincerely yours,

Howard K. Travers
Chief, Visa Division

DEPARTMENT OF STATE
WASHINGTON

March 3, 1944

In reply refer to
VD 840.48 Refugees/5177

My dear Mr. Tress:

With further reference to the Jewish families interned in Camp Vittel and replying to your letter of February 8, 1944 the Department has received a telegram from our Embassy at London, dated January 18, 1944 which states that the matter of the passports of these persons would be investigated further by one of the officers of the Intergovernmental Committee when he arrived at Bern to which city he was then en route.

For your further information the Department has received a telegram from Bern dated January 31, 1944 which states that cables from London have been received from Abrahams of Israel by Karakhan Muller a Geneva member of the Agudath Istanbul giving the following information:

1943, December 22: A meeting between the High Commissioner and the Parliamentary Committee; through Miss Rathbone, arranged for this morning and a delegation to the Foreign Office have prepared for. After reaching Sir Herbert Emerson have taken steps here with the Paraguayan Government authorities as the Paraguayan papers which are held by Refugees in Vittel. At the end of the present month I expect to go to Palestine from London, regarding this matter and others also. You are requested to acknowledge this cable's receipt.

1943, December 24. A cable was sent to the Paraguayan Government by Sir Herbert Emerson and an interview has been arranged with the Foreign Office on Tuesday for Chief Rabbi.

1944, January 2. The following is confidential. On Tuesday I saw Sir Herbert Emerson. The Paraguayan Government, because of intervention by the Intergovernmental Committee and because of Polish Embassies at London and Chile having

Mr. Michael G. Tress, Chairman,
Agudath Israel Youth Council of America,
Incorporated,
113 West Forty-second Street,
New York 18, New York.

the German government eventually announced that it would not deport any additional holders of the passports. Approximately 2,000 holders of such passports survived the war.[22]

Despite the fate of the Vittel deportees, the Latin American passports showed themselves sufficiently useful that Mike also explored ways of procuring additional ones. In late July 1944, he met with the Ambassador of the Dominican Republic, who asked how much his organization would be willing to pay for 10,000 Dominican passports. Mike doubted that anything like that number could be used, but offered to pay $10 for every passport.[23] In the meantime, he carried on discussions with the State Department to ensure that the State Department

---

22. Wyman, *The Abandonment of the Jews*, p. 279.

23. Minutes of July 26, 1944 meeting of Mike and Rabbi Joseph Yarmish with Dr. Don Roberto Despradel, Minister of the Dominican Republic.

would do nothing to obstruct recognition of any Dominican documents that were purchased.[24]

Another opportunity to provide some diplomatic protection for captive Jews came in the form of a directive from the WRB that parents, spouses, or minor children of U.S. citizens be allowed to follow a special visa procedure, whereby they would receive visas upon reaching the American embassy in any neutral country.[25] The U.S. would at the same time inform the German government, through these neutral countries, that those listed for receipt of visas should be treated as holders of American visas and accorded the full protection of international law given to foreign nationals caught in a war zone.[26]

The WRB also acted to save 5,000 Hungarian Jewish children from the Nazi vise. Recha Sternbuch learned from a Hungarian diplomat that the Nazis were prepared to release these children to Switzerland provided the United States issued visas for them.[27] On September 13, 1944, Lawrence Lesser, the assistant director of the WRB, showed Mike a telegram to the American Embassy in Bern instructing it to issue visas to every Hungarian child who arrived safely in Switzerland.[28]

ON OCTOBER 5, 1944, ISAAC STERNBUCH IN BERN SENT ONE OF THE most hair-raising cables to date. Himmler, he wrote, intended to liquidate all the inmates remaining alive in the concentration camps. As detailed in a confidential letter from the Polish Embassy in Switzerland to the Joint's Saly Mayer, dated October 1, 1944, the plan called for "a combined action by one motorized S.S. artillery division and a squadron of bombers to destroy the camp [Auschwitz-Birkenau] and to make all traces disappear, the minute the order is given in Berlin."[29]

Averting the Final Disaster

---

24. Minutes of meeting between Mike and Rabbi Kalmanowitz and Assistant Secretary of State Adolph Berle on August 3, 1944.

25. Though the procedure still required the filing of a financial affidavit, it no longer required the parties seeking a visa to first present themselves to an American consul in order to start the procedure. The visa could be issued before they reached the neutral country and thereby hopefully provide some protection to its intended recipient.

26. Minutes of September 13, 1944 meeting between Mike and Lawrence Lesser and Dr. Aksin of the War Refugee Board.

27. Minutes of September 28, 1944 meeting between Mike and John Pehle and Lawrence Lesser of the War Refugee Board.

28. Minutes of September 13, 1944 meeting between Mike and Lawrence Lesser and Dr. Aksin of the War Refugee Board.

29. Friedenson and Kranzler, *Heroine of Rescue*, p. 141.

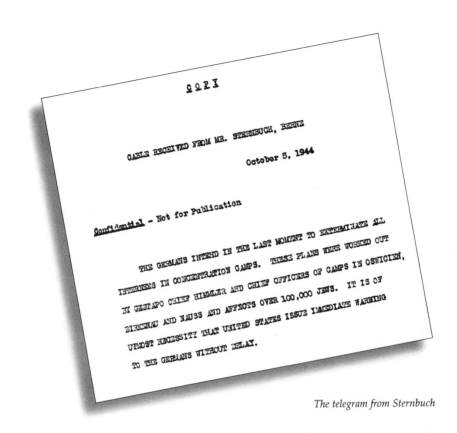

The telegram from Sternbuch

Hundreds of thousands of Jews faced death in the next few weeks unless something was done, yet it was far from clear that anything could be done. Germany's eventual defeat was no longer in doubt, but the Nazis retained the means and will to kill all the remaining Jews. Allied forces were still too far away to halt the slaughter, and it was clear that no Allied military resources would be deployed to save Jews.

Nor was there any reason to doubt the credibility of the Sternbuch cable. With the war lost, the only goal still left to the Nazis was the realization of what Himmler himself had once described as their most enduring achievement: the extermination of the Jewish people. Though Himmler had earlier shown interest in achieving a separate peace with the United States and Britain — Eichmann's offer to Brand may have been an exploratory feeler in this direction (See Chapter 16 pp. 289) — by October he likely realized that only unconditional German surrender would end the war. Thus Jews lost their value as bait to achieve more favorable terms. Even if Himmler took seriously President Roosevelt's earlier war crimes warnings, he knew that he could only be killed once and that the atrocities already committed surely merited execution. The Nazi leadership may well have reasoned that their best hope vis-a-vis a war crimes tribunal was killing every witness. No supposition about what had occurred could ever rival the stark horror to which survivors could testify.

The best hope of saving the threatened Jews lay in convincing those charged with executing Himmler's directive, from camp commandants on down, that they still had something to gain by not following orders. The same day the Sternbuch cable arrived, John Pehle told Mike that the WRB had already drafted a strong warning, to be issued by General Eisenhower, to those in charge of the camps holding them responsible for the safety of any Jews still alive.[30]

Less than a week later, Mike and Rabbis Kalmanowitz and Goldstein took up with Breckenridge Long the possibility of declaring all concentration camp inmates "prisoners of war." Long said he would study the proposal, but Pehle told the three men the same day that it was a non-starter because the War Department would never agree to anything which might complicate the situation of Allied servicemen or subject the Allies to possible German counterdemands. Moreover, there was no reason to believe that the Germans would ever grant such status to Jewish inmates.[31]

In desperation, Mike and Reb Jacob Rosenheim spent Shabbos day, October 14, at the White House.[32] They did not succeed in obtaining an audience with the President, but late in the afternoon they met with Mrs. Roosevelt. The First Lady told them that the President was very involved with the problem of camp inmates and that a war crimes warning to be issued by General Eisenhower was waiting for the President's signature and would likely be issued within 24 hours. She also promised to speak to the President that evening concerning Agudah proposals that she address a plea to German womanhood and that prominent Americans of German descent call on the German people in the name of German culture and decency to rise up against

30. Minutes of Mike's October 5, 1944 meeting with John Pehle and Lawrence Lesser of the WRB.

31. Minutes of Mike's October 11, 1944 meetings with Assistant Secretary of State Breckenridge Long and John Pehle and Lawrence Lesser of the WRB. The Orthodox spokesman also met with the Spanish Ambassador in an effort to have General Franco intervene to stop the extermination.

32. Mike's minutes of the meeting mention only himself and Rosenheim. Historian Monty Penkower, however, adds Rabbi Kalmanowitz and Meir Schenkolewski to the delegation. See, Penkower, *The Jews Were Expendable*, p. 255.

Washington Report – October 14, 1944

Discussions held with Mrs. Franklin D. Roosevelt by Mr. Jacob
Rosenheim and Mr. Michael G. Tress:

Mr. Rosenheim and Mr. Tress visited Mrs. Roosevelt at the White
House on Saturday, October 14th at 4:00 p.m. and discussed with
her the cable report received that the Gestapo Chief Himmler
had ordered the extermination of all Jews in concentration camps.
Mrs. Roosevelt stated that she had spoken with the President
about it the same morning and that the President had expressed
his concern and was willing to do everything possible that could
be done. She told us that the proclamation by General Eisenhower
was awaiting the President's signature and in all probability
would be sent to him within the next twenty-four hours. At the
same time, we suggested that the President issue a proclamation
in the form of an appeal to Germans, stating that all those who
would act mercifully in the saving of the Jews would be treated
in due regard after unconditional surrender. Mrs. Roosevelt
stated that she hoped the President would issue such proclamation
and to get Prime Minister Churchill and Marshal Stalin to do
likewise.

She also informed us that the President was thinking about the
feasibility of the plan of declaring these Jews prisoners of
war but did not know whether this could be practically carried
through.

A further proposal was made that Mrs. Roosevelt speak to German
womanhood and this was taken under consideration. Another
proposal given was that prominent Americans of German descent
be asked to issue a proclamation to call upon German culture
and decency to stop this needless extermination.

The interview ended with Mrs. Roosevelt's assurance that she
would speak to the President the same evening to present our
proposals and further discuss what could be done in this matter.

Mike's notes of meeting with Mrs. Roosevelt

the Nazis.[33] About the prisoner of war issue, the First Lady expressed
her husband's view that any threat to harm German P.O.W.'s in retalia-
tion for the murder of Jews would only spark an endless round of
retributive violence that would endanger Allied P.O.W.s as well.[34]

In fact, General Eisenhower's war crimes warning, which was
dropped in leaflets all over Germany, was delayed until November 7,

33. Minutes of Mike's October 13, 1944 meeting with Mrs. Roosevelt in the White House.
34. Penkower, *The Jews Were Expendable*, pp. 255-56.

Chapter Seventeen: IN THE CORRIDORS OF POWER □ 305

five weeks after it was first drafted by the WRB. Addressed to the German people, the proclamation warned them not to obey any orders, whatever their source, to harm those in concentration camps and forced labor brigades. The warning concluded:

> The Allies, whose armies have already established a firm foothold in Germany, expect, on their advance, to find these people alive and unharmed. Heavy punishment awaits those who, directly or indirectly, and to whatever extent, bear any responsibility for the mistreatment of these people.

Whether the warning had any effect is impossible to say though some survivors later reported a softening in the behavior of camp commanders in the last months of the war.[35]

Section Four

REBUILDING
FROM THE ASHES

Chapter Eighteen

VIEWS FROM THE RUINS

THROUGHOUT THE WAR MIKE AND RABBI Shlomo Ort, the head of the Jewish Servicemen's Bureau, had been in regular contact with hundreds of Orthodox servicemen. With the Allied invasion of Germany in April 1945, those contacts suddenly paid a completely unexpected dividend. Orthodox soldiers provided the Agudath Israel Youth Council with detailed information concerning the situation of the *shearis hapleitah* (survivors of the Nazi death camps) in the American zone of occupation.

AS SOON AS AMERICAN FORCES ENTERED GERMANY, Mike began receiving letters from Orthodox servicemen.

Eager to Help Many of them shared their feelings at seeing firsthand how efficient the Nazi death machine had been. One wrote, "I've read stories in the papers, but after hearing them [from the survivors], it is unbelievable to think that people such as the Germans should be permitted to live." Henry Cohn wrote of his brief exposure to a concentration camp in Austria, "I was there only a few minutes, but I saw enough to last me a lifetime."[1]

On June 5, 1945, Mike addressed a letter to all the soldiers with whom the Servicemen's Bureau had been in contact in the European theater. In it he asked that soldiers send lists of any survivors with whom they came in contact, together with the names of any known relatives in America. He also requested detailed information on the physical and mental state of the *shearis hapleitah* and their most pressing needs.

Mike's letter unleashed a torrent of pent-up feelings. From the number of replies received, it is clear that many of the Orthodox soldiers had been eager to help their surviving brethren but had felt frustrated by the lack of an organized structure in which to do so. "Your letter is the first indication that [anyone] is trying to do something for the pitifully few co-religionists still in this country," wrote Wilbur Marcus from Giessen, Germany.[2] Henry Hook stationed in Innsbruck, Austria echoed that sentiment: "Your letter of June 5 did not arrive a minute too soon."[3] The typical response to Mike's request for information concluded with some expression of gratitude for having been asked to help.[4] Even those soldiers who were stationed in rural areas of Germany, where there were no Jews left, wrote to express the hope that at some time in the future they would be able to help.

Prior to Mike's letter, Orthodox soldiers had already shown a great desire to do whatever they could for the remnants of European Jewry they encountered. As early as March 25, Saul Mendlowitz, who had gone through France, Belgium, and Holland with the 10th Infantry Division, had written to Mike, "Being right here on the scene, I feel as though I can be of great service. There are many people seeking contact with relatives in the States, and civilian mail is very slow."[5] Irving Berent, stationed from mid-May close to Feldafing — one of the German

---

1. From Henry Cohn in Augsberg, Germany to Mr. Tress, July 2, 1945.

2. Wilbur Marcus to Mr. Tress, June 12, 1945.

3. Henry Hook to Mr. Tress, June 12, 1945.

4. See e.g., Heshy Ginsberg in Langres, France to *Chaverim*, June 17, 1945; Melvin Kass in Innsbruck, Austria to *Chaverim*, June 21, 1945; Harry Roth to *Chaverim*, June 19, 1945.

5. Saul Mendlowitz to Mike, March 25, 1945.

army bases near Munich converted into camps for displaced persons — immediately began writing letters on behalf of survivors seeking relatives in the States. Over the next month, he sent out 200 letters to relatives of survivors he met.[6]

Mike's letter, however, gave a focus to the energies of Orthodox servicemen. A number of soldiers and chaplains sent in names of Jews that they had run across in the past several months.[7] In addition, much valuable information was received about existing lists of survivors that had already been compiled. An army chaplain named Klausner had worked hard to compile lists of all the survivors in the many DP camps in the Munich area, and another member of the chaplain's corps had sent the names of 5,000 Hungarian Jews in Feldafing to the Jewish Telegraph Agency. Other lists were forwarded to the Joint Distribution Committee.[8] The compilation of these various lists and combing through them for the names of those with relatives in America would become a major activity of the Youth Council Refugee and Immigration Division over the next several years.

A number of Jewish soldiers wrote to suggest that food parcels could be sent directly to them using the Army Post Office (APO) or to Jewish chaplains, who tended to remain in one place longer than the frontline troops.[9] And as news of the Youth Council's eagerness to help spread, Orthodox chaplains, such as Captain Hersch Levazer, responded with offers to distribute religious articles and kosher food.[10]

Moshe Swerdloff, a young accountant with Lend Lease in London, flooded the Youth Council offices with suggestions. From the volume of his missives to New York, it would seem that most of his day was spent thinking about what could be done both for the *shearis hapleitah* and for Jewish servicemen on the continent. He proposed producing a monthly newsletter to be distributed in the DP camps to provide spiritual uplift for the survivors. Elsewhere he wrote about the importance

---

6. Irving Berent to Mr. Michael Tress, June 18, 1945.

7. Chaplain Samuel Blinder to Agudath Israel Youth Council of America, May 13, 1945; Arthur Hoffing to Mr. Tress, June 15, 1945; Sgt. Jerome Shoenberger in France to Mr. Tress, August 13, 1945 (re: discovery of the grandson of Rabbi Chaim Halberstam of New York).

8. Chaplain Major Judah Nadich to Mr. Tress, June 19, 1945; Joseph Wechsler in Aalen, Germany to Mike, June 27, 1945; Rudy Tauber in Bamberg, Germany to Ernst Tauber (with attached letter on Jewish situation for Mike), July 28, 1945.

9. Irving Berent to Mr. Michael Tress, June 18, 1945; Harry Brown to Agudath Israel Youth Council of America, June 25, 1945.

10. Chaplain Hersch Levazer to Michael Tress, undated night letter; Chaplain Isaac Rose to Rabbi Ort, no date shown.

of informing Orthodox soldiers of the different laws governing Shabbos observance now that actual combat was largely over. In his three years in England, Swerdloff had become very close to Harry Goodman, one of the leaders of World Agudah. Many of his ideas concerned how the Youth Council could pool its resources with the British Agudah, which had already succeeded in placing a number of its operatives on the continent. In addition, Swerdloff had become friendly with the chief Jewish chaplain in London. The latter was a reform rabbi, and gave Swerdloff pretty much of a free hand in matters concerning the religious needs of American soldiers and the survivors.[11]

THE RESPONSES TO MIKE'S REQUEST FOR INFORMATION ON THE situation of the *shearis hapleitah* paint a harrowing portrait. "On the day

No End to the Suffering

of liberation," wrote Selig Chaim Tetove, "the survivors were in high spirits. They thought their American liberators would right all the wrongs of the Germans."[12] But while liberation had lessened the threat of death for many of the survivors, it had by no means ended it. Nearly 30,000 Jews died of disease and malnutrition in Bergen-Belsen alone after the liberation.[13] Six weeks after liberation a group of young survivors near Augsberg, Germany was subsisting on half a loaf of bread a day and some potatoes.[14] Sixty to eighty Polish Jews in a camp near Nuremburg, which was under the supervision of the U.S. 3rd Army, lived in conditions of extreme filth, with ten to sixteen people crowded into rooms designed to hold no more than six.[15] The Jews in the Bamberg area slept on straw and were entitled to no more than 2,000 calories a day, far below that required to rebuild the health of those broken by the starvation conditions of the concentration camps.[16] Polish Jews who had worked as slave laborers for the Nazis, Selig Chaim Tetove wrote from Innsbruck, were receiving only 800-1,000 calories a day, a fifth of what American soldiers were entitled to.[17]

The survivors had expected to be the beneficiaries of an outpouring of sympathy from the nations of the world in general, and their Allied

---

11. Moshe Swerdloff to Michael G. Tress, March 13 and July 8, 1945.
12. Selig Chaim Tetove in Linz, Austria to Mr. Tress, July 15, 1945.
13. Interview with Moshe Braunfeld.
14. Harry Brown to Agudath Israel Youth Council of America, June 25, 1945.
15. Sgt. Gorinfeld to Mr. Michael Tress, no date shown.
16. Cpl. Rudy Tauber in Bamberg, Germany to Mike, June 10, 1945.
17. Selig Chaim Tetove in Linz, Austria to Mr. Tress, July 15, 1945.

liberators in particular. But they were soon disappointed. Abe Septimus wrote home to his brother Sol of his amazement to find that German civilians were entitled to the same rations as the Jewish survivors, no matter how many years the latter had spent in concentration camps. The 60 to 80 Polish Jews in the camp near Nuremberg were still afraid to reveal their Jewish identity because the camp was completely run by Poles awaiting repatriation to Poland. The Poles controlled work assignments and the dispensation of all items in the camp. Sergeant Gorinfeld witnessed rations being taken away from Jewish teenagers "for Poles who never saw the inside concentration camp except as guards."[18] A group of armed Poles attacked a settlement of Jewish survivors at Neve Freiman.[19]

The task of administering Germany was an overwhelming one for the Allied conquerors, and in many cases they opted for the easiest course of leaving the locals in charge. As a consequence, Jews found themselves again being "pushed around" by Germans only months after the Nazis were vanquished.[20] German police entered a DP camp near Nuremberg with loudspeakers, shouting, "All Jews into the street." One Jew was killed and four more wounded.[21]

Morris Drucker met a group of Jewish survivors in Cham near the Czechoslovakian border. They complained bitterly to him that no one seemed concerned with their plight and that the Americans were "too easy" with the Germans. Drucker reported that the Germans controlled all the stores. A Jew, he wrote, would be told that items were not available, and then watch a German enter a few minutes later and walk out with the same item he had requested.[22]

The manner in which the Allied authorities applied their laws had the effect of discriminating against the few surviving German Jews. By repealing the 1933 Nuremberg Laws, which deprived Jews of German citizenship, German Jews were placed on the same footing with other German civilians. The prohibition against fraternizing with enemy civilians applied to them as well as Germans, and Jewish soldiers were therefore banned from talking to German Jews. "They were tortured

---

18. Sgt. Gorinfeld to Mr. Michael Tress, no date shown.

19. *Darkeinu*, April 1946, p. 2. The information in *Darkeinu* appeared on a page entitled "Round the World." The paper's information was presumably taken mostly from stories carried by Jewish wire services like the Jewish Telegraphic Agency.

20. Cpl. Rudy Tauber in Bamberg, Germany to Mike, June 10, 1945.

21. *Darkeinu*, March 2, 1946, p. 2.

22. Morris Drucker in Southern France to Mr. Tress, June 23, 1945.

because they were Jews. Now we can't talk to them because they are Germans," one soldier commented acidly.[23]

Though the Allies repealed the Nuremberg Laws, which had deprived many Jews of their property and businesses or forced them to sell to Aryans at a pittance, they froze all ownership as of the time they took over. As a consequence, German Jews were unable to reclaim their former property. "All this injustice," Private Sam Brooks noted in a letter to Mike, "is supported by our government. Jews are at the mercy of the town mayor and their neighbors. . . . Unless something is done quickly, Hitler's dream of exterminating the Jewish race in Germany will come true."[24]

The bitterest indictment of the liberators' attitude to the surviving Jews came from Selig Chaim Tetove in Innsbruck. He described how he had collected leftovers from the army mess every night for a group of Jewish refugees from Poland. But when the cook discovered where the leftovers were going, he insisted on throwing them out instead. Tetove complained to the commanding officer about the waste of perfectly good food. So the cook began giving the leftovers to the Austrian women who worked in the hotel instead. Tetove continued:

> The average G.I. sees to it that he gets food to his Austrian girl-friend but treats the D.P. like a leper — wouldn't go near him with a forty-foot pole. Anyone who says anything against the men treating the Germans as equals and fraternizing with them while despising the concentration camp victims is extremely unpopular with the rest of the men. If this war was fought against the Germans and to liberate oppressed peoples, you would never know it from the attitude of the average G.I. (and especially the officers).[25]

In a pitched street battle between Jews and Germans in Zielsheim, U.S. soldiers were accused of having sided with the Germans.[26]

There were, of course, many exceptions to this picture of poor treatment of the Jews left in occupied Europe. Often Jewish soldiers were able to use their positions to help their co-religionists. A number of Jewish immigrants from Germany served with the occupying U.S. army

---

23. Aaron Berger to Mr. Tress, June 18, 1945.

24. Sam Brooks to Mr. Tress, June 18, 1945.

25. Selig Chaim Tetove in Linz, Austria, July to Mr. Tress, July 15, 1945.

26. *Darkeinu*, February 1946, p. 2.

Rudy Tauber and Lothar Kahn in Bamberg

and were much in demand for their ability to translate from German into English and vice versa. Lothar Kahn, who had been active in the Williamsburg Zeirei prior to being drafted, for instance, served with the military government in Bamberg. He was placed in charge of interrogating local officials to determine whether they were Nazi sympathizers. "Much to my delight," he wrote Mike, "I was able to throw out Nazi mayors and install anti-Nazi mayors. Once I get on the trail of these Nazi ... they are done for!!!"

Kahn and Rudy (Shmiel) Tauber, another Zeirei boy stationed in Bamberg, took it upon themselves to solve the plight of Polish Jews coming into Bamberg after their release from the concentration camps. Kahn's major "pretty much let [him] do whatever [he] want[ed]" with respect to these refugees. If they needed passes to move to another area, he was able to secure these. But the major problem was that many of the refugees were simply stranded in Bamberg with nothing to do and no place to go. Kahn wrote to Mike that he had secured permission to requisition a large house for the refugees, and that he would soon throw out the German inhabitants and bring in Jewish refugees. He described his plans to create a kosher kitchen and *shul* on the premises, and

The first minyan in liberated Bamberg

concluded, "You see, dear Mike, the Agudah is still working even over-seas and in the army."[27]

DESPITE INDIVIDUAL SUCCESSES, LIKE LOTHAR KAHN'S IN BAMBERG, the overall situation of the *shearis hapleitah* remained very bad. Their

Growing Despair
mental state was in many ways even worse that their physical state. After touring the American zone in early 1946, an UNRRA official told a press conference, "If we don't clean out the DP camps, we will have mass suicide."[28]

Jewish refugees were in a far worse position than those of other nationalities liberated from Nazi slave labor. Polish nationals, for instance, could look forward to being repatriated to Poland. But for the Jews there was no place to go. Most of those from Poland had no desire to return there. The Poles, they told Jewish soldiers with whom they came into contact, were no better than the Nazis.[29] One soldier stationed near Frankfort met a group of survivors of Buchenwald and Dachau at Friday night services. Most of them would not consider returning to Poland, and one of them told the soldier that he would kill himself before going back to Poland.[30]

---

27. Lothar Kahn in Bamberg, Germany to Mike, July 4, 1945.

28. *Darkeinu*, March 1946, p. 2.

29. Wilbur Marcus to Mr. Tress, June 12, 1945.

30. From an unidentified soldier near Frankfort to Chaver Tress, June 26, 1945.

The Polish newspapers printed the names of Jews killed in pogroms upon returning to their hometowns, and members of the Polish government proclaimed openly that a Poland free of Jews was within grasp. Morris Drucker ran into a Jew from Warsaw who had fled to Germany carrying reports of pogroms all over Poland, and who had only been able to escape by posing as a Russian.[31] The vast majority of survivors wanted to go to Palestine, but the gates were still firmly shut by the British.

The bright hopes for Allied beneficence that the survivors had held at the time of liberation had long since been dashed. Perhaps even more painful was what they perceived as the indifference of American Jewry to their plight. In February 1945, Leonard Willig wrote to Shlomo Ort from Luxembourg, "All their hopes and prayers are directed to their more fortunate brethren in America to lend a helping hand. I have tried to console them with the thought that their desperate plight is close to our hearts."[32] One soldier wrote Mike in response to his June 5 letter, "Most of them have very great faith in American Jewry and were ready to hug me when I showed them your letter."[33]

Three months after liberation, there had been almost no contact between the major Jewish relief organizations and the survivors. There were no doubt many obstacles to setting up an operation on the requisite scale confronting the Joint Distribution Committee (JDC) and other relief organizations. With the Allies struggling to set up a functioning military government in occupied Germany, for instance, it was often impossible to know where the appropriate lines of authority lay. But whatever the case, the fact remains that the refugees perceived themselves as having been abandoned.

Chaplain Samuel Blinder informed Mike in early June that he was constantly being asked, "Where are the JDC and other Jewish organizations?"[34] Some survivors were driven in desperation to attempt to return to Poland. Selig Chaim Tetove wrote of them, "We bear much of the guilt. They are beaten in spirit and mind, as well as in body. They see nothing being done for them here, nothing but being subjected to slow malnutrition. No promise of someplace to go. Three months after liberation, they still see no relief group from the JDC or clothing, or

---

31. Morris Drucker in Southern France to Mr. Tress, June 23, 1945.

32. Leonard Willig in Luxembourg to Rabbi Shlomo Ort, February 16, 1945.

33. From an unidentified soldier near Frankfort to Chaver Tress, June 26, 1945.

34. Chaplain Samuel Blinder to Mr. Tress, June 6, 1945.

[anyone who can begin the] mental healing by drawing a picture of a new life."[35] In late August, Irving Berent wrote a relative in New York, "There are 16,000 Jews in Bavaria with no clothing. Large relief organizations have not yet brought their supplies into Germany. Winter is fast approaching and our people have nothing to wear."[36]

The feeling that after having lost five years of their lives they were still consigned to a limbo with no end in sight, and a generalized sense of being forsaken, led to widespread depression among the *shearis hapleitah*. According to Selig Chaim Tetove, the refugees were "improved physically but, if anything, deteriorated mentally from the time of the rescue. . . . The displaced persons from Western Europe were quickly repatriated but [the Polish Jews] have no place to go. . . . They lay around in assembly camps denied work while German P.O.W.s work the mess halls and get rich handouts." Tetove described the continual assault on every aspect of human dignity to which the survivors

A letter from a serviceman

---

35. Selig Chaim Tetove in Linz, Austria to Mr. Tress, July 15, 1945.

36. Irving Berent to Morris Wein, August 22, 1945.

had been subjected for years. In the concentration camps, if the person sleeping next to them died in the night, they tried to hide the fact from the guards as long as possible so that they could continue to collect the dead man's food ration, even if it meant sleeping next to a corpse. Basic amenities that free people never even consider — washing one's face, brushing one's teeth, using a handkerchief — were denied the inmates. The continuing assault on their dignity even after liberation was rapidly taking its toll on the survivors.[37]

Rudy Tauber wrote Mike that he was "expecting a wave of suicides daily."[38] The need for mental and social rehabilitation as much as food was a theme of many letters. A number of soldiers suggested sending Agudah volunteers and rabbis onto the continent as soon as possible just to give the *shearis hapleitah* a sense that someone cared about them and their future.[39]

Abram Spiro, an army chaplain stationed in Nuremberg, had taken responsibility for approximately 700 Polish Jews living nearby. Many of

Packing Pesach packages. At center, in shirtsleeves, is Beirach Rubinson.

37. Selig Chaim Tetove in Linz, Austria, July to Mr. Tress, July 15, 1945.
38. Rudy Tauber in Bamberg, Germany to Mike, June 10, 1945.
39. Sgt. Gorinfeld to Mr. Michael Tress, undated.

them, he noted, had been hardened and coarsened by the dehumanizing life in the concentration camps, and bringing back "all the Jewish values they inherited from their ancestors" would require "a concern with their welfare, an interest in their spiritual lives, a warm and throbbing heart."[40] Another soldier in the same area wrote, "Their greatest need is the moral help of knowing that there is someone who does care about them."

ALONGSIDE REPORTS OF THE GROWING DESPAIR OF THE REFUGEES came others of the remarkable clinging to their faith of many of the survivors. Joseph Wechsler wrote to Mike in early July to tell him that arrangements for a slaughterhouse in Augsberg with a reliable *shochet* were almost complete and that Feldafing had been described to him by Rabbi Yosef Yonah Horowitz as "resembl[ing] a *beis medrash* in prewar Warsaw more than anything else."[41] Another serviceman in Innsbruck sent to the Agudah offices a plea for help from the Innsbruck Committee for Jewish Refugees, which was attempting to register Jewish refugees, find them accommodations, and provide food and money to Jews in the area. The head of the committee was a young survivor named Jakob Mendelsson-Fischer, who had lost all 43 members of his family in the camps of death and was the grandson of Uscher Mendelsson, one of the founders of the world Agudah movement.[42] Morris Drucker helped form a group of Jewish refugees in the Straubing area, and was amazed that they seemed to be more interested in the fate of Jews collectively than of themselves individually.[43] By November, Rabbi Alexander Rosenberg, working for the Joint Distribution Committee, was able to report that *mikvaos* and *shechitah* had been established in most of the DP camps and that the religious groups in the camps were strong and well organized.[44]

Even in Poland, efforts were made to recreate some semblance of religious life. Isaac Lewin returned to Poland on a fact-finding mission and reported that seven Agudah branches had been reestablished in various cities since the war.

Sparks of Hope

---

40. Chaplain Abram Spiro to the Refugee and Immigration Division, September 27, 1945.

41. Joseph Wechsler in Aalen, Germany to Mike, July 11, 1945.

42. Henry Hook to Mr. Tress, June 12, 1945.

43. Morris Drucker in Southern France to Mr. Tress, June 23, 1945.

44. Paul Forchheimer to Harry Goodman, Michael Tress, and Dr. Raphael Moeller, October 28, 1945.

The thirst to resume a normal religious life is reflected in the large number of letters from soldiers requesting the necessities of religious life — e.g., *tefillin, tzitzis, siddurim, chumashim,* sets of Talmud — for the survivors.[45] Rudy Tauber, one of the Williamsburg group, pointed out in a letter to his family the significance of religious items, such as *tefillin* for the survivors: "They mark the end of the period when they couldn't observe anything."[46]

Food was everywhere in short supply on the war-torn continent, and kosher food still almost impossible to obtain. It was a bitter pill for the survivors to discover that even after being "free," they were still required to eat unkosher food to stay alive.[47] Several soldiers wrote describing a group of 34 young Hungarian girls they had discovered near Eshwege who would not touch any meat.[48]

Selig Chaim Tetove wrote again — this time from Marseilles, just prior to shipping out for the Phillipines for the ongoing war against Japan — of a pre-agricultural school set up by the Zionist organizations to prepare young survivors for life in Palestine. Even in this group — some of them quite young orphans — there were many who still insisted on *kashrus* and *davening.* There was, however, little hope that their needs would be attended to by the JDC inasmuch as those needs constituted, from the Joint's point of view a "minor" problem, at most, in light of the overwhelming task confronting it. The letter made clear that meeting the religious needs of the survivors would largely devolve upon the slender shoulders of Agudath Israel.[49]

The outpouring of letters from Orthodox servicemen provided Mike with a clear, if frequently grim, picture of the situation in Europe. It was now up to him to develop a plan that would utilize the resources still available to the Youth Council on the continent in the form of Jewish servicemen.

---

45. Abe Septimus in Eschwege, Germany to Sol Septimus, August 17, 1945.

46. Rudy Tauber in Bamberg to Ernst Tauber, July 28, 1945.

47. Sgt. Gorinfeld to Mr. Michael Tress, undated.

48. George Auman to Mr. Tress, July 8, 1945; Abe Septimus in Eschwege, Germany to Sol Septimus, August 17, 1945.

49. Selig Chaim Tetove in Marseilles, France to Mr. Tress, August 6, 1945.

Chapter Nineteen

FIRST TO THE RESCUE

What the Agudath Israel Youth Council lacked in financial resources and numbers, it more than made up for in dedication and ingenuity. While the Joint Distribution Committee — supported by the vast resources of the Jewish federations around the country — and other relief organizations dallied, the Youth Council was sending hundreds of packages into Europe daily. Months before the refugees saw any signs of the Joint, many were already benefiting from packages directed to servicemen and chaplains using the army post office (APO).

Of course, no matter how many 5-pound packages were sent through the APO, the

Packing Pesach packages for Europe

method was too piecemeal to ever meet more than a small fraction of the need. And in the long run, the amount of food and other supplies provided by the Joint dwarfed that provided by the Youth Council.

But recognition of those facts does not diminish the achievement of the Youth Council. The aid provided by the Youth Council came at a time when the spirits of the *shearis hapleitah* were declining daily and they were becoming increasingly embittered by the apparent indifference of both the Jewish and non-Jewish world to their unimaginable suffering.

The packages sent by the Youth Council, in addition to providing sustenance, sent a vitally needed message that the survivors were neither forgotten nor abandoned. Even after the larger organizations had finally mobilized their forces, the Youth Council had a crucial role to play in aiding those among the survivors eager to return to the religious life they had known before the war and whose needs were far from the purview of the secular relief organizations.

MIKE WAS QUICK TO RECOGNIZE THE POTENTIAL OF ORTHODOX servicemen and chaplains as conduits for food and religious supplies. It

Using the APO was that insight which enabled the Agudath Israel Youth Council to precede the mainstream relief organizations by months in providing relief to Jews in occupied Europe.

Loading packages for Europe

The principal means for getting supplies to Orthodox servicemen was through the APO. Doing so, however, meant putting the APO to uses for which it had never been intended. The APO was designed so that mothers of servicemen overseas could send cakes and the like to their sons. Each package was supposed to be preceded by a specific request from a soldier abroad.[1] Obviously the system was never intended for the volume of packages to which the Youth Council would subject it or for the purposes to which it was put. Yet the Agudah philosophy of rescue allowed neither propriety nor even legality to stand in the way when Jewish lives were at stake, and relief of the starving remnants of European Jewry was no exception.

Less than a month after Mike's June 5 letter to all Orthodox soldiers in the European theater, the first packages had started to arrive in Europe.[2] Many of the packages were routed through Moshe Swerdloff in London, and he in turn sent them all over Europe — to Munich, Vienna, Nuremberg, Paris — as needed.

One day, shortly after his arrival in the Munich area following the evacuation of Buchenwald by American forces, Lieutenant Meyer

1. Interview with Heshy Leiser.
2. Letter from Selig Chaim Tetove to Mr. Tress dated July 15, 1945, acknowledging receipt of 14 of the 50 packages sent June 22, 1945.

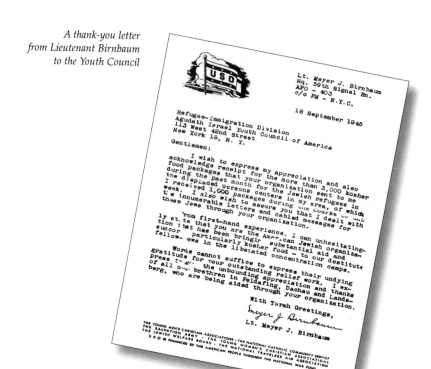

Lt. Meyer J. Birnbaum
Hq. 59th Signal Bn.
APO - 403
c/o PM - N.Y.C.

18 September 1945

Refugee-Immigration Division
Agudath Israel Youth Council of America
113 West 42nd Street
New York 18, N. Y.

Gentlemen:

I wish to express my appreciation and also acknowledge receipt for the more than 3,000 kosher food packages that your organization sent to me during the past month for the Jewish refugees in the displaced persons centers in my area, of which I received 1,000 packages during this course this week. I also wish to assure you that I dealt with the innumerable letters and cabled messages for these Jews through your organization.

I can unhesitatingly state that you are the American Jewish organization that has been bringing substantial aid and succor — particularly kosher food — to our destitute fellow-Jews in the liberated concentration camps.

Words cannot suffice to express their undying gratitude for your outstanding relief work. I express the unbounding appreciation and thanks of all our brethren in Feldafing, Dachau and Landsberg, who are being aided through your organization.

With Torah Greetings,

Meyer J. Birnbaum
Lt. Meyer J. Birnbaum

THE YOUNG MEN'S CHRISTIAN ASSOCIATIONS · THE NATIONAL CATHOLIC COMMUNITY SERVICE
THE SALVATION ARMY · THE YOUNG WOMEN'S CHRISTIAN ASSOCIATIONS
THE JEWISH WELFARE BOARD · THE NATIONAL TRAVELERS AID ASSOCIATION
U S O IS FINANCED BY THE AMERICAN PEOPLE THROUGH THE NATIONAL WAR FUND

Birnbaum was standing in the mail call. He was disappointed when his name was not called for a letter. That disappointment turned to shock, however, when at the end of the mail call, the soldier in charge nodded to a pile of about 40 packages still left and said, "The rest are for Birnie." In time, even Birnbaum's army jeep was insufficient to carry all the packages he received and he needed a truck for the volume of packages to be distributed throughout the four large camps in the Munich area — Feldafing, Fahrenwald, Landsberg, and Dachau.[3] In one month alone, Birnbaum received more than 3,000 packages from the Youth Council.

But even more important to the survivors than the packages Birnbaum brought them was the sight of a young American officer running around day after day for months to attend to their needs and struggling in his broken Yiddish to offer whatever encouragement he could.

The entire packing operation was manned by Youth Council volunteers. Initially most of the packing operation was done out of

---

3. On September 2, 1945, Sgt. Moshe Swerdloff in London wrote to Mike that he was forwarding 50 to 100 packages a week to Lt. Birnbaum in Feldafing. This number did not include packages sent directly from America.

Williamsburg. Working men would come in at night after work and pack until the early hours of the morning. Around 11 o'clock they would be joined by yeshiva students after night *seder* or returning from their evening college classes.[4] Often the yeshiva students would enclose personal messages to the recipients of their packages. Meyer Birnbaum still remembers receiving packages from Yaakov Goldstein, then a student in Torah Vodaath, in which was enclosed the following message: "Please give me a blessing that I *shteig* in my learning. Please give me a blessing that I find an appropriate *shidduch*. I'm your partner. I send these packages, and I hope they arrive in good condition."[5]

In other locations, Bnos girls worked sorting through used clothing collected for the *shearis hapleitah*. That which was appropriate was cleaned and then packed.[6] In an abandoned church in Williamsburg, which had been purchased by Louis J. Septimus, *tefillin, sifrei Torah,* and other *tashmishei kedushah* (religious articles) were collected for the DP camps.[7]

In late 1945, the Youth Council took over a rat-infested, abandoned store at 14 Avenue B on the Lower East Side. That store was soon transformed into an efficient food-packing operation which remained active for two years. Long tables were set up the length of the store and the packages were passed down conveyor-belt fashion and filled by volunteers. The store was in operation all day, six days a week. Yet with the exception of Heshy Leiser, who ran the entire operation, the workforce was entirely volunteer. Leiser never knew who would show up to pack on any given day, but somehow the requisite number of volunteers always appeared.

The volunteers came in all ages. A Rabbi Katz with a yeshiva for premesivta boys on the Lower East Side used to send over groups of his boys — affectionately known as the *ketzelach* (little cats) — on Sundays. Five or six volunteers could pack 500 to 600 five-pound parcels in a day. (The cartons packed for army chaplains could weigh up to 72 pounds.) In addition to the parcels sent to soldiers, Mike had arranged with the International Red Cross to send food to Jews behind the Iron Curtain in Hungary and Romania. Relatives of Jews in those countries could bring in whatever food they wanted for packing and shipment to the Red Cross. The lines of Jews eager to send food and other necessities to their relatives still in Eastern Europe often stretched around the block.

4. Interview with Rabbi Yaakov Goldstein and Heshy Moskowitz.

5. Birnbaum and Rosenblum, *Lieutenant Birnbaum*, p. 151.

6. Interview with Rena (Zirkind) Ebert.

7. Interview with Heshy Leiser.

*A group of Pirchim preparing packages from Europe. Overseeing the operation is
Rabbi Shlomo Ort. To his right is Pinchos Schaum.*

Packing was only part of the task. No less problematic was mailing the
parcels once they were packed. Each package was supposed to have been
individually requested — a requirement that would have slowed the
whole operation to a trickle. Fortunately, the operation was blessed with
siyata d'shmaya (help from Heaven) in this regard from the very beginning. The first time that Leiser showed up at the post office with 50
prestamped parcels and a handful of requests, the clerk asked him
whether he had requests for all of them. He replied that he had requests
and that he knew the addressees wanted the packages. The clerk yawned
deeply and told Leiser, "I'm tired. You stamp them [as APO approved]."
He did not ask to see the requests. Shortly thereafter, Leiser discovered
that the packages could be brought directly to the back loading dock of
the post office. He simply told the workers, "The guy inside told me to
unload these here." There was never a time when a shipment was turned
back. "I saw so much *hashgachah* (Divine Providence) working for
Agudah you cannot imagine," Leiser says, summarizing the period.

That is not to say that the packing operation never ran afoul of the
authorities. At one time, salamis furnished by Williamsburg butcher

Eugene Lamm were being sent abroad. Unfortunately, the requisite permit for shipping out of state was lacking, and Leiser had to appear before the New York City postmaster and promise not to repeat the mistake.

Two items were worth their weight in gold in war-ravaged Europe: silk stockings and cigarettes. Sending either through the APO was illegal. But with cigarettes, it could at least be plausibly argued that they were needed by the displaced persons for whom they were destined and were not intended as goods for the thriving blackmarket. By sending the refugees cigarettes, the Youth Council was able to greatly improve the economic situation of the *shearis hapleitah*. Somehow a postal inspector discovered the cigarettes in one shipment, and Leiser received a call from the postal authorities that the cigarettes would have to be removed from the entire shipment before it could proceed. He sent down a crew of ten *ketzelach*, together with a steel strapping machine for rebinding the packages, to the Long Island postal service center where all the APO mail was gathered.

When the *ketzelach* returned, Leiser asked them how they had fared. They told him that they had taken the cigarettes out of every package, but had put them back inside when they repacked the packages. At one point, a red-haired Irish supervisor had come into the room in which they were working, but he kept his head tilted resolutely towards the ceiling the entire time he was in the room, and said nothing other than to ask them when they would finish.

Running the packing operation was a grueling ordeal. Leiser, frequently accompanied by his new bride, often did not turn out the lights until one o'clock in the morning. "I never would have stayed involved for those years, or afterwards in the Food for Jerusalem campaign, except for Mike," he remembers. "He was the center of everything. He was a spellbinder — he cast a spell over us and pushed us beyond what we thought we were capable of."

Among the Shearis Hapleitah

THE WORK OF THE YOUTH COUNCIL WON WIDESPREAD RECOGNITION among those working on behalf of the remainder of European Jewry. Herbert Kahn, stationed in France, wrote to Mike in October, "Lothar [his brother in Germany] has written several times about the excellent work you are doing sending packages to the *shearis hapleitah* in Germany, and only praise can be heard about the Refugee and Immigration Division wherever you meet a Jewish soldier

Lothar and Herbert Kahn

who has been actively working for the survival of our poor brethren in various European countries. Your excellent work finds no counterpart over here even among organizations with much larger budgets."

But as always, Mike was impatient to do much more. He chafed under the budgetary constraints that limited all the Youth Council's efforts. In addition, he knew that the most important need of the *shearis hapleitah* was some hope for the future, a vision of a life still awaiting them. That could not be sent through the APO; for that he would have to go to Europe himself.

Mike had already been actively involved in pushing the concerns of the *shearis hapleitah* with the United Nations Relief and Rehabilitation Agency (UNRRA), headed by Herbert Lehman, the former governor of New York. Using his contacts with Lehman, he secured a commission with UNRRA, which would allow him to tour the DP camps in Europe. He left the United States for England on the Queen Mary November 30, 1945 for a Knessiah Mechinah in London organized by the World Agudah to plan the future of European Jewry. From London he went to the continent where he spent over a month living in virtually every DP camp in the American Zone of Germany and Austria. That journey to the DP camps and the stories of how Mike lived among the *shearis hapleitah* themselves would become the stuff of legends on which every youngster in Agudath Israel was raised.

Mike's visit was eagerly anticipated by the DPs. Many of them had grown up in the thriving Agudah movement in Poland, and would no

Mike in Europe

doubt have been shocked if they had known how numerically insignificant the American Agudah still was. For them the president of the American Agudah movement was something akin to royalty. The name Tress was one that they had heard over and over again. Meyer Birnbaum, for one, never stopped talking about him, and all the DPs knew that the parcels he distributed all came through the Youth Council. When army chaplain Hersch Levazer identified Yosef Friedenson in Buchenwald as the son of Eliezer Friedenson, one of the leaders of the Polish Agudah and editor of the *Bais Yaakov Journal*, the first thing he told him was, "I'm going to write to Mike Tress."[8] In addition, many of the DPs had been in contact with the Refugee and Immigration Division of the Youth Council prior to the Nazi invasion of their respective countries and so were familiar with the Youth Council.

To understand Mike's impact on the survivors, it is necessary to first grasp their frame of mind. By and large, they were extremely bitter, "almost disappointed that they had remained alive."[9] Those who came from Orthodox homes felt that they had been abandoned by their fellow

---

8. Interview with Joseph Friedenson.

9. Interview with Moshe Braunfeld who was in Bergen-Belsen at the time of liberation.

Orthodox Jews, and many were prepared to go to *Eretz Yisrael* with the Zionists or anyone else who could help them leave Europe and offer some type of vision of the future.[10] As far as remaining religious was concerned, their future hung by a very slender thread. Unless one made a concrete decision to remain *frum*, remembers Moshe Braunfeld, by the next day it could be too late. For him that meant deciding not to eat any *tarfus* after liberation even though the available food was still highly inadequate.[11]

The younger survivors had to make a concrete decision whether to return to being the religious Jews they had been before the war or to simply grasp at whatever life presented them. Their decision required sage counsel and guidance. But there was virtually no one left alive who could help them — no parents and no rabbis.[12]

For those who felt let down not only by the world but by their fellow Jews, the love and concern Mike showed them changed their entire attitude to life; for those still unable to believe that tomorrow they would not be walking into a gas chamber, he gave hope where there had been none.[13]

Everywhere he went, Mike immediately impressed the refugees as completely different from the vast majority of those who had come to the camps. "Most of those came stayed for a few hours, went away, and returned home to write articles in the Anglo-Jewish press of their great achievements," recalls Yosef Friedenson. Not Mike. He immediately sent away his jeep, canceled the hotel that UNRRA had arranged for him, and joined the *shearis hapleitah* in the camps, eating and sleeping with them his entire time in the camps.

Mike radiated love and compassion to the survivors. He came to Feldafing carrying 200 letters from relatives in the States, and insisted on delivering each one personally. Beirach Rubinson met Mike in Zielsheim and immediately felt personally attached to him. Everyone wanted to tell him their story, often over and over again. And they could see that he wanted to hear, wanted to feel their pain. He spent hours at a time listening to the bitter memories of those who had survived. Everwhere he went, he carried with him a notebook, in which he jotted down what he saw and heard.

---

10. Interview with Mrs. Pearl Beinisch, author of the acclaimed Holocaust memoir *To Vanquish the Dragon*.

11. Even most of the religious survivors considered him a *meshuganeh* (crazy person) for not eating *treife* meat in his still badly undernourished condition.

12. Braunfeld interview.

13. Beinisch interview.

Mike did not just listen. He told Moshe Braunfeld and everyone else he spoke to the same thing: "Anything we can do, we will do."[14] That included securing visas to the United States and helping the survivors find jobs when they arrived. After his visit, people felt for the first time that it was possible to go to America.[15] In one emotional speech after another, he assured the *shearis hapleitah* that they were not alone, that the Jews in America cared deeply about them.

His presence also gave a big push to the branches of Agudath Israel which had already been set up in almost every DP camp — between 15 and 20 branches in all. Agudath Israel was crucial to the religious rehabilitation of the *shearis hapleitah* because it gave them a feeling of connection both to their pasts and to other Jews around the world.

Twice in his stay in Feldafing, Yosef Friedenson observed Mike break down in tears. The first time was at the end of the fifth of *Shevat seudah* celebrating the *yahrzeit* of the *Sfas Emes* when everyone got up to dance. The second was when he visited Chayei Sarah, the girls' home that the Agudah branch in Feldafing had established, and he saw over 100 girls, almost all orphans, *bentsching*.

14. Braunfeld interview.

15. Interview with Joseph Friedenson.

ONE OF THE EMOTIONAL HIGH POINTS OF MIKE'S TRIP WAS HIS DIScovery of the Stoliner Rebbe in Feldafing. Mike's mother had been a fol-

Discovering the Stoliner Rebbe

lower of Rabbi Yaakov Perlow,[16] the Stoliner Rebbe in Williamsburg, and Mike himself was close to the Rebbe. Prior to his departure for Europe, Reb Yaakov told Mike that his brother Rabbi Yochanan Perlow was in Feldafing, but that he was almost certainly concealing his identity.

Rabbi Yisrael Yaakov Leuchter, then a young survivor from Czechoslovakia and today the principal of a well-known Talmud Torah in Jerusalem, had noticed soon after his arrival in Feldafing a fellow survivor who had somehow managed to retain his beard and still wore a *kapote*. When he asked the man how he had avoided having his beard cut off by the Nazis, he replied mysteriously, "I was a partisan. Some partisans fire with a gun, others shoot in another way. Everyone shoots in his fashion." Rabbi Leuchter recognized an aura of holiness about the mysterious stranger. Over the course of the winter he attached himself to the older Jew, who

The Stoliner Rebbe, Rabbi Yochanan Perlow, as he appeared in his passport picture upon leaving the DP camp

referred to himself only as Reb Yochanan the partisan, and who lived in a cold and damp basement, which lacked the most elementary comforts even by the primitive standards of Feldafing.

Indeed no one in Feldafing knew who Reb Yochanan was. Around Rosh Hashanah, he received a letter, and when some of the Chassidim from Warsaw noticed that his last name was Perlow, they asked excitedly if he was related to Reb Areleh Perlow of Warsaw.[17] His only comment was: "What does it matter?"

---

16. Rabbi Yaakov Perlow had no children of his own, but was especially beloved by the children of Williamsburg, to whom he used to pass out pennies.

17. Reb Areleh was another brother of Reb Yaakov and Reb Yochanan. In all, there were five brothers, each of whom was a *rebbe*. Reb Areleh was famous in Warsaw for *his chesed* activities and as the address for all those in need.

Mike's first question upon arriving in Feldafing was: "*Vu voint da der Stoliner Rebbe? Far allem vill ich gein tzum Stoliner Rebbe* (Where is the Stoliner Rebbe? Before anything, I want to meet the Stoliner Rebbe)." No one was sure whom he was talking about, but Rabbi Avraham Ziemba guessed that he might be the mysterious partisan living in the basement. During a reception for Mike in the office of the Agudah branch in the camp, Rabbi Ziemba went down to the basement to see Reb Yochanan and told him that the visitor from America was very eager to meet him and would come down to see him. Reb Yochanan, however, preferred to come up. As soon as he entered the room, Mike, who immediately recognized him as the brother of the Stoliner Rebbe of Williamsburg, started shouting, "*Shalom Aleichem*, Stoliner Rebbe. *Shalom Aleichem.* I have regards from your brother."

Reb Yochanan was very upset to have been revealed. "*Sha, sha, gornisht,*" was his only reply. The Chassidim, however, were electrified by the news that a famous *rebbe*, the son of the "Holy *Yanuka*,"[18] was in their midst.[19]

MIKE CAME BACK FROM THE DP CAMPS SEARED BY THE EXPERI-
ence. Years later, he told Yosef Friedenson, "I became a new person in

Back from the Abyss

the camps. For months I could not get the fifth of *Shevat niggunim* out of my head."

On the one hand, the faith and courage of the survivors had inspired him beyond words. He told Moshe Braunfield in Zielsheim, "*HaKadosh Baruch Hu* has given me a great *zechus* (privilege). I came to be *mechazek* (to give courage), and you have been *mechazek* me." For the rest of his life, he did not stop speaking of the dancing of the survivors at that fifth of *Shevat yahrzeit* celebration. He did everything in his power to impress on American Jews the unbe-

---

18. So named because he became Rebbe at the age of four, after the deaths within a year of his grandfather, the Bais Aharon, Rebbe Aharon HaGadol of Karlin, and his father, Rabbi Yisrael Perlow. He was one of the more interesting personalities among the later generations of *rebbes*. Recognized as an outstanding genius by the age of eight, he surprised his peers with his love of music, and his skill as a violinist. Famous in his lifetime both for his greatness in Torah genius and for the number of miracles attributed to him, the Holy *Yanuka's* fame continued to grow after his passing, and his *kever* (grave) in Frankfort continues to attract those who come to Europe to pray at the graves of *tzaddikim. Interview with the present Stoliner Rebbe, Rabbi Boruch Meir Yaakov Shochet, the grandson of Reb Yochanan.*

19. The story of Mike's discovery of the Stoliner Rebbe is based on the account of Rabbi Avraham Ziemba in *Dos Yiddishe Vort, Teves-Shevat* 1957, and an interview with Rabbi Yisrael Yaakov Leuchter. There are some slight variations between the two accounts, but all the principal details are the same.

lievable power of Jewish faith he had witnessed. When Beirach Rubinson came to America in May 1946, still barely more than a 70-pound skeleton, Mike took him everywhere with him to show the resilience of the Jewish soul. Everywhere he went, Rubinson, who had lost his wife and five children, taught the *niggunim* to "*Ani Maanim* (I believe)" and "*Al Tiru* (Do not fear)."

At Camp Agudah, the boys were obviously ill at ease in the presence of such an emaciated survivor until Rubinson got up at *Shalosh Seudas* and led them in dancing. When he sang the Skulener Rebbe's "*Z'chor Davar*" at the first Zeirei convention after the war, all the assembled burst out in tears. The words of Psalm 119, to which the Skulener Rebbe's *niggun* was put, resonated with special meaning in the immediate aftermath of the Holocaust: "Remember the assurance to Your servant, by which You gave me hope. This is my comfort in my affliction, for Your promise preserved me. Willful sinners taunted me exceedingly, but I did not swerve from Your Torah . . . ."

At the wedding of Mike's oldest daughter Henie Meisels, the *kallah* walked up the aisle to the *niggun* of "*Ani Maamin.*" Those who had grown up in the movement, with the memory of Beirach Rubinson teaching them "*Ani Maamin,*" recognized in that choice of music an expression of Mike's deepest feelings. For them it was the emotional high point of the wedding, and many could not contain their tears.[20]

But if he had been inspired by the faith of the *shearis hapleitah,* Mike was also haunted for the rest of his life by their suffering. Though he had known more of what was happening in Europe than virtually any other American Jew, the experience of seeing and hearing what Hitler, *ym"sh,* had accomplished was still overwhelming.

His heart was too big for what he had seen and heard. He lacked the self-protective devices that normally keep a person from being overwhelmed by tragedy. No matter how many stories of indescribable suffering he listened to, each new one cut him like the first. The normal human capacity to grow dulled to pain was absent in him. So was the ability to distance himself from another's pain — the suffering of a fellow Jew became his own.[21]

Those who greeted him upon his return from Europe were shocked.

20. Interview with Mrs. Daniella (Nussbaum) Buxbaum.
21. Interview with Herman Treisser.

He got off the plane with only the shirt, pants, and shoes he was wearing. Everything else — socks, coat and tie, suitcase — had been left behind. But the shock went far beyond the sight of seeing their invariably immaculate leader in such a disheveled condition. "When he got off the plane, you saw in his face that he had been in the depths of *Gehennom,*" Sylvia Klausner remembers. For months afterwards he walked around as if in a trance, his speech punctuated by frequent groans.[22] Though the doctors had their explanations, many of those closest to him remain convinced that the disease which claimed him at a young age had its origins in the DP camps and that he had never fully recovered from the horror he witnessed there.

---

22. Interview with Rabbi Yaakov Goldstein.

Chapter Twenty

A MESSAGE
FROM THE DP CAMPS

IKE RETURNED FROM THE DP CAMPS DETER-
mined to arouse his followers to do everything
possible to relieve the terrible suffering — both
spiritual and physical — he had witnessed.
Over the next five years, no one did as much to
make known the plight of the *shearis hapleitah*
in the Orthodox world. Those who heard him
felt that they were listening to the wretched
survivors themselves tell their story.[1]

No one who had not witnessed what he
had, Mike knew, could imagine in concrete
human terms the extent of the destruction of
European Jewry or how bad the plight of the

1. Interview with Rabbi Menachem Porush, who represented Agudath Israel in the Israeli Knesset for over 30 years.

survivors remained nearly a year after their liberation. American Jews to a large extent still imagined that the survivors had been the beneficiaries of an outpouring of humanitarian aid as the Allies recognized the awful price in human suffering of their previous indifference. Mike's task was to remove all such illusions.

Ad for Mike's speech at Hotel Pennsylvania

Mike began his campaign to lift the wool from the eyes of his followers with a mass gathering at the Hotel Pennsylvania the evening of February 10, 1946. The over-flow crowd — more than 500 people were turned away for lack of room[2] — had come for only one purpose: to hear from a broad-shouldered, clean-shaven young man in the uniform of the United Nations Relief and Rehabilitation Administration (UNRRA). As he made his way to the podium, Mike nodded to the many well-wishers who greeted him. No one who knew him could fail to note the toll that his trip to Europe had taken on him: His face was etched with lines of suffering far beyond his 36 years and the warm, open smile that was his trademark was absent.[3]

Mike's speech that evening was, in the view of many present, the most powerful they ever heard.[4] Melech Terebelo almost fainted when Mike described the conditions in the DP camps, and felt that he had witnessed them himself. The effect on Mike of what he had seen was itself the most eloquent testimony to the human devastation he had witnessed. "Mike just stood there and cried," remembers Rabbi Shlomo Ort. "You could see he was totally broken."

The speech had been billed "What I Saw in Germany," but Mike began by announcing that his subject that evening would be a different one:

---

2. *Darkeinu*, March 1946, p. 2.

3. Interview with Mrs. Malka Mashinsky.

4. Interview with Rabbi Shlomo Ort.

At the Knessiah Mechinah. Seated L-R: Mr. Harry Goodman, Mike, Dr. Hillel Seidman,
the Bobover Rebbe. Chaplain Hersch Levazer is speaking.
N. Schpringer, Secretary General of the British Agudah, is standing in the background.

I am not going to tell you what I saw in Germany. I am not going to report to you about things that I may have seen, about physical things. Instead I want to bring to you a word from those of our brethren, those of our fellow Jews who have remained alive.

THAT MESSAGE BEGAN WITH AN ACCOUNT OF THE KNESSIAH Mechinah in London organized by the Agudath Israel World Organ-

The Knessiah Mechinah

ization. There Jews from all over Europe, the surviving remnants of the Jewry in their native lands, had gathered to describe the situation in their respective countries and to begin to prepare for the future.

And more than anything else, [we] gathered to weep together. Men came from Bergen-Belsen, from Hungary and Czechoslovakia, from Barre and Rome, from Holland and Poland. We came to weep with them and hear what they had to tell us.

At a session devoted to youth, young men had spoken of their hopes for rebuilding Jewish life in their respective countries:

If you could only imagine for yourselves these young men, each of them arising [as a representative of his country], and each of them standing up with such deep *emunah* [and] with such hope that the *Yiddishkeit* in their country can be rebuilt. . . . These young people, who only yesterday were in Auschwitz and Treblinka, and Dachau, ... desire to see Zeirei Agudath Israel, yeshivos, Bais Yaakovs, and everything else that is vital to Jewish life rebuilt.

If you could have heard Celia Orlean rise and say that in Bergen-Belsen, in spite of the suffering, there were 400 young woman organized in Bnos and Bais Yaakov groups, then you would know that we Jews are an eternal people, that we Jews will live forever because implanted in our hearts and souls is a living truth.

Mike described some of the leading personalities at the conference — the Weitzner *dayan*, Rabbi Zvi Hirsch Meisels, who served as the *rav* of Bergen-Belsen; the Bobover Rav; the young Nitra Rosh Yeshiva, Rabbi Chaim Michoel Ber Weissmandl — who came to tell of the "*schrekliche churban*" of their communities. When Rabbi Meisels described the preceding Rosh Hashanah in Bergen-Belsen, the thousands at the conference wept along with him:

Every day there was a quota on the children, every day a certain number of children had to be sent to the crematoria for extermination. On this Rosh Hashanah, a group of 400 children were told that they should prepare for the bath. They knew what it meant to prepare for the bath.

So these children sent word to Rabbi Meisels that he should find some way to come to their room. They wanted to hear the *shofar*. Rabbi Meisels went in the middle of the night. Life had no value for him. Some of his own children were in this group. He did not care anymore whether the Nazis caught him and killed him.

So he came into the room. The children saw him and said, "*Blost shofar far uns* — Blow the *shofar* for us." And he blew the *shofar*. One of the children said, "*Rebbe, far vus muzzen mir shtarben? Mir villen leben* — Why must we die? We want to live. Why must we go to the crematoria when their children are walking upon this earth?"

MIKE'S NEXT STOP WAS PARIS, WHERE THOUSANDS OF REFUGEES
had gathered since the liberation. But freedom had brought no end to
Paris their suffering. Mike portrayed their desperation and the task
incumbent on American Jewry to help them:

> I'll tell you about one group of women, 33 girls from Bergen-
> Belsen, that I met on my first day in Paris. They came from
> Hungary and Czechoslovakia and had smuggled their way
> across the border into Paris, yet after all that they had been
> through, they could not find any place to live or food to eat.
> Sitting here, we cannot fully comprehend what has been done
> to Europe. There is not sufficient food for the populace, let alone
> enough for those who cross over borders. And we insist that
> these young women from Bergen-Belsen, each representing a
> whole generation of life, each of them depicting a whole world
> of suffering, must be housed and provided with some measure
> of comfort. Is that too much to ask? …
>
> The following day another group came from the French
> Zone, a group of 84 men and women, with the same plight of
> nowhere to go and no one to turn to. . . . Every day more and
> more people are coming into Paris, needing to be placed in
> hotels and homes. . . . Only today I received a cablegram that …
> "the first transport of children saved from Czechoslovakia and
> Poland has arrived. The second transport is expected to arrive
> next week, but financial support is desperately needed. These
> children have been smuggled out and must be cared for until a
> place of refuge can be found."

FROM PARIS, MIKE TRAVELED TO FRANKFORT, WHERE HE DONNED
the uniform of UNRRA for his visits to the DP camps. He described
In Germany what it was like for him as a Jew to find himself in
the land of his people's murderers:

> I tell you, my friends, I tell you from the very depth of my soul,
> that the moment I planted my foot on German soil, I wept
> bitterly. That on this soil, in this country, there were men and
> women walking around alive with their heads held high. And
> yet, these same men and women have perpetrated the most
> dastardly crime in history against the Jewish people. In every
> corner, in every face, in every "thing" that I saw in Germany —

Dais at the DP camp speech. L-R: Rabbi Herbert Goldstein, Rabbi Moshe Sherer, Rabbi Elias Karp, Rabbi Gedaliah Schorr, Herman Treisser, Sol Septimus, Dave Maryles.

I won't use the term human — I saw our own six million dead. And when I stepped out into the Bahnhoff in Frankfort, my heart bled and broke, seeing these arrogant people alive, and behind us, behind us the ruins of our own people, of our nearest and dearest. It required all of my strength and fortitude to restrain myself from reacting physically. It required every bit of my energy to stop from crying aloud, "MURDERERS! MURDERERS OF THE WORLD!"

THE FIRST OF THE DP CAMPS MIKE VISITED WAS ZIELSHEIM, WHERE between 3,500 and 4,000 Jewish men and women were housed. The

Where Are the Children?

men's camp was named Kibbutz Chofetz Chaim and the women's Ohel Sorah after Sarah Schenirer. As he spoke to the survivors, Mike began to notice something missing:

The men were between 16 and 35. I had anticipated seeing children. I went to the yeshiva that they had set up, and young men were there learning, but there were no children. Then it began to dawn on me that among these lost people in Zielsheim there were no old or young.

In my naive way, I asked, *"Vu zeinen die kinder? Vu zeinen alle kinderlach?* — Where are the children? Where are all the children?" And the answer was: *"Es is nisht da kein kinderlach* — There are no children."

Chapter Twenty: A MESSAGE FROM THE DP CAMPS □ 341

In all of Germany, there are a maximum of 100 Jewish children. In Poland alone, out of 3,500,000 Jews, there were over 800,000 children. The methodical, scientific Germans eliminated those children under the ages of 12 who could not be put to good use. There was also no value to men and women over the age of 60. They were the first to go.

The time in Zielsheim was a continual emotional roller coaster for Mike. Despair over the suffering endured, and still being endured, alternated with moments of uplift at the sight of the spiritual spark still burning:

> My heart broke a thousand times, yet at the same time my heart was filled with the greatness and devotion of our people. These young Jewish men and women had such deep *emunah* and they were filled with such hope and *bitachon* that it is beyond the human imagination to fully visualize what great strength rests in their hearts and in their souls after what they have lived through, after what they have died through. They still believe in *Hashem Yisbarach*, they still believe in the Torah. And they still believe in the greatness of our people.
>
> In Zielsheim, I met our *chaverim,* and I can tell you that their embrace was a warm one. They took me around and went everywhere with me. I was the first *shaliach* from the outside world. "*Ihr kumt nisht nuhr tzu nemmen bilder fun unz, ihr kumt alts a chaver* — You are not coming only to take pictures of us, you come as a friend," they told me.

DURING MIKE'S TWO DAYS IN ZIELSHEIM THERE WERE TWO TENAIM. One of the *chassanim* had learned in Bobov and the other in Nitra; one of

We Have Only HaKadosh Baruch Hu the *kallahs* was from the Bais Yaakov Seminary in Cracow and the other from Lodz. The speech of one of the *chassanim* at his *tenaim* captured for Mike in six words the situation of the survivors.

> I have to tell you a story about the night of the *tenaim* because it will help you visualize the entire situation of our people there. People ask me, "What did you see in those places in Germany?" **In the entire land, I did not see one complete human being.** This was made clear to me in Zielsheim. On the night of the *tenaim,* we were all sitting at the table singing the same *niggu-*

nim, the same songs, that we sing here. There were about 130 of us. If you had shut your eyes you would have thought that you were at a *Melaveh Malkah* in Williamsburg or Boro Park. And when you opened your eyes and looked around and saw for yourself who was sitting there, you could only describe it by repeating the words of the *baal simchah*, the *chassan*, himself:

"*Ihr vaist as bei yeder simchah, seiner da drei mechutanim: der Tatte, der Mammeh und HaKadosh Baruch Hu* — At every *simchah*, there are three *mechutanim*: the father, the mother, and *HaKadosh Baruch Hu*. We don't have a father, we don't have a mother. We have only *HaKadosh Baruch Hu*."

He had only the Almighty to turn to. It is with such *emunah* and *bitachon* that these young men live all alone in this world. When I was in Zielsheim, there was also a *Chanukas Habayis*. They had built a *mikveh* with their own hands. They made no appeals for funds. They just built it with their own hands.

That is why I say that my heart broke a thousand times, and yet, at the same time, my heart was filled with hope for these young men who have been through the *lageren* (camps). Let us understand what it means for a man or woman to have lived through a *lager*. It means having lived through a hell on earth beyond human powers of description. Anyone who has remained alive from Auschwitz or Treblinka, from Dachau and Buchenwald, from all of these places of horror, has lived through *Gehennom*.

FROM ZIELSHEIM, MIKE TOOK HIS LISTENERS WITH HIM DEEP INTO Germany, to the camps around Munich — Feldafing, Fahrenwald,

Giving the Lie to UNRRA Landsberg — and on to Garmish, Bad Gerstein, Gaulding, and St. Otillien. General Morgan, the commander of UNRRA in the American zone, had painted a rosy picture of the survivors for the world media, and Mike proceeded to refute his description:

[General Morgan] stated that there was an organized movement to bring Jews out of Poland into Germany. He said that those Jews were coming well fed, well clothed, with rosy cheeks and their pockets bulging with banknotes. And I say to General Morgan, or to any of his advisors who gave him such reports, that he should have visited the German museum in Munich when I was there. I saw those Jews who had just crossed the border to Munich from Poland. And in a hall the size of this one ... there were seven or eight thousand Jews lying on the floor. They were hungry, their clothing torn and ragged, and they were either too sick or weak to move. Were these the Jews that were well fed with rosy cheeks and pockets full of money? ...

There was only one bit of truth to his statement, and that bit of truth we are not ashamed of. We are proud of it. There is an organization that is helping these Jews to escape from Poland and bringing them across Slovakia into Germany. In Poland no Jew is safe. More that once I sat in on meetings where we planned the smuggling of our people across those borders. We are proud of the fact that we are bringing our Jews out of these countries where there is no hope for them.

Later in the speech Mike detailed the diets on which the survivors subsisted and the clothing they wore:

I want you to know that 40 percent of the Jews are tubercular. They do receive food, but only enough to gradually die from. If one had to live from the food portioned out to them alone, he could not survive for long. Day after day, their diet consists of sardines and bread and tea and jam. Day afer day. There are no fresh foods or fruit, there is no meat. We are normal, healthy human beings, and we could not survive on such an insufficient diet. There are not enough calories to live on.

You are anxious to know what they wear. Do not visualize what you yourselves wear. The truth is that they don't have clothing. They don't even have the basic necessities. I have seen ... 16-year-old boys and girls walking around with cardboard tied around their feet where the snow was knee high.

Mike coupled his description of the clothing worn by the *shearis hapleitah* with an uncharacteristically sharp criticism of the donations to date. He goaded his listeners to greater generosity:

We are very magnanimous, and in our great generosity, what do we do? We rummage through our closets, and we find clothing that has been saved from one Pesach to the next. And this is

Mike speaking about the DP camps

what we give to them, and I tell you the clothing that is donated is quite poor. It is true that you cannot send new clothing, but try to send clothing that is at least cleaned, that is repaired. It is a psychological blow to these people when you tell them to trade rags for rags. They would rather go around in their original rags than have to put on these new rags.

MIKE DID NOT LULL HIS AUDIENCE WITH CLAIMS THAT SPIRITUAL fortitude was sufficient to overcome the degradation of the physical conditions in which the survivors lived — the lack of **Breaking** food, clothing, and sanitation. He made it clear that **the Spirit** physical degradation of that magnitude breaks the spirit as well as the body:

> Our people are driven to doing terrible things. These *lager* Jews are driven to finding any way of attempting to live. Otherwise they would die. You must realize what it means to be a *lager* Jew and to have to fight for every minute of your existence.

The situation, he said, was a continuation of that in death camps themselves when "there were times when our own people were being transported from their homes in cattle cars, hundreds of them in cattle cars. And when the father sitting next to his son suffocated to death because of a lack of oxygen, the son would rejoice in the additional air to breathe."

> Here it is ten months after the liberation, and our people still have to resort to all sorts of transactions. What is more tragic

that anything else is to see them standing at the door, with their hands outstretched, begging for food and clothing, begging to live.

Living Among the Survivors

MIKE HAD GONE TO THE DP CAMPS WITH THE INTENTION OF LIVING among the survivors on the theory that there was no other way to truly gain an understanding of their problems. He pictured the barracks in Landsberg where he stayed:

> In the barracks of Landsberg, perhaps four to six people can fit in a pinch. Yet in these rooms, 16, 20, even 24 people can be found sleeping in double and triple-deckers on beds that are nothing more than wooden planks.
>
> As a guest from the United States, I was given a straw sack to sleep on. I had the privilege to sleep on a straw sack. No coverings, no sheets or pillows, not even such elementary sanitary facilities as a water supply. And this a full ten months after the liberation. . . .
>
> Yet in Landsberg, a *lager* of about 5,000 Jews living under these conditions, there were 75 Jews who had formed a yeshiva. There were 75 *chaverim* from Zeirei Agudath Israel and Poalei Agudath Israel learning together.

At this point, Mike reached the emotional high point of his speech. He related two incidents from his nights spent sleeping with the *shearis hapleitah* — incidents which, in his own words, left him so shattered that he did not think that he could continue with his trip:

> Well, after a good day of hard toil, you tell yourself that you can accustom yourself to anything. So finally I was able to fall asleep, even on that straw sack. In the middle of the night it was pitch dark. Suddenly, one of the survivors gets up and lights a candle. I awoke and looked at that man and watched what he was doing. I saw him going around with his candle looking in every corner, looking under the bunks, looking all over. Then he put out the candle and shouted, "*Zei zenen nisht dah! Gevald, ich hab zei alein farbrent* — They are not here. I burned them myself."
>
> Suffice it to say that I did not sleep any more that night. In the morning, I said to those around me, "What was this?" And they told me that this man had lost his wife and six children, which

[in that place] was nothing new. But what was different was that he was the one who had put the coal into the crematorium where they were being burned. And so he went around every night looking for his wife and six children, seeking them even though he knew that they were not alive.

In another *lager*, in another bunk, on another night, I was again awakened. This time it was a young boy. He was calling, "Mama, Mama!" He just kept crying over and over for his mother. I got off my bed and went over to him and just held him. I hugged him and kissed him, and I told him, "I don't know where your Mama is, and I don't know where your *Tatte* is, but I know that you'll never be alone again."

When he repeated the word "Mama," Rabbi Feivel Rosenzweig recalls, people broke out wailing in the hall.

MIKE JUXTAPOSED THE DEGRADING CIRCUMSTANCES IN WHICH the *shearis hapleitah* found themselves to scenes of desperate clinging to
Grasping the Divine spark:
at Straws   Now let me tell you about Feldafing. It was the fifth of *Shevat* when I was there, the *yahrzeit* of the *Sfas Emes*. For Gerrer Chassidim all over the world, in every one of the *lageren,* there was a *kiddush Hashem.* In Bergen-Belsen, in Fahrenwald, in Zielsheim, in Bad Gerstein, in every one of the *lageren,* they celebrated their first free *Hei Shevat.* At that *simchah,* they talked of last year. They said, "Who would have thought last year, in the concentration camps, that this year we would be able to sit around a table again and celebrate this great festival?"

This is the greatness of our people. After what these people had been through, to still be so grateful to *HaKadosh Baruch Hu.* My heart broke again and again because I could see what they couldn't. **I saw men trying to act human, grasping at every straw to try and live like a normal human being.**

At Landsberg, I again saw a group of our *chaverim* sitting around a table. They said that they were going to have a *shiur.* So I came. There were 40 young men sitting there around the table. They were just sitting there, so I waited. I wondered when they were going to bring in the *sefarim.* Finally, they brought in one page of a *Gemara*. One page of a *Gemara*, and around that page these 40 young men were learning their *shiur*.

And that was already a change for the better. At one time, there were 400 men using one pair of *tefillin* a day. They got up early in the morning, made the *berachah*, put on the *tefillin*, and passed them to the next one until all 400 men made the *berachah* on that one pair of *tefillin*.

That is what you call *emunah*. That is what you call *bitachon*. That is what you call *klahrkeit* (clarity). The situation has now improved greatly. Now only 15 or 20 use one pair of *tefillin*.

THE GREATEST WISH OF THE SURVIVORS WAS TO LEAVE GERMANY and to begin the rest of their lives. No normal life was possible in the

For Eretz Yisrael
camps; nor could they even begin preparing themselves as long as they remained there. Many had lost their entire youth in the concentration camps, and they were desperate not to waste any more years:

As I told you, they are grasping at every straw to return to some form of normalcy. But above all, they want to leave. They feel that they are on a boat, a boat that just keeps going on and on. But where will it stop? They said to me, "What will be the end of us? What will happen to us? We will not remain on this soil." They have vowed that not one of them will remain on that soil drenched with the blood of their own.

Where do they want to go? The answer is obvious. Of course, they all want to go to *Eretz Yisrael*, and they cannot believe that the ears of the world will be deaf to their plea. . . . But they see reality. They know that the great nations of the world forgot them when they were being slaughtered in the millions. They have had to face reality.

Until they can go to *Eretz Yisrael*, they want to leave the land that they call the *farshaltenne land*, the accursed land. We too must ask: What will be their final destination? Where will they go and what will happen to them? In Germany, Austria, Italy, the American zone, the British zone, in all of these places, there are altogether a maximum of 140,000 Jews, 140,000 *lager* Jews.

When I say "*lager* Jews" every muscle in my body vibrates with the word. For these Jews there are no walls, there are no barriers, there are no iron cells that they will not break rather than remain on that soil.

I say this because I have spoken to many thousands of them, spoken to them personally, and I know of their deep will and desire and hope to go to *Eretz Yisrael*. Yet they are realistic enough to know that until they can go to *Eretz Yisrael*, they would like to see the doors of this country and of other countries open to them. Instead they get proclamations that are quite empty, proclamations that mean nothing.

MIKE'S PURPOSE THAT NIGHT WAS NOT TO PULL THE HEARTSTRINGS of his audience but to mobilize them for a campaign far beyond their

Beyond Tzedakah

numbers — a campaign to supply kosher food and decent clothing, to provide *sefarim* and *tashmishei kodesh*, and to continue the affidavit work necessary to bring as many as possible to the United States as long as Palestine under the British Mandate remained a virtually closed door:

> Visualize for yourselves what these people need. Visualize for yourselves what needs to be done for them. Even though we are a small organization, we have already sent thousands of pounds of food, thousands upon thousands of pounds of kosher food. They have no kosher food. No kosher meat. Both the American and British governments believe that the German populace should not be deprived of their livestock. So the Jews are dependent for any form of nourishment on the outside world. These packages that we send may be small things when you think of them. But my dear people, multiply them by thousands. It is true that a small percentage gets lost. But at least 80 percent arrives. And in a country whose transportation system is in chaos — where there are no roads and no postal system — something should get lost. But even if a greater percentage were lost, we would have to continue because we know that these supplies give life to so many thousands of people.

Above all, Mike told his audience, a complete revision of their way of thinking about aid for the *shearis hapleitah* was needed. The normal categories of *tzedakah* no longer applied as far as they were concerned. All that was done for them should not be conceived as *tzedakah* but as *pirsumei nisa* (the publicizing of a miracle) and a *kiddush Hashem*:

My friends, I want you to fully understand, that for the *lager* Jews, we are practically their only hope. What do we have to do? First, we must change our mental attitude towards these people. Until now when we gave our *tzedakah*, whether in the form of a contribution or as a pledge, we gave as a form of charity. To give charity is noble thing, a worthy thing. We Jews know how to give *tzedakah*.

But my dear friends, we must have a different attitude when dealing with these Jews. These people are no longer charity cases. These are *lager Yidden, Yidden* who have lived through hell on earth. For every one of them, it is a *nes min HaShamayim*, a miracle from Heaven, that they remain alive. These are Jews who should be carried around in our hands. When in our generosity, in our great bounty, we help these Jews, we don't give them *tzedakah*.

The trouble with us is that we have lived too long in *Galus*, and we have become like the people of *Galus*. These Jews, this handful of our people that have remained alive, must be given a form of aid that comes from our very hearts. If need be, they must be given everything that we possess to lighten their burden. We must see to it that they have their food and that their other needs are met. They don't ask for much.

MIKE HAD SEEN ON HIS TRIP HOW IMPORTANT IT WAS TO THE *shearis hapleitah* to feel that they were not completely abandoned. As

Don't Forget Us needed as material aid was, no less great was the need of these Jews who had lost everything — family, friends, the entire world in which they had grown up — to feel that they were not all alone and uncared for. Everywhere he had gone, the Jews he met begged him to stay:

> They said to me when I left, they grasped my arm and said to me, "*Farlast unz nisht. Ihr last unz uber alein. Mir zainen vaiter alein. Farlast unz nisht. Shickt unz noch a shaliach fun America. Fun die yugend vas hat gefeel far unz* — Don't leave us. You are leaving us all alone. We will again be alone. Do not leave us. Send us another *shaliach* from America, from the youth that feels for us."

Already they were thinking about Pesach, about how they would celebrate the redemption from bondage in Egypt while still in the camps. Mike promised that he would make sure that they were able to celebrate a proper Pesach:

> They said to me, "Pesach is coming." And I promised them, "When I return to America, I'll go door to door, and I'll awaken Jews to the idea, 'Es kummt Pesach.'"
>
> I shudder at the thought that these Jews will not have a Pesach. I came home and told all of my *chaverim* on the Executive Board, "We can't let a day go past. We must provide a Pesach for these Jews. We must show those few who have remained alive that we have not forgotten them and that we will extend a helping hand across the ocean."
>
> And so this small group of *chaverim* have resolved to send in the next three weeks more than 300,000 pounds of kosher food for Pesach to the Jews in the different countries of Europe. True, we are going to appeal to you tonight, but don't be afraid. . . .
>
> These words describe a vision left of Feldafing, of Fahrenwald, of Landsberg, of those Jews gathering together, waiting and hoping that we will think of them.

When Mike was done, there was silence in the hall. It was as if the audience had taken a collective punch in the solar plexus and all the breath had been knocked out of it. Only after a long pause did the audience erupt in applause, but by then Mike had already descended from the dais and left the hall.

Chapter Twenty-One

KEEPING FAITH WITH THE SURVIVORS

M

IKE'S SPEECH AT HOTEL PENNSYLVANIA was the opening salvo in a campaign to arouse American Jewry to the requirements of the *shearis hapleitah.* Those needs were both physical and spiritual. On the physical level, the immediate needs were food and clothing; on the spiritual, a reason to live and some hope for the future. The latter could not be supplied, but at least those items the survivors needed to resume their lives as observant Jews — *sefarim* and *tashmishei kedushah,* such as *tefillin, taleisim,* and *chalafim* (knives for ritual slaughter) — could be.

A Responsibility Sought

The work of helping the survivors to rebuild their shattered lives was not just a responsibility that the Youth Council accepted in response to requests from abroad. Mike actively sought out the task. In a letter to the Sternbuchs in Switzerland and Mrs. Renee Reichmann in Tangiers shortly after the liberation, he wrote:

> We are very anxious to be of help to our brethren in the liberated countries and one of the projects which we are now in the midst of is sending religious articles and also kosher food packages to the children. We would be very grateful if you could forward to us, as quickly as possible, lists of those children under your supervision and who are in need of this aid. . . .
>
> We also wish to inform you that we are very anxious to expedite the procuring of visas to the United States for any case that you may have. In this respect, we will need the vital information, and we are enclosing a sample form as to the questions that should be answered.[1]

There was, in fact, no need to solicit requests for aid. By war's end, the Youth Council was the best-known Orthodox relief organization, and those concerned with the needs of religious survivors naturally turned to it for assistance. Within weeks of liberation, requests started pouring in from all over Europe. From Switzerland, Rabbiner Dr. S. Ehrmann wrote that there were several thousand Jews in the various internment camps capable of learning but without any *sefarim* to do so. In one camp, Rabbi Yonason Steif of Budapest had already established a yeshiva. In addition to *sefarim*, there was a desperate need for *tefillin* and *mezuzos* caused by the unavailability of parchment.[2] Rabbi Zev Tzvi (Victor) Vorhand cabled from Upper Austria requesting an advance of $800 in order to build two *mikvaos* in the DP camps in the area.

Meanwhile in England, the British Agudah was busy organizing teams to provide assistance to newly liberated Jews in the DP camps. Harry Goodman, chairman of the British Agudah, called upon the Youth Council to provide the *sefarim* necessary to establish schools and yeshivos. (One such yeshiva had already been set up in Bergen-Belsen by Rabbi Shlomo Baumgarten.) In addition, Goodman pointed out the necessity for *tefillin, siddurim,* and other religious articles for survivors

1. Mike Tress to Isaac Sternbuch, May 1, 1945; Mike Tress to Renee Reichman, May 1, 1945.
2. Rabbiner Dr. S. Ehrmann to Agudath Israel Youth Council, May 25, 1945.

Rabbi Michael Munk

in the DP camps.[3] In another telegram, Goodman described the plight of 300 Jews who had returned to Oslo and were virtually without food to eat.

Even a year or two after liberation, the lack of religious articles had not been fully cured. Herman Rosenberg, an Orthodox relief worker with UNRRA, described an orphanage that had been established for 150 Polish orphans from very Orthodox homes. But there were no *tefillin* or *siddurim* for the youngsters, let alone *sefarim*. "What is left of the Jews of Europe is a terrible remnant who have lost their faith and their morals," Rosenberg wrote. "A minute fraction is left and we cannot even give them the physical necessities of the faith."[4]

More than two years after liberation, Rabbi Michael Munk summarized his six weeks in the DP camps in the Berlin area. He found that the yeshiva and Bais Yaakov that had been established were discriminated against by the Camp Central Committee, and many of the Bais Yaakov girls were forced to work half a day in factories to maintain themselves. "Would you believe that people still have to join in groups of four or five for one pair of *tefillin*?" he asked. A number of 15 and 16-year-old boys, who were finally able to start their Jewish education for the first time, had not yet been able to put on *tefillin* because none were available. Nor were any *tzitzis* to be found.[5]

The response to the pleas for help was not long in coming. Even prior to the liberation of the camps in Europe, the Youth Council had already set up depots for the collection of clothing in a number of the religious neighborhoods in New York. Seventy thousand pounds of clothes were ready for shipment to Europe and *Eretz Yisrael* by January 1945.[6] In the

3. Telegrams from Harry Goodman to Agudath Israel Youth Council, July 24, 1945 and July 31, 1945.

4. Herman E. Rosenberg to the Agudath Israel Youth Council, August 11, 1946.

5. Rabbiner Dr. Michael Munk to Mr. Tress, August 5, 1947.

6. *Orthodox Tribune*, January 1945, p. 9.

Rabbi Moshe Sherer, Lester Udell, and Mike

four months after V-E Day, while the major Jewish relief organizations had still not managed to set up their European distribution networks, the Youth Council shipped 129,000 pounds of food and 155,000 pounds of clothing. Together with these went: 500 pairs of *tefillin*, 2,000 *siddurim*, 1,200 *chumashim*, 2,500 *sefarim* of various types, and 200 *chalafim* for kosher *shechitah*.[7] The Youth Council supplied 25,000 Jews with all their Pesach food needs for 1946,[8] and the next year that number grew to 36,000.[9]

In addition to its own shipments, the Youth Council also worked closely with Agudah groups in Europe, often supporting their work with direct cash payments. On June 16, 1946, M. Muller in Paris wrote to Mike congratulating him on the consummation of an agreement whereby the Youth Council would establish a Paris branch to be run by the French Agudah. The purpose of the office was to furnish aid to survivors pouring into France from Poland. Muller wrote that in the previous four weeks over 100,000 Jews, 40 percent of whom were religious, had returned to Poland from Russia, and that few wanted to remain in Poland, where a Jew with a beard risked

7. Report of Activities from May 8, 1945 to September 8, 1945.

8. Internal Youth Council Memorandum dated February 17, 1946.

9. Rabbi Moshe Sherer to Mr. Jacob Rosenheim, Feb 26, 1947.

R' Silver in Europe

his life every time he stepped into the street. He estimated that it would cost at least $100 to bring each Jew from Poland to France, and once in France living expenses would run between $15 and $25 a month.

In mid-1946, Mike convinced his long-time friend Louis Septimus to leave his accounting practice for three months and to accompany Rabbi Eliezer Silver on the latter's journey all over Europe for Vaad Hatzala. While in Paris, Septimus found a donor to establish a restaurant where refugees from Poland and other European countries could receive free kosher meals.[10]

Another major activity of the Youth Council was reuniting the *shearis hapleitah* with their relatives in the United States. The Refugee and Immigration Division had a department, headed by Irene (Silverman) Dzikansky, devoted exclusively to this task. A list of 35,000 survivors was compiled within a few months of the liberation of the camps, and the Youth Council began responding to requests from American Jews to determine whether their relatives in Europe were among the survivors and from survivors eager to locate relatives in the States. In the four

---

10. Interview with Louis Septimus.

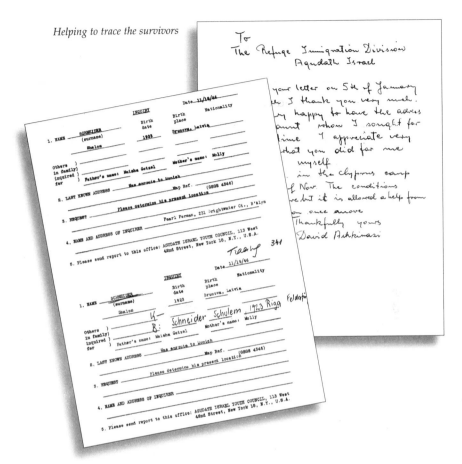

months after the end of the war, this department reunited 500 survivors with family members and responded to 2,500 queries.[11]

The process was an arduous one, and even the successful cases could often take a dozen letters to bring to a successful conclusion. The widely divergent European and American spellings of the same name, the frequently outdated addresses possessed by the survivors, and the fact that they often knew only the Jewish name of their American relatives, not the English name by which they were listed, made tracing difficult. The work, which continued for several years, however, was crucial. Finding relatives gave the survivors a feeling that they were not completely alone in the world. In addition, a concerned American relative could be of great assistance in obtaining an American visa.

The annual budgets of the Refugee and Immigration Division in 1946 and 1947 attest to Mike's success in arousing Orthodox Jews to come to

11. Report of activities from May 8, 1945 to September 8, 1945.

the aid of the *shearis hapleitah*. In 1941, the Youth Council's total annual budget was $4,000; by fiscal year 1946, the budget of the Refugee and Immigration Division alone had grown to close to a million dollars. Of the $928,298 raised by the Refugee and Immigration Division that year, $664,640 represented in kind collections of food, clothes, and religious items for Europe. Another $30,000 of direct financial aid was sent. Total revenues of the Division were approximately seven times as great as those for the preceding year.[12] The following fiscal year in kind contributions of food, clothing, and *tashmishei kedushah* declined over 50 percent, as the sheer horror of what had occurred in Europe began to wear off. But the $568,000 raised by the Refugee and Immigration Division — $310,000 of which was in kind contributions — still represented a substantial achievement.

It would of course be wrong to attribute the success of the still small organization's fundraising efforts solely to Mike's impassioned oratory or to his dedication to the *shearis hapleitah*. In part, the generosity of the Orthodox community was a reflection of the shock that greeted the first revelations of the extent of the Holocaust. And for some, no doubt, postwar generosity was a means of exorcising guilt feelings about not having done more during the war.

Yet from the time he challenged his listeners in his Hotel Pennsylvania speech, Mike spearheaded the fundraising efforts. To raise the money needed he spoke at every possible forum. He knew better than anyone how much could be achieved by motivated youngsters, and did not ignore the yeshivos and Bais Yaakovs. The impression left by his speech at Rebbetzin Kaplan's seminary still lives today in the minds of those who heard him. Here is how one woman describes it 50 years later:

> His face was contorted with pain. He looked like someone who had seen a vision and had been left transformed by the experience. The words spilled out of his mouth, and it seemed that he relived each story as he told it.

---

12. The expenditures on Camp Agudah and Youth Council organizational activities totaled $90,000 over approximately the same period, i.e., less than one tenth of the expenditures of the Refugee and Immigration Division. That ratio reflects the predominance of relief work.

At the same time, however, Camp Agudah was running an annual deficit of $13,000 and the costs of the organizational activities exceeded revenues by several thousand dollars. (By contrast, the deficit of the Refugee and Immigration Division was little more than $1,000 out of revenues of nearly $1,000,000.) The willingness to incur relatively large deficits on Camp Agudah and organizational activities is a reflection of the continuing commitment to the original purposes of the Youth Council.

We felt we were there watching the Nazi soldiers beating children, seeing the smoke of the crematoriums, witnessing the bewildered, hopeless blank faces of the survivors — both those who could no longer cry and those who could not stop crying.

We listened with fear and pain, as his stories of the unspeakable pierced our *neshamos*. Tears poured not just from our eyes, but from our souls.

When Mike was done, the girls felt an overwhelming need to do something. One girl called out, "What can we do? Don't tell us to *daven* or learn; we need to do something concrete — we want to do something now!" Mike replied that the relief work required vast sums of money, and that they should run a fundraising campaign.

The girls never made it to lunch that day, and with the permission of their teacher, they did not make it to their afternoon classes either. Going off in pairs, they invaded the New York City subway system with Mike's words ringing in their ears. No one told them what to say, but they had been inspired, and the words came as needed. At the end of the day, the girls had collected nearly $5,000; one pair of girls brought in $500 themselves.[13]

AS ESSENTIAL AS THE RELIEF WORK WAS, IT WAS AT BEST A STOPGAP measure. The survivors needed, above all, to begin reconstructing their

Bringing to a New Home

lives, and that they could not do as long as they remained in the limbo of the DP camps on soil soaked with Jewish blood. The majority of the *shearis hapleitah* wanted to go to *Eretz Yisrael*, but with the British White Paper still in effect that option entailed running the English blockade and the risk of ending up in another internment camp in Cyprus. That left the United States as the destination of choice for most. (Even after the creation of the State of Israel in 1948, many of the survivors still in Europe preferred the United States to the dangers of the war-torn, new state.)

Mike had given his word to the *shearis hapleitah* that he would do everything in his power to bring them to America, and much of the work of the Youth Council in the five years after his return from the DP camps was devoted to making good on that promise. For Mike that commitment was not just organizational but personal. He made every effort to be there himself when ships carrying large numbers of

---

13. Interview with Mrs. Phyllis Weinberg.

survivors arrived from Europe, and new arrivals could often be found sleeping in the tiny Tress apartment on Clymer Street.[14] A sign on the door read: There's always room for one more.[15]

Affidavits of financial support remained the key to bringing in immigrants. Such affidavits were now easier to obtain, especially from non-religious Jews, than they had been before and during the war. The extensive media coverage of the sufferings of the survivors made a powerful emotional appeal, and the postwar economic boom also caused people to be less fearful about undertaking the financial risks involved in signing affidavits. In the first year after the liberation of the camps, the Refugee and Immigration Division, headed by Mr. Oscar Schiff, processed 4,000 affidavits, more than in the entire wartime period.[16]

For nearly two months, Mike and Lieutenant Meyer Birnbaum, who had been present at the liberation of Buchenwald and remained in the DP camps for another four months, went around to groups of non-Orthodox Jews (see Chapter 6 pp. 88-89). Mike confined himself to introducing Birnbaum and making a pitch for affidavits when he had finished speaking. The whole project was vintage Mike. Though he was a powerful speaker who had been enthralling audiences for more than a decade, and Meyer Birnbaum was a complete novice, Mike did not hesitate to place himself completely in the background. He had no need to be the one making the dramatic presentation. The only question in his mind was who would be more effective, and he knew that Birnbaum in his army uniform, adorned with a chestful of medals, would have a greater impact on the audiences he was aiming at.

The postwar immigration work was multifaceted, but it all operated on one common assumption: that it was much easier to keep someone in the United States once he was already there than to obtain an immigration visa from one of the European consulates under the existing quota system. Thus the Refugee and Immigration Division focused much of its efforts on non-quota visas — student visas, visitors visas, and non-quota immigration visas.

Students had to demonstrate that they had a country to which they could return, and in some cases even post a security bond to ensure that they would do so. But as a practical matter, someone who had already

---

14. Interview with Herman Treisser.
15. Interview with Rabbi Shlomo Rotenberg.
16. *Darkeinu,* June 1946, p. 3.

been in the country a few years was much more likely to secure a permanent visa, especially if he or she had married an American in the interim. That made a student visa highly sought after, and some institutions did a brisk business in accepting overseas students for a fee. Others, however, extended themselves fully to help as many young refugees as possible enter the country. Among the latter group, Torah Vodaath, the Bais Yaakov Seminary run by Rabbi Baruch Kaplan and his wife Vichna, and Yeshivas Chofetz Chaim stood out.

Mesivta Torah Vodaath, for instance, applied for permission to accept an additional 300 students even though its enrollment at the time was only 200. That request required providing the government with detailed financial records designed to show that the yeshiva was capable of absorbing such a large influx of students. There were those who suggested to Reb Shraga Feivel Mendlowitz that Torah Vodaath should at least charge a minimal fee to cover the expenses of processing the various paperwork connected to each student visa. He refused, however, on the grounds that when one does a *chesed*, he should do it completely.[17] The Refugee and Immigration Division obtained affidavits from rabbis testifying to the suitability of those seeking student visas.

Under the 1924 Immigration Act, there were two exceptions from the normal quota restrictions which greatly aided the Refugee and Immigration Division's efforts — those for clergymen and academics. Many of the Orthodox survivors could, without too much effort, be shoved into these categories. All that was needed was an employment contract from either a synagogue for a rabbinic position or from a yeshiva for a "professor" of Talmud. Of course, there were only a limited number of positions for rabbis, assistant rabbis, and professors of Talmud in the relatively small American Orthodox world, and competition for the employment contracts, like that for acceptance as a student, was intense. Nor did the State Department Visa Division turn a completely blind eye to the number of contracts being issued, and in many cases a determination was made that the hiring institution was already amply supplied with rabbis or Talmudic professors, as the case might be.

Consuls abroad often looked askance at the number of supposed rabbis being processed, and it was therefore necessary to secure affi-

---

17. Interview with Rabbi Moshe Lonner, long-time principal of Mesivta Torah Vodaath.

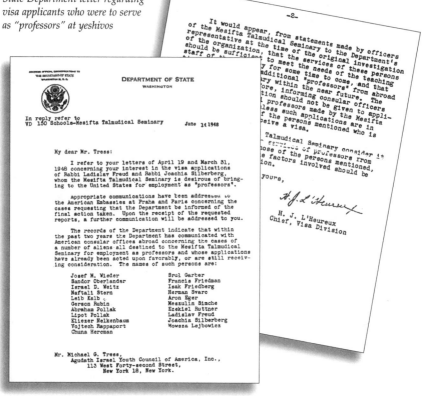
davits attesting to the qualifications of those seeking entry under non-
quota visas. The Youth Council maintained an office in Brussels in the
late '40s, and a large number of those seeking entry as rabbis or professors of Talmud came through there. One day the chief visa officer
expressed skepticism to the Youth Council emissary about the qualifications of one of the candidates. "Another one of your rabbis?" she said.
The emissary offered to bring the applicant in the next day so that she
could test his knowledge. It happened that the candidate in question
was the Vishnitzer Rebbe, and after the visa officer took one look at him,
she never again questioned the legitimacy of one of the non-quota
cases.[18]

    Mike also hatched a number of stratagems to bring survivors to
America on visitors visas. One of these involved inviting 250 to 300
survivors at a time to America to participate in Agudah-sponsored
conferences. American immigration law then specified that a person

18. Interview with Herman Treisser.

already in the country on a visitors visa could not apply for a permanent visa while still in the country. To apply for a permanent visa, he had to first travel to Canada or some other country and apply through an American consulate there.

The first obstacle in this process was thus obtaining from Canadian authorities permission to enter Canada. Nor could this obstacle be taken lightly. Exclusion of American visa-seekers was a cardinal point of Canadian immigration policy.[19] In addition, the United States State Department actively discouraged Canadian authorities from letting those holding United States visitors visas enter Canada. And the American consulates in Canada imposed long waiting requirements on those seeking to exchange their visitors visas for permanent ones.[20] The latter step created major hardships for those who had entered Canada only in order to apply for an American immigration visa, since they frequently lacked the resources to stay in Canada for any amount of time and the Toronto community itself was too small to accommodate them on a long-term basis.[21]

As formidable as these obstacles were, Mike, with help from a group of dedicated Zeirei members in Toronto, managed to overcome many of them. The Toronto ZAI began in 1943 when a group of religious young men decided to band together. They were unsure of exactly what type of affiliation they wanted and decided to invite Mike — "the one name the whole world knew" — to speak to them. He readily agreed. Mike's speech, Rabbi Feivel Rosenzweig, the leader of the group, would recall, "had a lightning effect. If there had been any doubts before his appearance, there were none afterwards."

But not until the late '40s, when Mike started spending weeks at a time in Toronto in connection with immigration work, did the local Zeirei really take off. Though the original impetus for him spending so much time in Toronto was immigration work, Mike took advantage of the time to transform those he was working with as well. He became, says Morley Auerbach, "our mentor and *gadol*. He was our inspiration and we turned to him for everything. Even when he wasn't in Toronto, we spoke to him daily."[22] Archie Zacks, a successful local businessman,

19. M.A. Solkin, Executive Director of Jewish Immigrant Aid Society of Canada, to Michael Tress, January 18, 1950.

20. Interview with Rabbi Feivel Rosenzweig.

21. Many of those waiting in Canada for permanent visas stayed in the boarding home of Mrs. Channah Urman, who later married Rabbi Yaakov Kamenetsky.

22. Interview with Morley Auerbach.

became a "chassid" of Mike's and, as a result of the latter's influence, developed into a major supporter of yeshivos.[23]

When Mike was in Toronto, his days were filled with trips to the Canadian immigration offices to secure entrance permits and to the American embassy to obtain permanent immigration visas. Feivel Rosenzweig, Morley Auerbach, Ruby Menzelevsky and a few other ZAI members were involved in acquiring entry permits from the Canadian government, frequently posing as relatives of the Jew in need of an entry permit. They also accompanied Mike to the American embassy to serve as character witnesses for those seeking United States immigration visas. Mike told Auerbach and Rosenzweig, "When I go down to Washington, I take along two *Yidden* with beautiful white beards [a reference to the Kopyczinitzer Rebbe and the Boyaner Rebbe] to stand on either side of me. Here I've got you."

Auerbach's description of how Mike worked — interesting in itself — also offers a clue to his *modus operandi* on his frequent trips to Washington, D.C. during World War II and thereafter. He completely mesmerized the office staff at the American consulate, Auerbach remembers. There was no such thing as a secretary telling him, "Please sit down Mr. Tress and so-and-so will be with you." He simply marched into whatever office he needed, dragging whoever was with him in his wake, without wasting a minute. He was able to convey his sense of urgency to all around him — even gentiles — and make them share it. This nonstop approach continued all day long. "I never saw anyone work so hard," recalls Auerbach. "In the evening he would say, `Just give me fifteen minutes on the couch, Morley.' As you watched him sleeping, you felt the *kedushah* in the room. And then it was up again for a quick dinner and a long night of meetings."

The hard work paid off. In one case, Mike, working through the Jewish Immigrant Aid Society (JIAS), obtained permission from the Canadian government for 250 rabbis and religious teachers to enter Canada, a concession that the executive director of JIAS labeled amazing.[24] The methods employed by Mike's cohorts were often unorthodox. When Canada clamped down on the entry of those holding American visitors visas, some Zeirei members rented a pleasure boat on the American side of Lake Michigan on the Fourth of July, dressed up a group of would-be immigrants in white suits to look like partygoers,

23. Rosenzweig interview.

24. M.A. Solkin to Michael Tress, January 18, 1950.

TELEPHONE ELGIN 9840

A. B. ZACKS
WHOLESALE DRY GOODS

112-114 YORK STREET

TORONTO, CANADA

July 3, 1947

Mr. Michael Tress,
President, Agudath Israel Youth Council of America,
133 West 42nd St.,
New York 18.

Dear Mr. Tress;

I wish to inform you that Rabbi Nochim Percowicz obtained his visa yesterday and left for New York last night. I am sure that you will be pleased with this information.

I want to thank you for your intervention in this case and for your prompt attention to my letter.

With kindest regards and my very best wishes,

Sincerely,

A.B. Zacks

and ferried them across to the Canadian side of the border. And when the American consulate imposed a long waiting period for those holding visitors visas who came to Canada to apply for immigration visas, Feivel Rosenzweig convinced a young woman working in the American consulate to expedite the handling of these cases, a strategy that worked well until she was arrested. Among those who obtained their immigration visas while in Canada were the Satmar Rebbe, the Bobover Rebbe, the Sigheter Rebbe (today's Satmar Rebbe), and the future Mirrer Rosh Yeshiva Rabbi Nochum Partzovitz.

Mike always operated on the assumption that pushing people to help their fellow Jews is one of the best ways to raise the level of their own *Yiddishkeit*. So it proved to be in Toronto. The same young men who played such a vital role in the immigration work went on to create one of the most vibrant Zeirei chapters. In the late '40s and early '50s, the

Toronto ZAI opened the city's first full-day *cheder,* introduced *chalav Yisrael* on a commercial basis, and started its own newspaper.[25]

Mike did not forget the broken survivors he met in the DP camps even when others urged him to turn his focus elsewhere. He had promised them that he would not rest until everything possible had been done to help them begin their lives anew, and he did not. But there was one more debt still to be paid — this one not to those who survived but to those who did not. Thousands of Jewish children were left in the hands of gentiles for safekeeping during the war, and Mike now turned his energies to saving them for the Jewish people.

25. Auerbach interview.

Chapter Twenty-Two
THE SAVE-A-CHILD FOUNDATION

O
N A BLUSTERY WINTER DAY IN LATE 1947, DR. YAAKOV Griffel[1] encountered the European representative of the Agudath Israel Youth Council outside a kosher restaurant in Prague. With his customary sense of urgency, Dr. Griffel did not even suggest that they step inside to the heated restaurant. Ignoring his shivering companion, he proceeded to unfold the tragic tale of thousands of Jewish children on the verge of being lost to the Jewish people forever.

---

1. Dr. Griffel was one of the true giants of wartime rescue efforts on behalf of European Jewry. For a full account of his life work see Joseph Friedenson's *Dateline: Istanbul* (Mesorah Publications, 1993).

Griffel's attempt to get the Youth Council involved in reclaiming Jewish children was typical of his method of operation throughout his life. He always tried to remain behind the scenes and enlist others in undertaking the tasks at hand. Only when he saw that something was not

Dr. Yaakov Giffel

As the Nazis conquered large parts of Europe, Griffel explained, desperate Jewish parents had hidden their children with gentile families or given them over to convents and monasteries for safe-keeping knowing that this represented their children's best hope of physical survival. The vast majority of these parents had been caught in the Nazi net and never returned. Now their children were being raised as Christians.

Dr. Griffel asked the Youth Council emissary whether the Youth Council would be interested in a major effort to return these children to the Jewish people. The Youth Council emissary immediately contacted Mike for his reaction. Typically, Mike put himself in the position of the parents of these children and thought of how greatly they would have suffered to know that their children were being raised as gentiles. He directed his European representative to immediately begin exploring the practical steps necessary to reclaim these lost children. Thus did the Save-A-Child Foundation come into existence.

Over the next year and a half, the Save-A-Child Foundation would become one of the Youth Council's most important projects and claim a

---

being done adequately by others would he get involved directly. *Interview with Herman Treisser.*

Dr. Griffel eventually did become directly involved in the return of Jewish children raised by gentiles. In 1953, he founded Children's Salvation, which had much the same mission as the Save-A-Child Foundation though on a broader scale encompassing Poland. The major financial support for the organization came from the Kopyczinitzer Rebbe, and Mike played an important role in getting the Rebbe involved in this project. Though he was always prepared to involve Agudath Israel in any project concerning the saving of Jewish lives, where others were able to do the work and allow Agudath Israel to concentrate on matters more directly within its specific purview — such as building up Agudath Israel institutions in *Eretz Yisrael* — Mike was happy to let them do so. *Treisser interview.*

Dr. Griffel's work with Children's Salvation continues even today. Dr. Aryeh Kimmerman, who worked with him in Israel, has compiled a list of 1,000 Poles who were either hidden as children or are descended from women who were hidden. The list includes only descendants who are halachically Jewish.

large part of Mike's time. Like all the postwar work, Save-A-Child Foundation came into existence only because Mike was able to convince his "kitchen cabinet" of a half dozen or so close supporters — including Louis and Sol Septimus and Nathan Hausman — that this was work that could not be left undone. Mike's attitude towards the project is best captured in a June 7, 1949 letter to Edouard Longerstaey, the Belgium Consul in New York: "We need not stress that the Jewish people has sacrificed over two million children, and that we cherish every child that has

Moshe Swerdloff in uniform

remained alive. . . . [We] will continuously exert every effort to bring these children back to their faith and heritage."[2]

A decision was made to focus initially on Belgium, where the Youth Council had already established an office. Work in Western Europe did not present the same host of problems as efforts behind the Iron Curtain. Mike's next task was to find the appropriate person or persons to conduct what promised to be extremely sensitive work requiring both intelligence and courage. For that task, he selected Moshe Swerdloff and his recent bride Estelle, one of the first graduates of Rebbetzin Kaplan's Bais Yaakov Seminary.

Swerdloff was well known to Mike from his wartime activities on behalf of the Youth Council while stationed in London. There he had been the chief coordinator of the Youth Council's initial postwar relief work in Europe. He compiled the only complete list of Orthodox servicemen in the American-occupied zones and was the conduit through which many of the first packages of food and clothing from the Youth Council were sent to homeless Jews on the continent. Swerdloff returned to America with a letter to Mike from Harry Goodman, head of the British Agudath Israel and one of the leaders of the World

2. This letter was written following a meeting with the Belgian consul devoted to an attempt to gain the support of the Belgian government for the return of the Jewish children.

Agudath Israel. In that letter, Goodman suggested that if the Youth Council should ever decide to have its own European representative there could be "nobody better able to fill the job than Swerdloff" who has "gained the affection and respect of all our friends throughout the land [for] his untiring devotion and all-out efforts in ... relief and rescue. . . ."[3] Mike was now prepared to accept that suggestion.

The decision to go to Belgium was not an easy one for the Swerdloffs. For Moshe Swerdloff, accepting the assignment meant he would have to begin his fledgling accounting practice again from scratch, and Mrs. Swerdloff was in the early stages of her first pregnancy. In the end, however, they decided they had no choice but to accept the assignment from Mike. For them the work represented the repayment of a debt that was owed by *Klal Yisrael* to the martyred parents of these children.[4]

FOR ALL THEIR ENTHUSIASM AND IDEALISM, THE SWERDLOFFS CON-
fronted considerable obstacles in their efforts. They set sail for Europe

Obstacles to Success March 20, 1948, nearly three full years after the end of the war. By then, all the children whose gentile care-takers recognized a responsibility to return them to the Jewish people were already living with Jewish relatives or in Jewish institutions. After the war, Mr. Yonah Tiefenbrunner established an orphanage in Brussels for Jewish children left orphaned by the war. Initially, the orphanage was small, but children began to trickle in on a daily basis. Eventually, there were approximately 100 children in the orphanage. Among these were children returned by gentiles who had saved them from Nazis.[5]

Those who were not returned had in many cases been living with gentiles or in Catholic religious institutions for eight years. Over that

---

3. Harry Goodman to Mike Tress, September 28, 1945.

4. Interview with Moshe Swerdloff.

5. Interview with Mrs. Miriam (Censor) Zupnik of Lakewood, New Jersey.
   Returning to Antwerp at the age of twenty-one after surviving two years in Auschwitz, Mrs. Zupnik went to work for Mr. Tiefenbrunner. She felt that there must have been some reason that she was still alive after the horrors of Auschwitz, and she wanted to serve Hashem in some concrete way. Working with Jewish orphans was her way of repaying Hashem for having been saved from the fire. In the orphanage, she witnessed many poignant cases. One little girl, who was returned by her gentile caretaker, came in wearing a crucifix, with which she could not be convinced to part. After a few days, however, she said, "If this is not my G-d, then I don't have to wear it any more." Today that little girl is the mother of *yeshivaleit*.

Miriam (Censor) Zupnik (center) with refugee children at the orphanage

period of time, they had come to think of the gentiles with whom they lived as their parents, and strong bonds of love had formed between the children and their caretakers.

Moreover, almost all the children thought of themselves as Catholics. Most of them had no memories of their natural parents or of having been born Jewish, and nearly all of them had been baptized. In the cases of those sheltered in convents and monasteries, the children's parents were often forced to agree to their children's baptism as a precondition for acceptance. Even those children old enough to have dim memories of their natural parents had received heavy doses of indoctrination against being Jewish. During the war, they were told that their very lives depended on concealing their Jewish origins and, after the war, that their only hope, in the event of another outbreak of murderous fury directed at the Jews, lay in being known to one and all as devout Catholics. A high percentage of the Jewish children in gentile hands were being trained to be either nuns or priests. Their Catholic protectors seemed to feel that some special merit was attached to placing Jewish children in religious vocations.[6]

---

6. The current Archbishop of Paris, Cardinal Lustiger, is one example of a Jewish child directed towards a life as a Catholic clergyman.

Chapter Twenty-Two: THE SAVE-A-CHILD FOUNDATION □ 371

Above: Children in the orphanage's dining room. Yonah Tiefenbrunner is at the left, Miriam (Censor) Zupnik is seated at left at the table, Mrs. Tiefenbrunner is at right at the table

Other obstacles too remained in the Swerdloffs' path. Funds were in short supply, and yet money was crucial to the success of the work. Even where the gentile caretakers could be persuaded to give up the children in their care, they often demanded to be compensated for all that they had provided the children over the years. There was little choice but to pay whatever they asked, even though the figure was often inflated by the illusion that world Jewry was desperately eager to ransom back these children.

If close relatives of the child could be located, there was the possibility of legal proceedings to have the relative appointed guardian of the children, at least where they were still minors. These proceedings, however, were often hotly contested and required substantial legal fees. Nor was success guaranteed. Belgium was a devoutly Catholic country, and even where close relatives of a child were still alive, the courts often refused to recognize them as the child's guardians.

Finally, the Swerdloffs were able to count on little in the way of tangible support from the local secular Jewish organizations. These organizations did provide lists of children known to be in gentile hands. But when it came to providing money to ransom the children — and certainly when it came to the illegal tactics that the Swerdloffs and those working with them contemplated when all else failed — the secular organizations were not interested. They feared that publicity over efforts to take the children back might generate renewed anti-Semitism. In addition, they often took the position that it was in the children's best interests to remain with foster parents, who had taken great risks on their behalf and who loved them, rather than to be uprooted again. On more than one occasion, Moshe Swerdloff was told by leaders of the secular Jewish establishment, "You feel the responsibility more than we do because you are more religious than we are."[7]

Given the various difficulties with which the Swerdloffs had to contend, the chances of success in any given case were slight. Falk Meiseles, who took over from them when they returned to America in March 1949, estimated that in the most promising cases the likelihood of success was no more than 20 percent and in other cases 5 percent.

THE SWERDLOFFS BEGAN THEIR WORK WITH A LIST OF 300 TO 400 names of Jewish children who had been hidden all over Belgium, many

Modus Operandi

in rural areas. The prewar Belgian Jewish community was a close-knit one, and in many cases there were survivors who had some knowledge of where children had been hidden.[8]

Once the children were identified, the first step was to try to establish some contact with them. This work was primarily done by the older orphans in Mr. Tiefenbrunner's orphanage under the direction of Miriam Censor, a young survivor of Auschwitz. Miss Censor's blonde hair and fair complexion had allowed her to walk freely on the streets of Antwerp for a year after the Nazi invasion, and she could travel anywhere without arousing suspicion. She and her assistants were fluent in both French and Flemish, the two languages of Belgium, and would travel to the places where Jewish children had been identified as living. There they attempted to find out everything they could about the

---

7. Swerdloff interview.

It is not completely true that the secular Jewish organizations never provided any funding. After the Swerdloffs returned to the United States in March 1949, their work was continued by Falk Meiseles, who was funded by the Youth Council. In a number of letters to Moshe Swerdloff, he mentions the receipt of funds to ransom Jewish children from the Society for the Aid of Jewish War Victims. The Society's aid was always conditioned on its total anonymity with respect to Meiseles' work.

8. Interview with Mrs. Miriam (Censor) Zupnik.

children and their circumstances, and, if possible, befriend them. Every week this group of operatives would gather with the Swerdloffs to review their progress of the week.

Once the first stage had progressed as far as it could, the next stage was to approach the children's guardians. Where they had succeeded in locating living relatives of the children, the Swerdloffs, or one of those working with them, would approach the gentile family together with the relative or with a power of attorney signed by the relative. Usually, however, no such relatives could be readily located. In such cases, the Swerdloffs attempted to find Jews in the United States with family names similar to those of the children's natural parents. These "relatives" were encouraged to write to the children, and the Swerdloffs posed as their representatives.

Whether the Swerdloffs posed as the representatives of real or fictitious relatives, the process of haggling with the children's guardians now began in earnest. This was often a protracted affair taking weeks or even months. Initially the guardians almost invariably refused to consider parting with the children, whom they had raised as their own. Their protestations of love for the child were usually echoed by the child himself. Eventually, however, the threat of legal proceedings over custody and the promise of handsome compensation for the expenses of raising the child sometimes succeeded in persuading the gentile guardian to part with the child. Even in such cases, however, the battle was far from over. The gentile might agree to part with the child on Wednesday and renege after being harangued by her parish priest on Sunday. Then the whole process would begin anew.

While negotiations were proceeding with the gentile guardian, the Swerdloffs tried to get the guardian's approval to take the child on day outings. There was no chance of convincing the children to think of themselves as Jewish in the brief time available. *"Je suis baptime* — I am baptized" was the usual response to all attempts in that direction. The Swerdloffs learned to bite their tongues when they took the children to kosher restaurants and the children crossed themselves before eating. At best, they could hope to acclimate the children somewhat to the Jewish world so that they would not view it as something completely foreign to them.

No matter how straightforward the case, complications always arose. In one case, a Polish Jewish mother had placed one daughter with a

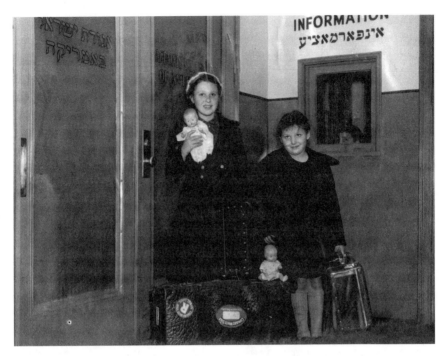

Two sisters smuggled out of a Catholic mission

wealthy Catholic woman and a second daughter in a convent. The mother survived the camps, and returned to Belgium a destitute refugee. Her daughters, then nine and eleven, were being well cared for and living in considerably more material comfort that she could possibly provide them. The mother, who was not religious, decided that her daughters were better off where they were than they would be with her. It took all the Swerdloffs' powers of persuasion to convince the mother that it was her duty to reclaim her own flesh and blood and raise them herself. Before the mother consented, they had to rent for her an apartment, something possible only on the black market in the postwar real estate market, and promise that they would secure for the entire family a visa to the United States. They did eventually succeed in bringing the whole family to the United States.

In the case of Maurice Westreich, the gentile woman who had raised him agreed to let him go to relatives in Israel, and was duly compensated for the expenses of his upbringing. But when the time came to fetch Maurice, she fell on the floor weeping convulsively that she could not bear to part with him, and the 13-year-old boy promptly followed suit. When at last the Swerdloffs had removed the boy, there still remained a problem of how to get him to Marseilles, France where he was to sail for Israel. Moshe Swerdloff and his partner decided to smuggle the boy, who lacked proper papers, across the French border. That would be easier if the boy were asleep, and to assure that he was, they put some knockout drops in his water. Being unaccustomed to such activities, however, they did so in such a clumsy fashion that the boy noticed and refused to drink the water. To demonstrate that there was nothing wrong with the water, Swerdloff's partner drank part of the glass and the boy drank the rest. Unfortunately, the drops left Swerdloff's partner groggy, while the boy was still wide awake.

Nevertheless, they managed to get Maurice across the border and into France, but in Marseilles the Jewish Agency refused to accept him for transport to Israel on the grounds that they did not wish to be accomplices to a kidnapping. Only Swerdloff's threat to go to the Jewish press with the story of how the Jewish Agency preferred to leave a Jewish boy in gentile hands rather than bring him to Israel caused the Agency officials to relent.

THE MANNER IN WHICH THE MONEY WAS PAID TO THE GENTILE caretakers left Swerdloff and those working with him vulnerable to

Arrest charges of kidnapping since there could never be a formal contract transferring guardianship in return for payment. Once the money had been paid, the gentile recipient could always go to the police and charge that the child had been kidnaped. That in fact happened in the Westreich case. In the end, however, Swerdloff and his partner were able to persuade the woman who had raised Maurice to drop the charges in return for a train ticket to Marseilles to see him off.[9]

Swerdloff, however, was not always so lucky. On January 5, 1949, he and Herman Treisser, a national vice-president of the Youth Council, who represented the Youth Council in Europe while also working on his own export-import business, were arrested in Brussels and charged with kidnaping. The police were, in fact, looking for Treisser in connection with the alleged kidnapping of one Morris Gottlieb, whose former guardians had filed charges when they learned that the boy was in *Eretz Yisrael*. Two plainclothes policemen made a surprise raid on the Youth Council's Brussels' office late on Friday afternoon, nabbing

---

9. Treisser interview.

Treisser and Swerdloff in the process and confiscating all their records. The two were forced to ride in a police van on Friday night and thrown into separate cells, where the only accommodations were dirty straw mattresses placed on top of cinder blocks and covered with a filthy blanket.

The two were arraigned in front of a gruff magistrate the next day and told to sign a paper that they had not kidnapped Morris Gottlieb. Both refused because of Shabbos. (Swerdloff had not even arrived in Belgium at the time of the alleged kidnapping.) After the initial hearing, the two were handcuffed and herded, togeth-

Moshe Swerdloff, Herman Treisser and Estelle Swerdloff in Antwerp, 1941.

er with a motley crew of common criminals, into a van for transport back to prison. In the van, they were each chained into a tiny compartment. The two spent the next four nights in separate cells, each with a cast of characters whose life histories would, in Swerdloff's words, have "fill[ed] a book."

In the meantime, Mike had sprung into action to secure Treisser and Swerdloff's release. As soon as he heard of their arrest, he immediately wired the heads of the major Zeirei branches in New York and elsewhere of the need to raise $5,000 for their defense. In Toronto, the members of the still new Zeirei chapter rang the doorbell of every Orthodox Jew in the city over the next three days. Meanwhile Treisser and Swerdloff were subjected to several days of grueling and hostile questioning by the local magistrate. In the end, however, they were released without ever standing trial. Mike used his connections in the State Department to put pressure on the Belgium government to drop the charges.[10]

---

10. The account of Treisser and Swerdloff's arrest is based on a first-person article by Moshe Swerdloff in the April 8, 1949 issue of *Jewish Opinion*, a publication of the Agudath Israel Movement in America, pp. 1-2.

THOUGH THE CHARGES AGAINST SWERDLOFF AND TREISSER WERE
trumped up, and they had never actually seized a child from his or her

Unorthodox Means guardian, it is nevertheless true that Swerdloff and
those working with him were not overly concerned
with legal niceties whenever there was a possibility
of saving a Jewish child from spiritual destruction. In this they followed
the tradition of the Youth Council during the war. Then too the Youth
Council had never balked at the employment of illegal means per se
when Jewish lives could thereby be saved. The only question had been
a practical one of balancing the consequences of being caught against
the chances of success.

No case better illustrates how far the Save-A-Child operatives were
prepared to go than that of the Halbersberg sisters. The two sisters had
been placed by their father in a convent on the Belgian-Holland border
as the Nazis invaded Holland. As a condition for their admission to the
convent, their father was forced to agree to their baptism. After the war,
an uncle on their mother's side was located in Paris. On his first attempt
to visit his nieces in the convent, he was told that they did want to see
him because they were no longer Jewish and wished to become nuns.
He attempted to visit them once more and this time he was told that
they were now in a convent in Holland. After that, he wanted nothing
more to do with the case.

Subsequently, Rabbi Moshe Halbersberg, formerly the *rav* of
Waldenberg in Poland and the brother of the girls' father, passed
through Belgium on his way to *Eretz Israel*. He was very eager to do anything possible to save his nieces, who were sixth-generation descendants
of the Seer of Lublin. Only after the Bishop of Liege was persuaded to
intervene did the convent superior allow him access to his nieces. Rabbi
Halbersberg eventually obtained permission to take his nieces on a
week-long holiday, but only on condition that he agree to return them to
the convent. He agreed to do so, but refused to sign a paper to that effect.

From the first day of the vacation, the girls, who were already 18 and
14 years old, expressed their desire to return to the convent. Every
morning they went to church, and they never ate without crossing
themselves. Their uncle was desperate for some stratagem to get them
out of the country.

Falk Meiseles went to Paris to see whether he could again interest the
other uncle in the case. But the uncle, fearing that he would be asked to

do something illegal, refused to see him. Meiseles did not give up. He called the girls in Brussels, and posing as their uncle's son, invited them to Paris for a few days' visit. They replied that they would be happy to come to Paris but lacked proper travel documents.

At that point, Meiseles returned to Brussels. The girls told him excitedly about the invitation and asked him if he could arrange to get them into France illegally. He assured them that it was the easiest thing in the world, which it definitely was not. Next they asked him to accompany them to Paris since they spoke no French. Meiseles at first demurred, but when pressed agreed. Thus the girls felt that he was doing them a big favor by accompanying them, even though the whole success of his plan was contingent on his continual presence.

In Paris, Meiseles told the girls that their uncle had gone for a short stay in the south of France and that they would join him. On this pretext, he booked train tickets for Marseilles from which all ships bound for Israel left. In Marseilles, the girls began to become suspicious, particularly when their uncle could not be located. Meiseles called Rabbi Halbersberg, who had in the interim come to Paris, and the latter promised to arrive in Marseilles within two days with the other uncle in tow.

Rabbi Halbersberg succeeded in persuading the maternal uncle to join him in Marseilles. But once the girls had seen their uncles, they were eager to return to their convent. Meiseles then arranged for the delivery of a fake telegram that the smuggler who had brought the girls to France in the first place had been caught and could not help them return. Then he placed a phone call in the girls' presence. Speaking in French, he pretended to be talking to another smuggler. He then informed the girls that he had found another smuggler, but that they would have to walk through a forest over barbed wire. The only alternative was to take a boat from Marseilles to Belgium. He asked the girls which they preferred, and they opted, as expected, for the latter.

Meiseles then arranged with the Jewish Agency for a first-class berth for the girls on a ship leaving for Israel in a few days. He also gained the Jewish Agency's agreement to let the girls be examined by a private doctor rather than at the Jewish hospital with all the new immigrants bound for Israel, which would have certainly alerted them to the ploy.

All Meiseles' planning almost came to naught when he arrived at the ship with the two sisters and found it painted with the Israeli flag. One of the sisters asked if the insignia was not Hebrew, but Meiseles assured her it was Greek. She then wanted to know why there were so many Jews on the ship. She readily accepted, however, his explanation that when somebody takes a ship, rather than a train, from one country to another he is either smuggling something or his papers are not in order. Since Jews are known to be heavily involved in smuggling, he continued, it was natural that there should be so many on the ship.

Shortly thereafter, the stewardess came to escort Meiseles to his compartment. All that was left for Meiseles to do was to convince the captain to let him disembark, against all regulations, after all passengers were already on board. The sisters meanwhile were on their way to Israel together with their uncle Rabbi Halbersberg, who, unbeknownst to them, was on the same ship.[11]

IN ADDITION TO THE CHILDREN RESCUED THROUGH SAVE-A-CHILD Foundation, there were a number of other positive results from having

Other Activities a tangible Youth Council presence in Europe. The Swerdloffs also used their time in Belgium to help refugees still trying to gain entry to the United States. Mr. Swerdloff established a good relationship with the American consul in Brussels and was thereby able to expedite a number of cases. Another Youth Council representative commenced negotiations for the return of 160 Jewish girls in a convent in Czechoslovakia. These negotiations did not bear immediate fruit, but were subsequently brought to a successful conclusion by other parties.

In another instance, Reb Jacob Rosenheim, head of the World Agudath Israel, succeeded in obtaining through the State Department 400 immigrant visas for families in Hungary. But the American consul in Budapest refused to issue the visas. The European representative of the Youth Council flew to Budapest to meet with the consul, who claimed that he lacked sufficient manpower in the embassy to process the visas. The Youth Council representative called his bluff and told him that he would provide all the necessary secretarial assistance to complete the paperwork. Sixty or seventy families thus received their visas

---

11. This account is based on a letter from Falk Meiseles to Mike dated April 4, 1949. The story has been simplified somewhat in the interests of concision.

over the next couple of days. (Only years later did the Agudath Israel representative learn that as soon as he left Budapest the consul again stopped processing the visas.)

The Youth Council was also able to help remove the remains of Rabbi Meir Shapiro from Poland for reburial in *Eretz Yisrael*. Rabbi Shapiro's brother Rabbi Avraham Shapiro reached Brussels after the war, and while there contacted the European representative of the Youth Council concerning his desire to have his brother's body brought to Jerusalem for reburial. After consulting with Mike, the Youth Council emissary went to Poland, where he was able to arrange the whole matter in four days through a relative of Rabbi Menachem Ziemba. The Youth Council paid half the expenses involved in bringing Rabbi Meir Shapiro to *Har Hamenuchos* in Jerusalem.[12]

Vital projects abounded in postwar Europe, and having an office in Europe meant that the Youth Council was able to participate in this work. After the declaration of the State of Israel, for instance, large numbers of Moroccan and other North African Jews fled to France in the wake of anti-Semitic riots in their native lands. In France, many of them were forced to live in camps maintained by the Jewish Agency in anticipation of their eventual emigration to Israel. This population was largely traditional in its observance, and Herman Treisser on behalf of the Youth Council tried to convince both the Joint Distribution Committee and Youth Aliyah to recognize this fact by supporting the children of the Moroccan refugees in religious institutions under Youth Council auspices. To this end, the Youth Council even obtained a house in Paris with facilities for hundreds of children.

Treisser's negotiations, however, met largely with a dead end, and he eventually decided to travel to Marseilles on his own to find children whose parents were interested in providing them with a religious education. On the instructions of Rabbi Mordechai Pogramansky, perhaps the brightest star of prewar Telshe Yeshiva and then a Rosh Yeshiva in France, Treisser made no promises of superior physical conditions for the children — only that they would receive a proper Torah education. Though almost all the parents to whom Treisser spoke were eager that their children receive a Torah education, they were fearful that the Jewish Agency would cut off the daily stipend on which they lived if

---

12. Interview with Herman Treisser.

they turned their children over to Treisser. Thus Treisser signed up only 28 boys aged 10 to 14. In the end, he was unable to bring even this number to Paris. When the Jewish Agency heard what he had done, they threatened the parents of the boys with loss of financial support, and Treisser brought only 10 children back with him to Paris.

This small number was still more than the Jewish Agency could tolerate, and the Marseilles police were informed that the children had been kidnapped. The head of Youth Aliyah in France offered to have the police investigation called off in exchange for the children. Treisser consulted Rabbi Pogramansky, who told him that it was absolutely forbidden to return Jewish children to the hands of the secularists, who had a long record of deliberately destroying all religious feeling in youth under their control. Rather than bring the children to the home in Paris as planned, the Youth Council had them hid elsewhere. Eventually these children went to Israel where they were among the first residents of Sdei Chemed Youth Village established by the Zeirei Agudath Israel of Israel.[13]

THE SWERDLOFFS HAD COME TO BELGIUM FILLED WITH ENTHUSIasm and high hopes for reclaiming hundreds of Jewish children living

Success and Failure with gentiles or in Catholic institutions. Those hopes were highly unrealistic given the inherent obstacles to success, the intricacy of each case, and limitations of both manpower and resources. In the end, no more than 50 to 70 children were brought back to the Jewish people.[14]

That itself represents an inestimable achievement, but the Swerdloffs could not help but view their year in Belgium with a sense of failure. "Our disappointment could not have been greater," Mrs. Swerdloff said later. The children whom they had gotten to know and for whom they had been unable to do anything weighed heavily upon them. Some of

---

13. The entire episode is recounted in a February 24, 1949 letter written by Mr. Treisser (and signed by Moshe Swerdloff) to Dr. Yaakov Griffel in New York.

14. This estimate is that of Herman Treisser, who remained in Europe after the Swerdloffs had returned to New York. It is extremely difficult to say with any exactitude how many children were rescued. Today, almost 50 years later, Moshe Swerdloff can remember clearly no more than 10 to 15 cases that he saw all the way through to completion. But in letters written while in Europe, he mentioned 73 children saved, and elsewhere Mrs. Swerdloff wrote only that the number did not exceed 100. Even taking into account the lower number that Mr. Swerdloff recalls today, this number does not include cases begun by the Swerdloffs and successfully completed after their departure and new cases undertaken by Falk Meiseles. Meiseles' letters to Moshe Swerdloff are filled with descriptions of both types of cases.

these children were close relatives of world-renowned Torah scholars.

In one case, an aunt who had survived the war in Morocco came to Belgium in the hopes of gaining custody of her sister's two children. As it became clear that the children, who were already in their mid-to-late teens, had no intention of returning to the Jewish people, the Swerdloffs watched the woman, who had no children of her own, age 20 years over the space of a few months.

Of the hundreds of Jewish children in Belgium living with Catholic families or in Catholic institutions, the Swerdloffs were able to save only a relatively small fraction. There were hundreds more children in the same situation in France and Holland, and thousands in Poland. But the Swerdloffs and the Youth Council could at least take pride in the fact that they had remembered these children's martyred parents and had not simply abandoned them. And Mike could take satisfaction in the fact that not once did the Swerdloffs fail to take a child out because there were insufficient funds to ransom him or her.[15]

Rabbi Mordechai Pogramansky

15. Letter of Falk Meiseles to Moshe Swerdloff dated June 13, 1949.

Chapter Twenty-Three

THE POSTWAR AGUDAH

ETWEEN 1948 AND 1950, THE AGUDATH ISRAEL Youth Council and Agudath Israel of America were

Another Day Older and Deeper in Debt

gradually amalgamated into one organization with Mike as the Administrative President, thus ending a division which had drained resources and energies over the years.[1] But for Mike the creation of a united Agudath Israel of America gave little relief: It just meant that now he was responsible for covering the accumulated debts of two organizations rather than one.

Those debts were the central fact of Mike's life

---

1. See Chapter 5 fn. 39 and Chapter 10 fn. 44 for a discussion of the two separate Agudah organizations.

Mike and Rabbi Shlomo Lorincz

throughout the late '40s and '50s. Rabbi Shlomo Lorincz, on his first trip to America in 1948 as a representative of Zeirei Agudath Israel in *Eretz Yisrael,* was astounded by the amount of time Mike spent each day trying to cover the bills coming due that day. Not until the banks closed in the afternoon did he have a chance to sit back and turn his attention to the projects at hand. Many times Rabbi Lorincz saw him place compresses on his head in an attempt to find relief from the pressures on him.[2] Those constant pressures took their toll, and in the opinion of those who worked closely with him, Mike aged much more in those years than would have been expected from someone still barely 40.[3] Summing up Mike's public career, Rabbi Lorincz says, "He never had an easy day in his life."

Yet such was the aura that surrounded Mike that requests for funds did not stop pouring in from around the globe. Even those who had witnessed firsthand the pressures with which he was struggling wrote letters critical of the amount of money they were receiving from Agudath Israel of America. Asked how they could still have pressed Mike for funds, Rabbi Shlomo Lorincz explained:

> If he had ever given us a firm no, we would have slackened in our demands. But he could never say no. He so much wanted

2. Interview with Rabbi Shlomo Lorincz.

3. Interview with Rabbi Joseph Elias.

to help. He had so much faith that somehow a way would be found to do everything that needed doing that we also believed him, and so we kept pressuring him.

The *Ramban* asks how Bezalel could have possibly built the *Mishkan* (Tabernacle) and fashioned its vessels. No man, the *Ramban* points out, could have possessed the skills required, and certainly no one who had grown up as a slave in Egypt doing brute physical labor. Nevertheless Bezalel went to Moshe and told him, "Impose this task on me, and I will do it," and Hashem responded by imbuing him with supernatural skills.

Mike had the same attitude. And since we saw that he had indeed had *siyata d'shmaya* in everything connected to building Zeirei and the wartime work, we became convinced he could do anything.[4]

The Agudah staff in those years shared Mike's idealism. Idealism, in fact, was often all the staff had to live on since salaries were frequently not paid for months at a time.[5] (Mike himself would never take his salary while others had not been paid, and at the time of his *petirah* he had accumulated a large pile of salary checks he never cashed.) The best testimony to the idealism of the office is that key staff continued to work as hard as ever despite being paid only intermittently. Comptroller Charlie Young's wife, for instance, was only able to force him home before nine or ten at night by threatening not to eat anything herself until he appeared for supper.[6]

The natural thing for a leader in Mike's situation to do would have been to institute a regime of fiscal responsibility — i.e, cut staff, undertake only those new projects that could pay for themselves, consolidate rather than expand. Mike, however, was constitutionally incapable of doing so. The financial bottom line could never be his bottom line. Every Jew lost to assimilation caused him personal pain, and if he could think of some way of reaching him, he had to try. He was possessed by visions of a transformed American *Yiddishkeit* and teemed with ideas as to how to bring that transformation about.

In the end, Mike's choice was vindicated. Had he undertaken only those projects for which adequate funding was already there, Agudath Israel would have closed its doors in the '50s, and there would have

---

4. Lorincz interview.

5. Interviews with Rabbis Joseph Elias and Shlomo Ort.

6. Interview with Mrs. Belle Young.

been no organization left to benefit from the growth of the Orthodox community — both numerically and materially — in the '60s and beyond.[7]

AN EXAMPLE OF MIKE'S CONTINUED ENTHUSIASM FOR NEW IDEAS and approaches was the Jewish Pocket Books Series published by **Jewish Pocket Books** Agudath Israel in the late '40s under the general editorship of Rabbi Joseph Elias. Not long after Rabbi Elias came to the United States from Canada in 1945 on a visa procured by the Youth Council, he approached Mike with the idea of producing a set of pocket books aimed at an English-speaking readership eager to learn more about the Jewish approach to contemporary issues.[8] Mike immediately realized the potential of the idea and sold it to the Spero Foundation of Cleveland, which undertook to cover the production costs. The series was one of the first ambitious efforts in English-language Judaica.

The 12 volumes produced nearly single-handedly by Rabbi Elias between 1947 and 1949 were almost all between 60 and 90 pages in length and focused on a single topic. They lack any of the eye-catching graphics of today's Jewish publishing. Just an unbroken chain of words on the page — no pictures or other adornment of any kind. Yet in the quality of writing and the sophistication of argument these slim volumes compare favorably with anything that has appeared since.

The choice of topics reveals a great deal about both the Jewish and secular worlds of the time. The works were almost exclusively philosophical in nature. No collections of inspirational stories or biographies were on the list. The editor took for granted that the major threat to the faith of the contemporary Jew lay in the realm of ideas, and not as today in the appeal of secular society to baser instincts. The volumes also assumed an educated readership. Taken as a whole, the series is designed to confront precisely those intellectual quandaries that might have presented themselves to the average Orthodox Jew of the day in the course of his or her college studies.

---

7. Lorincz interview.

8. Rabbi Elias first came to Mike's attention two years earlier as the publisher of *The Jewish Way*, a monthly journal of ideas that he put out in Montreal in 1943. That a young immigrant from Germany could publish an English-language journal adhering closely to Agudah ideology created quite a stir in Mizrachi-dominated Montreal. The local Mizrachi even offered to defray all the journal's expenses if Rabbi Elias would adopt a more non-partisan stance. Mike and Rabbi Elias met personally for the first time a year later when Rabbi Elias joined the Agudah delegation to the UNRRA Conference held in Montreal in late 1944. *Interview with Rabbi Joseph Elias.*

Jewish Pocket Books

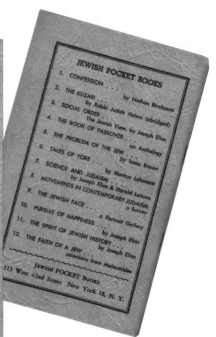

JEWISH POCKET BOOKS
1. CONFESSION . . . .
2. THE KUZARI . . . . . by Nathan Birnbaum
   by Rabbi Judah Halevi (abridged)
3. SOCIAL ORDER . . . . The Jewish View, by Joseph Elias
4. THE BOOK OF PASSOVER . . . an Anthology
5. THE PROBLEM OF THE JEW . . .
6. TALES OF YORE . . . . by Isaac Breuer
7. SCIENCE AND JUDAISM . . . by Markus Lehmann
   by Joseph Elias & Harold Leiman
8. MOVEMENTS IN CONTEMPORARY JUDAISM
9. THE JEWISH FACE . . . . a Survey
   a Portrait Gallery
10. PURSUIT OF HAPPINESS . . . .
11. THE SPIRIT OF JEWISH HISTORY by Joseph Elias
12. THE FAITH OF A JEW . . . by Joseph Elias
   selections from Maimonides
113 West 42nd Street   JEWISH POCKET BOOKS   New York 18, N. Y.

Thus a volume entitled *Social Order* explicitly contrasts the Torah's premises concerning the relationship of the individual to the community to those of laissez-faire capitalism, on the one hand, and Marxism, on the other. *Science and Judaism,* by Rabbi Elias and Rabbi Heshy (Harold) Leiman, drew on everything from the writings of Immanuel Kant to the Heisenberg uncertainty principle to demonstrate that the mechanistic "scientific" view of the universe as following certain immutable laws of cause and effect unguided by any motive force was not only philosophically undemonstrable but refuted by the most recent findings of physics and chemistry. On specific issues such as evolution, the truth of which had long since settled into unexamined dogma among the educated classes, the authors brought an impressive array of recent scientific evidence, particularly from genetics, to knock Darwin from his pedestal. In its general outlines, their refutation of evolution has been unimproved upon.

The Jewish Pocket Books proved a critical and popular success. To this day the 12 volumes in the series are treasured items by those who purchased them at the time. Unfortunately the project was less of a financial success, and the Spero Foundation declined to underwrite a second series on such topics as Jewish prayer and the *Yamim Noraim* (High Holidays). To his chagrin, Rabbi Elias discovered that it is easy to sell books at a low price but hard to collect the proceeds. Because each volume sold so cheaply, sellers did not immediately remit their payment, and by the time they did, they had often lost track of how many books they had sold.[9]

THE TASK CONFRONTING THE RELIGIOUS YISHUV IN *ERETZ YISRAEL* from the end of World War II through the mid-'50s was overwhelming.

Focus on Eretz Yisrael

For nearly a century and a half the *yishuv* had survived largely through contributions from Jewish communities overseas. Now those traditional sources of support had been reduced to ashes, and it was the *yishuv* itself that was called upon to absorb tens of thousands who had survived the consuming fire. In time, the newcomers would revitalize the religious community in *Eretz Yisrael,* just as their fellow survivors brought a new level of intensity to American religious life, but for now they needed everything: housing, jobs, and, for those whose youth had been cruelly ripped from them, a basic Jewish education. And no sooner had the first wave of new immigrants arrived in the late '40s, hundreds of thousands more Jews — presenting an entirely new set of problems — began to pour in from North Africa, Yemen and Iraq.

The Jewish Agency and the government not only discriminated against Agudah groups in the allocation of funds to deal with the needs

A cartoon from The Orthodox Tribune concerning the plight of young arrivals to Eretz Yisrael

SAVE THEM FROM SPIRITUAL DESTRUCTION!

9. Elias interview.

at hand, but actively competed with them to seduce the orphans from Europe and the children from Arab lands from the religious ways of their parents. With the government, the Labor party, and the Histadrut Labor Federation — which was also the largest employer — run as one integrated fiefdom, virtually all power in Israel was concentrated in the hands of the anti-religious Labor Zionists, and that power was often used brutally against religion.

Yet somehow the various Agudah groups in *Eretz Yisrael* rose to the challenge. Housing was built, trade schools established, agricultural settlements founded, and drop-in centers opened in the larger cities for religious soldiers, many of them orphans from Europe. Dormitory educational facilities and youth villages were created for uprooted youth from Arab lands and the younger orphans from Europe. (Eventually Israel had the largest percentage of children living in such facilities of any country in the world.) At the same time, the independent *chareidi* educational system nearly doubled in size in a few short years.

All this required vast sums of money that the impoverished *yishuv* was in no position to supply. The necessary sums could only come from one source: America. The head of the Israeli Agudah, Rabbi Itche Meir Levin, and young Agudah and Zeirei Agudath Israel activists, like Rabbi Menachem Porush and Rabbi Shlomo Lorincz, became regular visitors to America even before the Israeli War of Independence.[10]

On those trips their first address was inevitably Mike Tress and the Youth Council. The still small, and relatively poor, Agudah world could, of course, not supply most of the funds needed. But, says Rabbi Shlomo Lorincz, *neshamah,* not money, was the key to the success of the major endeavors in *Eretz Yisrael*:

> Without Mike Tress's interest and encouragement, the way he welcomed us with open arms and made sure that we were received enthusiastically by every Zeirei branch, and his assurances that whatever help he could possibly muster would be forthcoming, I don't know if we would have ever had the courage to assume the debts we did to start all our projects.[11]

Rabbi Moshe Sherer and Mike provided the logistical support for

---

10. Rabbi Itche Meir Levin represented Agudath Israel in the first Knesset and served as the Israel's first Minister of Social Welfare. Rabbis Lorincz and Porush both represented Agudath Israel in the Knesset for over three decades, with the former serving as head of the powerful Finance Committee from 1977 to 1984.

11. Lorincz interview.

many of these fundraising trips, and were often left with the difficult task of collecting pledges.

Mike also made crucial introductions that brought in the needed money. As Rabbi Lorincz put it, "I arrived in America knowing approximately as many people as I did in China." Mike introduced him to Rabbi Herbert Goldstein whose contacts extended throughout all segments of the Orthodox world and who was himself totally involved in the work on behalf of *Eretz Yisrael.* A narrowly based Agudah fundraising campaign could have commanded none of the support of campaigns led by Rabbi Goldstein. Among the major projects funded by Rabbi Goldstein was Sdei Chemed Youth Village near Rishon LeZion. Since its opening in 1950 under the auspices of Rabbi Goldstein's Children's Homes for Israel, Sdei Chemed has been home to thousands of boys who went on to establish fine religious families.

Though Children's Homes For Israel was not formally connected to Agudath Israel, it was hardly accidental that the incorporators were Mike, Nathan Hausman, Rabbi Moshe Sherer, and Moses Dykman, in addition to Rabbi Goldstein and Lester Udell, the president of Rabbi Goldstein's West Side Institutional Synagogue and long-time chairman of the Youth Council's Refugee and Immigration Division. Nor was it coincidental that the money raised went almost exclusively to projects begun by Zeirei Agudath Israel or Agudath Israel in *Eretz Yisrael.* Similarly, The American Religious Palestine Fund, headed by Rabbi Goldstein, became a major source of monies over the years for Agudah projects in *Eretz Yisrael.* Again, Rabbi Goldstein's co-directors, Beirach Rubinson and Heshy Moskowitz, were among Mike's closest associates.

Mike also used the political connections he had built up over the years on behalf of the work in *Eretz Yisrael.* Prominent politicians such as Congressman Franklin Roosevelt Jr. and Robert Wagner Jr., the future mayor of New York, not only lent their names to the establishment of a Great Americans' Children's Village in Israel, they even participated in meetings concerning the project, and Roosevelt made a special trip to Israel in connection with it.[12]

On one of Rabbi Lorincz's first visits to America, Mike arranged for him to be received by New York City's Mayor William O'Dwyer, an old

---

12. The June 17, 1949 minutes of the Central Committee of the Save-A-Child Foundation list Franklin Roosevelt Jr. and Robert Wagner Jr. as among those in attendance to discuss the founding of the Great Americans' Children's Village in Israel. A May 19, 1949 cable from Mike to Rabbi Itche Meir Levin is devoted exclusively to the upcoming visit of Roosevelt in connection with the project.

New York City Mayor Robert Wagner being presented with an award. L-R: Mike, Nathan Hausman, Mayor Wagner, Rabbi Herbert S. Goldstein, Louis J. Septimus, Rabbi Moshe Sherer.

friend from the latter's days as the director of the War Refugee Board. The reception was scheduled to take place during the three weeks preceding Tishah B'Av, and Rabbi Lorincz looked rather unkempt having not shaven in days. There was a general consensus that he could not be introduced to the Mayor of New York City looking as he did, but Rabbi Lorincz was uncomfortable with shaving during the three weeks. Finally, Mike decided that rather than pressuring Rabbi Lorincz to shave he would simply have to explain Rabbi Lorincz's appearance to the Mayor.

On the day of the reception, Mike told Mayor O'Dwyer that Rabbi Lorincz was not shaving because he was in mourning over the destruction of the Temple in Jerusalem, and that just as Jews do not shave when in mourning for a parent, so they do not shave during this period of mourning for the Temple. Rabbi Lorincz still did not speak any English and could not follow the conversation, but from the way that Mayor O'Dwyer and his entourage were staring at him in fascination, he realized that Mike's words had powerfully affected the Mayor.

Later he learned that the Mayor had asked Mike how long ago the Temple was destroyed, and Mike told him almost 2,000 years ago. The Mayor replied, "Now I understand why the Jewish people has always survived and will always survive. Any people that can mourn something that happened 2,000 years ago as they mourn the loss of a father or mother is indeed an eternal people."[13] The Mayor was so fascinated by Rabbi Lorincz's refusal to shave that he kept the Agudah delegation for almost an hour though each visiting group that day had been allocated only five to ten minutes.[14]

WITH THE END OF THE WAR IN EUROPE, MIKE'S FOCUS WAS ON relief work for the *shearis hapleitah* still in Europe and on securing visas
Chinuch Atzmai to bring them to America. But even at that time, *Eretz Yisrael* was not forgotten. As Rabbi Lorincz put it, "Mike Tress had a head big enough for two pairs of *tefillin* (see *Eruvin* 95b). He could concentrate on the survivors in Europe without ignoring *Eretz Yisrael*." Already in 1945, clothing valued at $40,000 was shipped to Israel by the Youth Council. Nshei Agudath Israel — founded in 1947 — concentrated from the beginning almost exclusively on *Eretz Yisrael* projects. At its height, the organization was supporting 43 nursery schools and kindergartens feeding into the Chinuch Atzmai system and contributing to many of the dormitory educational facilities originally built with funding from Rabbi Herbert Goldstein's Children's Homes for Israel.[15]

With the establishment of the State of Israel and the simultaneous declaration of war by her Arab neighbors, the eyes of the entire Jewish world were turned apprehensively to *Eretz Yisrael*. Agudath Israel was no exception, and during the siege of Jerusalem, a six-month Food for Jerusalem campaign was undertaken. Trucks with loudspeakers traversed New York City, and a theatrical agency provided actors to make appeals for the starving Jews of Jerusalem. One of the most effective was a black actor who used to begin, "I'm collecting and I'm not even Jewish. . . ." The campaign netted over $60,000, and sent a great deal of desperately needed food to the besieged city. On December 24, 1948, over 64,000 pounds of food, including 13,000 pounds of meat, was sent.[16]

By the time Israel's immediate survival was assured, most of the *shearis hapleitah* in Europe had already found permanent homes or

---

13. An almost identical remark is attributed to Napoleon after witnessing Jews in *shul* sitting on the floor and crying on Tishah B'Av.

14. Lorincz interview.

15. Interview with Mrs. Josephine Reichel, Rabbi Goldstein's daughter, who was President of Nshei Agudath Israel for 19 years. The original presidium consisted of Rebbetzin Clara Frankel, Esther Knobel, and Sylvia (Schonbrun) Klein.

16. Interview with Heshy Leiser, director of Food for Jerusalem.

Above: Packing food parcels for Jerusalem, 1947
Below: Rabbi Herbert S. Goldstein overseeing a shipment of food packages to Jerusalem

Mike addressing a rally protesting the conscription of women into the Israeli army
Seated L-R: The Ozerover Rebbe, Rabbi Simcha Elberg, the Sadigerer Rebbe,
the Novominsker Rebbe, the Boyaner Rebbe, the Bluzhover Rebbe, Rabbi Avraham Kalmanowitz,
Rabbi Mendel Zaks, Rabbi Yaakov Teitelbaum, Rabbi Yaakov Kamenetzky, Rabbi Mordechai Gifter

intended to go to Israel, and Mike was able to focus to a much greater extent on the needs of *Eretz Yisrael*. In a letter to Rabbi Itche Meir Levin on October 17, 1949, he wrote, "I would also like you to know that we are reorganizing our work and all of our efforts will be directed to practical and positive work in *Eretz Yisrael*." Mike's own experience in America had left him with great confidence in the power of an aroused youth, and he was particularly drawn to the projects of Zeirei Agudath Israel in *Eretz Yisrael*.[17]

The American Agudah also did not remain aloof from political developments in *Eretz Yisrael*. In the early '50s, Agudath Israel organized mass demonstrations to protest the Israeli government's decision to

---

17. Many of the ZAI projects were aimed at the large group of young religious immigrants in their late teens and early 20s. This group had been deprived of yeshiva learning due to the war, and most were already too old to reintegrate into the traditional yeshiva framework. Many of them were drafted immediately after their arrival, and others were interested in learning a trade so that they could earn a living and start a family.

Kibbutz Kommemiut, for instance, was one project whose founders were almost all drawn from this group. Led by its *rav* Rabbi Binyamin Mendelsohn, Kommemiut eventually spearheaded all *shemittah* observance by farmers in *Eretz Yisrael*. Rabbi Mendelsohn left a community of several hundred families to come to Kommemiut. At the time of his arrival, one could only walk around the primitive settlement wearing high boots due to the omnipresent mud. Rabbi Mendelsohn told his horrified wife, "Better to walk in filth than to look at it."

Kfar Achiezer in Bnei Brak provided a home for single, young immigrants, ensuring that they could live in a religious environment with a *mashgiach* and *shul* on the premises and a regular program of Torah classes.

Under the guidance of Rabbi Eliyahu Dessler, the Israeli Zeirei also worked out an agreement with the army whereby groups of young men not suited for full-time yeshiva studies would live together on specially created settlements, where they would learn a trade and receive six weeks of army training. *Interview with Rabbi Shlomo Lorincz.*

Chapter Twenty-Three: THE POSTWAR AGUDAH ☐ 395

draft women. And when Rabbi Israel Grossman was convicted of defaming the state for a colorful description of the pernicious effects of drafting women soldiers, Mike and Rabbi Samson Raphael Weiss of Young Israel led a delegation to Washington, D.C. to lodge a protest with Israel's ambassador to the U.S. Abba Eban.[18] Eventually Rabbi Aharon Kotler called off the mass demonstrations because groups not connected to Agudath Israel used them as a forum for violent attacks on the very existence of the state, which Rabbi Kotler felt was counterproductive in terms of arousing favorable public opinion.[19]

The major project of Agudath Israel of America on behalf of *Eretz Yisrael* in the early '50s was Torah Schools for Israel. With passage of the Israeli Education Law of 1953, what had previously been four separate streams of government-supported education was reduced to just two — the secular system and the state religious schools controlled by Mizrachi. At that point, an independent educational system called Chinuch Atzmai came into being to preserve the sanctity of traditional Torah education. Though the government covered 60 percent of the basic operating costs of the schools, the remaining 40 percent had to be privately funded. In addition, the government subsidy did not cover any costs associated with building or acquiring new schools — something of vital importance with the influx of large numbers of new immigrant children from Arab lands. The subsidy also only covered the hours of the average Israeli school day, which was then little past noon, while the classes in *chadorim* and Bais Yaakov often went far later into the afternoon.

The costs of funding the school system with 268 schools and 26,000 students were enormous.[20] The entire system was repeatedly threatened with strikes by teachers who did not receive their salaries for months at a time, and the fear that both teachers and students would desert to the state religious system was constant.

Rabbi Aharon Kotler in America and the *gedolim* of *Eretz Yisrael* placed the viability of Chinuch Atzmai and ensuring its ability to

---

18. The story was carried by the JTA and published in local Jewish papers across the country on May 29, 1953.

19. Interview with Rabbi Moshe Sherer.

20. As of 1955, Chinuch Atzmai included 65 Torah schools for boys serving 8,786 boys; 63 Bais Yaakov schools with a total enrollment of 8,657; 110 kindergartens and day nurseries serving 5,689 children; 20 evening schools for 871 working youth, and 10 seminaries in which 2,070 girls were studying.

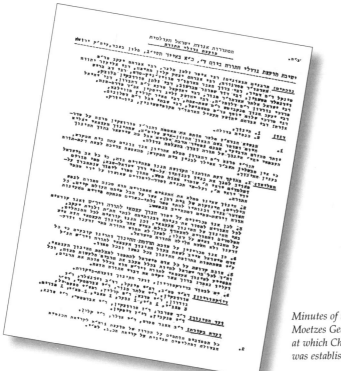

Minutes of the meeting of the Moetzes Gedolei HaTorah at which Chinuch Atzmai was established

expand to meet the needs of the mass of Sephardi immigrants at the top of their agenda. In 1953, for instance, while representatives of other Israeli political parties came to America to raise money for their election campaigns, the three Agudah representatives in the Knesset devoted themselves to raising money for Chinuch Atzmai.

Chinuch Atzmai meeting

Ad for a Toronto rally

Given the priority assigned to Chinuch Atzmai by Rabbi Kotler, Chinuch Atzmai became the most important endeavor of Agudath Israel of America. Torah Schools for Israel, the American fund-raising arm of the movement, was located in the Agudah offices at 5 Beekman Street, and a large percentage of Mike and Rabbi Sherer's time was occupied with Chinuch Atzmai.

In 1955, however, Reb Aharon decided that Torah Schools for Israel would be able to raise more money if it became totally independent. The identification with Agudath Israel, he felt, prevented many from contributing.[21] From an institutional point of view, the loss of Chinuch Atzmai was a serious blow to Agudath Israel. But that made not the slightest difference to Mike. He sat down with Rabbi Henoch Cohen, whom Reb Aharon had appointed to head the newly independent Torah Schools for Israel, and went over the lists of the major contributors in a number of cities. Shortly thereafter, Mike and Telshe Rosh Yeshiva Reb Eliyahu Meir Bloch traveled to Toronto to make an appeal on behalf of Chinuch Atzmai. Mike himself made successful appeals in a number of *shuls* in Williamsburg, including that of the Tzelemer Rav and the Stoliner *shtiebel*.

Even today, Rabbi Cohen recalls with awe the way Mike continued to throw himself into Chinuch Atzmai. "Some become *askanim*," says Rabbi Cohen, "because it's a job. But Mike became an *askan* to serve *Klal*

---

21. Rabbi Kotler had already been successful to a large extent in making Chinuch Atzmai a non-partisan issue in the American Orthodox world. The 1954 national conventions of the Rabbinical Council of America and the Orthodox Union both called for support for Chinuch Atzmai. A letter from Rabbi Joseph B. Soloveitchik, in which he stated that whatever one's feelings toward Agudah, Chinuch Atzmai was "in no way a partisan issue [and] everyone, regardless of his political sympathies or antipathies, should give them a helping hand," played a significant role in this regard.

Yisrael. Many work hard for their own organization, but he worked hard for any valuable project. It made no difference to him whether it was an Agudah project or not, as long as *Klal Yisrael* needed it."

MIKE DID NOT PERSONALLY VISIT ERETZ YISRAEL UNTIL 1954. THE occasion was the fourth Knessiah Gedolah of Agudath Israel, and the

The Fourth Knessiah Gedolah

first since Marienbad in 1937. Until that visit, says Rabbi Menachem Porush, who accompanied him throughout his stay, Mike's thoughts about *Eretz Yisrael* were primarily in terms of *Mashiach's* time. The sight of the pulsing, vibrant religious life was a surprise and an inspiration. In the center of the old *yishuv* in Jerusalem — in its yeshivos and Chassidic courts — he found an intensity of religious life as yet still unknown in America.[22]

But if Mike was surprised by what he found in Jerusalem, he surprised others as well. Some of the delegates to the Knessiah Gedolah did not quite know what to make of the clean-shaven stranger from America. True, many had corresponded with him over the years, and all

Going to the Knessiah Gedolah. L-R: Herman Treisser, Mike, Dr. Isaac Lewin, Rabbi Benjamin W. Hendeles, Rabbi Simcha Elberg

22. Interview with Rabbi Menachem Porush.

Fourth Knessiah Gedolah

knew of what he and his bands of inspired youth had achieved during the war, but his modern appearance still caused them to react with a certain suspicion.

Until he got up to speak at the Knessiah Gedolah that is. In the course of his address, he quoted the verses in *Tehillim* (122:8-9): "For the sake of my brothers and friends, I will speak of peace in your midst. For the sake of the House of Hashem, I will request good for you." "When there is a dispute between two Jews," he said, "then it is incumbent upon us to seek peace because all Jews are brothers. But when one is acting not for himself but for the *Ribbono Shel Olam*, then there is no room for compromise, and one must seek only that which is objectively good." The last thing the audience had expected to hear was such fiery *mussar* from the well-dressed young man from New York.[23]

That *drash* was only one of the highlights of the speech. As he did so many times, Mike described the fifth of *Shevat* celebration of the *yahrzeit* of the Sfas Emes in Feldafing. He pictured a room in which there was "not one whole human being" — not one who had not lost many of those nearest and dearest to him or whose body had not been permanently scarred in the death camps. Yet somehow they had found the courage to get up and dance that day. And then he proceeded to describe a certain survivor named "Maimon" who had been passing out

23. Told to Yitzchak Zvi Tress by Rabbi Berlin, Rosh Yeshivas Rav Chaim Ozer in Bnei Brak.

the shnapps at the *yahrzeit* celebration. At that moment, one of the listeners rose to his feet and shouted, "I am that Maimon." Whenever he told the story for the rest of his life, Mike did not forget to mention being reunited with Maimon at the Knessiah Gedolah.

The Last Hurrah

THE HUNGARIAN REVOLUTION WAS THE OCCASION FOR MIKE'S last great undertaking. On October 23, 1956, fighting broke out all over Hungary between the Soviet forces then controlling the country and those seeking an independent Hungary. The next day Imre Nagy, who had been previously removed as Prime Minister by the Soviet Union, was reinstated. He proclaimed an end to one-party rule and Hungary's neutrality in foreign affairs. After an initial retreat, however, Soviet forces moved to reassert control on November 4, and within two weeks were again firmly in power.

In the chaos that prevailed from the beginning of the revolution to its defeat by the Soviets, over 200,000 Hungarians fled the country, including close to 20,000 Jews. Even after the Soviets had regained power, the situation within the country was sufficiently in flux that it was still possible to escape over the border into Austria.

A group of 15 Austrian Jews of various factions operating out of the office of the Vienna Agudah initiated an "Underground Railroad" which hired smugglers to take individuals and families over the Hungarian border into Austria. In addition to paying the smugglers, the Underground Railroad kept border guards on both sides of the border on its payroll. Because of the illegality of the operation, the Joint Distribution Committee refused all participation despite the urgent need to act quickly.

The situation in Hungary provided a rare opportunity to fulfill the *mitzvah* of *Pidyon Sh'vuim* (redemption of captives). Tens of thousands of Jews who had previously been thought to be permanently trapped behind the Iron Curtain could suddenly be saved from spiritual death. Time was of the essence; each passing day brought that much closer the final resealing of Hungary's borders by the Soviets. The rapid jump in the price charged by those smuggling Jews across the border from $60 to $100 per person reflected the growing difficulty in crossing the border.

Here was a situation requiring dramatic and immediate action. There was no time to worry about the daily bills coming due. Mike was presented with a mission that he could throw himself into body and

The Hotel Continental in Vienna

N.Y. Times article about Hungarian refugee home

soul. Just as during the war, a few hundred dollars was again the difference between life and death.

Between December 5, 1956 and January 5, 1956, Agudath Israel of America transferred over $45,000 to Vienna to aid in the rescue operation. But Mike was not content to watch the action from afar. In mid-December, he flew to Vienna to oversee the Underground Railroad and to do what he could for the 15,000 Hungarian Jews, 4,000 of them religious, who had already streamed into Vienna. The situation was chaotic when he arrived, and his organizational skills were greatly needed. In the three weeks he was in Vienna, he purchased a 104-room hotel on behalf of Agudath Israel that served as a temporary home for 500 Jews and opened up three kosher kitchens that provided kosher meals for a thousand Jews every day.[24]

One day Mike was arranging transportation for a group of Jews headed for America by ship. He overheard a little girl ask her father, "Where are we going?" When her father told her that they were going

24. These facts are all taken from a confidential memo entitled "Eyewitness Report on Operation Bricha from Michael G. Tress, Who Just Returned from Vienna." The memo is on the stationery of the Hungarian Rescue Fund and dated January 1, 1957.

Hungarian girls in Vienna

to America, the little girl wanted to know, "And from America where are we going?" That brief exchange made a powerful impression on Mike, and whenever he told the story afterwards, he always added, "This is *galus*."[25]

On his return to America, Mike went on a whirlwind speaking tour, just as he had after the war to bring the message of the *shearis hapleitah*

Mike with Hungarian refugees in Fluchtheim

25. Interview with Rabbi Yisroel Belsky.

Mike looks on as Llewelyn Thompson, American Ambassador to Austria, presents Hungarian refugee children with scholarships to Camp Agudah and Camp Bnos.

to America. He had lost none of his power to move young and old to put the needs of their fellow Jews at the forefront in a moment of decisive challenge. In one Bais Yaakov, for instance, the graduating class donated to the Hungarian rescue all the money they had saved to rent graduation gowns.

There was again visa work to be done; though the United States was far more generous in accepting Hungarian refugees than it had been in accepting Jews during the war or afterwards. Perhaps President Eisenhower was embarrassed by the American failure to offer any support to those fighting for freedom in Hungary or perhaps the memory of what he had seen in Buchenwald and other liberated camps as a consequence of restrictive American immigration policies remained with him. But whatever the case, the immigration quotas were temporarily waived.

In one instance, however, Mike had to obtain a special bill from Congress to gain entry for a mother who had remained in Austria with a mentally defective child, to whom the U.S. consulate refused to grant a visa, while her husband and other children came to the United States. The desperate father stopped Mike every *Motzaei Shabbos* to inquire whether there was any progress in his wife's case. Finally, Mike pre-

Mike with Hungarian children and New York Governor Averell Harriman

vailed on Eleanor Roosevelt to become involved in the case and the so-called Mermelstein Bill was passed in Congress to admit the mother and her child.

Agudath Israel was also actively involved in easing the usually traumatic acclimation to a new country. Heshy Leiser, who had worked for the Youth Council for a number of years after the war, left his job for five months at Rabbi Moshe Sherer's request to work at Fort Kilmer, New Jersey, one of the major absorption centers. Thousands of refugees a day were being brought into Fort Kilmer in December, 1956 when Leiser arrived on the scene. Somehow he was given the first place in the reception line, which made it easy for the religious Jews coming off the planes to find the Agudath Israel representative. One older Jewish woman saw the sign Agudath Israel and assuming that Leiser must be a *rebbe* rushed over and kissed his hand.

When the Hebrew Immigration Aid Society (HIAS), which was coordinating the Jewish efforts on the scene, needed a secretary, Leiser mentioned a woman named Judy Weinberger, who spoke Hungarian fluently. Through her, he was able to obtain the lists of the latest arrivals, which vastly simplified the task of locating religious Jews on the sprawling army base. For the newcomers who had relatives or who were claimed by one of the Jewish communities involved with

Hungarian Jews — Adas Yereim (Vien) or Satmar — the stay in Fort Kilmer was relatively short. But for others it lasted months. A *milchig* kosher kitchen was set up by Rabbi Paysach Raymond of New Brunswick, a *sefer Torah* borrowed, an *aron kodesh* built by the Army, and *tefillin* obtained for many whose own were of very questionable quality. Leiser provided advice on immigration matters, and he took refugees into Brooklyn on special passes to make housing and employment arrangements.

As in the postwar period, Agudath Israel was also involved in finding housing and providing furnishing for the new immigrants. One family with 14 children arrived by boat and were taken to an apartment in Williamsburg that had been prepared with food, pots and pans, and furnishing. The mother of the family told her children, "Only a *malach* (angel) could have done this. The first thing we must do is find that *malach* and show our *hakaras hatov* (appreciation)." The mother went around collecting Shabbos clothing for all her shabbily dressed children so that they could greet their *malach* in fitting attire. Then she marched them off to meet Mike.[26]

Journey to Morocco

SHORTLY AFTER HIS RETURN FROM HUNGARY, MIKE WAS ONCE again on his way abroad. This time his destination was *Eretz Yisrael* for a meeting of the Vaad Hapoel of World Agudah. That session of the Vaad Hapoel was devoted primarily to the fate of Moroccan and North African Jewry. In both their native lands and upon arriving in *Eretz Yisrael,* the principal challenge confronting Moroccan Jewry was the same: the concerted efforts by left-wing Zionists to destroy the religious beliefs of the young. Mike heard stories of newly arrived Moroccan children being gathered in front of an *aron kodesh* that was then opened to reveal agricultural implements inside. The children were told, "These are your new gods."[27]

The Vaad Hapoel appointed a three-man delegation consisting of Mike, Rabbi Simcha Elberg, and Rabbi Binyamim Hendeles to travel to Morocco to survey the situation firsthand. There they found 30 emissaries of the left-wing Mapai and Mapam parties busily engaged in enticing the young to Israel. Sporting long beards, quoting Biblical verses, and speaking ceaselessly of the *kedushah* of *Eretz Yisrael,* these

---

26. This story was told to Leah Trenk by a neighbor who was one of those 14 children.

27. Interview with Shmuel Baruch Tress.

emissaries played on the naiveté of Moroccan Jews. When Mike and his colleagues asked religious Jews in Jewish Agency transit camps whether they expected to remain religious in Israel, they gave replies such as:

> I'm going to Kibbutz Devorah Haneviah.

> I am going to Kibbutz David Hamelech. I will be among the first to see *Mashiach*. Can a person who is not religious meet *Mashiach*?

> What kind of question are you asking? *Eretz Yisrael* does not allow anyone who is not religious to live within its borders.[28]

The Jewish Agency policy favored whenever possible taking only the young — those most capable of serving in the army and working hard, as well as those most easily shaped into "new Jews" freed of religion. Older Jews, especially religious ones, were told that they were physically unfit for the journey.[29]

Though most of Moroccan Jewry was still religious in 1957, the seeds of destruction had been sown. A majority of the Jewish children, over 35,000 in all, were enrolled in the *Alliance* school system run by assimilated French Jews.

Upon his return to the United States, Mike addressed himself to the question posed by some of his followers: Why, given all the problems confronting American and world Jewry, have you focused on Morocco? Mike gave three answers. First, Moroccan Jewry constituted the largest remaining repository of traditional Jewish *emunah* in the world, and had the greatest potential to strengthen Torah Jewry. Second, the Moroccan community was without either the financial or spiritual resources to defend itself. Without outside help, it could not solve its own problems. And finally, the community was under sustained and deliberate attack from the Zionists who viewed North Africa youth as the largest reservoir of manpower for the new state.

In response, he called for pressure to force the Jewish Agency to allow religious emissaries from *Eretz Yisrael* to guide the *aliyah* of those who wished to emigrate and to cease directing 80 percent of the children to *kibbutzim* and other left-wing institutions upon their arrival in Israel.[30]

But Mike was enough of a realist to know that the ability of world

---

28. Rabbi Simcha Elberg, "So Spoke a Moroccan Jew," *Dos Yiddishe Vort*, Adar 1957.

29. Rabbi Binyamin Hendeles, "False Alarms and True Misguiding," *Dos Yiddishe Vort*, Adar 1957.

30. Elemelech Tress, "Let Us Not Forget Them," *Dos Yiddishe Vort*, Adar 1957.

Orthodoxy to bring any such pressure to bear was slight and that any plans depending on the goodwill of the Jewish Agency were doomed to failure. The main thrust therefore had to be on providing Moroccan Jewry with the spiritual resources to save itself. That would mean vastly increasing the number of religious schools to compete with the *Alliance* and building yeshivos to produce native-born *talmidei chachamim*. To that end, Mike worked closely with the leading American Sephardi philanthropist Isaac Shalom on the development of the Otzar HaTorah network of schools in Morocco under the direction of Rabbi Zusia Waltner.[31]

While in Morocco, the Agudah delegation also succeeded in converting Rabbi Baruch Toledano, chief rabbi of Meknes, to the Agudah point of view, with important consequences. For the first time there was an influential rabbi who actively challenged the Zionists and who was willing to expose the wolf in sheep's clothing that lay behind the *Alliance* motto, "*Kol Yisrael chaverim* — All Israel are friends." The emphasis Rabbi Toledano placed on pure Torah learning not only saved his own family — all of his sons became *roshei yeshiva* — but numerous other Moroccan boys as well.[32]

Mike's interest in North Africa Jewry was not a fleeting one. His last public papers are virtually all fundraising letters on behalf of the 100,000 Algerian Jews — 20,000 of whom were religious — who fled to France in the early '60s in the wake of the Algerian civil war. He and Rabbi Sherer succeeded in 1962 in obtaining 1,000 visas for Algerian Jewish boys to study in yeshivos in the United States. But Rabbi Elie Munk, who was coordinating efforts on behalf of the community in France, expressed doubts that there would be many young boys prepared to leave Europe, and suggested that the primary thrust had to be on building up *chadarim* and yeshivos in France.[33] Mike did make efforts in this regard, but by then his vital energy was almost sapped.

---

31. Otzar HaTorah ran 23 schools throughout the country, including six residential institutions with a high standard of Torah learning in Tangiers. There was even a *kollel* of 50 in Tangiers. In the late '40s, Rabbi Waltner brought two transports of Moroccan boys to study in England in the Sunderland Yeshiva and Rabbi Zaidel Semiatizsky brought another group to the yeshiva of his father-in-law Rabbi Moshe Schneider in London. Later Rabbi Semiatizsky, who was one of the leaders of the European Agudah, established a girls' seminary in Morocco. *Interview with Rabbi Zusia Waltner.*

32. Interview with Rabbi Shlomo Lorincz.

33. Rabbi Elie Munk to Rabbi Sherer and Mr. Tress, July 20, 1962.

Chapter Twenty-Four

AT HOME

THE EMOTIONAL DEVASTATION WROUGHT ON offspring and spouses is already a convention of biographies of famous men. Countless such biographies detail the sufferings caused by the frequent absences of the father and the unrealistic demands placed on progeny to live up to the standards of their renowned father. In many cases, the private behavior of famous figures is revealed to have been at substantial variance with the public persona.

Mike Tress stands out in stark contrast to this pattern. Even prior to his marriage, he received a blessing from Rabbi Elchonon Wasserman that through the merit of working for the *klal* he would in turn merit to produce generations of *yirei Shamayim*. The degree to which that blessing has been fulfilled is a lasting tribute to both

Mike and his wife Hinde, who bore the major responsibility for raising the children.

The Tress children perceived their father in precisely the same terms as the other youngsters upon whom he had such a decisive impact. And the values with which they were raised were exactly the same as those which Mike preached in the public sphere. The precise fit between his private and public personalities is but another reflection of the extent to which "*tocho k'boro*," his inside was like his outside.

THE TRESS HOME WAS AN UNUSUALLY HAPPY HOME. STATEMENTS like: "I just smile when I think of being born into that home," "I can't

A Happy Home

imagine being born into any other family," or "I can just remember happy times; I loved being home," come naturally to the Tress children.[1] It was an easy-going house in which the neighbors' children loved to play and from which the Tress children rarely felt the need to venture. It was not unusual for mother and daughters to punctuate household chores or cooking by dancing together. Even after marriage, the Tress daughters would hurry home from Cleveland every *bein hazmanim* (intersession), with their young children in tow.

The first time the oldest son Shmuel Baruch brought his *kallah* to the house, she could not cross the threshold because a couple of the oldest grandchildren had emptied some egg cartons all over the floor, breaking most of the eggs in the process. Arriving on the scene, Mrs. Tress's only comment was: "Look at what a good time the *kinderlach* had."

This picture of a warm, loving home is confirmed by the many visitors. No family in Williamsburg had more guests.[2] Young men visiting New York in search of *shidduchim* made the Tress home a regular base of operations. Mike did not ask out-of-town visitors whether they wanted to come for Shabbos; he simply announced that they were coming. If they demurred, he would insist, "All it means is that we'll add a little more water to the soup." (If the soup was diluted, no one ever noticed. "Fifty percent pepper and fifty percent all other ingredients" was one visitor's description.)[3]

Isadore Rubenstein was one of the many young men who used to come from Toronto. He remembers a house filled with children —

---

1. Interviews with Mike's daughters Eska Reidel, Leah Bloch, and Basya Rosenblatt.
2. Interview with Gavriel Beer.
3. Interview with Binyamin Urman.

"every year another one crawling on the floor and the older ones a bit bigger." Yet despite all the children, there was not a lot of screaming and running around. The children were too happy at the table to want to play elsewhere.[4] At the Tress Shabbos table, one felt his extra Shabbos *neshamah:* A meal never passed without a *dvar Torah* from one of the boys, the food was excellent, and the singing loud and filled with feeling. Guests with nice voices were especially enjoyed.[5] Dinner done, Mike would do the dishes himself. The Friday night rule was that Mrs. Tress was not allowed up from the table.

After the meal, Mike would go to 616 Bedford Avenue for a *leil Shabbos shiur* with the boys. Invariably he returned from 616 Bedford Avenue with a large contingent of new recruits for more singing and the eating of Mrs. Tress's baked delicacies. Even those in *mesivta* and beyond, who were no longer active in Pirchei, returned for the Friday night singing in the Tress home. Sometimes Mike would take the boys to the *tisch* of one of the many rebbes he was close to: the Kopyczinitzer Rebbe, the Boyaner Rebbe, the Skverer Rebbe, or the Bluzhover Rebbe.

In the '50s, Yankel Rosenbaum and Rabbi Yisroel Belsky used to bring the older boys in the Williamsburg Pirchei to sing together with Mike on the last day of Pesach. The boys looked forward to this visit all year long.[6]

The *gedolim* too enjoyed the spirit of the home. Rabbi Yaakov Kamenetsky was a frequent Friday night visitor. The Tress children would pepper him with questions. After the 1959 Soviet launching of the first Sputnik, for instance, one of the children asked him whether he thought a man would one day walk on the moon. Reb Yaakov replied that he thought so because the moon is not considered part of the Heavens. Other times, Reb Yaakov dropped by during *Shalosh Seudos* to talk to Mike. Rabbi Eliyahu Meir Bloch was another visitor when he was in New York from Cleveland. The Tress children still remember with amusement how one morning the Telshe Rosh Yeshiva asked for an egg cup in which to eat his egg. They had no idea of what he was talking about, though to him it was obvious that an egg could not be eaten without an egg cup.

America's Torah leaders were a constant presence in the lives of the Tress children. As a toddler, the oldest daughter Henie used to go

4. Ibid.
5. Interview with Isadore Rubenstein.
6. Interview with Rabbi Yisroel Belsky.

around chanting, "Kalmanowitz, Kalmanowitz," so many times had she heard her father speak of the Mirrer Rosh Yeshiva, with whom he worked together constantly during the war. Before his children's weddings, Mike took the *kallah* and *chassan* separately to the Kopyczinitzer Rebbe, the Boyaner Rebbe, and the Skverer Rebbe for *berachos*. Those honored under the *chuppah* at the wedding of Mike's oldest daughter, Henie, included the Boyaner Rebbe, Rabbi Moshe Feinstein, Rabbi Yaakov Kamenetsky, the Kopyczinitzer Rebbe, Rabbi Aharon Kotler, the Ponevezher Rav, Rabbi Yosef Shlomo Kahaneman, Rabbi Eliezer Silver, and Rabbi Gedaliah Schorr. Rabbi Chaim Stein of Telshe Yeshiva was the *mesader kiddushin*.

The rhythms of the Jewish calendar were felt clearly in the Tress home. Each time of the year had its special family customs. Every new item of clothing had to be worn first on Shabbos even if eventually intended for weekday wear. On Purim, dozens of *Shalach Manos* were sent, with the Tress children forming an assembly line — one cutting the cakes as they came out of the oven, another wrapping, a third packing, a fourth labeling, and the rest delivering.

Erev Shavuos, hundreds of flowers were delivered to the Tress home from a florist in Manhattan. Mike himself would put together beautiful gladiola arrangements, and the Tress children would then take them to various families and to decorate the Zeirei headquarters at 616 Bedford Avenue. Rabbi Yerucham Leshinsky remembers how those flowers lifted the spirits of his whole family the first Shavuos after their arrival from Europe. Before Pesach, white organdy curtains were purchased for the living room. When these went up on *Erev Pesach*, even if it was five o'clock in the morning, it signaled that the Pesach preparations were complete. One of the chief joys of the family's move to 586 Bedford Avenue in 1950 was that for the first time there was a place to build a *sukkah* in which the whole family and their many guests could eat.

MIKE WAS AN EXCEEDINGLY BUSY MAN. THROUGHOUT THE '40S and '50s he traveled extensively, and during the war years and the

Quality Time

intense refugee work in the aftermath of the war, there were long periods in which he rarely ate supper at home before 11 p.m. Yet he still found time to be present as a father. When he was home, the children felt he belonged to them and that he was happy to be with them. Until Mrs. Tress broke her leg in

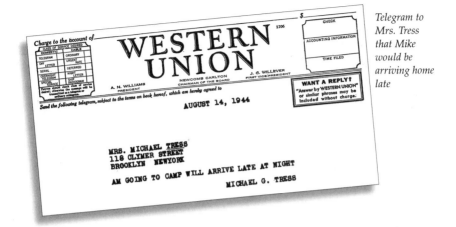

WESTERN UNION

Charge to the account of

$ CHECK

1206

ACCOUNTING INFORMATION

TIME FILED

A. N. WILLIAMS
PRESIDENT

NEWCOMB CARLTON
CHAIRMAN OF THE BOARD

J. C. WILLEVER
FIRST VICE-PRESIDENT

WANT A REPLY?
"Answer by WESTERN UNION"
or similar phrases may be
included without charge.

Send the following telegram, subject to the terms on back hereof, which are hereby agreed to

AUGUST 14, 1944

MRS. MICHAEL TRESS
118 CLYMER STREET
BROOKLYN NEWYORK

AM GOING TO CAMP WILL ARRIVE LATE AT NIGHT

MICHAEL G. TRESS

1948, there was no phone in the house so that people would not infringe on his time with the family. When Mike needed to communicate with his wife, he sent a telegram. (Of course, the lack of a phone did not prevent people from coming to the door.)

No matter how late he came home, Mike always had time for his children. The children would hop out of bed as soon as they heard him at the door and race downstairs for the honor of taking off his overcoat and hanging it up. A daughter once discovered to her horror that she was trying to wrest away the overcoat of a beggar who had come to the door and whom she had mistaken for her father. Once his coat was hung up, the children would sit down and join their father while he ate his supper. Even at that late hour, he took the time to help with homework or writing compositions. One of the Tress girls once won a state contest for an essay on Theodore Roosevelt with which Mike helped her.

He took a keen interest in what the children were doing. Every week he found time to speak to the boys' *rebbis*. The conversation at home never dealt with what he was doing but on what was going on in the children's lives.

Sometimes Mike would make up stories while imitating the sound of the wind whistling through the trees or of various animals. He could produce poems on the spot, and frequently entertained the children with his verse. The most famous example in family lore is "Dr. Diamond the Penicillin Man" composed one day when Mike and several of the children were all home sick. As soon as Dr. Isaac Diamond, a famous Williamsburg physician, entered the room where Mike and the children were together, they all popped up and started singing in unison:

Hurray for Dr. Diamond, the penicillin man
He gives you one and two and three and jabs it in again
Hurray for Dr. Diamond, he always comes on time
You call him in the morning and he comes next day at nine
Hurray for Dr. Diamond, he's always tried and true
Listen to him always because it's good for you.

On Shabbos, Mike would take the kids out for a walk. The local firehouse down the block was a regular stop, and the firemen knew all the children by name. On these walks, Mike would point out the homes of the various *rebbes* and *talmidei chachamim* who resided in Williamsburg. On Sundays in the summer, there were outings to Clove Lake Park on Staten Island for which the family packed every imaginable kind of sandwich. Once there, Mike would put on a cap and play ball with the boys. Every Chanukah, Mike took the children over the Williamsburg Bridge to his old neighborhood on the Lower East Side. He had a way of turning all these outings into adventures.

The demands on their father's time were a fact of life that the Tress children accepted without bitterness. "I never felt deprived," says his daughter Donya Pichey. "I was just proud to be his daughter. We loved to walk in the street with him and see the way so many people stopped to talk to him and looked to him for help." A favorite game of the girls was to sit at the window on Shabbos and count how many people accompanied their father home. They noted how he always paid special attention to those most in need of it.

Every Friday afternoon, Mike would return home laden with bags full of clothes for the children. The salesladies at Lanes and Klein's knew to set aside any dress with long sleeves for him. Though Mike's taste in clothes made his daughters the envy of all their friends, he was no master at picking out his children's sizes, and the children took turns going back the next week to return what did not fit. But what remained, even with the children whose weekly present had to be returned, was the good feeling of knowing that their father was thinking about them and his joy in giving them presents. On his return from his nearly two months in Europe in 1946, one of the first things Mike did was to go down to Ludlow Street on the Lower East Side and buy presents for his wife and children.[7]

---

7. Interview with Abe Dicker.

Mike instilled his children with the same sense of unity and team-work as in his Pirchei groups. The children grew up without a sense that there were favorites, though the girls might occasionally complain that the boys had fewer chores. Mike went to great lengths to prevent jealousy. One time three of the girls had to have their tonsils out. When they arrived home after the operation, they each found the identical doll on their pillow.[8]

Just as he led without a harsh word, Mike rarely had to discipline his children; their innate respect for him and desire to please made that unnecessary. If Mike asked one of the children to do something and the child did not respond immediately, he would simply say, "O.K., I'll have to ask someone else," and the first child would jump to it.

MIKE PREACHED THE SAME MESSAGE AT HOME THAT HE DELIV-ered to his Pirchei groups. His children grew up hearing him repeat time

Tress Family Values

and again, "*A Yid muz tahn, auftahn vet der Ribbono Shel Olam* — A Jew must do, but accomplishment belongs only to G-d," just as did his Pirchei boys.[9]

Chesed flowed in the Tress home. The house was always filled with visitors, some of whom would stay for months at a time. At one point, an invalid relative lived with the family for six months. She was given the largest room in the house and her own private bathroom, while the rest of the family made due with three large bedrooms and a small bath-room. After the war, the family took in two sisters from Europe pending their adoption by an American family. The girls were still suffering from the aftereffects of severe malnutrition and used to wake up screaming in the night with nightmares of the ordeal they had been through.

Many of the guests were of the type not always welcomed elsewhere. One European immigrant, who suffered from epilepsy, was a welcome guest, and used to come by to pick up issues of *Dos Yiddishe Vort*. Another honored guest was a European *talmid chacham* who had been left traumatized for life when the Nazis murdered his *kallah* under the *chuppah*.

The children were also involved in these *chesed* projects. They were taught to greet each person who came to the house, even the most downtrodden beggars. The children learned from their parents that the criterion for purchases was not who offered the best prices or even what

---

8. Interview with Eska Reidel.

9. Interview with Yisrael Berger.

type of merchandise was most required, but which salesman needed the money the most.

Mike deliberately avoided ever taking the children with him to the Agudath Israel offices. He did not want people fussing over the President's children for fear that they would become conceited. At Camp Agudah and Camp Bnos explicit instructions were given that no privileges were to be given the Tress children. But that did not prevent them from feeling a special responsibility for taking care of their "father's camp." Litter on the ground was picked up as if it were in their home, and if a guest appeared to be lost, a Tress daughter was likely to be the first to offer directions.

The family financial situation was never easy, but the children were never conscious of it. Mike's attitude towards money was that it was not to be wasted but it was not that important. He used to say, "If it can be replaced by money, it's not that important." One day Mike's daughter Henie commented wistfully that the family could have been rich if only he had not sold all his stocks. Her father replied, "We are rich — in everything that counts."

When Mike was in Houston for open-heart surgery towards the end of his life, an offer was made to redecorate the house while he was away. Mrs. Tress turned it down because she knew that material things would have little meaning for him. During the *shivah* period, visitors to the house saw that he had retained nothing for himself of the large sums raised for the *klal*.

The same attitude towards money manifested itself in the *shidduchim* of the Tress children — both those in his lifetime and afterwards. Though Mike was the preeminent Orthodox layman in America, not only respected but loved, he never looked for either money or *yichus* in seeking spouses for his children. His sons-in-law were chosen for their own personal merits and nothing else. The values for which Mike stood were reflected in his children. Each of his sons and sons-in-law learned for many years in *kollel*, and many of them have remained in learning and *chinuch*.

IN THE EYES OF MANY BOTH WITHIN AND OUTSIDE THE TRESS family, the Tress child most like his father was Rabbi Avraham Gershon

Rabbi Avraham Gershon Tress, zt"l

Tress. The natural *middos* of the Tress home were honed in him over the course of 20 years of intense yeshiva learning, the last 13 as a member of the Telshe Yeshiva *kollel*.

From a young age, Avraham Gershon showed his father's love of people and desire to help. One of his camp counselors describes him as so sweet "that if he put his finger in a cup of tea you wouldn't need to add any sugar."[10] "If you felt the slightest bit depressed," remembers Rabbi Ephraim Silverman, a friend from Telshe, "Avraham Gershon was the one you wanted to see. His face shone with such light."

R' Avraham Gershon Tress zt"l

"Its not just that he smiled at everyone he saw," a student recalled after his passing. "When he saw someone approaching, his whole face lit up. . . . When he smiled at you, it was because he saw something special. . . ."[11]

He was renowned in Telshe for his *hasmadah* (diligence). Rabbi Mordechai Gifter, the Rosh Hayeshiva, once wrote Mrs. Tress urging her to convince Avraham Gershon to leave the *beis medrash* earlier. Rabbi Gifter was afraid that he was damaging his health. When he said a *sevara* in the *Gemara* his face would flush bright from excitement and mental exertion. People used to come into the *beis medrash* just to watch him learn. Yet at the same time, he was the one who always made himself available to teach the pertinent *halachos* to any new *chassan*, no matter how many others he was already teaching. And later as Rosh Yeshiva in Kol Yaakov, "[he] was," in the words of one student, "always available. He gravitated back toward the *beis medrash* and the *bachurim* like a magnet."[12]

Like his father, Avraham Gershon's first question was always: What does *Klal Yisrael* need? When he joined in founding Yeshivas Kol Yaakov in Monsey, there were many who expressed surprise that he had chosen to teach *baalei teshuvah*. He had been offered a number of positions as a *maggid shiur* in advanced yeshivos — positions that seemed more in

---

10. Interview with Chaim Kahan.

11. From the words of remembrance of his *talmid* Rachmiel Abramowitz.

12. Ibid.

keeping with his abilities as a *lamdan*. To those who wondered at his choice, he had a simple answer: "Does the *Aibeshter* (the One Above) want me to be a Rosh Yeshiva or to do His will?" He felt the biggest contribution he could make was inspiring Jews from limited backgrounds.

The *bitachon* he showed throughout his life, and especially in the last year of his life as he battled cancer, was another Tress legacy. "*Veiter gegangen* (keep going)" was his watchword. A tape exists of the *shiur* he gave three hours after the first tumor was discovered. Listening to it, it is impossible to discern that the voice is that of someone in his mid-30s who had just been told that his life was in imminent danger.

One day in the middle of *shiur*, he was informed that a summer bungalow in which he had invested a good deal of his money had just blown up due to a gas leak. "Was anyone hurt?" was all he wanted to know. Assured that no one was, he let out a laugh and continued teaching the *Gemara* as if nothing had happened.[13] Yet despite being so far removed from the material world, he was able to advise his students on every aspect of life. That advice reflected deep sensitivity and understanding — above all, it was "simple, straight, and *glatt*," as if it came straight from a higher world.[14]

Even in the final throes of his disease, he did not slacken in the *mitzvos bein adam lechaveiro*. One night, shortly before his passing, he was gasping for breath. The doctors wanted to drain his lungs, but before doing so they sought the permission of his older brother Shmuel Baruch. Though the doctors told Avraham Gershon that he could choke to death if the fluid was not drained immediately, he refused to let them wake his brother in the middle of the night. "I'll pull through the night," he insisted. The next morning he made his brother Mendel open the curtains so that he could see that it was really morning before he would let the doctors call. When his mother came to visit, he forced himself to eat whatever she brought so that she would not know how bad the situation was.

Nor was he less scrupulous with the *mitzvos bein adam leMakom* (*mitzvos* between man and G-d). To the very end, he insisted on standing when his *tefillin* were being put on because it says in *Shulchan Aruch* that one should put on his *tefillin* standing up.

Though to his friends and students he was a walking *mussar sefer*, there was still much that was kept hidden behind his easy manner. One

---

13. Words of remembrance of his student Yaakov Astor.
14. Ibid.

night, when his father was very sick, one of Avraham Gershon's close friends happened to come into the Telshe *beis medrash* at three in the morning. There he found Avraham Gershon pouring out his heart in *Tehillim*, the tears streaming down his face. Though he also said *Tehillim* during the day, only when he stood alone with Hashem did he permit himself to give full vent to his deepest inner feelings.

A Good Investment

DURING HIS LAST YEARS, MIKE WAS FREQUENTLY FORCED TO SPEND much of the winter in Florida. On one of those vacations, he found himself seated in a lounge chair next to a man eager to discuss his investments. When the man had finished detailing his stock portfolio, he asked Mike what he was invested in. Mike answered simply, "My children are my investments."

He had invested well.

Chapter Twenty-Five

THE SUN SETS AT MIDDAY

M ike's final years were not easy ones. From 1961 until his passing in 1967, he suffered from coronary disease that made it increasingly difficult to work. Besides being debilitating, the disease left him in constant, and often excruciating, pain.

For a man still in his early 50s, who had always been able to work almost around the clock, the frustration of not being able to contribute was the worst of all. Mike was a dreamer always busy hatching plans for raising the level of *Yiddishkeit* in America, and there was much left to do before those dreams were fully realized. Though no one could have imagined in 1931, when Mike first entered the

Rodney Street Zeirei, what would be accomplished over the next 30 years, each accomplishment had only whetted his imagination more.

Mike was by no means ready to rest on his laurels and spend his time reminiscing about the past. "He wanted so much to get better so that he could continue working," recalls Rabbi Shlomo Rotenberg. As soon as he felt the slightest improvement, he would immediately start looking for something to do or someone to help.[1] He was willing to try any type of operation, no matter how experimental, which offered him the hope of getting better so that he could work again.

Only occasionally would he permit himself the pleasure of reflecting on what he had done. Sitting by the parlor window, he would look out onto the sidewalk. There he could see, passing by, many who had been brought to America under the auspices of the Agudath Israel Youth Council. Even then, he always referred to those who had been rescued as "one of *our* cases," eschewing any reference to himself personally.

There was much that might have embittered a lesser man. The family debts continued to mount. At the same time, there were many to whom Mike had loaned money over the years who had not repaid the money despite having prospered in business. Gavriel Beer and a few others who were close to Mike wanted to try and collect the monies, but Mike would not let them. He did not want to embarrass those who had forgotten about their old obligations.

That lack of bitterness was characteristic. Leon Keller once went collecting with Mike in an attempt to pay off the mortgage on the building at 616 Bedford Avenue. One of those they visited had lived for some time at 616 and his training in the diamond industry had been paid for by the Youth Council. The man pulled out a large role of bills and handed Mike five dollars. Keller was incensed at the paltry gift, but Mike took it in stride. "Don't be a disappointed Jew," he told Keller. "If you do someone a favor and expect a thank-you, you'll be disappointed."

Mike's tremendous store of *bitachon* protected him from bitterness and kept him going in those last years. As soon as he came into the house, he needed alcohol compresses to lessen the headaches caused by poor circulation, but he never complained about the terrible pain he was in. Self-pity was anathema to him.

One of his younger daughters, Shevy, used to spend long hours

---

1. Interview with Mike's daughter Donya Pichey.

sitting next to her father trying to make him more comfortable. When the pain was particularly intense, he did not cry out or complain, but merely held her hand more tightly. He used to call her his "nurse" and make her feel very important.

In the mid-1960's, Melech Terebelo, who had been one of the most active volunteers in the wartime rescue work, decided to pay a sentimental visit to the Agudath Israel offices. He happened to come in on one of those rare that days Mike was in the office, and found him sitting there with two small notebooks, apparently toting up a series of figures. Terebelo asked what he was doing. Mike showed him one ledger: "This is the list of all my hospital expenses, medical bills, and operations." Then he showed him the other ledger: "And here are all the expenses for my children's weddings. I figure this page [i.e., the one with the expenses for the weddings] just about covers this one [the one with the medical expenses]," Mike told him. The joy in his family compensated for all his personal suffering.

Had he been the type, Mike might at least have taken solace in the respect and affection shown him by the spiritual leaders of the generation. He enjoyed their complete confidence because they knew he was totally subservient to their decisions, and at the same time, they relied on his knowledge of the American milieu and his instinctive sense of how to reach the *"pashute Yid."*[2] Rabbi Aharon Kotler, lying in the hospital only weeks before his *petirah,* sent his son Rabbi Shneur Kotler from the hospital to the wedding of Mike's daughter Donya Pichey. Reb Shneur was reluctant to leave his father's bedside, but Reb Aharon told him, "If Mike Tress is making a *chasanah,* I want to be represented." Among those who came to visit Mike when he was very weak one winter in Florida were: Rabbi Yaakov Kamenetsky, the Ponovezher Rav, the Boyaner Rebbe, the Kopyczinitzer Rebbe and Rabbi Shneur Kotler. Long after Mike passed away, Rabbi Moshe Feinstein still made a point of being at every Tress family *simchah.*

Despite his ideological opposition to Agudath Israel, there was always a feeling of friendship and admiration between the Satmar Rebbe and Reb Elemelech Tress. Agudath Israel Youth Council had played a major role in bringing the Rebbe to the United States, and the Rebbe would frequently stop Mike to talk when he saw him in Williamsburg, calling, "Meilech, *cum nor aher* — Meilech, please come here."

---

2. Rabbi Menachem Porush compares the trust the *gedolim* had in Mike Tress with that they had for Reb Jacob Rosenheim.

Towards the end of his life, Mike came to Cleveland to visit his children learning in Telshe Yeshiva. When he came into the *beis medrash,* the Rosh Yeshiva Rabbi Mordechai Gifter ordered everyone to stand up "for the *gadol hador.*"[3]

The affection in which he was held in the Orthodox world was unparalleled. A young Bnos girl in the '50s, hearing her parents discussing the upcoming presidential elections, asked in surprise, "What's the question? Mike Tress is president." One of the inevitable perils of community service is the accusation that one has fallen in love with the prestige of the office. Mike was almost unique in that such an accusation was never uttered about him, even in private.[4]

By 1967, Mike's condition had deteriorated to the point that his doctors told him that there was no alternative to heart by-pass surgery. Such surgery was still in its infancy. Only two doctors in the whole world, Drs. Denton Cooley and Michael DeBakey in Houston, performed the surgery. Insurance did not cover such experimental operations, and Mike did not have the $3,000 dollars necessary to pay for the surgery.

Somehow the Kopyczinitzer Rebbe heard of his plight and came to Mike with the sum needed for the operation. Mike could not be sure of surviving the operation and so did not tell the Rebbe that he would pay him back. At best he could say, "The Rebbe will be paid." The Rebbe replied, "No, it is you who will be paid," meaning that Hashem would surely reward him for all that he had done on behalf of *Klal Yisrael.* As soon as he heard that, Mike was sure the operation would be a success.[5]

Prior to the surgery, he cheered up his family with his jokes and good spirits.[6] His doctors in Houston, Dr. Cooley and Dr. Christian Barnard, could not stop talking about his easy-going manner and serenity prior to what was at the time extremely high-risk surgery.

Shortly after the surgery, his daughter Devorah flew down to Houston to see her father. She had been told that he was extremely weak, and was shocked when she saw her father at the airport waiting to meet her.

"Pa, how were you able to come to the airport?" she asked him.

3. Interview with Aaron Rubinson, who was in Telshe Yeshiva at that time.

4. Interview with Rabbi Shlomo Lorincz.

5. Told to Yitzchak Zvi Tress by the Rebbe's son Rabbi Sysche Heschel.

6. Pichey interview.

In a barely audible whisper, he replied, "If you could make such a long trip to see me, the least I could do is to come here to greet you."

As Mike had hoped, the open-heart surgery was successful, and for six months he regained some of his former vigor. Unfortunately, medicine prescribed for a relatively minor condition caused his blood to thin and brought on a stroke Shabbos morning, *Parshas Korach* 5527 (1967). He smiled and nodded "Good Shabbos" to a group who came over from the *minyan* at 616 Bedford Avenue to see why he had not been at *davening*. But over the next week, his condition gradually deteriorated, and he drifted in and out of consciousness. When unconscious, Mike was heard repeating the names of his children over and over again.

The following Sunday evening, the second day of *Tammuz* (July 9, 1967), Mike passed away. His *levayah* the next day was attended by virtually every figure of prominence in the Orthodox world and thousands of others who had known him personally or felt they had. A visitor from Jerusalem expressed surprise when he saw the Satmar Rebbe preparing to accompany the *levayah* of the leader of Agudath Israel, but the Rebbe silenced him immediately: "He was a *tzaddik* and a *tahor*."[7] (The Satmar Rebbe also paid a *shivah* call to the Tress family.)

As the *aron* was being carried to 616 Bedford Avenue, the clear blue skies suddenly gave way to a sun shower just above the *aron*. Rabbi Shlomo Rotenberg, standing next to Mike's son-in-law Rabbi Michoel Meisels, commented, "The *Gemara* (*Sanhedrin* 47a) says that rain on the *mitah* (bier) is a *siman tov* (good sign) for the *niftar* (deceased) in Heaven."

One of the *maspidim* commented, "He was together with the *gedolim* in this world, and he'll be together with them in the next." Rabbi Gedaliah Schorr, his friend of a lifetime, wept inconsolably. "Whatever one could say about him would not be enough. Elemelech Gavriel Tress was responsible for bringing Torah to the shores of America," he said. His fellow Rosh Yeshiva in Torah Vodaath, Rabbi Yaakov Kamenetsky, echoed that assessment: "Because Reb Elemelech Tress created a strong Agudah in America, when the *gedolim* came from Europe they had a base of *Yiddishkeit* from which to work. Without that, far less would have been accomplished."

---

7. Told to Yitzchak Zvi Tress by Rabbi Yosef Sheinberger, one of the leaders of the Eidah Hachareidis in Jerusalem.

The most eloquent testimony to the love of the spiritual leaders of the generation for Mike Tress did not come from any of the *maspidim*, but from one who could not attend. The Kopyczinitzer Rebbe was informed as soon as Mike suffered his stroke. Even though the Rebbe was at his Shabbos table when the news reached him, he broke out crying. Shortly thereafter, he took to his bed and never recovered, passing away soon after Mike. The Rebbe's son, Rabbi Sysche Heschel, has no doubt that news of Mike's stroke hastened his father's passing.

Sometime after Mike's passing, his son Zvi went to Rabbi Yaakov Kamenetsky with two questions. First, he wanted to know how his father could have died so young after receiving a blessing from Rabbi Elchonon Wasserman for *arichas yamim* (length of days). Reb Yaakov replied that length of days is measured in deeds not time, and by that standard his father had indeed merited a "very long" life. But Zvi was still bothered by the fact his father had suffered so much during his final years. Reb Yaakov told him that the verse in *Mishlei* (19:21), "Many are the thoughts in the hearts of man, but Hashem's counsel shall stand," means that no Divine intention is ever completely revoked. *Chazal* tell us that originally Hashem intended to create the world according to the attribute of strict justice alone, but that He saw the world could not exist on that basis and therefore added the attribute of Divine mercy to the Creation. But, said Reb Yaakov, the original Divine intention to create the world only on the basis of strict judgment

MICHAEL TRESS, 56, LED AGUDATH ISRAEL

Michael G. Tress, president of Agudath Israel of America, which promotes Orthodox Judaism through educational programs, died Sunday night of a stroke in Maimonides Medical Center, Brooklyn. He was 56 years old and lived at 586 Bedford Avenue, Brooklyn.

Mr. Tress, who headed Agudath Israel for more than two decades, was credited with helping in the rescue and relief of thousands of Jews from Eastern Europe during World War II.

He spurred the State Department to issue emergency visas for oppressed Jews and he visited displaced persons camps after the war for the United Nations Relief and Rehabilitation Administration.

He was born in New York and graduated from City College. He had been an executive with Lamport Company Inc., a textile concern.

Mike's obituary in The New York Times

remained to a degree. In every generation there are a select few working to be judged according to the attributes of strict judgment. "Your father was one of those," Reb Yaakov told Zvi.

A few days after Mike learned that he needed open-heart surgery for which he had no means to pay, his daughter Eska noticed in the paper that Esquire Shoe Polish had been sold to Revlon for $3,000,000. Of that, one third would have been Mike's share had he not sold his stock. "Just think, *Tatte,* how different everything would have been if you had just held onto those shares," Eska said to her father.

"*Baruch Hashem,* how different," was Mike's only reply.

It was a *Baruch Hashem* that could have been echoed by tens of thousands of Jews around the world.

INDEX OF PERSONALITIES

A

Aaron brothers   62
Abramowitz, Rachmiel   417
Ackerman family   145
Adler, Emil   138, 151, 185, 222
Aksin, Dr.   297, 302
Alter, Rabbi Avraham Mordechai
   see Gerrer Rebbe
Altusky, Rabbi   84
Ashkenazi, David   357
Astor, Yaakov   418
Auerbach, Morley   97, 109, 363-364
Auman, George   320
Ausband, Rabbi Isaac   262

B

Bagry, Donya   258
Bagry family   145
Bagry, Rochel   145, 149, 254
Bagry sisters   58
Bagry, Velvel   254
Bakst, Rabbi Leib   262
Barenbaum, Rabbi Michel   262
Barnard, Dr. Christian   423
Baruch, Bernard   298
Basch, Eli   100
Baumgarten, Rabbi Shlomo   353
Bechofer, Jerry   271
Beer, Gavriel   21, 22, 89, 99-100, 103-
   104, 235, 421
Belsky, Berel   72, 143, 287
Belsky, Channah   57-58, 60, 72, 174-
   175,
Belsky, Rabbi Yisroel   86, 218, 220,
   411
Bender, Rebbetzin Basya   124
Berent, Irving   309-310, 317
Berger, Aaron   313
Berger, Moshe   28, 113, 136, 249, 252,
   261, 265
Bergman, Clara   173
Bergson, Peter   236
Berkowitz, Rabbi L.   153

Berkowitz, Mottel   89, 119
Berle, Adolph   296, 302
Berliner, Hirschel   51, 53
Biberfeld, Dr. Henry   293
Birnbaum, Dr. Nathan   47, 80, 165
Birnbaum, Lieutenant Meyer   47, 77-
   78, 97, 110, 111, 146, 323-325, 329,
   360
Blau, Rabbi Moshe   50
Blinder, Chaplain Samuel   310, 316
Bloch, Rabbi Eliyahu Meir   180, 226-
   227, 238-239, 398, 411
Bloch, Leah   79, 410
Bloch, Rabbi Moshe   255
Bloom, Congressman Sol   159, 206,
   258
Blum, Pvt. Marvin   209
Blumenthal, Rabbi Chas.   208
Bluzhover Rebbe   83, 184, 395, 411
Bobover Rebbe   113, 169, 338, 365
Bohlen, Chester   296
Borchardt, Rabbi Max   247
Boyaner Rebbe   115, 148, 181, 254,
   259, 364, 395, 411-412, 422
Brand, Joel   289, 303
Braunfeld, Moshe   330, 333
Brawer, Menachem Mendel   255
Brenner, Alexander   185
Breslauer, Rabbi Dr. L.   165, 176, 190
Breuer, Dr. Isaac   166, 165, 191-192
Breuer, Rabbi Dr. Joseph   143, 271
Brick, Yussie   229
Brody, Feivel   229
Brooks, Sam   313
Brown, Harry   310-311
Bunim, Irving   65, 125, 139, 237-238,
   253, 295
Bursztyn, Dr. Naftali Hertz   255
Buxbaum, Daniella   174, 177-178

C

Celler, Congressman Emanuel   196
Chafetz Chaim   20, 51, 68, 80, 82,
   204, 215
Chavkin, Rabbi Roy   138

Chazan, Rabbi Elya   262
Chill, Shmuel   58
Chodorov, Rabbi Mendel   53, 84
Chortkover Rebbe   20
Chuster Rav   226
Cohen, Rabbi Henoch   398
Cohen, Simon   125
Cohn, Henry   309
Cooley, Dr. Denton   423
Coughlin, Father Charles E.   241
Coulter, Eliot   258

D

DeBakey, Dr. Michael   423
Debreziner Rav   289
Dembroff, Mendy   110, 113
Dershowitz, Aharon Menashe   31
Despradel, Dr. Don Roberto   301
Dessler, Rabbi Eliyahu   395
Deutsch, Adolph   289
Deutsch, Deborah   33, 58, 146
Deutschlander, Dr. Leo   122-123
Diamond, David   206
Diamond, Dr. Isaac   413
Diskin, Rabbi Yehoshua Leib   146
Diskin, Rabbi Yeruchum   145-146
Drebin family   145
Drebin, Reb Kalman   145
Drillman, Amelia   59
Drucker, Morris   312, 316, 319
Dubois, Josiah E.   240
Dykman, Moses   184, 391
Dzikansky, Irene   356

E

Eban, Abba   396
Ebert, Rena   74, 176
Eden, Anthony   245
Eger, Aron   362
Ehrenfeld, Rabbi Shmuel   see
    Mattesdorfer Rav
Ehrmann, Rabbiner Dr. S.   353
Ehrmann, Shlomo   49
Eichenthal, Fishel   50-51, 53

Eichenthal, Moshe   53
Eichmann, Adolph   289, 303
Eiger, Rabbi Akiva   228
Einsiedler, Jacob   53
Eiseman, Rabbi Gedaliah   262
Eisenhower, Dwight David   304-305, 404
Eiss, Chaim   280-281, 299
Elbaum, Rabbi Yechiel   113
Elberg, Rabbi Simcha   84, 395, 399, 406
Elias, Rabbi Joseph   165, 169, 293, 387-388
Eller, Rabbi E.M.   277
Epstein, Rabbi Ephraim   48-49
Epstein, Rabbi Moshe Mordechai   49, 50
Epstein, Rabbi Moshe Yechiel   see
    Ozerover Rebbe
Estes, Bernard   30

F

Falik, Florence   33
Falik, Judah   33
Farkas, May   59, 177
Feigenbaum, Yisrael   50, 53-54, 90, 168
Feinberg, Sam   21-22
Feinstein, Rabbi Michel   160
Feinstein, Rabbi Moshe   84, 181, 412, 422
Felderbaum, Rabbi Dovid   83
Feldman, Rabbi Moses J.   120
Fensterheim, Moe   72
Fensterheim, Shirley   59
Feuereisen, Yitzchok   229
Finkelstein, Shaindel   177
Fink, Jerry   118
Fink, Mottel   56
Fink, Rabbi Anshel   53, 56, 67, 72, 129
Fink, Rabbi Yoel   129, 134
Firstenberg, I.   277
Fishelis, Shmuel   229
Fisher, Anshel   50, 53
Flanzgraben, Rabbi Yaakov   44
Fogel, Charles   51, 53

Fogel, Herzl   50
Fogel, Joseph   50-51, 181
Follman family   122
Forchheimer, Paul   319
Francis, Alexander   119, 154, 185
Franco, General Francisco   304
Frankel, Rebbetzin Clara   177, 393
Frankel, Rabbi Shabse   262-3, 270, 300
Frankel, Yehudah   229
Freedman, Mr.   300
Freudiger, Philip   289, 291
Freud, Ladislav   362
Friedberg, Isak   362
Fried, Herschel   90
Friedenson, Reb Eliezer Gershon   329
Friedenson, Yosef   330-331, 333
Friedman, Rabbi Avraham Abba   89, 118-119
Friedman, Francis   362
Friedman, Rabbi Mordechai Shlomo   see Boyaner Rebbe
Friedman, Rabbi Mordechai Sholom Yosef   see Sadigerer Rebbe
Friedman, Rabbi Moshe Yechiel (Murray)   92-93, 170
Friedman, Rabbi Yisrael   see Chortkover Rebbe
Fruchthandler, Ephraim   33
Fruchthandler, Ruth   33
Fuerst, Rabbi Isaiah   166

G

Garber, Srul   362
Garfinkel, Rabbi Noach   51
Gartenberg, Leo   53
Gartenhaus, Leo   53
Gassner, A.   138
Gelbwachs, Yisroel   229
Gellman, Aryeh Leib   49
Gelman, Rabbi   143
Gerrer Rebbe   20, 80, 82, 124, 166, 263-264
Gewirtz, Claire   57

Gifter, Rabbi Mordechai   395, 417, 423
Ginsburg, Heshy   309
Glass, Sarah   58
Gleicher, Avraham Abba   50, 51
Gleicher, Moshe Yehudah   50, 53, 187
Gleicher, Robert   53
Goldberg, Chaplain Capt.   208
Goldenberg, Rabbi Bernard   187, 189
Gold, Jack   50, 251
Goldman, Albert   104, 105
Goldman, Israel   195
Gold, Pearl   177
Gold, Rabbi Zev   116
Gold, Reb Shea   47, 50-53, 90, 251
Goldstein, Rabbi Herbert S.   158-160, 162, 176, 184, 199, 204, 274, 290-291, 295, 300, 304, 341, 391, 392-394
Goldstein, Rabbi Yaakov   39-40, 42, 93, 103-104, 143, 110, 235, 325
Goldstein, Rebbetzin Penina   92
Goodman, Harry   311, 319, 353-354, 369
Gordon, Yaakov Mordechai   50, 53
Gorinfeld, Sergeant   311-312
Gottlieb, Morris   376-377
Greenbaum, Aaron   89
Greenbaum, Rabbi Berel   33, 58, 74, 89
Greenberger, Louis   53
Greenhaus, Donya   58
Greenstein, Rabbi Philip   183
Greenwald, Rabbi Levi Yitzchok   see Tzelemer Rav
Greenwald, Sidney   20, 41, 91, 93, 158, 160, 170, 219-220, 226-227
Greenwald, Yaakov   170
Griffel, Dr. Jacob   269, 367-368
Griffith, Mrs.   258
Grodensky, Shalom   128
Grodzenski, Rabbi Chaim Ozer   81, 89, 167, 180, 261-262
Grodzitski, Rabbi Yehoshua   107
Gross, Bernard   168
Gross, Max   56, 63, 134
Grossman, Baruch   229

Grossman, Rabbi Israel   396
Grossman, Max   62
Grozovsky, Rabbi Reuven   17, 107,
   115, 118, 262
Gruber, Dr. Ruth   277
Grunfeld, Rebbetzin Dr. Judith   122

H

Hager, Rabbi Chaim Meir   *see*
   Vishnitzer Rebbe
Halbersberg, Rabbi Moshe   378-380
Halbersberg sisters   378
Halperin, Kaila   59
Hamburger, Esther   124
Hammerman, Mr.   153
Hamm, Harold   56
Hamm, Irving   56
Hamm, Morris   56
Harogsohn, Hartog   293
Harriman, Governor Averell   274,
   405
Harrison, Leland   290
Hasenfeld, Israel   53
Hausman, Nathan   53, 56, 122, 135,
   178, 184, 253, 369, 391-392
Hecht, Ben   237
Heiman, Rabbi Shlomo   115, 117,
   128, 265
Hendeles, Rabbi Binyamin Wolf   84,
   160, 172, 399, 406
Hershkowitz, Binyamin   119
Hershkowitz, David   297
Herskowitz, Leah   57
Hertzman, Rabbi Chuna   362
Herzog, Rabbi Yitzchak Isaac   116,
   195
Heschel, Rabbi Avrohom Yehoshua
   see Kopyczinitzer Rebbe
Heschel, Rabbi Sysche   219, 224, 248,
   425
Hildesheimer, Rabbi Dr. Meir   47
Himmler, Heinrich   303-304
Hirsch, Binyamin   48, 50, 53, 168, 181
Hirsch, Rabbi Samson Raphael   188
Hirschel, Shabse   53

Hodell, Miss   300
Hoenig, Anne   58
Hoenig, Rabbi Dr. Sidney   58
Hoffing, Arthur   310
Hook, Henry   309, 319
Hoover, J. Edgar   242
Hopfer, Rachel   58
Horowitz, Nathan   51
Horowitz, Yosef Yonah   319
Horthy, Admiral Miklos von
   Nagybanya   234
Huberman, Anshel   50
Hull, Cordell   245, 293, 296, 298, 300
Huttner, Ezekiel   362

J

Jacobson, Rabbi Wolf   176
Joffen, Rabbi Avraham   180, 262
Jolson, Al   41
Jundef, Shevy   109, 421
Jung, Rabbi Dr. Leo   56, 158, 176, 249

K

Kahan, Benno   256
Kahan, Rachel   256-7
Kahana, Rabbi Meir   117
Kahaneman, Rabbi Yosef Shlomo
   see Ponovezher Rav
Kahane, Rabbi Levi Yitzchak   70, 71,
   141
Kahn, Herbert   327-328
Kahn, Lothar   76, 155, 210, 314-315,
   327-328
Kalb, Leib   362
Kalmanowitz, Rabbi Avraham   237-
   238, 274, 291, 295-296,
   300, 302, 395
Kalmanowitz, Rebbetzin   173-174
Kamenetsky, Rabbi Yaakov   83, 106,
   115, 143, 363, 395, 411-412, 422,
   424-425, 426
Kaplan, Rabbi Baruch   125, 143, 361
Kaplan, Rebbetzin Vichna   124-152,
   179, 358, 361, 369

Kaplan, Rabbi Yisrael Chaim 17, 180, 262
Kapustin, Alexander 296
Karelitz, Rabbi Meir 50
Karlin, Rabbi Aharon of 333
Karlin, Meyer 58
Karp, Rabbi Elias 54, 206, 341
Karpf, Rabbi Yitzchak 89, 91, 128
Karski, Jan 236
Kass, Melvin 309
Kastner, Dr. Rudolph 289, 291
Katz, Avner 53
Katz family 101
Katz, Rabbi Chaim Mordechai 84, 180, 238-239
Katz, Tillie 34, 59, 177, 179, 221
Kaufman, Irving 104, 220
Kaufman, Shaye 58, 214-215, 221
Keller, Leon 64, 102, 152, 421
Kimmerman, Dr. Aryeh 368
Kirschenbaum, Channah 58
Klaristenfeld, Michoel 108
Klausner, Chaplain 310
Klausner, Jack 33, 74, 93, 170
Klausner, Sylvia 77, 335
Klein, Charles 53, 54, 89, 168
Klein, Jonah 53, 206
Klein, Sylvia 393
Knobel, Esther 59, 393
Knobel, Joseph 53
Kohn, Rabbi Pinchos 167
Kolatch, Sender 56
Kook, Rabbi Avraham Yitzchak 116
Kopyczinitzer Rebbe 16, 115, 226, 247-248, 259, 364, 368, 411-412, 422-423, 425
Korff, Rabbi Baruch 274, 300
Kotler, Rabbi Aharon 16-18, 66-67, 82, 84, 106, 122, 125, 160-161, 180, 226, 235, 237, 262, 265-268, 274, 295, 396, 398, 412, 422
Kotler, Rabbi Shneur 422
Kowalski, Rabbi M. 282
Kowalsky, Rose 177
Krakowsky, Milton 208
Kramer family 122
Krane, Robert and Ruth 72, 254-255

Kranzler, Dr. David 151-152
Kranzler, Gershon 75-76, 88, 98-99, 112, 128, 130, 136, 155, 163-164, 166-167, 179, 185, 249, 252, 256, 288
Krohn, Hindy 145
Kurzman, Marcus 170

L

Ladislav, Rabbi 362
Lamm, Eugene 185, 221-222, 327
Lamm, Marion 177
Lamm, Solomon 185
Lamport, Samuel 34
Landesman, Esther 58
Lanton, Moshe 53
Lashinsky, Rabbi 143
Lehman, Governor Herbert S. 168, 328
Leibowitz, Rabbi Dovid 115-116, 187
Leiman, Henchie 33, 58
Leiman, Rabbi Heshy (Harold) 33, 72, 172, 388
Leiser, Heshy 325-327, 393, 405
Leissar, Herbert 206
Lejbowicz, Mowesz 362
Leshinsky, Rabbi Yerucham 412
Lesser, Lawrence 297, 302, 304
Leuchter, Rabbi Yisrael Yaakov 332
Levazer, Chaplain Hersch 181, 310, 329, 338
Levenberg, Rabbi Yehudah 177
Levin, Rabbi Aaron 167
Levin, Rabbi Itche Meir 111, 159, 194, 390
Levitan, Yosef 85
Levovitz, Rabbi Simchah Zissel 180, 262
Lev, Rabbi Joseph 47
Levy, Irene 33
Levy, Mr. 158
Lewin, Dr. Isaac 61, 197, 262-263, 276, 283, 293-294, 319, 399
Lieber, Arnie 170
Lieber, Moshe 143

Lieber, Yossi   229
Liebowitz, Julie   25, 63-64
Linchner, Rabbi Alexander   72, 120
Link, Gyla   289-291
Lipshitz, Rabbi Chaim Uri   97, 101, 105, 142, 181, 184, 187, 235, 247
Lipshitz, Rabbi Dovid   84, 262
Lipshitz, Grand Rabbi Moshe   181
Litmanowitz, Zelda   177
Litvinoff, Ambassador Maksim Maksimovich   296
London, Meyer   39
Long, Breckenridge   240, 242, 258-259, 262-263, 266-268, 304
Longerstaey, Edouard   369
Lorincz, Rabbi Shlomo   168, 385, 390-393
Lubinsky, Rabbi Chaim Pinchos   135, 175
Lublin, Seer of   378
Luski, Rabbi Moshe   263
Luzzato, Rabbi Moshe Chaim   116

M

Machlis, Leon   221
Mandelbaum, Rabbi Reuven   44
Mandelbaum, Staff Sergeant Wilfred   211
Mandel, Julia   176
Mandel, Pincus   53
Mandel, Rebbetzin Fruma Leah   57, 61
Marcus, Wilbur   309, 315, 317
Marshall, Justice Louis   38
Maryles, Dave   56, 71, 74, 88, 89, 122, 151, 168-169, 206-207, 221, 341
Mashinsky, Rabbi Heshy   33, 75, 85, 89, 97, 117
Mattesdorfer Rav   143
Mayer, Ben   185
Mayer, Saly   290, 302
McClelland, Roswell   290
McDermott, Colonel Arthur V.   208
McDonald, James   259
Meiseles, Falk   373, 379-380, 383
Meisels, Henie   334, 441-412, 416

Meisels, Rabbi Michoel   424
Meisels, Rabbi Zvi Hirsch   339
Mendelowitz, David   53
Mendelowitz, Yitzchok   72
Mendelsohn, Rabbi Binyamin   395
Mendelsson, Uscher   319
Mendelsson-Fischer, Jakob   319
Mendlowitz, Abish   118, 219-220
Mendlowitz, Channah   58
Mendlowitz, Reb Sharga Feivel   15, 17-20, 58.67-68, 88-89, 91, 115-119, 122, 126, 143, 148, 171-173, 227, 254, 361
Mendlowitz, Rivka   58
Mendlowitz, Saul   309
Menkis, Pesachya   53, 56
Menzelevsky, Ruby   364
Metchik, Irwin   108
Metzger, Itche   50, 53, 90
Metzger, Mendel   50, 53, 90
Miller, Asher   229
Mintz, Bracha   177
Mittman, Isaac   53
Modzhitzer Rebbe   262
Moeller, Dr. Raphael   319
Mordechovitz, Rabbi Shimon   84
Morgan, General   343
Morgenthau, Henry   239, 266, 295, 297-298, 300
Moskowitz, Herman   185
Moskowitz, Heshy   76, 89, 119, 154, 187, 213-214, 249, 391
Mostel, Milton   53
Muller, M.   355
Muni, Paul   237
Munk, Rabbi Elie   408
Munk, Rabbi Michael   113, 354

N

Nachman, Etta   239
Nachman, Schimon Leib   239
Nadich, Chaplain Major Judah   310
Nagy, Imre   401
Nekritz, Rabbi Yehudah   262
Nelkenbaum, Eliezer   362

Nerl, Martin   189, 195
Newhouse, Rabbi Avraham   124
Newman, Esther   59
Newman, Frank   72, 267, 273
Nitra Rav   287, 290
Novagrodsky, Dr. Solomon   152
Novominsker Rebbe   70, 71, 181, 226, 395
Nussbaum, Efraim   226

O

Oberlander, Sandor   362
Ochs, Rabbi David   84
O'Dwyer, General William   277
O'Dwyer, Mayor William   391-392
Olshin, Hymie   62
Orlean, Celia   339
Ort, Rabbi Shlomo   89, 119, 154, 206, 208, 308, 310, 316, 326, 337
Oshry, Rabbi Ephraim   109, 110
Oysher, Moshe   71
Ozerover Rebbe   395

P

Pachtman, Yisrael   53-54
Pam, Rabbi Avrohom   72
Pappenheim, Liza   177
Partzovitz, Rabbi Nochum   365
Pearson, Drew   300
Pehle, John   240, 284, 296, 302, 304
Pejsach, Rabbi Avraham   263
Pekier, Rabbi Alter   161
Penkower, Monty   304
Perl, Alter   93, 103, 170206
Perlow, Rabbi Aharon   332
Perlow, Rabbi Nachum   see Novominsker Rabbe
Perlow, Rabbi Yaakov   56, 64, 332
Perlow, Rabbi Yisrael   333
Perlow, Rabbi Yochanan   332-333
Pichey, Donya   414, 421-423
Pilchik family   122
Pincus, Rabbi Avraham   124
Pincus, Chava   123-124, 179

Plotzker, Abe   53, 56
Plotzker brothers   54, 56
Plotzker, Charlie   56
Plotzker, Joseph   53, 56
Plotzker, Max   56
Plotzker, Yossi   229
Plotzky, Rabbi Meir Don   47
Pogromansky, Rabbi Mordechai   381-383
Pollack sisters   58
Pollak, Abraham   362
Pollak, Lipot   362
Ponevezher Rav   412, 422
Portugal, Rabbi Eliezer Zusia   see Skulener Rebbe
Puritz, Molly   58, 177

Q

Quinn, Rabbi Nesanel   28, 33

R

Rabinowitz, F.D.   170
Rand, Rabbi Oscar   181
Rapaport, Chaim   85
Rappaport, Vojtech   362
Rauchwerger, Staff Sergeant Leon   211
Raymond, Rabbi Paysach   406
Reichel, Josephine   393
Reichel, Rabbi Oscar   185
Reichmann, Renee   353
Reidel, Eska   79, 410, 415, 426
Richter, Charles   281-283, 285-286
Riegner, Gerhard   245
Riis, Jacob   38
Ringel, Pfc. Oscar   208-209
Rivlin, Rabbi Moshe   95, 130
Robinson, Edward G.   237
Roosevelt, Eleanor   295, 304-305
Roosevelt, Franklin Jr.   391
Roosevelt, President Franklin Delano   196, 239-242, 250, 250, 259, 262, 293, 303
Roseman, Louis   210

Rosenbaum, Yankel   411
Rosenberg, Rabbi Alexander   319
Rosenberg, Herman   354
Rosenberg, Rabbi Yisrael   49
Rosenberger, Yosef   76, 115-158, 161-162
Rosenblatt, Basya   410
Rosenheim, Reb Jacob   48, 61, 64-65, 82, 160, 165-166, 173, 181-182, 195, 99, 203, 233, 280, 292-293, 295, 297, 304, 380, 422
Rosenholtz, Dave   208
Rosenman, Samuel   240
Rosenzweig, Rabbi Feivel   98, 106, 347, 363-365
Rosenzweig, Joseph   234
Rotenberg, Channah   177
Rotenberg, Rabbi Shlomo   64, 81, 98, 106, 143, 165, 169, 172, 191, 270-271, 421, 424
Roth, Abe   206
Roth, Ferdinand   289
Roth, Harry   309
Roth, Max   239
Rubenstein, Isadore   410
Rubin, Gerson   362
Rubinson, Beirach   100-101, 318, 330, 334, 391

S

Sabbath, Adolph   296
Sadigerer Rebbe   395
Saltz, Elimelech   53
Sandhaus, Moshe   72
Sanft, Meyer   53
Satmar Rebbe   16, 289, 365, 422, 424
Schaum, Pinchos   326
Schecter, Herschel   89
Schenirer, Sarah   57-58, 122-124, 173, 341
Schenkolewski, Meir   249, 262, 293, 295, 304
Schiff, Jacob   38
Schiff, Oscar   360
Schiff, Rabbi Sheah   89

Schmidman, Rabbi Yitzchok   226
Schneider, Rabbi Moshe   408
Schneider, Schulem   357
Schonbrun, Irving   53, 62
Schonfeld, Pesach Dovid   53, 56
Schonfeld, Rabbi Dr. Solomon   174, 286
Schorr, Aaron   56
Schorr brothers   54, 56
Schorr, Dovid   53, 56
Schorr, Moshe   56
Schorr, Rabbi Gedaliah   50, 53, 56, 66-67, 71-72, 85, 89, 115-116, 122, 129, 143, 226, 265-266, 288, 341, 412, 424
Schorr, Rebbetzin Shifra   254
Schpringer, N.   338
Schreiber, Max   53
Schutzman, Rabbi Meir   84
Schwab, Rabbi Mordechai   274
Schwab, Rabbi Shimon   51, 165, 169, 178, 197
Schwartz, Berel   90
Schwebel, Aaron   226
Seidman, Dr. Hillel   338
Seif, Abraham   53
Seif, Aron   53
Seif, Seaman Morris   211
Semiatizky, Rabbi Zaidel   408
Septimus, Abe   56, 312, 320
Septimus, Alice   58
Septimus brothers   54, 56, 74, 252
Septimus, Edythe   59
Septimus, Harry   56, 98, 134
Septimus, Louis J.   42, 53, 56, 68, 69, 79, 122, 139, 143-144, 222, 236, 252, 254, 276, 325, 356, 369, 392
Septimus, Max   56, 89, 134
Septimus, Morris   53, 56
Septimus, Norman   56
Septimus, Sol   53, 56, 207, 270, 312, 320, 341, 369
Shalom, Isaac   408
Shapiro, Rabbi Aron Yeshaya   143
Shapiro, Rabbi Avraham   381
Shapiro, Rabbi Meir   50, 66, 167, 381
Shatzkes, Rabbi Aharon   262

Shatzkes, Rabbi Moshe   262
Sheinberger, Rabbi Yosef   424
Sherer, Basya   25, 27-29, 144, 163
Sherer, Rabbi Moshe   21, 24, 27, 29, 38, 49, 84, 87, 98, 101, 112-113, 125, 127, 175, 178-180, 184, 187, 189, 219, 223-224, 277, 341, 355, 391-392, 405
Sheridan, Pvt. Alfred   208
Shertok, Moshe   289
Shkop, Rabbi Moshe   180, 262
Shmulevitz, Rabbi Chaim   262-263
Shoenberger, Sgt. Jerome   310
Shoulson, Rabbi Chas.   208
Shup, Rabbi Noson   261
Shurin, Rabbi Aaron B.   169
Shurkin, Rabbi Yaakov Moshe   143
Sicherman, Cpl. D.   208
Sigheter Rebbe   365
Silberberg, Rabbi Joachia   362
Silber, Pvt. Harry A.   208, 210
Silber, Meilach   93, 169-170, 191, 221
Silbermintz, Aaron   185
Silbermintz brothers   74
Silbermintz, Rabbi Joshua   41, 75, 83, 89-93, 94, 112, 139, 171-172
Silbermintz, Seymour   116, 138, 142, 168
Silbermintz, Teddy   220
Silverman, Rabbi Ephraim   417
Silver, Rabbi Eliezer   16, 83-84, 106, 167, 180-181, 237, 261, 276, 295, 356, 412
Simanowitz, Fishel   90
Simanowitz, Pesha   59, 177
Simche, Messulim   362
Simon, Private Arthur   206
Simon, Dr. Jonas   181
Skulener Rebbe   334
Skverer Rebbe   109, 411-412
Slutsky, Mr.   252
Smart, Joseph   276-178
Smith, Gerald L.K.   241
Smith, Pfc. Mac   208
Solkin, M.A.   363
Soloff family   122
Soloff, Reuven   127

Solomon family   101
Soloveitchik, Rabbi Joseph B.   398
Sonnenfeld, Rabbi Yosef Chaim   80
Sorotzkin, Rabbi Zalman   160
Spero, Earl   253
Spiegel, Moshe   223
Spinner, Avraham   121
Spira, Rabbi Yisrael   see Bluzhover Rebbe
Spiro, Chaplain Abram   318-319
Spitzer, Rabbi Asher   47
Starfer, J.A.   191
Stauber, Aaron   53
Staum, Abe   251
Steffens, Lincoln   42
Steif, Rabbi Yonasan   83, 143, 226, 289, 353
Steinberg, Alex   53
Steinfeld, Julius   235-236, 251, 277, 285
Steinhardt, Laurence A.   240
Stein, Rabbi Chaim   412
Stender, Nathan   208
Stern, Rabbi Dr. David   54, 65, 85, 122
Stern, Naftali   362
Sternbuch, Isaac and Recha   232, 284-285, 289-290, 299, 302-304,
Stettinus, Edward   274
Stoliner Rebbe   see Perlow
Strahl, Isaac   53, 58, 61-62, 126, 181
Strahl, Ruth   177
Sulzberger, Arthur Hays   189
Surkis, Pfc. Gabriel   208, 211
Susswein, Hirsh Meilech   53
Svaro, Herman   362
Swerdloff, Moshe and Estelle   310-311, 323-324, 369-370, 372-378, 382-383

T

Taft, Robert   258
Tannenbaum, Abraham   185
Tannenbaum, Rabbi   143
Tanzer, Jacob   53
Tauber, Ernst   310

Tauber, Cpl. Rudy   310, 311-312, 314, 318, 320
Taub, Rabbi Shaul Yedidya   *see* Modzhiter Rebbe
Teitelbaum, Rabbi Moshe   *see* Sigheter Rebbe
Teitelbaum, Rabbi Yaakov   228, 395
Teitelbaum, Rabbi Yoel   *see* Satmar Rebbe
Teitz, Rabbi Pinchas M.   49, 84
Tenenbaum, Dr. Joseph   283
Terebelo, Elimelech   19, 119, 138, 337, 422
Tetove, Selig Chaim   311, 313, 316-317, 320, 323
Thompson, Dorothy   80
Thompson, Llewelyn   404
Thumim, Rabbi   226
Tiefenbrunner, Mrs.   372
Tiefenbrunner, Yonah   370, 372-373
Toledano, Rabbi Baruch   408
Trachtenberg, Lieutenant Meyer   211
Treisser, Herman   205, 277, 341, 376-378, 381-382, 399
Tress, Rabbi Avraham Gershon   416-419
Tress, Gershon   25-27
Tress, Henya   25-28, 30
Tress, Hinde   33, 58, 144-146, 149, 270, 410-413, 416-417
Tress, Mendel   110
Tress, Morris   27
Tress, Shmuel Baruch   109, 410, 418
Tress, Yitzchak Tzvi   109, 425, 426
Tropper, Devorah   103, 423
Truman, President Harry S   280
Turkel, David   134, 285
Twersky, Rabbi Yaakov Yosef   *see* Skverer Rebbe
Tzechoval, Rabbi Moshe I.   278
Tzelemer Rav   143

U

Udell, Lester   152, 160, 253, 355, 391
Ulio, General J. A.   203-204

Ullman, Benjamin   93, 170, 206
Ungarischer, Rabbi Don   150-151
Unger, Rabbi Shmuel David   *see* Nitra Rav
Urman, Binyamin   96
Urman, Channah   363

V

Vishnitzer Rebbe   362
Vorhand, Rabbi Zev Tzvi (Victor)   353

W

Wachtenheim, David   53
Wachtfogel, Rebbetzin   124
Wagner, Robert   87, 223, 391-392
Walkin, Rabbi Aharon   47
Waltner, Rabbi Zusia   408
Wasserman, Rabbi Elchonon   19, 68, 82-83, 86, 125-130, 140, 146-148, 155, 197, 409, 425
Wasserman, Rabbi Simcha   143, 295
Wechsler, Joseph   208, 310, 319
Weill, Kurt   237
Weinberg, Mattis   123-124
Weinberg, Rabbi Mordechai   89
Weinberg, Morris   53, 125, 168
Weinberg, Rabbi Noach   123
Weinberg, Rabbi Shneur and Phyllis   102
Weinberg, Rabbi Yaakov   123
Weinberger, Judy   405
Weinberger, Rabbi Mickey   226
Weiner, Sidney   185
Weinrib, Joseph   51
Weinstein, Marvin   170
Weintraub, Mollie   177
Weisberg, Anne   33
Weissmandl, Rabbi Michoel Ber   232, 287-289, 247, 269, 339
Weiss, Rabbi Samson Raphael   396
Weiss, Rabbi Shlomo   287
Weitman, Rabbi Moshe   89
Weitz, Israel D.   362
Weizmann, Chaim   195

Wenger, Yitzchok   229
Wengrovsky, Charles   170
Westreich, Maurice   375
Wieder, Josef M.   362
Wiederkehr, Yisrael   50, 53
Wilhelm, Reb Binyomin   44, 46, 58
Wilhelm, Lucy   58
Willig, Leonard   316
Wise, Jonah S.   189
Wise, Stephen   194-195, 237, 292-293
Wisliceny, Dieter   289
Wolbe, Rabbi Shlomo   176, 274
Wolf, Rabbi Arnold   54, 93, 138
Wolf, Rabbi Ephraim   19, 89, 93, 112,
    119-121, 154, 185, 221
Wolfson, Rabbi Moshe   18, 92
Wyman, David   234, 236, 246

Y

Yaffe, Channah   58
Yaffe, Rabbi Mordechai   143

Yarmish, Rabbi Joseph   301
Young, Avraham Chaim   229
Young, Charles   54, 89, 168, 180, 182,
    187, 221, 223-224, 386

Zacks, Archie   363
Zaks, Rabbi Mendel   17, 180, 262,
    395
Zamore, Bessie   33
Zanzipar, Celia 18, 111, 173
Zehnwirth, Zelda   177
Ziemba, Rabbi Avraham   333
Ziemba, Rabbi Menachem   235, 381
Zirelson, Rabbi Yehudah Leib   167
Zirkind, Mr.   103
Zohn, Rabbi Shachne   143
Zupnik, Miriam   370-373
Zweig, Avrohom   229
Zweig, Shimon   229

GLOSSARY

ahavas Yisrael — love of his fellow Jews

agunos — women unable to remarry

Aibeshter — the One Above

aliyah — being called to recite a blessing on the Torah; moving to *Eretz Yisrael*; ascension

arichas yamim — long life

aron — bier

aron kodesh — synagogue ark, where the Torah scrolls are kept

askan (pl. **askanim**) — activist

azoi — like this

baalebas (pl. **baalebatim**) — layman

baalei teshuvah — those who return to traditional Jewish observance

baal simchah — one making a festive meal

bachurim — young men

Bais Hamikdash — the holy Temple in Jerusalem

Baruch Hashem — thank G-d

beis medrash — house of study

bentsching — reciting Grace After Meals

berachah levatalah — a purposeless blessing

berachah (pl. **berachos**) — blessing

bimah — reader's table in the synagogue

bitachon — faith in G-d

bitul Torah — disturbing Torah study

bnei Torah — Torah students

borei pri ha'eitz — lit. Who creates the fruit of the ground; latter part of blessing before eating fruit

bren — spiritual intensity

chalafim — knives for ritual slaughter

chalav Yisrael — milk supervised by a Jew

chametz — leaven

chanukas habayis — celebration of the dedication of a home

chareidi — one who is rigorously observant

chasan — groom

chasunah — wedding

chaver (pl. **chaverim**) — friend, comrade

chavrusa — study partner

chassidim — followers of a chassidic leader (Rebbe)

Chazal — our sages

chazzan (pl. **chazzanim**) — cantor

cheder — lit. room; small Jewish school

cherem — ban of excommunication

chesed — kindness

chevra mishnayos — mishnah study group

chibas haaretz — love of Eretz Yisrael

chilul Shabbos — desecration of Sabbath

chinuch — Jewish education

cholent — hot stew eaten during the Sabbath day meal

Chumash (pl. **Chumashim**) — one of the Five Books of the Torah

chuppah — wedding canopy

cum nor aher — please come here

daas Torah — Torah outlook

daf — folio page of Talmud

daled amos — lit. four cubits

daven — to pray

dayan — rabbinic judge

dina d'malchusa dina — the law of the land is binding

dinei nefashos — laws of life and death

dinim — laws

din Torah — rabbinic trial

drash — homiletical interpretation

drashos — sermons, hermenuetic exegesis

dvar Torah (pl. **divrei Torah**) — Torah thought

emunas chachamim — faith in the Sages

Eretz Yisrael — the Land of Israel

erev Shabbos — Friday

erliche — honest

farshaltenne land — accursed land

fleishig — meat

fregt a kashe — asks a question

frumkeit — religiosity

gadol hador — Torah leader of the generation

galus — exile

gaon — genius

gartel — a belt worn at religious services

gedolei Torah — Torah giants

gedolei Yisrael — Spiritual leaders of the Jewish people

gehoibeneh mentsch — an elevated person

Gemara — the Talmud

girsa d'yankusa — knowledge aquired during one's youth

glatt kosher — kosher meat without question

goldene medinah — "The Golden Land" — The United States; land of opportunity

goyishe — non-Jewish

grammen — rhymed verses

hachnasas orchim — hosting guests

hadras panim — glowing countenance

haftarah — the reading from the Prophets which follows the Torah reading

haggadah — the text used at the seder

HaKadosh Baruch Hu — G-d

hakafos — the dancing around the reader's table in the synagogue on *Simchas Torah*

hakaras hatov — appreciation

halachah (pl. **halachos**) — Jewish religious law

hartzige mentsch — one full of heart

Hashem Yisbarach — G-d

hashgachah — rabbinic supervision on food; Divine Providence (usually: *Hashgachah Pratis*)

hashkafah — Torah outlook

hasmadah — diligence

Hatikvah — Israel's national anthem

hatzalah — rescue

hatzalas nefashos — involving saving a life

havdalah — ceremony performed at the ending of Sabbath and Festivals

bein hazmanim — intersession

hechsher — stamp of approval

heter — lenient rabbinic ruling

hiddur mitzvah — beautification of a commandment

hislahavus — enthusiasm

Hy"d — acronym for *"Hashem yikom dammo"* — may G-d avenge his blood; used for martyrs

Judenrein — free of Jews

Kabbalas Shabbos — prayer welcoming the Sabbath

Kaddish — prayer, often recited in memory of a relative

kallah — bride

kapote — rabbinic frock

kasher — to make kosher

kashrus — Jewish dietary laws

kavod haTorah — honor for Torah scholars

kedushah — holiness

ketzelach — little cats; kittens

kever — grave

kibbutz (pl. **kibbutzim**) — settlement

kiddush — prayer said over wine at Sabbath and Festival meals; a snack served after this prayer is recited

kiddush Hashem — sanctification of G-d's name

kinderlach — children

kiruv — bringing one closer to Jewish tradition

klahrkeit — clarity

Klal — community

Klal Yisrael — Israel's collective body; the Jewish people

kodesh kodashim — lit. holy of holies

Kohen (pl. Kohanim) — descendant of Aharon

kollel — post-graduate yeshiva, usually for married students

kolleleit — those attending kollel

Kol Nidrei — first prayer of the Day of Atonement

kulo — entirely

Lag B'omer — the 33rd day of the omer

lager (pl. **lageren**) — camp

lamdan — Torah scholar

landsleit — those from the same town or area in Europe

landsmanshaft (pl. **landsmanshaften**) — group of Jews sharing a common place of origin in Europe

lashon hakodesh — Hebrew; the holy tongue

latzanus — scoffing

leil Shabbos shiur — Friday night class

levayah — funeral

maalos — positive attributes

Maariv — evening prayer

maasim — deeds

maggid shiur — instructor

malach (pl. **malachim**) — angel

marbitz Torah — teacher of Torah

mashgiach (pl. **mashgichim**) — supervisor of kosher food; dean of students

maskilim — "enlightened ones"; forerunners of Reform Judaism

maspidim — eulogizers

mechazek — encourage

mechilah — forgiveness

melachah d'oraisa — Biblically prohibited activity

melamed (pl. **melamdim**) — Torah teacher

Melaveh Malkah (pl. **Melaveh Malkahs**) — meal after Sabbath ends

menahel — principal

menuchas Shabbos — Sabbath rest

mesader kiddushin — officiator at a wedding

meshamesh — serve

meshuganeh — crazy person

meshulachim — fundraisers

mesiras nefesh — self-sacrifice

mesivta — yeshivah high school

mezuzos — parchment scrolls affixed to the doorpost

middos — character traits

mikveh (pl. **mikvaos**) — ritual bath

milchemes mitzvah — a Divinely sanctioned war

milchig — dairy

minhagim — traditions

min Hashamayim — ordained by Heaven

minyan (pl. **minyanim**) — quorum for communal prayer

Mishkan — Tabernacle

Mishlei — Proverbs

Mishnayos B'al Peh — learning mishnayos by heart

mitah — bier

mitzvos bein adam lechaveiro — mitzvos between man and his fellow man

mitzvos bein adam leMakom — mitzvos between man and G-d

mockies — foreigners

mokir rabbanim — one who values Torah leaders

Motzaei Shabbos — Sabbath night

Mussaf — prayer recited on Sabbath, Festivals, and on the New Moon.

mussar — ethics

mussar sefer — book on ethics

neshamah (pl. **neshamos**) — soul

nes min HaShamayim — miracle from Heaven

niftar — deceased

niggun (pl. **niggunim**) — melody

pareve — neither meat nor dairy

pashute Yid — simple Jew

petirah — demise

peyos — sidelocks

pidyon sh'vuim — redemption of captives

pikuach nefesh — a matter of life and death; saving of lives

Pirkei Avos — "Ethics of the Fathers"; a section of the Mishnah dealing with ethical conduct

pirsumei nisa — the publicizing of a miracle

plumbe — seal on kosher meat and poultry

posek — decisor of religious law

psak — religious ruling

pushkas — charity boxes

rabbanim — rabbis

Rashi — primary commentator on the Bible and Talmud

rav — rabbi

rebbi (pl. **rebbis**) — teacher

Ribbono Shel Olam — G-d

Rosh Hayeshiva — Yeshiva Dean

ruach — spirit

schach — covering of a sukkah

schrekliche churban — awesome destruction

seder — study session; the festival meals on the first nights of Pesach

sefer Torah — Torah scroll

sefirah — period between Pesach and Shavuos

semichah — ordination

seudah — a meal

sevara — theory

Shabbos Shuvah — the Sabbath between Rosh Hashanah and Yom Kippur

shadchan (pl. **shadchanim**) — matchmaker

shalach manos — Purim gifts

shaliach — emissary

shaliach mitzvah gelt — money given to a traveller for distribution to charity

"Shalom Aleichem" — greeting

shalosh seudas — the third Sabbath meal

shammos — beadle

sha, sha, gornisht — quiet, it's nothing

Shas — set of Talmud; the entire Talmud

shatnes — garments containing mixtures of wool and linen

shearis hapleitah — survivors of the Nazi death camps

shechitah — ritiual slaughter

sheitel — wig

shemittah — the Sabbatical year, when the land in Israel may not be tended

shemurah matzos — specially supervised matzos for Pesach consumption

shidduch (pl. **shidduchim**) — arranged match

shiksa — non-Jewish woman

shittah — opinion

shiur (pl. **shiurim**) — class

shivah — the seven-day period of mourning for an immediate relative

Shivah Asar B' Tammuz — the 17th of Tammuz, a fast day

shochet (pl. **shochtim**) — a ritual slaughterer

shomer Shabbos — Sabbath observant

shteig — to grow in learning

shtetl (pl. **shtetls**) — small town or village in Europe

shtiebel (pl. **shtieblach**) — house of worship

shtreimel — fur hat worn by chassidim

shul — synagogue

siddur (pl. **siddurim**) — prayer book

sifrei kodesh — holy books

siman tov — good sign

siyata d'shmaya — help from Heaven

sonei betza — one who cannot be swayed by money

sukkah — hut used during the Festival of Sukkos

tahor — pure

talis (pl. taleisim) — prayer shawl

talmid (pl. talmidim) — student

talmid chacham (pl. talmidei chachamim) — Torah scholar

Talmud Torah — after-school Torah school

Tanach — acronym for "Torah, Neviim, Kesuvim"; the 24 books of the Bible

Tanya — a classic work of chassidus

tarfus — non-kosher

tashmishei kedushah — religious objects

Tatte — father

tefillin — phylacteries

tehillim — psalms

te'naim — engagement party

tichel — kerchief

tisch — chassidic gathering

tocho k'boro — his inside is like his outside

Tosafos — a commentary on the Talmud

treife — non-kosher

"treifene medinah" — "unkosher land"; appellation given by many in Europe to the United States prior to the World War

tzaddikim — pious ones

tzitzis — fringes; a fringed garment

tzores — misfortune

vieter gegangen — keep going

yahrzeit — anniversary of a death

Yamim noraim — High Holidays

yarmulke (pl. yarmulkes) — skullcap

yeshiva ketanos — elementary yeshivos

yeshivaleit — people in a yeshiva

yetzer hara — evil inclination

yetzias Mitzrayim — Exodus from Egypt

yichus — lineage

Yidden — Jews

Yiddishe kinder — Jewish children

Yiddishkeit — Judaism

yirei shamayim — G-d fearing

yishuv — settlement

ym"sh — acronym for "yemach sh'mo" — may his name be erased, refers to an evil person

Yom Tov (pl. Yomim Tovim) — Festival

zechus — privilege

zemiros — hymns sung at the Sabbath and Festival meals

zman — time; semester

zoght — says

This volume is part of
THE ARTSCROLLSERIES®
an ongoing project of
translations, commentaries and expositions
on Scripture, Mishnah, Talmud, Halachah,
liturgy, history, the classic Rabbinic writings,
biographies, and thought.

For a brochure of current publications
visit your local Hebrew bookseller
or contact the publisher:

Mesorah Publications, ltd

4401 Second Avenue
Brooklyn, New York 11232
(718) 921-9000